September 202

To Maryjo ᴓ

A glimpse into my story, and
the city where it took place.

Love,
Ed

Nathan Hughes

a novel by

Edward Garvey

Nathan Hughes

Eden Stories Press
ISBN 978-73517-4-3-9-6

To Mark –

our lives

together

and then some

Author Confession

As the main character in this novel is prone to, the author also tends to blur the lines between fact and fiction. Many of the inhabitants of this story bare, to varying degrees, occasional resemblance to people who lived or still live. Likewise, a few events reflect bits and pieces of what can be termed 'reality.' Having confessed to such a common tendency within the world of prose, this story may be best described as a figment of the author's imagination.

Separate from the above confession, the author recognizes (and gives undying thanks to) the many writers whose fragments of poems, plays, and lyrics found their way into this tale. These include Richard Brint, Emilio Castillo, Leonard Cohen, Josh Collins, Bob Dylan, Lowell George, Bart Howard, Mick Jagger, Stephen Kupka, Daniel Langton, Joni Mitchell, Van Morrison, Edith Piaf, Cole Porter, Keith Richards, George Sefaris, and Tom Stoppard. It is noted that any poem presented in its entirety within this tale was 'written' by the character within this tale, and that one of them ('Almost to the Sea') somehow found its way out of these pages to be first published in RavensPerch.

My deepest thanks to my love, my wife Susan – for her love and her love of words, and to our three children, Nicholas, Isaac, and Djahna (and their growing families) for being who they are – inspirations of the present and future, with a special thanks to Isaac for his creation of the cover. A grateful nod to Tony Morris and Corey Alicks for their encouragement and helpful criticism of an early draft. And finally, thanks to the publisher Jeffrey Kanode for his love of story, and his taking a liking to Nathan accompanied by his careful edits.

Contents

1964

1967

1970

1973

Nathan Hughes

1964

Chapter 1
Place

We are bound by place, or sometimes even more so by a sense of place. Many are born, live, and die embedded within one locale, surrounded by family, friends, and strangers, all who share that specific world. This connection to where we live can also happen instantaneously when traveling, leading to a 'coming home,' to where one truly belongs. Who is more influenced by this sense of place – the native, or the converted? And sometimes, another question forms – who views this attachment as a blessing, a support, and who finds it troubling, or even a curse?

• • •

Nathan Hughes was born both near the geographical center of a peninsular city, and at the chronological midpoint of the 20th century. Although there was no true line that kept rigid boundaries, Nathan's childhood was also near the mythical point where half his days (and nights) were enwrapped in fog, and half were spent in bright light (and under brilliant stars). Under either covering, and in any season, temperatures were often surprisingly cold, and days without wind rare.

The house that Nathan grew up in was a wooden structure, much of its dark brown front covered by vibrantly climbing ivy. Over the years, this adornment would vacillate between a professorial look when kept trimmed or something approaching a tree house when not. Most of Nathan's youth was in a home of the latter condition, with the consequence of little natural light inside. As with much of the city, the houses next door nearly abutted his family's, leaving the front windows (encumbered by ivy) and back windows (free from any embellishment) to catch exterior light. Hence, Nathan's warmest memories were set in the southern-exposed converted back porch, its walls composed mostly of large double-hung windows. Even with overcast skies, enough light entered to transform this back of the house into another world. And on days complete with glorious golden rays, the joys of childhood within this room were almost too giddy to be held.

Nathan's bedroom was also in the back of the house, on the second floor, though his room had fewer windows, and was thus less of a stark contrast to the rest of the house. The predominant feature in this room was the tapered ceiling which prevented one from fully standing at the side. For an adult that is. This nearly tailor-made-for-childhood room seemed to Nathan built just for him. It lent an intimate, womb-like feeling that would help lull him into deep sleep at night, no matter what the day had thrown at him. He would claim this as the source of his ability to carve vivid and intricate dreams. And from this immersion in the dream state would come his addiction to story, sometimes from the dreams themselves, but also from books, television, mouths of friends, and especially movies.

In contrast to the back of the house, the remainder was a gradient of shadows and, on a clear day, momentary patches of sunlight. Nathan's father, a poet and teacher, spent the days and nights when he was home mostly in the room off the kitchen aptly referred to as the den, seemingly hollowed out of the wood-lined walls. Here, desk and floor lamps were the only sources of light, save a single window that was usually blocked off with shade pulled down. However, this dim room, far from being dismal, smoldered from the passion of his father's writing.

It was the front room that changed the most, dependent upon the gardener's shears. Because of the northern exposure, the depth and breadth of the ivy coverage had an even more pronounced effect of reducing the light. When the windows were fully adorned, the room had at most the soft but quiet light of evening, even at the height of day. This lent a quality of privacy to any visit within. When empty, and Nathan passed by from the stairs, this room had a stately, formal air that he respected but avoided.

The kitchen, entered from the end of the dim hallway that began at the front door, drew the visitor into its warmth and aroma. More important in setting the tone of this room was Nathan's mother – this was her room, and it radiated from her inner spirit and outer beauty. Almost all meals were served gathered around its table. Because Nathan was an only child, the family and even a friend or two could easily fit between sink and stove.

As much as a house forms the immediate world of childhood, and thus lays a foundation of place within the growing psyche, the nearby neighborhood is a close second in importance. Directly across the street from Nathan's front door was a wide boulevard of trees, grass, paths, play structures, and courts that extended the acres of the immense parkland to the west well into the city streets to the east. As if the immense park was the pan and this skinny stretch of land its handle, neighbors simply referred to it as such, the Panhandle. As a toddler, he would ride in the carriage steered by his mother across the lighted intersection to the small swings and slides. As an older child, he would sneak out of the house, often with his friends, to run, dodging the onrush of cars and escape into the trees and brush. What Nathan liked best was the nearness to his house; the Panhandle was his park, his fields, his secrets. He was its master, and he knew every hiding place, every spot that would draw the oohs-and-aahs of his friends. And the older he became, the more territory he staked as his own.

Nathan stood with his best friend Jimmy at the bottom of his front steps on a Friday after school. He wanted to show off his latest treasure hidden across the street.

"Jimmy, you know the shed past the courts?"

"Yeah. It's always locked."

"Have you ever noticed the three windows on the back look like . . . a ladder?"

"Uh, no."

"Well, they do to me. Like they're begging to be climbed."

"And?"

"Well, you're in for a treat. Something more than special. I got to show you."

With a quick flick of his wrist against Jimmy's sleeve, Nathan grabbed a pause in the traffic and was across the street before Jimmy could react. Nathan was almost through the brush when he slowed and stopped before coming to the basketball court, waiting for Jimmy, his arm outstretched to stop his friend.

"We have to wait. The bums are out today, in full force, drinking and yakking it up."

Nathan didn't mind the drifters as much as Jimmy did. He thought of them as the drunken magi seated on their park bench thrones. At least on days like today that were not unbearably cold and windy. (*Where do they go when it's really cold?*) Nathan even liked talking with them, and not just saying, hey. They treated him more like adult than child, nodding their heads with hearty laughs at his jokes. He loved to hear the tales they spun no matter how farfetched. (*The more unlikely the better.*) Their storytelling was really a series of friendly but often combative challenges – who could outdo the other. But Nathan knew these outcasts made Jimmy uncomfortable, so he paused, wondering how to get from here to there without coming too close to the present gathering. (*Way too many magi today!*)

Nathan rubbed his thick wavy brown hair, his brow and eyes exaggeratedly knotted in thought. "Jimmy," he finally said, "I just don't see those guys leaving anytime soon and that shed's too much out in the open. I'll have to show you later." The two boys started walking slowly and without much purpose back to Nathan's house. Then, unable to contain himself, Nathan blurted out, "Jimmy, I gotta at least tell you. I mean, what I saw in the shed. Through the top window in the back." He dropped his words to a whisper. "There's a baseball bat up on the top shelf, with the end of it covered . . . with dried blood. There's a blanket partly over the handle, so you'd never see it from below."

"Ah, Nathan – that's just another of your stories. That shed belongs to the city park. It's where they keep all the gardening stuff."

"Cross my heart, Jimmy, I saw it yesterday. We'll go back, soon, when the bums aren't there."

"How in the heck could you tell it's blood – maybe it was just mud or something."

"No sir, there was plenty of light. This was a color, staining the bat, not something stuck on, and it looked just like dried blood. You know, browner than red."

"Maybe one of the gardeners whacked a gopher. There's a million of them. I was over near the merry-go-round the other day, and I couldn't believe all the burrows! You couldn't go five steps without tripping."

"So, why'd someone throw a blanket over it? No, this is more serious than some dumb gopher, Jimmy."

They walked again in silence. The wind picked up and they both pulled their jackets tight. They reached the street and waited for the flow of cars late on a Friday afternoon to disappear, then ran across the street, hurrying not for safety but because of the cold. They continued their run, up Nathan's front stairs, through the door, and up the inside stairs, not stopping until they both jumped together onto Nathan's bed, laughing. Jimmy pushed Nathan away from him.

"You expect me to believe you? A bloody bat, Nathan, you're *crazy*!"

"Your loss. If you're not interested, no sweat off my back."

"Just another tall tale from the Nathan dude. The make-believe man. The story-man. A writer just like his old man."

"You wait and see, Jimmy boy. You just wait and see."

Chapter 2
Red-Winged Blackbird

The neighborhoods to the west of where Nathan lived were once entirely covered by sand, all the way to the ocean several miles from his house. This half of the city was perfectly positioned between the sea with its mighty wind currents above and the dry heat of valley to the east to be at the mercy of the thickest of fogs. Sometimes mystical and even beautiful, it was the constancy that could induce states of persistent dullness of thought, even depression. This response was felt more by visitors or newcomers, those not toughened by years of acclimatization. For the native, the response was a willful focus on whatever lay ahead, 'weather be damned.' Similar for the greenery – the parks in these neighborhoods had adapted to this climate and blended their vegetation, and even terrain, into the cold wind and mysterious fog. The Grove, laying well below the residential streets in the southwest corner of the city, was such a park.

The special character of the Grove lay in its sunken center, a forever long grassy field surrounded by steep slopes covered with trees, mostly eucalyptus. So dense were these that the air was nearly saturated with its aromatic oils. The main entrance was to the east and included a short winding drive steeply downhill that ended in a small parking lot for those who worked there or attending events at an old Victorian lodge. No cars were allowed in the grove itself, so the field was mostly uninterrupted save the one cement path that meandered from one end to the other. At the far end of the field was a small lake, and at the western side of the lake, a natural maze of tall grasses. Much of this park and its border slopes were left untended in a natural state.

The head gardener, park naturalist, and some say 'mayor' of the Grove, John Scanlan, was familiar to all who knew its fields, especially the children who visited on school trips. Mr. Scanlan, a tall, sinewy man with a weathered face and deep melodious voice, was a dynamic teacher, who distilled both the science and mystery of the Grove into simple stories, wanting each student to be held by both the meaning and beauty of the lesson. Nathan had met him on previous school outings. But the more recent kinship he felt was formed by happenstance when he and Jimmy had hiked there recently. The boys had found him tending a plot of plants and were immediately welcomed into the specifics of his task. Eventually, the gardener shifted the conversation to something new to them.

"Now, have either of you ever heard of the aura of a plant?" They both shook their heads. "Something I usually don't mention during class trips, but from your questions, I think the two of you will find of interest. Plain and simple, auras can be thought of as the spirit of the plant. But that doesn't mean you can't see them. You can. If you're lucky enough to have 'the gift,' that is. The gift to see their colors. Now, I'm not talking the color of the plant itself, mind you. The aura comes from within, and it radiates without." Mr. Scanlan paused, then muttered to himself, "Not sure why I can see these at all, let alone so clearly." He smiled at the two boys. "Must have been 'front and center' when that blessing was handed out by my angel. Auras can tell us so much – the health of the plant, its stage of growth, and especially, when to harvest . . . for medicinal use, that is." The gardener could tell from Jimmy's expression that medicinal plants were a new idea. "I mean, when to collect the leaves or flowers or roots, if you need these to treat an ailment. Do either of your mams ever use teas or ointments from a plant? Maybe mint or chamomile if you have an upset stomach?" Jimmy shook his head, while Nathan showed a knowing smile. "Well, it matters when you harvest a plant for medicine, just as it does for food." He turned to Nathan whom he could see had some experience. "Does your mam ever talk about the quality of the tea she uses?"

"Only all the time," Nathan grinned.

"Well, there you go," Mr. Scanlan returned, his deep blue eyes set upon the brown pair of Nathan's. "All from the spiritual world. As real as the physical. And boys, auras exist in every living being, not just plants. One day, you might be caught by surprise. You might see an aura when you least expect."

• • •

Later that month at the end of the school week, Nathan's eighth-grade teacher announced that the annual class visit to the Grove would take place the following week. She assured them Mr. Scanlan would once again be part of the day. This morning however, Nathan was in shock as he read the Saturday paper in disbelief: the popular gardener had died in the violent winter storm that struck the city Wednesday night, apparently killed by a falling tree. His body wasn't found until late Thursday morning, and the police at first had kept their report from the newspapers. Then, Nathan read the last sentence: *The police are still investigating whether the death was indeed caused by a falling tree.* Without a moment's thought, Nathan's thoughts jumped to the bat hidden in the garden shed. (*I saw it when? Thursday afternoon. The day after he died.*) Nathan immediately ran down the hallway to call his friend. "Jimmy, you gotta meet me as soon as you can, in the Panhandle, at the garden shed."

Nathan waited impatiently near the shed for what seemed forever, pacing back and forth, looking around for any suspicious character who might also be looking around. Finally, he saw Jimmy heading his way.

"Man, what took you so long? Did you read the paper yet?"

"Just got up when you called."

"You know Mr. Scanlan, don't you? Well," Nathan paused, still not believing the news, "he was killed."

"Killed!" Jimmy said, stunned as Nathan had been. "How?"

"That's just it; it's not clear. Maybe by a falling tree, during that storm the other night. But it says the police are still investigating."

Jimmy's face was expressionless while taking this in, then his nose and eyebrows came together in disbelief at where his friend was heading. "Say, Nathan, why're we here, at this shed?"

"You gotta see the bat. You have to tell me what you think's on it."

Jimmy immediately replied, "Man, Nathan, what are you thinking? That someone killed him way cross town and then hid the bat inside here? That's beyond crazy."

"You better believe it's crazy." Suddenly, Nathan's view turned a hundred and eighty degrees – he wanted his guesswork to be wrong. Mr. Scanlan's death was bad enough. He didn't want it to be murder. "Come on, Jimmy. Up we go. Then you can tell me I'm crazy."

The three windows were framed one on top of the other, each with a ledge deep enough to hold at least half a foot and to grab with most of a hand. And wide enough for Nathan and Jimmy to peer side by side through the top window. The light inside was dim, but bright enough to see across to the top shelf. There was no bat – bloody, muddy, or otherwise.

"It's not there!" Nathan cried, and before he could take in his next breath, realized what Jimmy would think. "I swear, Jimmy, it was there – right between those boxes. You can see how they're pushed aside to make room." Another breath. "Someone must have taken it. Now this is really crazy."

"I don't know," Jimmy said, shaking his head. "I mean, Nathan, I don't know what to believe. Even if any of this is true, how're you ever going to convince anyone?"

"I don't know, Jimmy. Right now, I have no idea. About any of this. I swear I saw that bat."

• • •

When Mrs. Lowe shared the terrible news of Mr. Scanlan's death shortly after the morning bell Monday morning, Nathan was surprised so many had not yet heard.

"Mrs. Lowe," Nathan asked while raising his hand, "I read the police weren't sure about his death. That maybe it was a tree falling in the storm, but maybe it wasn't."

"I read that, too, Nathan. Because of our trip, I just called the park department. I was told the police are now ninety percent certain that Mr. Scanlan was killed by a tree. All the evidence so far matches." Mrs. Lowe paused. "So, out of respect for Mr. Scanlan, we'll be postponing our trip. Not sure for how long, but we'll set a new date when we can."

A few weeks later, Nathan and his classmates arrived at the Grove for the rescheduled visit. The bus temporarily parked at the top of the entrance, and most of the students plunged down into the park as if they were diving into a warm pool. They tore down the road that curved gently to the bottom, through the dim light of tall eucalyptus, slowing down only when they reached the bottom.

Nathan welcomed the frantic transition, as he was well inside the park before he thought of Mr. Scanlan, before he looked for him, knowing he wasn't there. Many of his friends hurried in a long run across the open grass. Nathan walked slowly, nearer but separate from his teacher and the few parents. He thought of how Mr. Scanlan, not that long ago, had introduced the auras of plants and trees. Nathan wanted so much to see, almost ached to feel this spirituality. Most of all, Nathan wanted to know that Mr. Scanlan was still here, somewhere in this park.

What he saw instead were trees, walls of a cathedral, a green carpet laid underneath. Even the sky that day was a rare blue, infinitely high overhead. Nathan felt Mr. Scanlan's presence. He felt the kind and oh-so-wise man in all he saw before him, in the countless greens of the trees and grass spread in front, and in the intoxicating fragrance of eucalyptus in the air.

This spell slowly dissipated the nearer Nathan came to his classmates. Some had started to kick a ball back and forth, quick to start the morning games. Nathan broke into a jog and joined just in time for team selection. Bases were thrown down. Soon, he was lost in a different state of mind, the freedom from thought that comes from kicking or catching a ball, immersed in the physicality of the game.

In the afternoon, after the few class lessons were complete, Nathan found himself by the edge of the lake at the far end of the large field, skipping stones with some of the other boys. Lost in his throws, the next time he looked away from the lake, he was alone. He decided to stay put, happy in the warm sun, hoping that one of his side-arm throws might impossibly skip to the far side of the calm water.

Nathan saw Maureen out of the corner of his eye and watched as she slowly wandered down to the water's edge. He tried not to pay any attention but could tell she was watching him. Finally, without looking at her and without knowing what he was going to say, Nathan blurted out, "You ever been to the other side of the lake? Over there?" He threw a stone as far as he could in the direction he had motioned with his head.

"Oh, yes, lots of times. It's one of my favorite places." Nathan kicked himself for saying anything, as Maureen continued. "There's a place deep in the grasses that's just like a secret room. You can hardly find it and when you're inside, you can't see out. It's shady and cool, usually too cool when it's foggy, but today, it would be perfect. Do you want to see it?"

Nathan had no interest in being led by her (or any girl), but he knew as soon as she asked that he'd go. He had often thought about exploring the other side of the lake, losing himself in the reeds and grasses, so he shrugged, "Sure."

"Oh, good," Maureen said, now standing right beside him, looking at Nathan closely, her eyes bright and mouth smiling. "I just know you'll like it. I'm guessing you like secret things." (*How did she know that?*) He had seldom talked with her before, not one-on-one, not alone. She turned around, away from him, waving her hand. "Come on, Nathan."

The invitation of her hand was enticing, her wave blending into the slight movement of the tall reeds surrounding them. But it was hearing her say his name that was unexpectedly personal. With this connection, his hesitancy vanished.

Around the bend, they did indeed enter, if not a secret world, a different one. The reeds and grasses were tall enough to almost block even the tallest trees. Not only did the view of the grove disappear, but the sounds also changed – the frogs and flying insects near the small lake, the sound of their own feet slapping the damp path, of their arms brushing the branches and reeds. And then, Maureen simply stopped and dropped to her knees. To Nathan, there wasn't much difference between the path and the secret room. As there was ample room for two, Nathan also fell to the floor of this room.

"Isn't this perfect? You can't hear anybody at all, can you? It's so quiet."

Nathan closed his eyes and felt the warmth of the sun. (*She's right about this being perfect.*) The two sat a few yards apart. Nathan kept his eyes closed, listening to the hypnotic hum of the insects. After a few minutes, Maureen's voice filtered through this steady sound.

"I usually come here and read or draw or just sit sometimes. I *always* lose track of time, and once my parents got worried. They still don't know about this place. I've kept it to myself. One time, I brought my dog here; *that* was a mistake. He just got restless and wanted to leave. He sat for a minute, then ran off. I didn't follow, not at first anyway. But then I heard him barking and he sounded lost, so I had to go find him. Do you know why I wanted to bring you here?"

Maureen had been making large circular patterns in the dirt with a pointed stick, her eyes focused on her drawing. When Nathan didn't answer her question, Maureen began to erase the sketch using her stick lengthwise.

"It's because I like you. I wanted you to see this secret room."

As she didn't look up, Nathan sensed that she wasn't really expecting him to say anything.

"Nathan, have you ever kissed a girl?" She finished one final sweeping motion across the dirt and looked directly at him.

"No." (*Something more than that.*) "Have you ever kissed a boy?"

She didn't answer, but instead turned toward Nathan and quickly went from sitting on her tucked-under legs to kneeling beside him. She put her bright round face next to his and paused, hoping he would be the one to move closer. He didn't, so she closed her eyes and pressed her lips forward to find his. Nathan felt the warm skin of her cheek as much as her lips, but then, he felt her lips slightly move against his. After a split second hesitation, he mimicked what he had just felt. As Maureen moved away, Nathan realized he had been holding his breath at the same time as he released it.

"There," Maureen said, "now we've both had our first kiss." And almost in unison, except he knew that she started first, they fell into momentary laughter.

She picked up her drawing stick and began another drawing. Nathan watched the first few straight lines form in parallel to each other, then was distracted by the sound of a bird's trill. At the farthest point in the horizon he saw a blackbird perched on top of a reed, its beak pointed up in song. At this sight, he remembered a lesson taught by Mr. Scanlan – red-winged blackbirds position themselves in sets of three, equal distance from one another. He heard Mr. Scanlon's resonating voice, "The three birds, they know how to form a triangle. A perfect triangle." Nathan now listened carefully to locate the other two birds. (*There's one. And now, another. I hear them both.*) He closed his eyes and pictured the three birds from directly above. (*Yes, a perfect triangle.*) From that image, his thoughts slowly drifted further upward so that at first, he saw the lake, then slowly, the field and the lake, and finally, the entire grove, all the while, the sounds from the surrounding water world vibrated in his ears. It seemed to Nathan as if these sounds kept his vision from floating higher still. Then Maureen was gently shaking his arm.

"Nathan, we better hurry. I think we've been here longer than we should." They jumped up and brushed themselves off. They had been sitting in a patch of sun and now, moving into the shade and a late afternoon chill, Nathan knew she was right. They opened the door of tall grasses, started to walk, and then quickly broke into a run down the path that led around the lake, back to the field and their classmates, who were just gathering jackets and packs to head back to the bus, no one running this time across the long field of grass. The towering eucalyptus now blocked the sun, but above, the sky was still crystalline blue, still without even a wisp of fog.

Chapter 3

Memories, Dreams, and Movies

Later that same afternoon, still held by the daylong trip to the Grove, Nathan lay on his bed, his lamp turned on early to balance the swirling gray outside, the fog that had chased him home from school. His thoughts drifted ill-formed from the beauty of the lake to Maureen's warm skin to more distant memories of Mr. Scanlan, and then jumped to the half-covered bat seen through a window while balanced on a ledge. He blinked, then blinked again harder, trying to clear this image, then testing it, daring it to stay. But then a more critical question – had he ever truly seen it? Retracing his steps, he climbed up the shed and looked through the top window. The bat was indeed there, one side of its top end indelibly marked with a dull reddish-brown. What should he do with this picture? (*Hide it in a drawer . . . inside my head?*)

The conclusion accepted by all was that Mr. Scanlan had died by accident, that no mystery should linger in anyone's imagination. Accidents tragically happen – the gardener had died in a violent storm. Nathan had talked more than once with his parents, and after finally letting go of the intrigue of stumbling upon a murder, he was left only with the reality of Mr. Scanlan's death. Nathan was surprised at the depth of the sadness he felt. Surprised because he had met this man only a few times. Maybe though, it wasn't the number of meetings, but the unexpected bond that he felt. (*When he looked at me, it felt he knew exactly what I was thinking.*) As Nathan gazed unfocused across the room, Mr. Scanlan's face slowly appeared as a painting on the opposite wall. For a moment, the intensity of his features was almost frightening, but then, the warm eyes and knowing smile calmed Nathan. The drawing then faded into the grand cathedral of trees from the morning's long walk across the field. But this too disappeared, leaving Nathan simply staring at an empty wall.

Nathan still struggled with the nagging question – had he truly seen what he claimed to have seen in the shed? If this memory didn't exist, where did this fiction originate? Could one part of the brain fool another so completely? And why? This progression of thoughts came to a dead end. Nathan simply had no answers – his precocious but still adolescent brain had taken these thoughts only so far. Instead, he found himself returning to the warmth of the small room within the grasses and to Maureen's round face pausing, then coming forward. He had to tell Jimmy about his first kiss.

• • •

Before dinner, Nathan wandered about the house by himself, first upstairs, then downstairs, finally settling into the kitchen to join his mother cooking, telling her of the walk through the Grove, surrounded by towering eucalyptus.

"Mom, why do some trees have such a strong scent? Eucalyptus is amazing. Especially when it's warm, like it was today. It comes from its leaves, right?"

"Nathan, you know I don't have answers to science questions, especially when they start with the word *why*," his mother laughed, her voice always seeming to dance more than walk across the air. "But you're right about eucalyptus; the oils you smell are in the leaves. The oil has healing powers, though people collect and dry the leaves just for their fragrance. I love their shape – long and slender. Plus, such a wonderfully strong papery feel to them when dried. And the olive color. They're really quite beautiful."

Nathan helped his mother slice vegetables in silence for the next few minutes. He enjoyed the quiet, and his mother treasured any chance to share simple tasks with her son, who was much too quickly losing the few remaining airs of childhood.

"Dad home late again?"

His mother sighed, bordering on imperceptible, but still noticed by Nathan, "Yes. An unexpected class. So, Love, just you and me tonight."

It certainly wasn't the first time Nathan and Ava were alone for dinner. Nathan's father Tommy often spent evenings at the university, preparing his seven o'clock class, one he particularly enjoyed because it attracted graduate students, and thus led to better chances to teach the intricacies of poetry. But tonight, Tommy was to teach a first-year English class for a colleague. Nathan could hear his father, "Nathan, I love my writing courses, but first-year English? – that's when I earn my salary. I have to actually teach!" Did Nathan see slight furrows on his mother's brow, concerns in her eyes, and did these match a disappointment in her voice? Just to encourage these to disappear, even if only from his imagination, Nathan affected the cockney English that had recently made her laugh out loud.

"Say, can aye take you to the movies tonight, me love? We can see Miss Poppins again. Ya know, *A sweep is as lucky as lucky can be.*" Nathan grabbed the broom from the corner and hobbled around in a stiff and wobbly dance, half talking, half singing. "*Nowhere is there a more 'appier crew than them wot sings, chim cher-ee chim cher-oo! on the chim chiminey chim cher-ee chim cher-oo!*" He ended by doffing an invisible hat and taking a deep bow, sending his mother into spontaneous laughter.

"Yes, let's do, Nathan. No school tomorrow, so yes, let's go out on the town." Ava gazed brightly into his smiling face. "Now, how many times will this be? Four, five? Or is it more?"

"Mom, stop it. I've only seen it twice."

"Yes, but one time you stayed to see the entire second showing. Or at least that was the line you gave me."

"Not what I said," Nathan said in feigned indignity. "I was just a little early, so I simply saw the end before the second showing. Anyway, what's wrong with seeing something you love more than once?" he added defiantly. "Besides, I haven't got all the dance steps down. Still working on my penguin strut." He stuck his hands into his pockets, pulling his pants up high, teetered around the kitchen, before careening, then crashing to the floor, sending his mother back into her giggles.

Nathan sang from the floor, spinning around in circles, *"Ohhh, it's a jolly holiday with Mar-ry, no wonder that it's Mary that we loooovvve!"* He jumped up and took endless bows, still more penguin than boy, as his mother stood applauding and wiping tears from her eyes.

"Well, shall we still go to the movie? I think I just saw a better version!"

"Haaahh! You're just being Mom. Thanks, but you're not getting out of accepting my invitation."

"Not intended. So, let's eat this great dinner and get moving. I'm *not* staying for the second show."

• • •

The neighborhood movie house was less than a mile from Nathan's home. The grand exterior, all the various trappings inside, and, of course, the story unfolding on its wide screen all contributed to the theatre being a large part of Nathan's world. This was one of many such theaters in the city, large enough in both seating and stage to house not only movies but live performances. In fact, this theatre had been built for Vaudeville more than forty years earlier, and only began to show movies during the height of Hollywood, when popular movies could fill the many seats. Nathan loved this palace. He would sit in one of the first rows, throw his legs over the seat in front, rest the back of his head on the top of the chair's velvet-covered back, and stare straight up into the enormous screen. It seemed to Nathan that recently fewer and fewer people were in the audience. (*Maybe a plus. More my own.*) With fewer distractions, Nathan could more easily enter the story onscreen. From his earliest experience, he always thought of movies as his own personal dreams. (*And dreams at night, my own personal movies.*)

Tonight, the movie house was less than half full. Ava looked at her son with a knowing glance, "Where should we sit tonight?"

"Wherever you want, Mom. This is for you." Nathan knew that the front rows were not his mother's favorites, in fact, she 'wouldn't sit there if you paid me' and he was still focused on making sure she was not worried about his father. "How about over there," he said pointing. "Smack dab in the middle."

After settling into their seats, Ava leaned over and whispered, "You know, Nathan, as many times as you have seen this movie, your father still hasn't seen it even once."

"Not too sure he'd want ta see it, Mum – not sure his cup a tay, if ya know wot aye mean."

"Oh, Nathan, don't be mean. I think he'd be like you – won over by its cleverness and charm. You know he's a true poet, body and soul, and fairytales are sometimes just simple poems. When done well, of course." She paused and looked into his eyes. "And besides, those penguins are pretty cute. Maybe even cuter than you."

Nathan bit his lip while listening to his mother. Even though he loved her voice so, he held her look steady. (*Yah, then why isn't he here?*) He replied, "All right, Mum, we'll have to drag 'is rear end back here. Before it leaves for good."

Ava shook her head. "Nathan, you're such a wonderful young man, much too advanced for your years and a bit odd at times, thank goodness," she said, giving his arm a squeeze. And with that, as if on cue, the house lights began to dim. Nathan sank even further into his seat. The unanswered questions and new experiences from the long day were now gone, to be replaced by the momentary anticipation of another waking dream. (*Even if I've seen this dream before.*) Then in complete darkness and without warning – that split-second explosion of light filling the broadest of screens, the sudden transition from darkness into another world. Nathan's eyes widened. (*Even if I've seen this world before.*)

Chapter 4

Bison

Weeks after Nathan and Maureen shared their first kiss, the two stood with Jimmy at the far end of the immense city park, close to the ocean but still within the park itself. It was past mid-afternoon on a day exceedingly thick with fog. Nathan was oblivious to the dreariness. (*At least it's not windy.*) The fourteen-year-olds were looking up a slope near a large circular pond where model boats sailed. All three when much younger had brought vessels to launch upon these shallow waters. Nathan had recently remembered the pond, and specifically, how difficult it was to keep his boat afloat in the strong winds. Wanting to compare notes, he had invited his friends to revisit their childhoods. Not to sail any boats, he added, simply to reminisce. Now finished with their tales of long ago, the tall hedges above the pond's back edge had caught their attention – the long row enticingly disappearing into the heavy gray cover. Maureen was first to notice a break within the nearly solid wall of shrubbery and quickly hiked up a slope to find a trail on the other side. "Hey, let's see where this leads," she said, quickly side-stepping the steep embankment beyond. Soon, the three stood at the top of a ridge with little to see through the fog, feeling as if they had somehow wandered together into the same dream. The ground gently fell away marked by a long running cyclone fence that faded into a gray veil in either direction.

"I've never seen a fence anywhere near here," Jimmy whispered, "and I've been here a million times. Well, not exactly here. It's like a different world."

"Different, smifferent, let's see where the fence goes," said Nathan, randomly heading to the right.

Before they had gone a hundred yards in the dim light, a hole in the fence appeared. A seam in the fencing had either fallen away from its pole by wear or had been cut, and Nathan, first to arrive, pulled the meshing back, and said without a beat, "In we go." First Maureen, then Jimmy, then Nathan entered, none knowing whether they were inside or outside, the fence being only a fence. They headed slowly downhill in the diminished light, weaving around the pines and cedars thick on this side of the hill. (*Just where are we?*) The trees thinned as the terrain became less steep, but the fog still encircled them, keeping the mystery alive.

Continuing down the slope, the three kept to a common pace, kept by a slight hesitation of the unknown. The individual features of the terrain were all second nature to the three – the straw-colored grasses, soft brown sandy soil, beach pines, cedars, here-and-there cypresses, and ever spreading manzanita were each well known in this end of the park. However, this specific combination of shrubs, trees, and grasses was unfamiliar. (*This is 'our park' – I can't believe none of us know where we are.*) Time slowed as they strained to see anything that would identify their location. But it wasn't a visual clue that finally made its mark. Not long after being on flatter ground, a guttural sound broke through the fog. All three stopped, in unison, holding their breaths to hear if the sound repeated. It did, rich and low and almost lulling. Loud and close enough to be surprising not to see its origin. The sound stopped again, and straining, the three heard a slight shuffling movement, which then itself disappeared.

After a brief pause, Nathan whispered, "Hey, you guys ever seen *The Hound of the Baskervilles?*'"

"Read the book," said Maureen quietly. "I've told you, Nathan, I'm not much of a movie girl."

"Oh yeah, forgot. I read it, too. After the movie. You see it, Billy?"

"Nathan, man, it's 1964. I'll leave the old black and white flicks for the story-man. But I think I know what you're thinking."

"Guys, I hate to break it to you, but that was no hound," said Maureen, not hiding her disdain of her friends' sense of hearing. "Closer to a cow, but . . ."

Maureen's eyes suddenly grew wide. "Nathan, Jimmy! It's a buffalo, I mean, a bison, or whatever they're called! You know the herd you never see from the main road." She slapped Nathan's arm with the back of her hand. "I was just here a few days ago, I mean there, on the road. We must have walked up and down that fence an hour looking for them."

"That means," Jimmy said in an excited whisper, "we must be in the trees you can barely see from the road. If we keep walking, in the right direction, we'll end up in that big open field."

This sudden realization froze each in the same way. The mysterious sound had just confused them, but now, even more, they were mystified by how this obscure small patch of land fit into what they had previously known of the larger park. Or thought they had known. What had been two separate and unconnected worlds were suddenly joined. (*That's why you never see the bison. They're here, hidden in these trees.*)

The fog seemed to thin, inviting the three to prove what they thought was true was indeed true. Without speaking, they deliberately walked onward, unintentionally spreading apart, led by different desires – Jimmy to see the thinning of trees and bushes become the field he knew from the opposite view, Maureen simply entranced by the continuing otherworldliness, and Nathan listening for the baritone music to repeat.

After only a moment, a form seemed to emerge from the wispy grayness to Nathan's right, away from his friends. Nathan stood as still as he could. (*Be patient. It will come.*) He squinted hard through the mist, then blinked several times to sharpen his vision. (*Is the fog getting even thicker?*) All of a sudden, the fog thinned to reveal a large animal. Indeed, a bison, four strong and shaggy legs, maybe twenty paces away, its body perpendicular to his, its head turned away. The tufty soft brown color of fur rising the full height of its hump blended into the light gray of the fog. Nathan unconsciously held his breath to guard the silence. As he slowly released his breath, the massive head turned equally slowly and squared two surprisingly small eyes on his. This visual joining lasted no more than a handful of seconds, long enough for Nathan's body – shoulders, neck, arms – to release the tension of surprise and awe. After a beat, the union deepened. (*Almost . . . spiritual?*) He felt himself sinking into and then past the beast's eyes. (*Into its soul?*) Nathan was hypnotized. Then, with the softest of snorts, the animal broke this momentary connection with a simple turn and ambled away – first its head, then hump, then rear, and finally its tail, all lost to the cover of overwhelming gray.

• • •

"Should we hike all the way back or take the streetcar?"

Nathan barely heard the question; the voices of Maureen and Jimmy, several steps ahead, were the smallest part of the overall sensations surrounding him. By now, well after they had found each other, somehow retraced their steps back up the grade, and located first the fence and then its tear, the three were circling the quiet string of lily-padded ponds that bisected the middle of the park. Nathan loved this mostly hidden section of park where the water from the creeks and small lakes farther east gathered. Three separate ponds were joined by underground channels and above these connections and surrounding the ponds, tall reeds and wildflowers rose into thick bushes covering the slopes. The paths that meandered through this dell eventually guided a visitor away from this meditative world back to the larger, more directional paths.

Nathan's mind was still charged with the vision. The bison, though not much bigger than cows he had seen close-up, seemed so much more powerful. What was different? The huge head and massive hump that rose behind the shaggy crown were certainly impressive. This vision was unique, and so breathtakingly close. But more powerful was the bond made between boy and animal, between Nathan and nature. This connection, this meeting within the temporary brightening of a thinning fog, left Nathan in a heightened state. He wanted (*no, needed*) to keep this within himself, so he slowed to further separate from his two friends.

Not only did Nathan want this vision for himself, but he was afraid he might somehow lose it, that it might vanish. (*As quickly as it had appeared?*) To keep it close and strong, Nathan willed it to grow even larger. (*The larger it is, the less likely to disappear.*) He began to turn this moment of transcendence into the beginnings of a story, a tale to tell friends and strangers. (*And, more importantly, to me.*) So many choices – which facts to keep, what elaboration was needed here, what exaggeration there. This brief experience tumbled about his young and rich imagination as he walked farther and farther behind his friends. But follow them he did, as the three wandered away from the park, two eventually leading the one by a full city block, to where the streetcars rattled and connected the ocean fog covering the western half of the city to the clear but cool late afternoon sky near the edge of the bay, far to the east.

• • •

By the time Nathan reached home, the plot of his story was set. (*Though not finished – stories are never finished.*) His mother listened as an audience of one. All events that led up to the vision remained intact, embellished only to make way for the storyline to follow. The slight gap in the fence had grown into a formal gate that should have been locked shut but wasn't, the padlock mysteriously hung upon the fence. He relished the beauty of the mystical fog and the amazement of the unknown becoming suddenly familiar. He made sure to laugh at himself for suggesting a hound could even come close to making the sound heard through the fog. Though he had to add, the dense secretive mist occupied the same importance as in the older more familiar story. But the real tale took flight from the moment the majestic beast turned and walked back into the emptiness.

"Its tail was all that remained, the rest was gone," Nathan said to his mother in awe. "It seemed to have walked through a curtain, exiting a stage. Then the tail disappeared, and the curtain closed. And when that happened, this thought, this idea just dropped from the sky – *I didn't have to just stand there.* I didn't have to look at where the bison had been. I could be part of this strange happening. I could follow this creature through the curtain. Into its world."

Nathan paused and looked intently at his mother.

"I didn't want this moment to end."

He paused again, closing his eyes to take the two of them into another world, one that didn't exist. Except that it did – his words would make it so.

"I followed quietly but not so quietly as not to be heard. I wanted to be heard. And every few steps, I could see a leg, the tail, sometimes a bit of the hump. I had no idea where we were, even less than when we first started down the hill. It was truly as if the bison were leading me, to somewhere it knew we should go. I trusted it. I trusted this world. The bison's world. Completely and totally. I wasn't certain, nothing was certain, but it seemed like a very long time had passed. Not that I noticed time at all. I was more and more, simply . . . connected. With this animal, this other being."

Nathan paused, again making sure he had his mother's full attention.

"And then, the creature stopped. I looked up to see where we were. At the gate that Jimmy, Maureen, and I had come through, the gate we had closed, but had left unlocked. The bison turned its massive head and fixed its gaze on me. Then it turned back and looked longingly at the gate. Then, again, back at me."

"Oh, Nathan, you didn't. Did you? Oh, Nathan, you couldn't have. Nathan Thomas Hughes, don't you dare tell me you let that poor animal out of that gate!"

Slowly, ever so slowly, the muscles beside and above Nathan's lips stirred, then moved upward, his eyes widened, and eyebrows arched. His shoulders rose slightly, and he held these curvatures for a moment, only a moment, before letting eyebrows and shoulders fall to rest. "Well, I guess we'll just have to wait for the late-night news to answer that question."

"I don't believe you, Nathan. I don't believe a single word you've said." But Nathan could see that she had no idea what was true and what was not. That the story had worked. (*Boy oh boy-o, had it worked!*) He could see that he had what he wanted, what he desperately needed – she had felt the magic, the magic that he had felt just a few hours earlier, the magic that, because of this story, remained alive in his thoughts and was now safe inside him, inside them both. (*Inside my mother. Locked inside me.*)

• • •

By the next day at school, the tale was set, and it was told – in the hallways between classes, outside during recess, in the cafeteria during lunch. How Nathan Hughes had let the bison out. How Nathan Hughes had freed the beast. Jimmy shared an afternoon class with Nathan and before it began, he came up to his friend and shoved him, hissing softly through a grin he tried to suppress, "This one takes the cake, Nathan. This one is way over the top! Everyone's talking about it. Where the heck did you ever find this load of malarkey?" Nathan simply answered with a smile, a beaming smile, taking his friend's annoyance as the grandest of compliments.

But Maureen hadn't seen Nathan during school, had only heard second-hand the story that stunned her with its disregard for the simple beauty of the day before. As she and Jimmy walked home, she angrily reacted to what she had heard from nearly every other person that day.

"I don't know what to say, Jimmy. I mean I don't even know where to begin. Yesterday was one of the most beautiful days ever. The magic we felt, that we *shared*. Or at least I thought we shared. He takes that special world, that special . . . place, and destroys it by turning it into a fairytale. Or worse . . . into an adventure story, where he's some phony hero freeing animals from captivity."

Maureen reached out in frustration and grabbed Jimmy's arm just above his wrist. "I mean, is he serious? From what I heard, it wasn't even told as a joke; he told everyone, as if it actually happened. How could he . . . lie, so completely?" She threw Jimmy's arm down as if trying to throw Nathan's story from her head.

How could he, thought Jimmy. Nathan is Nathan. Always has been, always will be. He tells stories; he *loves* stories. Sings the song. Finds the rhyme. How? Why? Never asked. Though there were times. Boy oh boy, there've been times. Like the story about the bloody bat.

And then, remembering that outrageous story, Jimmy let loose. "It's just who Nathan is, Maureen. It all just kind of blurs together. Tales that are clearly just tales, and tales that sound like the gospel truth. Sometimes I believe him when I know it's not true because, well, it's a story. But then there's times where he'll swear on his grandmother's grave. I guess it never got in the way of our friendship because it *is* our friendship. Or at least a big part of it." Jimmy paused and looked at Maureen. "I have no idea where this one came from. When I first heard it, I really had to bite my lip.

"One time . . . one time I did ask Nathan why a story had something I knew wasn't true. He looked surprised. He said that it just needed a bit of extra color. 'You know, Jimmy, that little bit of extra color is all it takes to make or break the story. I mean, the impact of the story. Whether or not it really grabs you.'

"So," Jimmy stopped, holding Maureen's gaze. "Best I can do. Closest I can get. Nathan's just, he's just the story-man."

They had stopped walking just when Jimmy had begun his attempt to explain his friend. Now, he could still feel his arm being gripped by Maureen minutes earlier. She muttered under her breath and turned down the street. Jimmy followed, not with her, but a long step behind. Jimmy had taken his explanation of his friend as far as he could. He could sense through the distance between them, as clearly as if his brain were wired directly into hers, that Maureen could not leave Nathan's story, his lie, behind. He knew, could almost see it spinning wildly in her thoughts. Much as those toy boats used to spin, bordering on tipping over. On that sailing pond in the park. Near the ocean. Blown by the uneven wind of this uneven city. Then Jimmy remembered the wonder of yesterday. Was it gone for him? For Maureen? Was that magic now lost? No, ruined? Certainly, not for Nathan. Jimmy thought back on Nathan's smile earlier at school. No wind was ever going to blow that tale of wonder from his friend, not from Nathan Hughes, not from the story-man.

Chapter 5
Northside Poetry

Nathan stood impatient under a marquee in the northeast corner of the city. He was anxious to claim his favorite location, front-and-center and in the fifth or sixth row, just below the level of the performer on stage. (*Certainly, no farther back.*) He needed to look up, just the slightest, at the performance. (*Need that slightest sense of awe.*) At the moment, his father was knee-deep in yet another conversation.

Nathan whispered in his mother's ear, "We really don't need to listen to another story of his first-year students. Let's make sure we get our seats."

Ava whispered back with barely a smile, "You mean, your seats."

Thomas J. Hughes, J. for James, though never referred to by his full name except on the cover of three published books of poetry, took Ava and Nathan to every annual reading by the city poets, including Thomas J., held in the Theatre for the Performing Artist, known simply as The Theatre. The reading was presented on the first Sunday after the spring equinox, as a fixed celebration of rebirth. Tommy Hughes had been an integral member of the city's renaissance of poetry since its beginnings, though not nearly as famous as the few who had made names for themselves, some with even worldwide recognition. His poetry, compared to many of the others, did not break new ground in content or style. Rather it spoke of classical themes such as love and friendship, and in classical forms, often sonnets, sometimes a pantoum. Hughes considered himself more craftsman than artist, but never resented his colleagues any success derived from novelty. Most importantly, all the poets believed religiously that poetry was best delivered aloud, by the human voice.

The annual reading was set in format. The time allotted each reader was ten minutes, and under no circumstance more than fifteen. The order was decided by picking names from a hat, with the hat itself becoming more and more worthy of a poem. The year of the great City Hall scandal had seen a replica of the mayor's dapper brown derby. And somehow a beret that was known to all save the odd change of color to a bright orange – some say to honor the city's beloved ball team – showed up the year the Pulitzer was awarded to arguably the most famous of the city's poets. This year's hat was a copy of the baseball cap that a neighboring impresario always wore to cover his balding top, and which had been clearly displayed recently on the front page of the city's newspaper when his nightclub had been closed, complete with chain and lock, for a much-too-explicit performance the night before. There was one change this year to the event's makeup. The organizers had dedicated a reading slot to a newer, younger poet to broaden the horizon for both the writers and audience.

Nathan and Ava were settled just after one thirty, with Tommy seated next to Nathan minutes after. By one forty-five, the hall was well on the way to capacity. Nathan watched his father's yearly habit of shuffling the order of his five or six poems, back to front, then this one to second, and after another pause with a slight grunted curse, a random flipping of pages. Tommy finally turned to Nathan, muttering with a smile, "Well, you know, Nathan, me boy, it really doesn't matter; they're all perfect gems. They can all stand alone. And in any order.

"I tell you what," he continued, spreading the pages like a small deck of cards. "I'll have you draw the first I read."

One poem poked out more than the others. (*Oh, you want this one first, do you?*) Nathan felt obliged, sliding the protruding sheet from the others. He took a peek at the title to make sure it wasn't the new poem his father had recently read to him. (*Abraham and Isaac. No need for that poem. 'My son, come here, the time has come.' Boy, that gave me the shivers.*) It wasn't, and Nathan slipped the poem, not on top, but at the bottom of the stack. (*So there.*) His father let out a soft sigh, "I wouldn't expect anything less from my one and only." Then out of the corner of his vision, Nathan watched one of his father's compadres make his way across stage, an upside down baseball cap filled with bits of paper.

"Good afternoon, my fellow denizens, I mean, citizens, colleagues, old friends, and soon to be new friends," his high yet resonating voice immediately capturing everyone's attention. "Welcome to this annual rite of spring in our fair, fair city. A celebration of renewal. We grow, we change – how we change – hardly ever staying in one place. Some making strong steps forward, or sideways if necessary. And more than we care to, backwards when that is unavoidable. And we write the same damn poem over and over and still over again. Thinking, believing, *knowing* that it is somehow maybe not new but, at least this time, for new ears. Will the poets," his hand dipped into and slightly stirred the papers in the cap, "take to the wings in the following order." Soon, the reading, at least the first half, was set. Nathan's wish had been granted. His father would read before intermission. As an added luck of the draw (and maybe mimicking Nathan's insertion of Tommy's chosen poem at the bottom of the stack), "Thomas J. Hughes" would be the last to read before the break.

It wasn't until Tommy leaned over and tapped his hand on his son's knee, whispering, "Wish me luck, boy-o," and excused himself without even a glance at his wife, that Nathan realized his father and mother hadn't spoken to each other all afternoon. (*Not a single word. Worse – they've been ignoring each other.*) As he watched his father climb the side steps and disappear behind the edge of the curtain, Nathan could not recall any time when his father read his poems, publicly or privately, that there was ever even a hint of tension between his parents. (*Not a single time.*) Just the opposite – his father's poems and especially the slow and measured cadence in which he read them, captured, reinforced, and echoed his and his wife's love for each other. Nathan sat with his head down, all thoughts or words of poetry quickly gone. Up to this moment, he had been fixed only on the reading, words that flowed as pictures and stories, sometimes simply beautiful sounds, sent on their way outward, toward the audience. Now, these songs were barely audible, as Nathan thought back to earlier that day before they had arrived at the theatre, even before leaving the house, trying to remember anything that might explain his parents' surprising coolness toward each other.

Nathan turned his head slightly toward his mother. He immediately saw the worry that lined her forehead. Vague suspicions he had barely noticed during the past few weeks resurfaced in this new context – a dinner missed, an unusually sharp response, the briefest of looks – and with these, Nathan wanted doubly to believe he was only imagining these doubts. What made him even more uncomfortable, on the edge of a physical misgiving, was a distance he perceived, not from his mother simply toward him, but what he now saw even in a glance – a distance separating her from the immediate world. (*Such an empty look. Our knees are almost touching, but she's . . . so far away.*) He sat immobilized, not knowing the word or touch that could bridge this gap.

Out of this feeling of separation, Nathan suddenly realized his father was on stage, at the microphone, reading his poems. (*When did he start?*) As if woken from a deep dream, he was slow to return to full attention. (*Which poems have I missed?*) More so, Nathan was still held by the totality of his mother's withdrawal. (*Is she even listening?*) Then, realizing he was only half-listening, Nathan fully connected with his father's rhythmic tempo, in time to hear the closing lines of what turned out to be his father's ending poem. ". . . *No one knows that this sweet mass they like to call the best is just as pleasant as an aimless walk. It moves along, the other grows and grows.*"

• • •

Nathan quickly crossed the street in a lull of traffic and headed toward the steep hill that seemed to rise into the sky itself. Moments before, still inside the theatre, he had abruptly turned to his mother and said before the applause for his father had finished, "Back after intermission." As he now hiked up the many blocks that led to the hill's summit, Nathan realized that those last lines were from the poem he had taken and put at the bottom. (*Why did he want me to pick that first to read? Had it just been written?*) Then, more a feeling in the pit of Nathan's stomach – could this poem be at the heart of his parents' sudden and complete avoidance of each other?

As an unconscious escape from these rambling thoughts, Nathan found himself stopping in the middle of a block, at a low iron fence that ran alongside a small city park. This oasis amidst the gray concrete held a large square grass court for lawn bowling, where several small groups of older men were gathered. The few times Nathan had been here before, the court was always full of these characters. This world oh-so-different from the theatre and his immediate thoughts distracted him. The air was laced with thick accents and pungent cigar smoke, both strong enough to easily cover the distance between Nathan and the closest few. He watched the scene before him, lost in the brightly colored balls being rolled across the clipped grass, coming to rest just next to other brightly though differently colored balls. These gentlemen all wore Old Country garb, complete with well-creased hats to shade against the bright spring sun. In studying them, Nathan wondered what made this place seem different. (*So slow. No, not so much slow, just how everything . . . fits together.*) The slowness of movement was indeed extraordinary. However, what caught his attention was how much everything, the game, the park, the men, blended snugly just so. (*Like a story. A visual story.*) The vision before him took on the features of the grand paintings that hung on large museum walls. (*Hung on the wall of this park.*) Nathan stood mesmerized.

Two boys, shoes slapping down the sidewalk, broke the spell and turned Nathan's attention to a family walking toward him. (*Such a large family!*) The older boys were followed by a stroller being pushed by the mother, and both arms of the father tugged by what looked like twin girls. Not only the size of family, but the immediacy of their joy, impressed Nathan and contrasted with his family – this quickly brought him back to the present moment. (*Intermission must be long gone. Better get back.*) He turned downhill. With the laughter and shouts of the family close behind, Nathan's thoughts stayed with the contrast just felt. (*So why don't I have any brothers or sisters?*) And from that question to others, most centered on his father. (*For a writer, he doesn't tell me enough stories. Not long-ago stories. Nothing like Mom's stories.*) Why had his father journeyed from one side of the country to the other? And why this city? Was it as simple as he once said, 'the farthest from home before reaching the ocean'? Each question barely registered before being replaced by another. The chatter of the family behind faded into the hum of the city. Soon, Nathan saw the theatre half a block away – its doors indeed closed. He hoped his mother wasn't worried. But quickly a second thought – maybe better to be worried about me than buried in that sadness he had seen while his father was on stage. (*Reading his stupid poems. Especially, that last one. 'The other grows and grows.' What did that mean?*)

• • •

From the back of the theatre, Nathan stood just inside the door he carefully closed. In a scan of the audience, he quickly saw his mother in her seat, the two seats to her right still empty. He was immediately brought back into the charged air of the reading, juxtaposed with the realization that something was wrong in his small family. A younger poet, a woman who Nathan didn't know, was at the podium. Her voice was warm, with an accent new to him. (*Not Spanish, but . . . whatever it is, it's beautiful.*) Her poems were simple descriptions of scenes remembered from childhood, from a distant world, a place filled with gardens and quiet afternoons. A poem of the color of trees at dusk.

"*Steel, olive, the almost yellow, these shades of green when struck by dim of light, become one green of evening tree. Dusk and past dusk, the fir, manzanita, alder lose themselves in not quite blue to pass through each a deeper gray, to become the slender hue of silhouette, the thickest reach of night.*"

And then, how the paths of a garden are more important than the flowers that fill the beds, and finding a set of new clothes draped across a fence in the middle of a countryside, ghost-like, without a soul in sight. Without thought, Nathan looked to his right. His father was standing parallel to where Nathan stood, near the door on the other side of the theatre. (*I'll bet his eyes are closed. Always closed when listening to a new poem.*) When the poet finished and walked off stage, Nathan was surprised to see Tommy abruptly turn and exit into the lobby. Nathan instinctively pivoted out the door behind him, just in time to catch his father leave the theatre, the sounds of the city lingering as the door slowly closed on itself. (*Where's he going?*) Nathan stood fixed, alone in the lobby, uncertain whether to follow. (*Do I really want to know?*) For a moment, he was nearly paralyzed with the choice before him, then an impulse took hold and led him back inside, back to his mother. As the next poet approached the podium, Nathan walked down the aisle and returned to his seat. Ava looked up and smiled, uncertain, as her son sat down, reaching out his hand to let it lie in her hands, sad on her lap.

Chapter 6

Woman in a Blue Dress

Ava Hughes and her son sat in the back room of their home, windows open and the spring sun flooding the room with bright light and unusual warmth. Nathan looked up from his book and studied the print that hung on the wall opposite the windows. A woman wrapped in a blue dress against a deep red background silently returned his gaze. The angle of the sunlight through the window cut the image diagonally, leaving one half in shadow while the colors of the print hit by the sunlight exploded in intensity. Nathan must have looked at this image a thousand times. He now saw it anew, as if he himself were split in two, one half open and fully exposed, the other half hidden. He turned to his mother, her head slightly bent, focused on her sewing. At this moment, nothing seemed amiss, nothing showed in her tranquil face. The timing of the thread being pulled through cloth was like the ticking of a quiet clock, as calming as a heartbeat.

The past week had been a new experience for Nathan. He wondered if this unspoken tension was as new for his parents, or if they had ever struggled in this way before. (*Even before I was born?*) As certain as he was of the friction, he was truly unsure of not only the specifics but also the depth of trouble. Had he imagined the unforgiving strain of that long afternoon just a week ago? (*No, not possible.*) He had not asked for an explanation or even an acknowledgement, and his parents in turn had not volunteered a telling glance, let alone words. He was unsure of how to bridge such a gap. (*Almost a gulf.*) If he could, it would likely be at a time such as now, during this moment of steadfast calm.

Ava interrupted his thoughts.

"Nathan," she said quietly without taking her focus from her stitch, "did I ever tell you about the time my brother Lawrence and I went to our uncle's farm? It was maybe a year or so before I moved away from home, so it must have been just after I turned fourteen." She paused to look at her son. "Just about your age."

(*Wasn't expecting a story. Not one from her childhood.*) He loved his mother's stories and smiled to himself. These were wonderful tales, but also glimpses into his mother's past. He wanted to simply wait for this story to begin, as if he was sitting in a darkened movie house, waiting for the magical flickering light to break upon the screen. However, he realized his mother had paused for some engagement from him, some verbal awareness. "No. Can't remember you even telling me of an uncle. Farm or no farm." Nathan stretched his arms up above his head, then nestled well into his chair in anticipation. "Did he live close to you?"

"Oh no, not at all. We were at least an hour from the pass and my uncle lived all the way down the other side of the mountains, on the high plains. So, most of a day by bus back then," she smiled at her son, "way back then."

She paused, intent on her stitch. Nathan couldn't tell if something had gone astray with her sewing, or if she was simply choosing the all-important first line of a story.

"It was late winter, and a very heavy snow had just fallen. A day or two before we left home, a man's body had been found near the top of the pass, frozen to death. I remember the bus slowly making its way up the mountain – all I could think about was that poor man and wondering what a frozen body looked like. I looked so hard out the window, trying to see any shape half buried in the snow. As we got nearer the pass, I focused extra hard out the window. Somehow staring at the incredible whiteness must have hypnotized me, because the next thing I knew, we were well beyond the pass. Much less snow on the ground, and color, a winter palette of evergreens, browns, and so many grays. But coming out of such pure whiteness, and from whatever trance I was in, the sensation was powerful." Eva looked up from her sewing and smiled. "And unforgettable.

"What I maybe remember most about the entire trip, Nathan, was realizing, really for the first time, how much I loved winter, *my* winter, winter in the high mountains. Everything about snow, the look, taste, touch, sound, even smell. To this day, when I think of snow, I think of all five senses. The different . . . qualities of snow, some soft, like feathers, and snow so hard and icy it could cut. The bitter cold, and then coming inside to the wood stove. Or the quiet cold when no wind blew – almost dizzy it was so fresh.

"You see, this was my first trip of any distance, and while it was still winter at home, by the time we came to a stop in the high plains, it was spring-like. To me at least. No snow anywhere, and the air anything but cold. I couldn't understand why anyone was wearing coats and hats. I remember laughing, 'It's so warm.' The difference I felt, Nathan, it made me giddy. We were in a big town, nearly a city, that I had never been to, but it was the disappearance of winter that was . . . it was simply beyond my understanding."

"I thought you said you went to your uncle's farm."

"And do I interrupt your stories?"

"Sorry," Nathan quickly returned. "Actually, I was wondering why you went on this trip. For some reason, it doesn't sound like a holiday or vacation or anything like that."

"Yes, my precocious son, it wasn't 'anything like that.' And that *is* part of the story, *and* you are still interrupting."

Nathan smiled and pretended to zip his lips shut.

"Our uncle was waiting to greet us outside the station in a very old truck. You know, Nathan, this may sound funny, but I don't remember his name, I mean his first name. And this was my mother's brother. It's quite amazing what details one remembers. Or forgets!

"So, why were we there? You're right, Nathan. It certainly wasn't anything like a vacation." Ava paused. "I know I've told you about my mother and her illness, her depression. One of the first attempts to 'solve the problem' was a change of scenery. A big change – back to where her folks still lived, in the Midwest somewhere. My sister went with her, as 'guardian.' Funny to think of a daughter as guardian of a mother. When still young that is. The plan from what Anna later told me was to give Mother a long rest from the stress of raising a family in a small mining town, in the middle of nowhere. However, whatever doctor they saw knew little about depression. So, of course, her 'problems' moved right along with her. Both Mother and Anna eventually returned home, though as you know from other stories, Mother didn't find peace there either. Really anywhere.

"With Anna and my mother in the Midwest, and my sister Vera already out on her own, I was left with Daddy and Lawrence. I certainly was old enough not to need much help, at least not until my father's leg was crushed. Feeling overwhelmed, he decided to contact my mother's brother. Have I ever told you about my father's accident?"

"Mentioned it. But no, never, you know, a story."

"Poor Daddy was on his back for months. While he was still in the hospital, the idea was for Lawrence to close the bakery for a several days, and the two of us to visit my uncle and quickly test the waters. Of my living with him.

"It wasn't really that I had to be 'taken care of.' It was more that Daddy was worried about my not having enough 'supervision.' Too much freedom for a young girl, who was 'growing up too fast.' Not that I knew what that meant. I had no idea. No boyfriends, not even romantic thoughts, but it was a small town, Nathan, and from what my sisters have since told me, Daddy was worried about my . . . becoming pregnant. And then to be stuck in that town, stuck going nowhere in the middle of nowhere. So, if he were bedridden, it would be safer for me to be somewhere else.

"I was young and a bit frightened, and for me this trip to a different world made no sense. But I was 'a trooper' as my father always said, and I swore to him that I would truly try. And I did. At least I think I did. Really, truly."

Ava had finished mending the shirt. "I think I need a short intermission in this movie," she smiled. "Can I get you something?"

"Not sure." Nathan's thoughts remained with his mother's story. "No, I'm fine. Thanks." He had been gazing out the window, not really seeing anything, mainly taking in the bright sun and colors of the few trees and neighboring houses. He returned to the print on the wall. The dividing line had moved up, as the sun was lower in the sky, and now, just the head, shoulders, and upper arms of the woman were in sunlight. Would the shadows below keep rising? (*As if she's about to drown?*) It was an odd perspective because her face still showed the same thin smile. (*No, she's simply swimming. Just treading water.*) The afternoon air in the room was colder, and Nathan shut the windows.

Ava Hughes placed a full teacup next to her finished sewing, settled back into her chair and waited for Nathan.

"Thank you for your patience, son. You know, for someone who loves to talk, and you do love to talk, you have such a wonderful gift of listening. It's almost the more important gift, you know. You certainly didn't get that from your father."

She took a quick sip of tea and then closed her eyes to find her way back to her story. She didn't have her sewing to help find a rhythm.

"Not much happened the first night at my uncle's. It wasn't really until my uncle apologized at breakfast that I realized how considerate he was. Maybe too considerate. He seemed quite lonely. He was worried that the make-shift bedding was uncomfortable! He said that he had been planning to buy an extra bed and mattress anyway, and if I decided to stay, he would do that right away. Whatever joy he noticed from what I said or did, big or little, he immediately noticed – favorite foods, books, even a favorite job! When he heard that I loved to sew, he said that could become my chore. Sewing! Maybe, I thought, this could be a perfect match.

"And the first day or two were close to perfect. I started to think that the decision might not be so hard, that not only could I stay, but maybe even be a help. Be a help to this loving, lonely man. Now, Nathan, you must understand, I wasn't consciously thinking such thoughts. But I was certainly feeling something like them. It was when Lawrence left for a few days – he had business in the city nearby – doubts began to appear.

"The first misgiving was easier to feel. Even easier to put into words when I tried to explain to Lawrence. I simply felt separated from everything I was used to. This farm on the dry, high prairie in early spring was as different as could be from my little coal-mining town still buried in winter. For the first time in my life, I knew how important 'home' was. A sense of place. Of where I belonged.

"The second uncertainty was more complicated. And frankly, I'm not so proud of how I responded." Ava Hughes gave a very short, ironic laugh. "Not that I really put any blame on myself, certainly not on that young girl.

"After only a few days, it became clear how quiet this farm could be, how quiet my uncle was. And nighttime was the quietest. I still remember, Nathan, how he looked sitting across the room in the firelight. That for all the kindness and love he had showed me, how sad he looked, and then, in a single moment, seeing in his face, seeing in his eyes, my mother's eyes. My sad, sad mother. A mother so sad she had to go away and leave me. And then the realization – of course, he's my mother's brother.

"I wish I could remember what I said, Nathan. I'll say right now I don't. What I remember is when my brother came back, I ran to him confessing that I didn't have the courage to live with someone I barely had met, but with a sadness I knew only too well.

"I was worried that Lawrence and my father would think I wasn't 'a trooper,' that they would feel that I had broken my promise to 'really truly try.' But neither were disappointed. Not at all. Even though I couldn't put my thoughts or feelings into words, it was somehow obvious, and maybe even to my uncle, that this idea . . . well, just wouldn't work. So, I said a very difficult goodbye, and it was back home for Lawrence and me, back up the mountain, back over the pass, back into my winter.

"I remember, on the long ride home, I was adamant that whatever disappointment, and guilt, I felt for not staying with my uncle, I would turn into caring for my daddy. And, Nathan, taking care of him became one of the happiest times of my childhood.

"Which made leaving him that much harder. But you've heard that story before."

• • •

Nathan lay in bed that night, and as was often his habit, used the moments before sleep to let the happenings of the day return and drift through his mind. He had not yet returned to his mother's story. The phone had rung just after she'd finished, and then evening began – his father came home, then dinner, then homework. No real tension tonight, Nathan realized lying in bed. (*Almost as normal as normal should be.*)

Now, in the quiet of his bedroom, he let the story drift back, bit by bit, and began to turn the pieces about, pausing to reflect on one, and then another. Although not completely understanding what she had meant, her words 'a sense of place' joined the tumble, and then came to rest, highlighted. His thoughts turned to his home and the world inside the house he knew so well. (*And outside . . . the fog outside.*) The dense fog he couldn't see from within, but knew instinctually surrounded his house, even clinging to his windows. (*Like a blanket.*) A blanket that sometimes overwhelmed, but tonight comforted. (*Like a thick blanket.*)

Ava's story stirred the deep love he had for his mother, for her spirit and the hardships she had lived through. Maybe this story was another small part of why she moved away from her home. (*At such a young age.*) But he didn't understand why she chose to tell him this story today. He heard again, '...after I turned fourteen. Just about your age.' (*Somehow, she was connecting with me.*) Had she read his mind? Could she sense his unformed questions about his family. Did she intend her story to reassure him that all families had confused stories? (*This was hers. But what is mine?*) Nathan was tired, and rather than entertaining any further questions (*probably no answers anyway*), he returned to the woman in the blue dress. When he had last looked, only her head was highlighted, bobbing up and down on the shadows cast by the thickening and thinning clouds, blocking then uncovering a late afternoon sun with overcast, eventually to grow into the nighttime fog that now enclosed his home. (*At least, she was still above water. At least, she hadn't drown.*) Nathan fell into sleep.

1967

_____

Chapter 7

Under Bright Lights

It was on Nathan's 17th birthday that an idea (*no, more an overwhelming feeling*) took hold in an unexpected moment of clarity – he wanted to be on stage. Under bright lights. He wanted to act. Though the word 'actor' did not come to mind, he simply wanted to be on stage telling stories, in a much more formal way than with friends and family. Maybe he needed a different audience, or craved a bigger one. Nathan had no idea where this sudden crystallization came from. In the past, he had considered trying out for a school play, and once he started writing a play with the intent of taking on the main character. But those were passing fancies that vanished in whatever next caught his attention. What fixed this revelation was the purest gift of fate that followed within the hour – a call from someone he had never met or even heard of.

"Hello, is this Nathan Hughes?" The voice, though new, was quickly in tune with Nathan, pleasant to both his ear and soul.

"Yes," replied Nathan, about to add a quip. But the new voice was off and running.

"Hope I'm not interrupting your day, Nathan, but I wanted to introduce myself. Terry Dwyer. Wanted to see if I might pique your interest in a project I'm starting." A pause. "Mr. Sheridan thought you might be interested."

(*Ah, Mr. Sheridan.*) Mr. Sheridan had taught Nathan's last English class, and the two had quickly formed a friendship beyond teacher and student. They shared a love of story, both on paper and, in particular, on the screen, and had recently discovered a small movie house a few blocks from the beach on the far western side of the city, a new kind of a theatre that brought movies to its screen from long ago or far away.

"Any friend of Mr. Sheridan's a friend of mine."

"The response I was hoping for! First, a quick background. I'm a drama teacher, and I should warn you – a card-carrying fanatic on all things dramatic. My current passion is to bring *new* theatre to those, uh, new to the theatre. We teachers do a great job with the classics, but are a wee bit timid exposing our students to the latest ideas." Yet another brief pause, which was perfectly timed to Nathan's ear for the narrative. "My idea is a summer workshop, for high school students, focused on plays just performed within the last year or so. All aspects of theatre – acting, directing, lighting, costumes. We won't perform the whole play, just a scene or two from a small number of plays.

"A friend runs the summer youth programs at one of the Ys, and we're close to finalizing plans. I've talked to friends and colleagues to find young talent who might have a knack to . . . help bring this together. Jerry – sorry, probably should keep to Mr. Sheridan – immediately mentioned you. And before you interrupt, he told me that you have no experience acting. Formally, that is. Even though he's encouraged you to do so." (*Yes, just the other day.*) "And he said you might also make an excellent director." This new but already familiar voice laughed, "Probably scaring you off, without taking as much as a breath. Do you have any questions?" Silence. "Or any reaction will do."

Nathan's head was swimming. He had let this man's unbridled energy flow, as a continuum, from his out-of-the-blue thoughts an hour before. Then Nathan realized a question had been asked.

"Uh," Nathan almost stuttered. "Must admit I'm, well, knocked over. But, in a good way. No, in a great way. It's, hate to use the word, but it sounds . . . perfect."

"Well," Terry started, then stopped. "Now *I'm* bowled over. Seems like we might be reading from the same script. Tell you what. Let me send you the flyer we're putting together – time and place of an intro meeting. It'll have my phone number if you have any questions. Oh, and one 'assignment.' You should come

43

up with a recent play, say first performed in the past year, two at the most, that you'd want to either direct or perform in. Maybe both!"

• • •

Gazing into the YMCA's large multi-purpose room a few weeks later, Nathan's mouth dropped. (*No stage!*) Although he had never been to any Y, he knew the focus was exercise and physical training, certainly not theatre. Even so, he had assumed the venue would have a stage and some type of lighting. (*For chrissake.*) Nathan stood just inside the doorway, exasperated, trying to imagine where and how and even why someone would perform a play in such a large empty space. Nathan didn't hear Terry Dwyer come up behind just as he muttered, "What the Jesus F. Christ was he thinking?"

"I think he was thinking, minimalist."

Startled, Nathan turned to meet in person the man who would be guiding his first experience on stage. Though the idea of a stage now seemed to be only abstract.

"Oh, boy. Mr. Dwyer? Jeez, what can I say..." Nathan keenly felt his face warm and knew this revealed more than anything he could stammer and simply looked down.

"Oh my, Nathan, worse things are said to me ten times a day. More importantly," Terry reached out his hand, "glad to meet in person. After all the phone calls."

Nathan looked up into a large smile, framed by a full auburn-colored beard, and somewhat shyly reached out to shake his hand. "Mr. Dwyer."

"Terry, you mean." He dropped Nathan's hand and silently assessed the full appearance of his new would-be actor.

"A good-looking young man, not too tall or short, and more importantly, your voice seems built for the stage. You project exceedingly well. Even when embarrassed – a talent in and of itself.

"But let me answer the question I think I heard. Remember what I said on our very first call – the workshop is geared toward the entire theatrical experience. Which includes what's referred to in the business as stage production. And not to be disingenuous – I did not select the Y for the workshop because it lacks a stage. But having no stage forces a director to focus, consciously, on how to stage, how to produce the play. Make sense?"

(*Yes, absolutely. Without something, you have to fill in the holes.*) Nathan nodded, his eyes now alert.

"Plus, rest assured, there will be a stage. Though as I said, it will be minimal. Not sure if we'll have everything we want, but we will have all we need." Terry paused to make sure of his connection with his new student. "Promised and guaranteed."

Nathan made a note to thank Mr. Sheridan yet again for his recommendation. To be made aware of all that lay behind 'putting on a play,' even if the barest of bones – what a too-good-to-be-true piece of luck.

"You know, Nathan, I think minimal staging, and I do mean minimal, is not only perfect for your play, but downright mandatory. After you told me your idea, I went out and bought a copy of *Rosencrantz and Guildenstern*. The play, at least the first scene you mentioned, is about as minimalist as it gets. Depending on how much of it you do, the only props you need are two bags of coins!"

Terry dug into his pocket for an imaginary coin and flipped it high into the air. With mouth opened, he stumbled about waiting for it to fall into his hand, turned it over onto the back of his hand, keeping it covered while his eyes locked on Nathan's, waiting for the answer. "Hmm, heads!" Nathan exclaimed. Terry took his hand off the coin, and with an exaggerated look of disgust, flipped the imaginary coin toward Nathan. Just then, two girls opened the double doors behind them.

"Ah, and the troupe begins to arrive!" Mr. Dwyer said, sweeping his right arm low. "Two of Trinity's finest, Judy King and Bobbie McGregor. Ladies – Nathan Hughes. Nathan's a rising senior at Jesuit High. You three will make the private school contingent of our core team, which, I admit, is truly meaningless information."

As the three of them shared hellos, Nathan noticed Bobbie looking at him, as if she had seen him before, although they had never met.

Mr. Dwyer continued, "Several more should be coming. Let's pull out some of those folding chairs over there and set up a circle." As the three went about this task, Bobbie said to Nathan, "I know you don't know me, but I feel that I know you. I'm Maureen Nolan's friend."

(*Oh. Maureen. That explains it.*) Nathan had not seen his on-again-off-again girlfriend for several months, and as often was the case, their latest falling out had been abrupt and awkward, leaving him once again filled with ill-defined guilt. "How is Maureen?" was all he could manage.

"She's . . . okay. Sorry, what an odd way to introduce yourself. Just heard her say so much about you, and, well, here you are. Caught me by surprise."

He could see this girl felt uncomfortable. (*Do I even make girls I don't know uneasy?*) "Hey, no problem. I say far stranger things when I'm caught off guard." He felt he should add something, any additional comment, about Maureen. "Maureen's such a great person – not sure why we keep breaking up. Must be me."

Bobbie started to reply, but quickly held her tongue.

Soon, eight students and one bemused teacher were seated in a circle. The mood was a mix of nervous glances and anticipation to get started on what had been a growing focus for each the past few weeks. Mr. Dwyer cleared his throat.

"First and foremost, a deep and sincere thank you. To each of you. Not only for your interest but your offer to help make this workshop happen.

"So first, the general announcement goes out today. The size and scope of the workshop will be dictated by the response. As mentioned, two goals. A broad survey of all that makes up what we call theatre. And to expose high school age students like yourselves to the most recent productions – pushing the boundaries of theatre or presenting commentary on important social or political issues. Of the here and now." Mr. Dwyer stopped to let the emphasis sink in.

"But the goal today is introduction, to each other and the initial thoughts you have for plays. Then, we'll discuss the next few weeks. By the time we have the larger group together, we'll have a full month to the performance. Not a whole lot of time, but most will be focusing on only one part of one play. So, before we start, questions?"

"Not quite sure how we're choosing the plays?" asked the boy directly across from Nathan. "There're eight of us here now, so likely, eight different ideas? Seems we'll have to choose, or vote, or something."

"Not sure, Mario," Mr. Dwyer responded quickly. "Today, I just want us to hear your ideas. Over the next week or two, we'll get a sense of the response to the announcement." Terry paused. "But to answer your question, if we have to, yes, we'll likely decide by a simple vote."

The girl next to Nathan spoke up while raising her hand, "Will there be tryouts? What if we have too many students responding?"

This question caught Mr. Dwyer off guard. "To tell the truth, Annemarie, hadn't thought of that. This was and is, and will be, a learning experience first and foremost, so never considered the need to whittle the number down. Let's just say we'll cross that bridge if we have to."

Terry Dwyer looked around the circle to gauge the commitment of these young thespians and saw enough nodding agreement. "Maybe we can start with some introductions. Basic name, rank, and serial number," Mr. Dwyer smiled. "And if you have a theatrical focus – acting, directing, staging. Or not! What you feel you bring to this project, and what you want to learn. Then, we'll go around a second time for your choice of plays. I'm a right-hand kind of guy, so we'll start with Judy here."

"Hi, everyone. My name's Judy King. Just finished my junior year at Trinity High. I should start with a disclosure. Terry has been my drama teacher and the director of our school play last semester. So, no teacher's pet jokes. Even if they might be deserved. (*Boy, Miss Confident or what?*) Recent experience – we did *Midsummer's Night Dream*, and in the spirit of the playwright *and* his love of gender switching . . . well, to tell the truth, too many roles for our small girls-only school, I played Lysander and Nick Bottom. Acting is my passion. I'll do my best to share what I've learned this past year. And I plan to learn even more in this workshop. Specifically," Judy said with a smile, "I want to learn how to play a female this time round."

Immediate laughter. Mr. Dwyer broke in, "I think we can make our first official decision of the workshop. Judy King will have a female role!"

As introductions continued around the circle, Nathan sat with his eyes half-closed listening more to the music and tone of the new voices than to any detail being said, though he occasionally heard bits and pieces. He heard that quiet and to-the-point Bobbie McGregor was not an actor but did play guitar, and that she wanted to learn the ins-and-outs of theatrical lighting. That the exceedingly lyrical Annemarie Haran was of course a singer and recently played Marian the Librarian. That Mario's last name was Hernandez and boy, was he one serious guy. Mostly Nathan half-gazed at the light coming in the bank of windows along the top of the far wall, toying with what he would say. He could tell the fog was coming in, as the sunlight would dim only to come back, then dim again, much like his thoughts – try something, then back off, then (*damn it*) go back – all the while sitting directly to Mr. Dwyer's left. His introduction would be last.

"And last and definitely least, name's Nathan Hughes. Just finished my third year at Jesuit. Listening to everyone's talent and experience, I'm the odd duck. Except for maybe Bobbie over there. Like her – never took a drama class or acted in my life. What I do though, constantly and for as long as I remember, is tell tales. Tall, short. Stories half true, half made up, not always with a purpose, or sometimes not even with an ending. Though I always try and have a punchline. Often, just to tell the tale. So, true story. (*Well, true enough.*) Two or three weeks ago, on my 17th birthday, I was sitting in my room, minding my own business, when a bolt of lightning hit me from out of nowhere. Knocked whatever I was thinking completely out of my head. All of a sudden, I had this urge to be on stage. And then, one thought, one whim quick to the next, there I was, on stage, playing Hamlet, for chrissake. The theatre was dim, and I was center stage, paused and so ready to launch into "To be," milking that pause for all it was worth, and I mean really milking it. I could just feel the energy of the audience, deep in my bones. Waiting. And I swear, right as "To be" was coming off the tip of my tongue, I hear my mother from downstairs, calling up. A phone call for me. I go downstairs, still very much on stage, still lost in this dream, and grab the phone." Nathan paused, then gestured with his right hand toward a smiling Terry Dwyer, "Struck by another bolt of lightning – Mr. Dwyer calling about this workshop, waking me out of that dream. So," Nathan said, now raising both arms up with a huge shrug of his shoulders, "no idea what I can bring to anyone here, but somehow, someone – maybe my guardian angel? – was whispering in my ear, *you need to be a part of this!*"

• • •

On a July evening of the first night of performances, halfway through the scenes from six different plays, Nathan stood behind the side door, opened barely a crack, to watch the performance before his. Highlights from the last six weeks were rapidly passing through his head like a movie on a screen. Mr. Dwyer *always* saying the right word of encouragement or guiding discussions toward agreements. Mr. Dwyer's close friend, Lenny "Amazing" Lehane, on how to design and build the stage for *Rosencrantz*. The surprising closeness of the students in so little time. New and already friends, especially Bobbie and Judy. And the star of the movie flickering through his head – Jack Evanston playing Rosencrantz to his Guildenstern. (*If it weren't for Jack . . .*)

It was Jack's crazy idea to build a large cube to place in the middle of the lower platform. "Look, you can sit on it, lean against it, jump off it, hide behind it, flip coins on it. It'd be something, you know, to react to."

It was Jack's idea for the actors in the troupe to wear black except for the Player, and to stand in the background. "Keep the emphasis on R-and-G."

And it was Jack's idea to have a hard metal flooring as one of the platforms. "It'll make a different sound when a coin hits the floor – you know, change up the sound of flipping coins."

As if on cue, Jack came up behind Nathan as he was looking out at the audience. "You see your Rentals out there?"

"Rentals?"

"Yeah, Ma and Pa Rental. The ones who pay the rent. Oh, yeah, you go to that private school, so no one pays rent. Your old man must own your house."

Nathan laughed and shook his head. "Yeah, well, he might own the house, but he's not getting his money's worth. Hasn't been living there for months."

"Oh, so he's got a girlfriend or something?"

"Unfortunately, the former. Your parents here?"

"Mom, yes. Old man – well, nope, never. No way, no how. And, no excuse, he lives at home. Though, he shouldn't."

Just then, the audience broke into applause, as the performance before *Rosencrantz* ended. All of a sudden Nathan shook uncontrollably, "Holy Mary Mother. Christ, Jack," he whispered, "I'm not ready for this."

"Man," Jack whispered back in exasperation, "give me a fucking break. This is what you keep saying you want!"

Nathan laughed and whispered, "No sympathy from you." His eyes were glued on Bobbie at the lighting box, her hand gliding the switches downward to transition into *Rosencrantz*. The room grew dim, then dark. Nathan and Jack carried the large cube, carefully stepping onto the lower platform. (*Geez, hadn't practiced in the dark and at night. Can't see a thing.*) Jack quietly pulled himself on top and sat cross-legged at the front edge. Nathan sat down in front, leaning his back against the cube. He pulled out a large metal coin and waited for Bobbie to slowly bring the lights back up. He closed his eyes, took a deep breath, then opened his eyes to a room packed full. (*Calm down. Breathe. No, deeper.*) Guildenstern slowly exhaled and made sure he flipped his coin up as straight as he could, as he knew Rosencrantz was to snatch the coin as it came down. Which he did. Guildenstern tilted his head, looking directly up in annoyance.

"Heads," said Rosencrantz, looking down at his friend, then checking that he was correct, pocketed the coin.

The performance was on. (*Well, I'll be God damned.*) Nathan was now officially under oh-so-bright lights.

Chapter 8

Out of the Fog

An hour after the final scene on the second night of performances, just after Nathan had said goodbye to Bobbie (*more than a friend?*), he saw his father standing near the front door of the Y. Few others were in the building, and he barely heard Mr. Dwyer and Lenny Lehane in the performance room. His father stood quietly, arms folded across his well-worn leather jacket as Nathan slowly approached. They had hardly seen each other the last few months, and not at all the past few weeks. To Tommy, his son seemed different, surprisingly more mature, likely influenced by just having seen Nathan on stage for the first time. Nathan swore under his breath that his father would have to say the first word. (*No, maybe, every word.*)

"Well, boy-o, that was some performance," Tommy Hughes said in his slow cadence. "I'm impressed. Mightily impressed."

(*Not talking.*) His father sensed Nathan's reluctance, and immediately suspected the cause.

"It's been too long, Nathan," he said, his eyes still set on his son's. Nathan briefly met his father's gaze, then looked down. "Son, look at me." Nathan did, but without conviction. "I need to apologize. Being as absent as I've been – I've made, well, let's just say mistakes, and I need to make that right. Hell, that's a weak thing to say." Tommy hesitated. "I need be your father again."

(*Yes, but that's not the problem.*) "Christ, Dad, that's not the problem," Nathan managed to reply through clenched teeth, almost in a whisper, but loud enough for his father to hear. Nathan clearly saw the response on his father's face. Nathan looked down, surprised at having blurted out feelings he hadn't consciously been aware of, shocked by the power of his words. All he could do was shake his head, fighting back the emotion rising in his chest. (*Tears? I'm feeling tears?*)

"What," his father said, then repeated, "what? Nathan, tell me."

Nathan fought against the unexpected feelings, taking a deep breath. He motioned toward the door, mumbling, "I need to get outside." Nathan pushed the doors open with a bang and head down, quickly walked past the lighted overhang outside into the night fog. He headed toward the nearby residential neighborhood, before he allowed himself to hear his father's call to wait. Nathan reluctantly stopped.

"Son, we have to talk this through. We can wait until you're ready, we can wait all night." Tommy's tone was both quiet and measured, and Nathan knew far too well his father would indeed wait as long as was needed for him to explain his feelings. (*If only I understood.*) Tommy briefly put an arm around his son. "Let's sit down. Over there."

Tommy Hughes could tell his son was struggling, but wasn't sure with exactly what. "Nathan, this is about you and me, isn't it? I mean, my living away from home, not seeing you, not spending time together?" No response. Tommy then tossed a thought into the night air, to see if his son would react. "How's it been with your mother?" Before he could finish the question, Nathan responded – a torrid of accusation and confusion.

"How could you have done this, Dad? How could you have hurt her? You've hurt her so much." Nathan looked at his father with the briefest of glance. "Do you have any idea?" He turned away again, shaking his head. "It's not about me. It's *not* about me."

His father clenched his teeth, about to respond, but Nathan started again.

"I mean, it's mostly about Mom, but not all, I guess. I don't know. It's so . . . confusing. I swore I didn't want you to come to the performance. When Mom told me, you know, she could come the first night and you the second, I told her, forget it, she should come both nights. I didn't want you here. If you weren't spending time with me, I . . ." All the fight not to give in vanished in the sudden realization of the pain and anger his father had caused him. (*It's true – it's not just Mom.*) Nathan's uncertain resolve shattered under this weight, and he wept. Uncontrollably.

Tommy Hughes muttered, "Sweet Jesus, Mary, and Joseph. Nathan, son, come here to me," and encircled his son, pulling him close. Time stood still for both, leaving only the intense and inseparable connection of father and son, the union of pain and love.

As he felt his son's sobs gradually ease, Tommy followed with an equally slow release. When he felt Nathan take one last deep breath, Tommy briefly hold the back of his son's head as he ended his embrace.

"Believe me, son, I know all about the pain I've caused your mother." He looked into Nathan's eyes. "And I can see the pain I've caused you.

"Nathan, I'm not perfect. Far from it. Moving out is what I had to do, but not in the way I did it. I need to do a better job." Tommy took a slow breath, then slapped his hands on his legs. "Starting now. This minute." His father paused for Nathan's full attention. "Let's you and me take a walk. If you're up for it." Tommy Hughes' voice was once again slow and steady. "Just the two of us." Nathan answered with a simple nod.

Father and son rose together, and Tommy asked, "Which way? I'm sure you know your way around this neighborhood better than I."

Just as Nathan was about to point the direction, he remembered how late it was. "Dad, wait a minute. I told Mom I'd call if I was going to be much after midnight," Nathan said, looking at his watch. "There's a phone booth over there."

Tommy Hughes watched his son's quick trot to the phone and shook his head, both in admiration of his son's thoughtfulness and kicking himself at the mess he had caused. "You damn fool. I hope you've really learned your lesson." he muttered.

Nathan soon returned. "She didn't say it, but I could tell how much she likes we're together."

"That I can believe," Tommy replied. The two quickly fell into a rhythmic sound of shoes on sidewalk, his father's hard leather soles echoing in the still air with Nathan's tennis shoes barely heard alongside. The fog was thick, with the temperature neither cool nor warm. Nathan could hardly see the houses as they passed. Most porch lights were turned off with the streetlamps every half block the only consistent lighting. Tommy lit a cigarette without breaking stride.

He inhaled deeply. "You know, Nathan, I spend most of my waking hours less than a mile from here, up the hill at State, but I've never been on this street before. It's truly like another world."

(*No, it is another world.*) As they walked for a moment in silence, Nathan thought of the many times he had hiked these streets the past month and a half. His world seemed so much simpler in this neighborhood. In nearly a daily ritual, he had explored these modest streets, sometimes alone, often with Bobbie and Judy or other of his new friends. Once, and only once, he had even dragged Jack reluctantly though the exceedingly quiet blocks.

His father continued. "You'd think this neighborhood had been here forever. But it hasn't. Wasn't that long ago it was just miles of sand. The university itself only moved up the hill in the early fifties." His father let out a short quiet laugh, shaking his head. "Amazing to think that was *after* you were born. You know, son, when I first moved to this city, the weather drove me batty. I hated the fog. Couldn't stand it. Can't say I love it now, but in a way, perhaps I do. Certainly appreciate it. What I like is how it softens the city. In a funny way, one might say it brings out more of nature, more of the natural world into . . . all this man-made hardness. At least this thick pea-soup weather." Tommy finished his cigarette with one final draw and flicked what was left into the fog. Nathan saw the bit of light hit the pavement, take a short bounce, then vanish. Most of the tension of a few minutes ago was also disappearing.

"But the thin gray overcast? That can be mind-numbing. Day after day." Tommy paused, then laughed. "Listen to me. I remember my folks always complaining about the weather in Ireland, all the endless rain. I was too young to remember. At least we don't have to worry about getting soaked to the bone. Just a wee bit damp, as Grandma Jenny would say."

Nathan smiled at the mention of his grandmother's name. Her cross-country visits were few and far between, but he could immediately call to mind her loving smile, could feel himself engulfed within her immense hug. Then, he realized that he hadn't even spoken with her for several weeks and was brought back to the reality of his father no longer living at home. (*Damn – can't get away from it.*) His father always initiated the call back east, and neither he nor Ava had yet embraced making the call. Nathan was lost in these thoughts and didn't hear his father ask a question until it was repeated.

"I just asked, son, if you want to keep walking or if we should turn back?"

Nathan quickly responded. "No, not at all. Let's keep walking." Deep down, he was happy just to be with his father, zigzagging through the dream-like fog. They walked in silence for another few minutes, still not passing a single car or person this late at night. When Tommy lit another cigarette, Nathan knew a new subject would follow.

"So, Nathan, I'm wondering about college. Yours, not mine, that is." His father paused to let the topic hang in the quiet air, hoping to give his son a chance to pass beyond any quick reaction.

"I know you've been focused on your workshop, and summer's only half over." Again, a pause. "But your last year of high school will start soon and, well, maybe time to start a conversation?"

(*Funny you should ask.*) Nathan slowly nodded in response. "In fact," he paused, thinking how to best phrase his thoughts, "in fact, Dad, as a prelude to college, I think I want to explore theatre. And I know I'm jumping ahead, but I've even thought about college drama programs."

This was indeed more than Tommy Hughes had expected. "Nathan. To be impressed a second time in a single night."

"I know this idea has happened quickly. Theatre, I mean. But it just feels right. The biggest plus has been Mr. Dwyer. He was the one telling us about the college drama programs in the area. He said that State's program was one of the best. If not the best." Nathan realized he was maybe sounding too naïve, maybe starry-eyed. "Anyway, first things first. He wants me to audition for the play his school's doing this fall. It'll be a chance to see if I have any real talent. And if I like theatre as much as I have this summer. If I get a part that is."

"I want to meet your Mr. Dwyer. I must say, that was quite the production this evening. Clearly, the man is a force to be reckoned with."

They reached the end of the block. Through the dense fog, they barely saw across a wide boulevard directly ahead. Tommy started to turn back just as Nathan realized where they were – across from the park he used to visit in grade school, the park in which Mr. Scanlan had tragically died. "Dad," Nathan said, "let's take a quick hike through the Grove. The entrance is just up the road," Nathan pointed to his right. "There's a path that comes back out a few blocks down, not that long. I've never been there at night. Though not sure how much we'll see in this fog."

"The Grove, is it? I remember the music concerts we went to, way back when. Do you remember those?"

"Not really. Mostly how far away from the stage we had to sit, it was so crowded. What I remember more is our school trips. And, of course, Mr. Scanlan."

"Mr. Scanlan," his father responded. "Remind me."

(*You don't remember?*) "Our science guide on those trips. With answers to every question you could think of." Nathan was surprised at how well he could remember not only Mr. Scanlan's physical features – his tall, rugged stature and well-lined face – but also how clearly his deep but lyrical voice, even the phrasing of his words, now echoed in his head. (*'All from the spiritual world. Remember that. One day you might be surprised.' Or something like that.*) "You don't remember him, Dad? He died in that winter storm."

By this time, they had reached the entrance to the Grove and had begun the descent downhill. The mystery of the road disappearing into the fog and trees was overpowering, and Tommy left his son's question unanswered. Rather, he said, "I stand corrected on what I said earlier, Nathan. *This* is another world, as if we are walking into a dream."

(*Or back in time?*) The sound of their shoes seemed to be even more noticeable, as the steepness of the slope added more force to each step. Nathan stopped, thinking he heard a low-sounding noise from much farther downhill. "Do you hear something, Dad?" They both strained to hear beyond the sound of their own breathing.

"If I do, only barely," Tommy said. "I'm trying to remember what's at the bottom of this road."

Nathan let his mind travel to that bottom, and remembered the structure he had always hurried past in a rush to enter the park. Though he had never stopped there, it had made enough of an impression. "It's a clubhouse of sorts, a large older Victorian. I think I remember Mr. Scanlan telling us you can rent it out, you know, for a gathering." Nathan paused. "Maybe someone's rented it tonight?"

Father and son continued down the steep hill. By the time they came to the next lamppost, it was clear that the fog was thinning. And that voices could indeed be heard, though still only as a low sound.

"Hope we're not crashing a private party!" Tommy said as they turned the last curve of the road. They were several hundred yards from the bottom when they were stopped by the realization that the sounds were not casual or lighthearted, but shouts and yells. At nearly the same time, a large dull yellow glow became visible through the fog. Figures could be dimly seen running crisscross through the parking lot. Then, all of the sudden, the most telling piece of the puzzle – the sound of a booming fire engine horn blasted through the night directly above them. They looked at each other in shock.

"Holy Mother, son – off the road!"

Nathan and his father ran quickly off the road then through the trees, more caught in a sense of chaos than knowing where they were going. They soon came to the parking lot in front of the lodge. At that moment, the first fire truck arrived and headed toward the large structure engulfed in flames. Several more trucks followed, and still more sirens could be heard in the distance.

"Crickey, Dad, the parking lot's not big enough for all the trucks!"

Tommy Hughes and his son stood on the edge of the lot, held by the intensely bright fire, its smoke bellowing skyward and intertwining with the night fog. The eerie mix of flames, smoke, and fog was spellbinding. Even though they were at least a hundred yards away, they could feel the heat of the fire through their jackets.

"Don't think I've ever seen anything so frightening but so beautiful at the same time," Tommy said.

Slowly their attention was drawn to the firefighters. Several hoses had already been hooked up, now throwing water from several directions onto the lower sections of the lodge. Tommy and Nathan watched in awe at the precision and teamwork, the slow but steady progress to subdue the fire. All of a sudden, Nathan's father turned toward him.

"Nathan, now will you look at that. At whoever must have been at the party. Or whatever it was. It looks like they know the firemen. They're not only talking with them but working with them. Look over there – those two, alone on a hose." His father paused. "Now you wouldn't think *that* would be allowed. Untrained men taking over like that."

As his father was talking, Nathan noticed what seemed to be a tall older man approaching from the chaos before them. As he neared, his features began to appear vaguely familiar. The man was walking with a quick purpose, his gaze fixed intently at his father and himself. Just as he sensed that his father's attention was now also on this man, Nathan's heart stopped.

"Oh, my God. It's Mr. Scanlan," Nathan said slowly in a frightened whisper. His eyes widened and locked onto the man's as he closed the final steps, stopping a few yards in front of them. Nathan focused on the beads of sweat that covered the man's face.

"Just who are you two and what the hell are you doing here?" the man growled. (*Sounds just like Mr. Scanlan. A very angry Mr. Scanlan.*)

Tommy Hughes didn't take kindly to the man's rough approach. "Now hold on, sir. No need for that tone." He slowed his speech even more than typical. "My son and I were simply taking a nighttime walk." He realized how far-fetched that must sound, considering the unusual circumstances. "As strange as that might sound, 'tis the truth." The two men's eyes were now fixed, the man sizing up

Tommy, and Tommy holding firm. "By the time we realized what was happening, well ..." Nathan's father let his sentence stop, assuming that their fascination with the pandemonium needed no explanation.

The man slowly released some of his tension and gave the slightest of nods with a grunt. He turned his head and saw that Nathan's look had not changed. He squinted and tilted his head slightly. "And just what are you staring at?"

Nathan indeed had not moved, had not changed expression from when he had identified the man coming toward them. Or at least who he thought this man was. His father was taken aback when he turned and saw Nathan's face, realizing then what his son had just said about Mr. Scanlan. Tommy Hughes thought, now, damn, just who *is* this Mr. Scanlan? This portrait of confusion held for what seemed an embarrassingly long time, before the man broke the silence, first with a gruff snort of awareness.

"Oh, yes. I've seen this look before. Mostly from ones your age." He shook his head slowly. "Never like this though." Another pause. "You're thinking of *John* Scanlan, aren't you?"

The spell was bending, though not quite broken for Nathan. As if a wand were waved too quickly in front of his face. "Yes. Yes. I am." The two sets of eyes continued locked together. "You are Mr. Scanlan, aren't you? I don't understand."

The man muttered under his breath, "Won't ever be free of this curse." He looked away with a deep breath. "John was my brother. My identical twin." He looked at Nathan and, seeing a look more of confusion than understanding, for the briefest of moments let go of the roughness that had been all too apparent. "My *identical* identical twin."

Nathan saw the man's lips move, heard the words, but their meaning didn't quite come together. (*This man was not my teacher?*)

"My name is Scanlan, but I'm not John. My name is Patrick. Pat Scanlan."

(*Mr. Scanlan. Not Mr. Scanlan.*) The spell broke. Not completely. But enough. (*Twins? Oh! Twins.*) "Sorry . . . it took me so long."

Nathan's father broke in, "That's okay, son. This is quite a night, quite unusual to say the least." He gave his son a quick squeeze around the shoulders. "I don't think I've ever seen anyone look so stunned."

The man spoke up, "Yes, well, sorry to have given you such a start." Then turning to Tommy said, "Sorry for being abrupt, but you and your son need to be off now. Still have a lot of work. Don't want anyone getting hurt." A nod of the head was the emphatic period to his sentence.

Tommy Hughes put his arm around his son and turned them both away from the tall man standing firm. He kept his arm over his son's shoulders as they walked away. When they reached the walking path that entered the grove proper, Tommy asked quietly, "You still up for taking the path you mentioned? The fog's thinner now and there's a full moon tonight. I think we can see where we're going." Nathan nodded. (*Full moon. Looking down on me?*) Tommy turned around briefly and saw that the man had gone. The fire was still burning, but noticeably less intense. What a strange night, Tommy Hughes thought. What a remarkably strange and powerful night.

As they made their way along the path that crossed the acres of grass, Tommy let his son walk in silence. His own thoughts went back to the firefighters working hand-in-hand with the partygoers, or whoever those were in casual clothes. That thought juxtaposed with Patrick Scanlan's all-too-certain command for Tommy and Nathan to leave, that he simply wanted them gone. Then Tommy realized that the men helping the firefighters were no different in anything they were doing, no different in how they were fighting the fire. Of course, Tommy thought, they were all the same. They were all firemen. The ones not in uniform must have been at an off-duty event. And if he were right, and a fire had somehow started, now that would be something to keep from the public. The public being a father and son taking a midnight walk through the park.

"Dad, we take this path ahead, up into the trees." It was Nathan's turn to interrupt his father's thoughts. "It'll take us out, back to the boulevard."

"Yes, well, lead the way, son. Trying to understand why we were so unwanted. I'm wagering that a fire was started at a firemen's ball, of sorts.

Something they would want to keep quiet." Tommy reached for a cigarette but stopped himself. "Last thing I should do here," he muttered. "I'll be very interested in seeing what's in the papers tomorrow. If there's any mention at all."

Nathan half-listened to his father's logic. It made sense, but he was still recovering from the ghost of his former teacher walking toward him, out of the bedlam beyond. The man's face was now seared into his mind. So much the same as the memory of his Mr. Scanlan. Except the one difference that couldn't be more different. (*And what did he say about a curse?*)

Halfway up the grade out of the Grove, something made Nathan look to his right. They were near one of few lampposts on the path, and its illumination allowed him to see into the trees and bushes along the slope. There was a large, curved stone set by itself at the far edge of the light. Nathan was immediately drawn to it.

"Dad, wait a second."

He approached the stone with fascination but also a misgiving. As he neared, he could see that the top was flat with words chiseled into its smooth surface. Before he could read them, he knew why the stone had been placed there. He closed his eyes before he read, bringing Mr. Scanlan's face, the kind and thoughtful Mr. Scanlan, into his mind's eye. Then, he read the etched words in the moonlight dimmed by the remaining fog.

John Scanlan. Lover of nature. Now, forever, a part of nature. January 17, 1964.

"Dad, this is where he died," Nathan called back to his father. "I never knew where it happened." Nathan looked up at the towering trees trying to imagine one of them falling. The loudness of the crack. (*Did he even hear it? Over the sounds of the storm?*)

Nathan bent over and touched the stone, and with the touch, closed his eyes. With the tips of his fingers, he slowly felt the edges of the chiseled markings while the base of his palm slid along the smooth surface. When all letters and numbers had been touched, he turned back to his father. They climbed the final grade and exited the park, leaving behind what seemed more dream than reality.

Re-crossing the wide boulevard, father and son briskly made their way through what was left of the fog. Unlocking his car, Tommy threw his cigarette onto the pavement, crushing it hard under his heel.

The drive across town was surprisingly quick, with few if any cars on the road this deep into the night. Nathan listened to his father quietly sing to a Sinatra song on the radio, . . . *on Jupiter or Mars. In other words, hold my hand, in other words, baby, kiss me . . .* (*Is he singing this to Mom, or his . . . girlfriend?*)

Tommy Hughes pulled into the driveway of the house he owned but did not live in, cut the engine with a conscious twist of hand, and then turned toward his son.

"A one-of-a-kind night." His father paused, waiting for his son to turn toward him. "Not sure if I understood everything that happened. But I did understand what happened at the beginning. And I know damn well that sharing all of it was, well, more than special." Tapping the side of his temple with his finger, he added, "This will be a memory that lasts."

Nathan looked straight ahead and slowly nodded, then turned, reaching out his left hand. His father grabbed it, encircling it with both hands. "I'll call you tomorrow. You know, just to check in," Tommy said to his son. "You okay?"

Nathan nodded and took in a full breath. "Dad, I take back what I said. About not wanting you at the performance." Nathan looked into his father's eyes, being reminded once again that the color was the same rich brown as his own. (*Maybe even browner?*) "I always wanted you to be there. I just wanted you to be there with Mom."

Tommy Hughes quickly reached out to his son, partly to hide a welling of tears, saying, "Come here, boy-o," and gave Nathan one last hug. "I love you so." Nathan turned to get out of the car, and with one final look back, focused first on the familiar slight upturn of his father's smile. Then was surprised to see that those brown eyes were no longer sharp and clear, but now, most definitely, covered with a film that wasn't there just a moment before.

Chapter 9

Bobbie

The day after the seemingly endless night, Nathan kept not only to his home but mostly to his bedroom and with the door closed. When he woke late in the morning and found himself alone, he was at first disoriented, but then remembered his mother was to start a new job that day. He spent the afternoon distracting himself by reading. He hardly ate and was not so much tired but oddly without energy. Occasionally, he put his book down and let his thoughts try to drift back to the previous night. However, those events were much too complex, and he simply let each form and then dissipate, like movement of water away from a thrown stone. The phone rang once or twice, but he ignored it. Even after remembering that his dad might call, Nathan could not push himself to go downstairs and call back. Late in the afternoon, he must have fallen asleep, as he was surprised to hear a knock on the door, followed by his mother's voice.

"Nathan, are you awake?" (*No, not really.*) Another series of knocks followed.

Nathan physically shook his head trying to clear what felt unmovable. "I'm wake," was all he could manage. Then, knowing all too well that she would accept nothing less than a full report, he added a half-hearted, "Down in a minute."

Her steps faded down the stairs, and Nathan softly mumbled, "Christ."

Beneath the sedated afternoon, Nathan could sense a mix of uncertainty and confusion. His mother's voice had quickly amplified the ambiguity that he had avoided during the day – last night's leap forward in resetting his relationship with his father contrasted with the unchanged reality of his mother's relentless hurt. (*I should still be mad at him.*) Then he remembered the sound of her voice last night when he called – she truly wanted him to be with his father, even if his father was her estranged husband. He had to trust that, as painful as the past few months had been, she would want to hear any positive step forward. And she would absolutely have to hear details. It was the latter that he was doing his best to avoid. He knew how much his mother enjoyed his stories, but he simply had no energy to weave a yarn. No energy to conjure up the details of breaking down in front of his father. And then, of their hypnotic walk through the fog. But more to the point, he was overwhelmed by the task of piecing together the tale of what followed. The still incomprehensible dream-like events inside the Grove. Normally, he would have immediately latched onto the strange and bizarre, but now he was avoiding them. (*Why? Have I finally met my match?*) Had reality won the day? How could such an unusual night be told with a simple step-by-step narrative, with no need to embellish? (*How can I exaggerate the unbelievable?*)

"Enough!" he muttered, again shaking his head, then roughly rubbing his hands through his hair, forcing himself to move. He pushed the mysteries of last night out of his mind, opened his bedroom door, and reentered the fully awake world. First and foremost were the various gaps between himself and his splintered parents. He knew the more important story to tell, and certainly the one his mother was waiting downstairs to hear. (*The other damn story will have to wait.*)

• • •

More than anything, it was Bobbie McGregor who became the center of Nathan's attention during the month of August. The first week after the workshop seemed to be filled with walks or phone calls or conversations in the enclosed back porch with either his mother or father. It wasn't until the following weekend that Nathan's thoughts returned to earlier that summer and his headlong immersion into the world of theatre. He thumbed through the notebook he had meticulously kept and was reminded of the endless specifics he was introduced to. Then he turned a page to see the funny little drawing of Bobbie he had sketched late one afternoon.

The moment returned to him in an instant. He was sitting on the floor, by himself, his back against the far wall. Most had left for the day, but Bobbie was working with Lenny, setting up portable lighting fixtures. Judy was the 'model,' standing in different poses as they explored various angles and heights and colors of the lights, and the effect of each on how Judy might be viewed by the audience. Nathan remembered being tickled at the diminutive Bobbie stretching on tiptoe to reposition the head of the lighting units, and how he tried to capture this stretch in his drawing. He then realized that it was now a full week after the performances. They had spent most days of summer together and had promised to keep in touch. (*Too soon to call?*) He turned the notebook to the back cover to make sure he had her number, then reached over to grab a quarter, smiling to himself, "Heads I call, tails I wait." It landed heads. (*Surprise, surprise.*)

"Hello." Bobbie's soft voice had the slightest upturn on the second syllable, almost a question. Nathan was surprised how effortlessly her voice resonated in his ears.

"Hey, Bobbie. Nathan. Am I interrupting?"

A pause, short but long enough to give Nathan a moment of doubt.

"Nathan, what a surprise. I, ah, well I wasn't expecting to hear your voice." Bobbie hesitated, but continued before Nathan could break in. "Such a nice voice to hear."

(*Hmm, yes. No, your voice is.*)

"So, remember we said we'd stay in touch? I was just thinking about the workshop. I don't know about you. It already seems ages ago." Nathan stopped in mid-sentence. (*Slow down, kiddo.*) "Well, I know it's only a week, but I heard this voice in my head saying, 'it's time to call.' You know, to stay in touch."

"Nathan, that's sweet."

"Well, not sure how sweet." Nathan had no idea of what to say next, the phone call had just happened. He quickly remembered talking movies with Bobbie and that she lived near the beach. "So, we should get together. Maybe a movie? There's a great little movie house near the beach. I'd love to introduce you."

"Wait, there's only one theatre near here – you don't mean the Sunset? I walk near there all the time. But every time I stop to see what's playing, well, I've never heard of the movie!"

65

(*Lucky me!*) "Perfect! I can *really* introduce you then. Properly introduce you. How about next week?"

"Next week?" Bobbie said thinking. "Just my job, but that's during the days. So, Nathan, you're not going to drag me to some boring old black and white movie?"

"Oh, I'll take it easy on you. At least, the first time. Let me check their schedule, and . . . at least I promise it'll be in English." Bobbie laughed, which reminded him of the many weeks together and how much he enjoyed (*no, more than that*) her mix of quick wit and love of banter.

"Oh, all right. But I promise you back – I'm holding you to your promise."

After goodbyes, Nathan ran up the stairs two-at-a-time, knowing exactly where he had left the movie schedule. He admired the Sunset's schedule itself, such a handsomely crafted brochure. Thick paper. Quality photographs. Such enticing annotations, sure to capture any movie fanatic's fancy. And whoever came up with the combinations for double bills was, well, a genius pure and simple. Nathan flipped through the pages to see what choices might impress Bobbie. It took only a heartbeat to realize the coming Wednesday could not be more perfect. Old. Black and white. And in English. The King's English. To top it off, Nathan had already circled the double bill for his own viewing, from the week-long retrospective 'Alfred Hitchcock's English Films from the 1930's.'

Although he had only seen a couple of Hitchcock movies in the theaters (*and a few more on TV*), Nathan was enough of a film buff to know that the rotund director of the macabre was a master of the visual story. He had just read that Hitchcock literally sketched each camera shot prior to shooting a single scene of a new film, and Nathan had vowed to see as many classics next week as possible. The choices to see with Bobbie were many, but the first night's showing of *The Lady Vanishes* and *The 39 Steps* had to be the one – such glowing reviews of both. Nathan bounded back downstairs.

"Hey, Bobbie. Nathan again. If all nights are the same to you, I have the perfect double bill. This coming Wednesday."

"Whoa, Nathan. That sure didn't take any time," Bobbie replied half-laughing, but also impressed. "What can I say? Yes, Wednesday night sounds great."

"First one starts at six. I'll be there early in case there's a line. But you get there when you can."

"It's a date, Nathan. (*A date!?*) See you in line!" Bobbie replied quickly, happily caught up in Nathan's enthusiasm. Her excitement triggered in his mind a subtle but sweet smile, the smile he now realized he had perfectly memorized during the long summer together.

• • •

Bobbie's family house was directly across from the thousand-acre city park and only a few blocks from the beach deep within the fog belt. The Sunset Theatre was even closer than the beach, and on Wednesday night, Bobbie walked away from the park, turning down the first cross street. She immediately spotted Nathan under the marquee in animated conversation with an older man. His back was to her and as she walked closer, she weighed a surprise tap on the shoulder or a simple call out of his name. She suddenly grew nervous and could not choose between the two.

"Nathan, hi," Bobbie finally called when only a few steps away.

"Hey, Bobbie," Nathan said, turning. "You're here. Hi. It's *so* good to see you." They gazed at each other, smiling, and for both, suddenly quite easily. Bobbie's nervousness vanished. "Bobbie, let me introduce you to an amazing man I just met, at least officially – I've heard his name for months. Herb Malakoff, this is my friend Bobbie McGregor. A movie buff like me, but her first time *inside* your theatre. I get the honor of introducing her to the wonders of the Sunset!" Turning to Bobbie, Nathan continued, "Mr. Malakoff is the genius who's transformed this theatre. There've been more than a few articles written about his concept of a film art house. Maybe each with a different description. But *all* of them credit the Sunset as being the first neighborhood theatre of its kind.

Anyway, running off at the mouth as usual. Mr. Malakoff was just suggesting I might work here. You know, part-time. I can't believe how perfect that would be."

From Bobbie's few glimpses, it was clear that Herb Malakoff was taken by Nathan's unbridled enthusiasm.

"It's not often that a man gets to hire a walking advertisement for his business," Herb laughed. "Nathan, come by some night before we open, and we can talk. Bobbie, pleasure meeting you. Please, enjoy inside and make sure you try the popcorn. I hear it's maybe worth the trip itself."

As they chatted, a line had formed, and Nathan and Bobbie maneuvered to the back. "I think still early enough for good seats," Nathan said, then added, "Say, forgot to ask, where do you like to sit?" He mentally crossed his fingers.

Bobbie could tell a loaded question when she heard it. She had no preference whatsoever and reasoned that with Nathan's enthusiasm for movies, he probably would want to sit close. "Really no favorites, but I guess somewhere closer to the front?" Then she added as innocently as she could, "Oh, shoot, I forgot to bring my glasses, so maybe closer is better? If you don't mind."

"Mind? Closer-the-better's my middle name!" (*Whoa, kiddo. Bring it down a notch.*) "You pick the seats, Bobbie. I'd go to the front row, but even my buddies can't take that close." Nathan shrugged. "What can I say. I like being *inside* the movie."

As they entered the front door, Bobbie thought, not ready for that close. However, stepping inside the lobby of the Sunset Theatre, any thought of seating vanished, giving way to immediate sensations different from any movie house she'd ever been in. The overall décor used its small size to wrap the patrons in a quick welcoming. Visually, the Sunset truly had the look of an art house, with handsomely framed posters of classic films on walls painted a royal burgundy. The intimate lobby was saturated with the aroma of the two offerings most associated with the Sunset – freshly made popcorn and the unexpected smell of espresso. But maybe the most noticeable sensuality was the eclectic music that filled the lobby. Tonight, a favorite of the house – the densely French Edith Piaf. As they entered and walked slowly through the lobby, Nathan snuck glances at

Bobbie, and saw what he had hoped to see – Bobbie's smile in full display and her eyes alive as she looked from poster to poster and then at the concession bar to the far left of the lobby. Then, realizing what song filled the air, he couldn't help but tease, "Don't worry – the movies tonight are *not* in French."

"Oh, Nathan. I take back what I said. All of this is, why, it's all wonderful. And what do you mean? I love Edith Piaf. Especially since I'm like her – a contralto. Maybe even more so! I'll have you know I sing a pretty mean 'Non, Je ne Regrette Rien.' Remind me, I'll do it for you one day. And with guitar!"

Bobbie's bit of French rolled effortlessly off her tongue, and speechless in delight, Nathan suddenly remembered that Bobbie's unspoken passion was indeed music. Although this talent was never on display during the workshop, he remembered how she had often rushed off from the workshop for another music lesson.

"I'll make absolutely sure to remind you to sing that." Nathan looked intensely at Bobbie, as if seeing her for the first time. She held his gaze for more than a moment, and then a moment longer, before shyly looking down.

(*Oh, sweet Jesus, am I, falling in love? In the lobby of the Sunset Theatre no less?*) As Bobbie looked down, Nathan realized that they were blocking traffic, and said, to break the spell, "Should we get our popcorn now or wait?"

"I think we better find those up-close seats of yours," Bobbie replied emphatically and took Nathan's hand, with a full and knowing look of affection. She led them both through the opened double doors and into the theatre, down the long central aisle toward the front. It was a few minutes before six, and well over half of the couple hundred seats were filled, but luckily the first two or three rows were mostly empty. She plopped down in a third-row seat while still holding Nathan's hand, neither of them ready to let go.

"Nathan, I have no idea what we're about to see!" Bobbie said suddenly. "I forgot to look at the marquee – I was so caught up with you and Mr. Malakoff." Bobbie finally released his hand, straightening her long skirt to fully settle into her seat. "You know, this is so fun – a complete unknown." Then turning to Nathan she continued, "I feel totally at the mercy of your whims!"

"*Whims?* Hey, look at it this way, Bobbie," Nathan said, recovering a bit from the head-spinning glimpse into the all-encompassing world of falling in love, "this many people on a Wednesday night at six o'clock for some old black-and-white?" As the music fell quiet and the lights gradually dimmed, Nathan reached over to take back Bobbie's hand, letting his hand rest on her lap. (*Whims, whimsy, whimsical, whatever - my heads a-spinning!*) Then, as the first burst of light struck the screen, he squeezed her hand in anticipation. In the blink of an eye, the light instantaneously condensed into the first image on screen – three bolded words, "The Lady Vanishes," perched on top snow-capped mountains, somewhere in the depths of Eastern Europe.

● ● ●

"You live nearby, don't you? I'll walk you home," Nathan said as they exited through the back door of the theatre. This exit led to a short walkway that led to the street going back to Bobbie's house.

"Hey," Bobbie said in surprise when they came to the street, "I must have walked past this a zillion times and never even noticed!"

"Yeah, the first time I came here, I just followed a couple leaving through that door. Toward the park?"

"Nathan, you don't have to walk me home. It's the opposite direction from your streetcar."

"Oh, tired of me already? After only a couple of movies? No way! You have to tell me how you liked those old boring black and white movies."

They were standing close, facing one another. Bobbie reached out with both hands and lightly touched Nathan's fingers. "I liked the movies, thank you very much, but I think I would have liked any movie tonight. Sitting next to you. Holding your hand. Why didn't this happen during the workshop."

Nathan's head began to spin again.

"Bobbie."

"Yes?"

"I," he started, then stopped, both his hands now entwined with hers. "I've never felt like this before. How I feel about you. It's ...it's a powerful feeling."

"Yes, it is."

"A bit scary."

"Yes. But also, wonderful. Don't you think?"

(*And now losing control.*)

While still holding hands, Bobbie reached up with her other hand to Nathan's face and gently held his cheek for the briefest moment. He felt the slight coolness of her hand against his skin, her forearm close to his chest. She lightly caressed his cheek before dropping her hand, softly saying, "Yes. You can walk me home."

They walked side-by-side, hand-in-hand, ever so slowly down the street toward the park. Nathan, looking down at both of their steps, focused on Bobbie's ankles and the small shoes just showing under her long skirt next to his larger shoes. (*Just who do these shoes belong to? This has happened so quickly!*)

"Scarier, or more wonderful?"

Nathan gave a short laugh. (*Uh-oh. She's persistent.*) "I can see, no ignoring your questions." He shook his head, "Can't say. More or less, that is. It's wonderful, but I don't know, it's, overwhelming. I feel a bit . . . out of control." Stopping and looking at Bobbie, he said, "But I do know one thing. *You* are 'more wonderful'." Then, drawn by a such a natural gravity, Nathan lowered his head and lips to meet her lips, their arms encircling, their bodies closer, then touching. Their first kiss stopped with lips partially open, both having briefly tasted the other. They slowly released their embrace, leaving them to continue their walk, now arms around each other.

"Oh my," Bobbie managed to whisper. Then just a bit more loudly, "and I thought I was just going to some boring old movies. Little did I know."

"Hmmm," Nathan sighed. "I'll second that." Then recovering just an ounce of pride, "The 'oh my.' Not the 'boring movie' part. You have to admit, Bobbie. Watching three hours of romance, well, it kind of puts one in the mood."

"Oh, so it was all planned, was it? I'll have to watch out for your tricks next time."

"Watch out all you want. Just make sure there *is* a next time."

Bobbie laughed softly, "You're right about one thing. Three hours of romantic banter does kind of wear off on you. In a good way."

They continued to walk slowly down the street, with Bobbie slipping her arm from Nathan's waist and taking hold of his hand instead. "Holding hands will be our show of affection," she stated matter-of-factly.

"Oh, I see."

"Yes, it's more romantic. And, well, I'm too short for the arm thing. I like my arm around your waist, but your arm around my shoulders? Doesn't work."

"Oh, I do see."

"Plus, holding hands was the first sign that, you know, we like each other. More than just friends?"

"Hmm. Yes, more than just friends." Nathan paused. "So, since we like each other, you know, so much, it's important to be honest with each other, right?"

"Ah-oh."

"You have to give an honest answer. Promise?"

"Not sure, but okay, I promise." Bobbie raised her free hand to show Nathan her crossed fingers. Nathan stopped and gently pushed her away in mock frustration.

"Tell me. Were those movies really that boring?"

"Oh," Bobbie laughed, proudly showing her fingers uncrossed, "I can absolutely promise. They were wonderful, Nathan. Both of them. Well, you know, it was a little like watching one long movie. I do have one criticism, though."

"What's that?" Nathan said smiling.

"It made me realize that English can also be a foreign language. I swear, I missed more lines in all that swallowed British mumbling. I sensed they were funny, but I couldn't understand half the lines!"

"What was your favorite? That you could understand that is?"

"Oh, that's easy. Can't remember it exactly. It was in the first movie, *The Lady Vanishes*, that was the first one, right? It's when the girl said something like, 'I've no regrets. I've been everywhere, done everything. Eaten caviar at Cannes, and blah, blah, blah. What's left for me, but marriage.'"

Nathan took back Bobbie's hand and pulled her close, saying, "So, not too disappointed in my pick? I can take you back to the Sunset?"

"You can always take me to the Sunset. And yes, you can drag me to any old, new, foreign, silent, whatever movie you want," Bobbie said laughing loudly. "Never in my wildest dreams did I ever imagine I'd be going out on dates only two blocks from my house. And oh, here we are!" They were at her house so close to the theatre, but so wonderfully far to reach.

"Bobbie – I know I spend way too much time talking about movies. You might be surprised to know I do like doing other things."

"Oh, such as?"

"No really, I'm just a normal guy, who just happens to be a bit," Nathan hesitated while Bobbie screwed her face waiting for whatever line he was about to offer. "Well, *obsessed* with a good story if you must know," he blurted out.

"Oh, I've heard about *that* obsession," Bobbie replied too quickly. She immediately knew that Nathan would know that she had heard 'that' from Maureen. "Oh crap, shouldn't have said that. Dumb, so dumb of me," Bobbie cursed while fiercely banging her hand hard against her other forearm.

Nathan's first reaction was indeed of the role his obsession played in the failed attempts at romance with Maureen, but he immediately turned his attention back to Bobbie who had tightly latched her arm across herself, grabbing onto the arm she had hit.

"Hey," Nathan said softly, reaching to take Bobbie gently by her shoulders. "Hey, what's this about?"

But Bobbie seemed not to hear him, so quickly had she turned inward. The feelings between them that had wonderfully deepened the past few hours had vanished in a blink of an eye.

"Hey. Bobbie." No response. She stood rigid; her eyes now tightly shut. Nathan was at a loss – he wanted to shake her. (*That can't be right.*) Instead, instinctually, he drew her close and slowly rubbed her back. After what seemed forever, he felt Bobbie finally take more of a breath, and then, maybe, did he feel her body releasing? He leaned back to look down at her face. Her eyes were still clenched closed.

"Bobbie. Hey. Where are you?" Nathan said quietly, almost whispering.

She shook her head sideways. Questions swirled in Nathan's mind, but he blocked them out and once again took hold of Bobbie. When she finally reached up to partially complete his embrace, he breathed a sigh, and slowly released her. She was still looking down.

"Hey." He gently touched her shoulder. "Let's sit down." Bobbie immediately went to the front steps and sat. Leaning forward with her arms crossed, she slowly rocked her head back and forth sideways, and then momentarily bent her head. Nathan sat down, fully turned toward her. Having no idea what to say, he tried to be patient and wait for Bobbie to speak, though he knew she wouldn't. (*Maybe she can't?*)

"You all right? I mean you don't have to say much."

"Oh, well, I've already said too much, haven't I?" (*At least she's speaking.*) "I'm so sorry, Nathan." Bobbie shook her head sideways again, as if trying to make the last few minutes disappear.

Nathan felt on the edge of a precipice without a safety net. Not for him, but for Bobbie. How could he possibly understand what had just happened, without triggering Bobbie to fall inward again? (*When in doubt, keep it simple.*) "Hey," he said reaching out again to hold her shoulder, "remember, we're more than friends now."

Bobbie looked up at Nathan, her eyes welling. "I'm so embarrassed – must have looked like some kind of freak. And I said such a stupid thing. *And* I feel so bad about Maureen. I mean, it's endless"

"Wait, what do you mean, about Maureen?"

"I took you from her."

"What!?"

"From that very first time we met. I thought you and Maureen were still, you know, together."

"Bobbie, wait. Maureen and I were not only no longer together, but I'm not sure we ever were – I mean in love. I never felt anything toward her like I felt tonight, toward you."

"Not sure that makes me feel any better. Kind of proves the crime. Don't you understand – I thought you two were still together, and never said anything to Maureen the whole summer. Even about meeting you. Pretty messed up, huh?"

"I don't understand," Nathan said quietly, mainly to himself, but then saw Bobbie's face respond, and quickly added, "I understand what you're saying, but I don't agree." Nathan took a deep breath. "Bobbie, look. You didn't steal me from anyone. The way I see it, we had a wonderful long introduction, this summer, where we got to know each other. But tonight, it was like, all of a sudden, we finally *met*." Nathan paused, trying to think of how to re-connect, how to return to the closeness he felt only a few minutes before. "You know when I first had that feeling? That we really met?" Bobbie shook her head. "It was in the lobby when you said you knew the Edith Piaf song. It was the way you said the name of the song – you almost sang it. It was so clear that you knew the song and that you could sing it beautifully, that even your French was perfect. And in that instant, the whole summer's introduction made sense, that I now knew a wonderfully special person. One that I really, *really* like."

Oh my, Bobbie thought, Maureen was right – you do have a way with words, Nathan Hughes. But can I trust you? Bobbie looked at him, at his eyes fixed on hers, at his entire body leaning, longingly toward her, all expressing an earnestness as real as she had ever seen. And his words did ring true; it *was* as if they had just met tonight. Really met. But as much as she wanted to ignore what just happened, the past few minutes were too powerful. And this was the second time Bobbie had experienced this inward feeling, or really, lack of feeling.

What causes it, and why? she thought. She finally reached out and took Nathan's hands. "I *do* know what you mean, about truly meeting tonight. Funny, for me it might have been seeing how Mr. Malakoff was looking at you. He was so taken by you, by your enthusiasm. And your enthusiasm can be very . . . attractive." Bobbie paused, then said, "Nathan, I don't understand what just happened." She paused again. "I guess there's no good way of ending this. Our first date. Yet, end it has." Bobbie looked up. "Call me tomorrow?"

Too many questions, and the only answer was a three-word commitment to another day. (*Tomorrow. That's enough. That's all I need for now. For this minute.*) Nathan nodded, "Yes. Of course." He stood holding the railing, and watched Bobbie walk up the steps to her front porch. As uncertain as the last few minutes had been, he couldn't help but let go of this confusion and simply latched onto what the world meant to him now, to Bobbie, to the oh-so rhythmic sway of her hips, the fall of her hair down her back. She reached the landing, turned, and blew a kiss down to him, then quickly unlocked and slipped through the front door. For the second time in little over a week, Nathan was left with a mind-numbing question about all that had occurred over the course of a very long night. (*Fact or fiction? This better be fact.*) All he knew for sure was that the streetcar ride back home was endless, much longer than the one he had taken in the opposite direction, only several hours earlier. Before he had fallen in love.

Chapter 10

Highs and Lows

Nathan awoke with a start to harsh and loud banging (*a fist on table?*) and still louder voices (*my parents!?*), sounds coming up the stairs through his closed door. He had heard their raised voices in the past, but never like this – a no-holds-barred anger from both, especially his mother. The voices were more sounds than words, not decipherable but clearly filling the house with rage. Simultaneous questions ripped through his head – What's going on? Why is his father even here? Should he go downstairs? And then, one he never imagined asking, Is his mother in danger? The last question followed by the first distinct words he could make out through his door, from his mother, "Get out! Get the hell out of my house!" A brief but telling silence lingered for a tense moment before the front door slammed, shaking the entire house.

Nathan quickly threw on whatever clothes lay close and ran downstairs, fearful for his mother. Half expecting to find her collapsed at the kitchen table, crying uncontrollably, he was surprised to see her standing, her back to him, at the kitchen counter, in full control but visibly seething.

"The bastard. How dare he even think that!" Ava was muttering, not to Nathan, whom she hadn't yet seen, but to herself.

"Mom!" Nathan cried out, hurrying to reach out and hold her.

Startled, as if shaken from a spell, Ava Hughes turned, with a look of anger mixed with confusion. The look disappeared into the all-of-sudden awareness of how loud, how frightening the just-finished fight must have sounded. "Oh, Nathan," was all she managed as they fell into a tight, rocking hug.

"Are you all right?" Nathan pulled away enough to ask while still holding his mother's upper arms. "What happened? What was Dad even doing here?"

Nathan's mother released him, at the same time placing a hand on the counter to steady herself. The emotion coming from her son's concern released the full impact of the fight. Ava turned, bewildered, to sit down, "I'm not sure what happened," she admitted, shaking her head in disbelief. "I've never been so angry with your father. Maybe with anyone. Ever."

"But why was he here? This early on a Saturday morning."

Ava let out a deep sigh, again shaking her head. "He wanted," she began, then took a breath, "I can't believe it, but he wanted to know," and she slowed her words even more, not so much for emphasis, but to check if each word were true, "if we, you, me, he, could go on an outing this holiday weekend," she looked at Nathan to see his reaction, "with Nira."

Nathan reacted first to the name. He had yet to hear his mother say it. Nira. Short for Ianira. Ianira Diaz. He pieced together the entire sentence, the unbelievable request.

"You're kidding!" was all Nathan could muster in disbelief. "Why, what outing? Why this weekend?"

"Lord only knows. I didn't even let him explain," she said, shaking her head again. "I just lost it. And then, all of a sudden, we were going back weeks. Months. To all the pain. And anger. And mistrust. The good will and hard work . . . it just went down the drain. He was like a little boy. Thinking we could be friends and..." Ava let her sentence end abruptly, her face blank, staring down the front hall past Nathan as if trying to recall the image of her husband storming out. She looked back at her son. "It's as if I didn't know him, Nathan. He's always been so grounded. Where in God's mercy did he get the idea that we could all be . . . together." Ava paused. "If he's ready for all of us to be friends . . . that's a bad sign."

Nathan had been standing quite still the whole time, a hand stuck on the back rung of his mother's chair. With her last words, he guessed that more (*much more*) needed to be said, would have to be waded through, if simply to give his mother the chance to put words to this new hurt. But he was wrong. After he pulled a chair beside her, sat down, and reached out to take both her hands, she looked at him, and said simply, "I've had it, Nathan. It's time to move on. Today. *Now*."

Nathan ached to see the weighted tiredness throughout his mother's body, especially heavy on her face, but couldn't help but be impressed by the steely resolve in her eyes, a resolve that tied him to her, and to this moment. "Let's you and me do something special this weekend," she said, their hands still grasped. "You start your last year of high school this coming week. That deserves something special, don't you think?"

"Hell, yes," Nathan shot back, along with a smile that dared to push the worry and tension aside. "Just you and me? Or should we round up some friends?"

"Oh, no, just you and me. Not ready to 'go public.' Maybe soon, but not yet." Ava Hughes momentarily closed her eyes and let out a deep breath, releasing just a tiny part of the morning's turmoil. A start, she thought, I have to start. She opened her eyes, and then returned her son's loving smile with the barest of her own. Nathan latched onto this smile, now just a thin outline of what he knew so well but had been more absent than present for too long. Then, out of nowhere, like the beginning of new story, an idea for an outing materialized in his head. A long and full and yes, damn it, special day, an excursion his mother had proposed more than once, but that somehow had never happened. (*Tomorrow – it will finally happen. Tomorrow. It's perfect.*)

• • •

Early the next morning, Nathan and his mother walked the few blocks from their home to wait for the city bus. As often in early September in this city, the sun was not only out, but underscored by the bluest of crystal-clear morning skies.

"Oh, Nathan, thank you, thank you, thank you," Ava almost squealed. "No idea where we're going, but I know it will be wonderful. What would I do without you?"

"Oh, Mom, you're such a little girl sometimes. You're being your wonderfully silly self, you know," Nathan said, feeling a reversal of roles. He looked at his mother in the surreally bright morning light and couldn't believe how refreshed she looked. The worn and heavy lines from yesterday had receded enough to reveal the graceful maturity he admired. Her eyes sparkled from both her inner resolve and a long-overdue full night's sleep.

Nathan had spent the better part of yesterday readying for their daylong trek and digging up the old knapsack buried in the basement. He even remembered to rummage through his father's dresser for the old family camera (*he won't be needing this tomorrow*), smiling when he found it loaded with a mostly full roll of film. He had given his mother two tasks – one, choosing her best pair of walking shoes, and two, finding whatever hat would securely stay on her head even if the wind came up. Lastly, he salvaged all but a few dollars from his remaining savings to cover the final treat. Thus, feeling prepared and a little full of himself, Nathan stood tall with both hands hooked onto the straps of the knapsack. As the Number Seven bus pulled up, he nodded to his mother, "Here we go, Mom. This is ours. And you'll need a transfer."

As it wasn't even eight a.m. on a Sunday morning, Nathan expected to board an empty bus. He was surprised to see this one at least a third full. He then remembered it was a holiday weekend, and that this line bordered the huge city park. (*Hmmm, I should take this bus instead of the streetcar to Bobbie's.*) Thinking of Bobbie reminded him that he still hadn't mentioned her to his mother. (*Definitely time.*) By now, he had spent more than a few evenings and weekend days with Bobbie. More to the point, most of his thoughts were now rooted to this gorgeously diminutive girl – loosely in shapeless daydreams, more tightly when remembering the lingering taste of her kiss, and often, impressed with those impossible questions she always seemed to ask. However, before he introduced the reality of a bona fide girlfriend to his mother, he had to say something about her floppy wide-brim hat with its strap cinched snuggly under her chin.

"You know, Mom, that hat you picked out really is too much. I know I said it had to cover your head, but it's, well, certifiably goofy."

"Oh, I don't care a tinker's whistle how I look. I was following my son's instructions, to the letter. Something that would stay on my head and keep the sun off my youthful skin."

"All right, all right. But you don't need it now. Here, let me put it in my bag. I feel like I'm sitting next to Pippi Longstocking."

"But you are, my son. You are sitting next to the grown-up Miss Longstocking. Didn't I ever tell you? I was twelve years old when the first book came out. My hair was much redder, and I wore it in two pigtails. And, surprise, surprise, everyone knew me as playful and overly friendly. It was Daddy who started calling me Pippi. Even though I read everything I could find, he loved to read me that book. I've lost the red hair and the pigtails, but you have to admit, I still have her spirit. Don't you think?"

"What can I say? How did I ever miss seeing it?" Nathan said shaking his head. "But you still need to put that hat away. Hand it over."

"Oh, all right. I must say, I kind of like the dumpy feel of it. A perfect way to deal with your father – hiding as a nondescript nobody." Ava took the hat off and plopped it onto Nathan's lap, then smiled as she re-fluffed her hair, "Better?"

"Much." As he leaned over to place the hat inside his knapsack, he struggled to come up with a perfect line to start his story of Bobbie. Ava intervened.

"So, Nathan. Tell me about your girlfriend. I've been waiting for you to say something, but, well, I don't have all the patience in the world."

Nathan's jaw dropped. "How in the..."

"Oh, come now, son. I know I'm your mother, but any stranger with two good eyes could have known someone of the opposite sex had come into your life this past month. Was it someone you met at the workshop this summer?"

Nathan again looked at his mother, his mouth now frozen in the same half-open look of incomprehension.

"So, let's start with the easy part. What's her name?"

"Mom!"

Ava patted her son on his hand. "I'm sorry. I'll stop. It's just that I'm so excited, and we haven't had a chance to talk. What with your father, and my new job, and, well, whoever you're trying to tell me about. And I'm not letting you."

Like any good storyteller, Nathan knew he always had to be quick on his feet, to adjust to surprises thrown from the audience. (*Best give in and get on with it.*)

"Yes, on all counts. Her name is Bobbie McGregor. And no, she wasn't *in* any of the performances. She did the lighting for half of them, including *Rosencrantz*. And before you start teasing, yes, you can say she's now the light of my life. And oh, crap, this is our stop."

Nathan jumped up to grab the pull-cord. Luckily, the traffic light ahead had just turned red, and the driver had slowed down. The bus half-pulled into the stop and the two quickly exited.

"We cross here to catch the next bus." Nathan pointed across the street.

"So, getting back to Bobbie," his mother said, not willing to be distracted.

"Yes, well, let's first get across the street without being hit."

"Oh, Nathan, you're so dramatic. And by the way, I want my hat back."

"Jeez, you're impossible," Nathan said, trying to keep pace with his mother's whimsy. He reached into his bag and handed her the hat "Here you go, Miss Anonymous. So, you want to hear more about Bobbie or not?"

"Yes, absolutely. Most interested in where you are in the spectrum of, hmmm, interest? More like, or more . . . you know? From all the telltale signs you've been leaving around, I'm guessing it's shifted, somewhat to the right?"

Nathan chuckled, "No beating around the bush with you. Well, having never been in 'more' before, I can say it is most definitely to the right of 'like.' But you're going too fast, Mom. Enough about me and how I feel. Let me tell you about her."

Ava chuckled back. "I'm sorry, Nathan. I must plead to a mother's mindset, her child always first. Yes, of course, tell me about Miss Bobbie McLeod."

"Bobbie Mc*Gregor*."

"Ooops. Sorry. Nice Scottish name. I assume, at least second generation, no accent?"

"No. Oh my God, if she had a Scottish accent, on top of everything else, I really wouldn't be able to handle how I feel about her. No, and neither does her mother, whom I met once."

"You've met her mother, and you're just telling me!?"

"Mom! I just met her mother the other day. And like you said, a few things have been going on in our house. Anyway, yes, it's time you know about Bobbie. And, yes, it's time you meet her. I was thinking of inviting her over for dinner."

"Of course, and I'm going to pull rank and insist she come for dinner before any rendezvous with your father."

"Absolutely. Don't even have to ask. I mean, demand." Nathan looked up the street to see the next bus approaching. "Here comes our transfer."

The Number 28 bus was even more full, but they managed to find two seats together. Ava Hughes took off her hat without having to be asked. She shook her hair out and said, turning toward her son and smiling, "I'm excited for you, Nathan. Tell me more."

"Not sure where to begin. Smarts or looks. What's funny is that all summer at the workshop she was focused on learning the ins and outs of lighting, so that was the context I saw her in. Especially everything with *Rosencrantz*. But no opportunity to become aware of, let alone even fully appreciate her real passion. Which is music. What a voice. *And* she plays a pretty mean guitar."

"What type of music?"

"Oh, that's the best part. A perfect mix. Of everything. All the recent greats – Beatles, Dylan, Joan Baez, plus such a wide collection. Some international music. Especially French. Wait until you hear her Edith Piaf songs. *Amazing.*"

"Sounds like the barometer is pegged way to the right, Nathan."

"Yeah, I guess it is, Mom. I guess it is."

"So, her looks. I'm guessing drop-dead gorgeous?"

"I think so! But not in the picture-perfect sense. More in the everything-is-just-right sense. Maybe the two most distinguishing features are her height and her hair. She's kind of short. Well, I'll just say it – she *is* short. Like in five-foot-even short. And I didn't ask; she told me. And beautiful black hair. Slightly wavy, long down her back, and usually braided. But only a single braid, no pigtails. This is *not* an Oedipus thing." Mother and son both laughed.

The questions and answers faded for a moment, lapsing into the enjoyment of simply being together. They both looked out the window as the bus passed out of the park and onto the long boulevard thickly bordered with trees. When the bus stopped at a red light, Nathan continued.

"But you know what might interest me the most are her damn questions. She's so, I don't know, direct. Well, not only direct, but amazingly perceptive." Nathan paused. (*Not getting this quite right.*) "I mean you ask direct questions all the time, but you're my mother, and that's what mothers do. At least you do," Nathan said half-smiling, half-smirking. "I've never known anyone my age to ask such tough questions. And I can't think of a single question that hasn't been either right on, for whatever we're talking about, or important in a larger context. For example, out of the blue, the other day she asks me my opinion about, not just the war, but about the draft. 'So, what would you really do if you were drafted?' One way or another, she's always challenging me. I can tell you, at times it's been hard. No, impossible! And, believe me, I haven't always responded, uh, politely. But her questions are becoming what I like the most." Nathan smiled and corrected himself, "Well, that's not quite true."

The bus entered the tunnel that bisected the large northwest corner of the city. Even in the faint light, Ava Hughes could see how deeply engaged her son was in describing Bobbie, that he had indeed shifted far to the right. She thought, how lucky that my son has found someone equally special to fall in love with. Being challenged is a good thing. Good for Bobbie, and good for Nathan to see that. Ava thought, maybe all the ingredients of truly being in love?

As the bus came out of the tunnel, her thoughts turned back to the present, and she puzzled, where in the world is he taking me? The bus exited off the roadway and the trees disappeared to present, directly ahead, the greatest engineering feat in all the city, no, one of the greatest in the country if not the world – the majestic vermillion bridge that crossed the waters where ocean met bay. Are we walking across the bridge, she wondered. She turned to Nathan with a questioning look. His return smile was immediate, indeed bursting because his secret had been kept and was now revealed in all its glory.

"Today's the day, Mom," Nathan simply said. "You know it's nearly two miles long, don't you, well over three round trip. You've said you always wanted to do this. You ready?"

"Oh, Nathan, am I ever," Ava Hughes exclaimed, reaching into Nathan's pack to grab her hat. With a wide smile, she securely plopped it onto her head, pulling the string band tightly up to her chin. "I've never been so ready my entire life!"

• • •

A few weeks later, Nathan sat alone on a bench in the Panhandle waiting for his father, jacket bundled tight and hands buried in his pockets. It was shortly after school, still well before Tommy's evening class, and late enough in the afternoon that the park was relatively empty. As Nathan waited, he thought back to the breakthrough night spent with his father. Although their relationship was not yet on solid ground, at least they were talking. (*No, gotta give him credit. More than just talking.*) The bond was strong enough that Nathan was comfortable asking his father what the hell he was thinking by asking if Nira could join them on a weekend outing. Plus, he needed to introduce Bobbie. He smiled to himself, imaging how different it would be from telling his mom – no way his dad knew anything about his love life.

Nathan saw his father approaching from the direction of the house, his old jacket zipped up. (*Must have parked in the driveway – did he see Mom?*) In another minute, Tommy, throwing down his cigarette, called out, "You picked a great place to meet on a day like this, boy-o. Let's you and I get something hot to drink. Indoors!"

"Absolutely. Wasn't that cold when I left the house, but as soon as the wind came up . . ." Nathan stood up and rubbed his arms for warmth.

"Diner or coffee house?" Tommy Hughes asked. Although most poets might prefer a café, Nathan knew his father's choice.

"No need to ask, Dad. Let's go to the diner on Hayes. I need to pick up some photos on the way."

They crossed the street bordering the park and headed up hill. "So, Nathan, you just started classes. Always an adjustment."

Nathan gave a short, sarcastic laugh. "Adjustment? How about being on another planet. I don't know, Dad, this has been the hardest back-to-school ever. I guess too much going on. Which I want to talk about. But, yes, a transition for sure."

"Tell me what you're taking."

"Jeez, let me think. Well, Chemistry for my science. Wish I could keep taking Biology. Done with Math. Intro to Psych. Third year Spanish. And then the fun stuff. Drama and my senior English class – Fiction into Film, a brand-new class taught by Mr. Sheridan. He told me his idea last semester. I couldn't believe how perfect it sounded. And from the first class, even better."

"Sounds like a good mix. But you didn't mention any religious study. Not that I would care in the least, mind you, but isn't that mandatory?"

"Ooops," Nathan said quickly, "do Freudian slips have to be sexual? Taking a senior elective on World Religion. Father Gautier's teaching it. He's cool. In a subtle, low-key kind of way. Very smart. And very liberal-minded, so I'm sure he'll do justice to every religion known to man."

"Shouldn't that be, known to God?" Tommy added, eyebrows raised.

"If there's a God, way too smart to have anything to do with such stupidity."

They turned down Hayes Street and stopped in the camera shop where the photos were ready for pick-up. As they headed back out the door, Nathan stuck the envelope in his pocket without looking. (*Not now. Too windy.*) The diner was two blocks farther down the street.

"And when's that play your Mr. Dwyer's directing?"

"Wow, Dad, what a memory. I'm impressed. Later in the semester. Though I should give him a call. Glad you mentioned that – it's probably been chosen."

They walked in silence for a few moments, before Nathan remembered that it was a new semester for his father also. "So, Dad, how's *your* semester? What are you teaching?"

"Nice of you to ask, son." Tommy nodded toward Nathan. "I've put together a new English course. For lack of a better name, I'm calling it, 'Primitive and Ancient Poetries.' A bit of a matter-of-fact title, but there you have it. It's built around a book I was lucky enough to preview: *Technicians of the Sacred*. A collection of poems, songs really, from across the globe and across time. Wonderful book."

"Sounds right up your alley."

"It is, it is. McClure turned me onto it. Hate to say it but must give credit where credit's due." Tommy Hughes paused for the briefest of beats. "And then of course, I have my usual evening poetry class. No undergraduate courses this semester. The rotation thing, you know, one semester on, the next off. So, all in all, looking forward to it. Truth be told, excited."

They reached the diner, glad to escape the cold wind that had chased them down the street. The restaurant was empty. They chose a booth in the back, both taking off their jackets. It was too warm a contrast to the outside air. The waitress who Nathan remembered from childhood greeted them. (*As part of the diner as the food.*)

"Let me guess – no need for a menu. Just something hot to drink."

They both smiled, as Tommy Hughes answered, "Now what gave us away, Irene? The frost bite markings on our lips? I'll have a cup of coffee. Black. Nathan?"

"This'll sound crazy, but I'd like a chocolate shake. I'm a bit hungry."

"Nothing crazy about that. It's kinda warm in here if you ask me. Coffee and a shake."

As Irene shuffled away, Nathan leaned over and whispered, "Christ, if she's warm, why doesn't she just turn down the heat!" They both shook their heads as if to say, "the 'charm' of the old diner."

Nathan wondered which topic to bring up first. (*If I start with Bobbie, it will be harder to talk about the argument. If we start with the fight, might be too pissed to tell him about Bobbie.*)

Irene placed the coffee down with a bit of a bang and slowly made her way back to the counter. Tommy lit a cigarette, carefully setting the match in the ashtray, and then answered the riddle of where to begin.

"So, Nathan, all in all, tell me how you would grade your summer?"

Nathan paused before answering. (*I guess Bobbie it is*). He was momentarily taken by his father's confident face. His mother couldn't have been more correct – how could such a man make such a blunder? (*Guess no one's perfect.*)

"All in all? Well, I'd give it, without a doubt . . . an A plus."

"Oh, sweet Lord," his father said in surprise, then took a deep drag of his cigarette, held it for a moment, and slowly blew the smoke out sideways. "I know the workshop was a success, but I'm wagering you must be referring to something else." Another pause. "Or maybe, some*one* else?"

(*Guess I'm not that hard to read. Well, let's get this out in the open.*)

Nathan nodded. "Yes, some*one* else. We met in the workshop. That's probably obvious. One thing has quickly led to another, and well, all in all, definitely an A plus. She's my first true girlfriend, Dad."

"And what's your first girlfriend's name?"

"Bobbie McGregor."

"And how has Miss McGregor stolen my son's heart?"

"Well, looks, brains. Way too much talent. And, all kidding aside, she challenges me like no other. Excluding Mom of course, but she doesn't count."

"I like brains, looks, and talent. Tell me, how does she challenge you?"

"The damnedest questions you can imagine! Every type in the book. Some I guess I deserve, and some, no one does. And out of the blue. Except they're never completely out of the blue, once you stop and think."

Irene placed the tall, fluted glass filled with thick chocolate drink in front of him. "And a chocolate shake. Anything else I can get you two?"

"I could use a tall glass of water, Irene."

As the waitress walked slowly away, Tommy winked at his son. "Giving her some exercise." He turned the conversation back to his son's girlfriend. "I assume that your mother knows all about Bobbie – has she met her yet?"

"This weekend. I've invited her for lunch. I've met her mother once, not her father."

"Siblings?"

"An older brother, but haven't met him. He left last month to go back to college."

"Well, maybe we can get together sometime so I can meet her. No rush. Last thing I want to be is a nosy parent. I still remember how much my mother was a pain in the you-know-what when I started to date your mother. That was a lesson for a lifetime."

Irene placed the glass of water down, and the tab next to it. She picked up the empty cup. "Need a refill, dear?"

"No, thank you, Irene."

Nathan listened to the scuffing steps of the waitress fade across the diner and paused in his tale of Bobbie – Bobbie's surprising mood shift popped into his thoughts. He hardly understood what had come over Bobbie when she had turned inward, so angry with herself. (*Didn't mention this to Mom.*) Yet, for some reason, he wanted to share this with his father. However, once again, his father broke into his thoughts.

"And how is your mother?"

Nathan looked up at his father, into those strong brown eyes. (*Damn, too much like mine.*) He wondered if his parents had talked. Did his father know that

Nathan knew about the fight, that Nathan had heard the fight, and more importantly knew why they were fighting? (*Oh, hell, just say it.*)

"You know, Dad, I heard you two fighting. Heard you slam the front door. It sounded as if the mirror in the hallway fell. And Mom told me what it was about."

Tommy Hughes' face showed no reaction. "I haven't been able to reach your mother at all since then, so I didn't know what you knew."

"Dad, how could you ask Mom to spend time, family time, with Nira? That's crazy. It's way too much to expect."

His father nodded slightly. He took his pack of cigarettes and rhythmically tapped the pack upside down on the table. He spoke slowly. "The intent was simply to be with my family. Obviously, short-sighted of me." He took a cigarette and lit it. "You see, Nathan, I haven't made any commitment to Nira. None whatsoever. So, I didn't see her being with us as . . . as any type of conflict. But I know now how your mother sees this, sees it only in black and white. Only as a betrayal."

Tommy pulled hard on his cigarette, exhaled, and then said, "Nathan, I wish to God I could learn without having to make such mistakes. I know I should be smarter. Anyone should be smarter about this one. I've called, wanting to apologize. But I guess she's not ready." He looked at his son. "What did you two do Labor Day weekend? There's no way either of you would let each other wallow in any kind of misery."

"That's what gets me so angry. Both of you know each other so well, know me so well. I guess I still just don't understand . . . any of this."

Tommy smiled bittersweetly. "Understanding each other is not all there is to a relationship, son. But, you know, you're right. I do know your mother, to the bottom of her soul, and that understanding may very well win the day. But I'm not there. I'm still very much here."

Father and son held each other's gaze, Nathan trying to recall any image from his childhood and Tommy trying to glean if his son understood even the smallest of his struggles. Nathan was first to look away.

"You know how Mom has always talked about walking across the bridge? I surprised her, somehow kept it a secret until the final bend in the road. We walked all the way across and back. Finished with a late breakfast at the Roundhouse. It was, well, words can't describe it. Wait, I have the photos right here." (*I have goddamn proof.*) Nathan excitedly reached for his jacket and grabbed the packet of photos, hurriedly opening the flap and pulling all out. Expecting to see images of his mother (*his wife, damn it*), himself, the bridge, spectacular views, Nathan was left speechless by the image of a smiling beautiful young Brazilian sitting on a park bench. A photograph of Nira Diaz. In an instant, he remembered the almost full roll of film in his father's camera. Then realizing the roll must have been partially used. By his father. In disbelief, he glanced at the second photograph, obviously taken by someone else – his father and Nira together, on the same bench (*and wearing that goddamn jacket no less*), his arm fully wrapped around Nira's shoulders.

"Jesus *fucking* Christ," muttered Nathan, throwing the photographs at his father, the stack flying across the table, while grabbing his jacket in a blur and fleeing toward the door. Remembering the sound of his father slamming the front door at home, Nathan caught himself doing the same and deliberately closed the door to the diner, without sound, and stepped back outside, into the unforgiving cold wind.

Chapter 11

Dancing on the Beach

Nathan found himself more than once thinking back to his walk across the bridge, to a moment when he stood near the middle of the immense central span and looked back toward the city. While his mother was nearby trying to capture the perfect panoramic photo, Nathan was focused on the peninsula that lay before him in the distance. From this view, the city was effectively an island, surrounded by mighty waters. What he sensed at the time and what had become clearer in returning to this moment was how exposed, how vulnerable the city was. Exposed not only to what he could see, but to all that journeyed across the mighty ocean to his right. A city on the edge of the world. This made perfect sense to him. With so much happening at home, at school, with Bobbie, and the upcoming new play, Nathan, too, felt exposed. So many stories starting, stopping, spinning inside him. He was just trying to hold on, buffeted by a constant wind. And yet, at times, the multitude of challenges was exhilarating.

Ignoring the more serious challenges, Nathan decided it was time to test Bobbie's agreement to sit side-by-side at any movie. It was high time for not only another black and white movie at the Sunset, but a black and white film in another language. And not just any such film, but a recognized masterpiece of the French New Wave – a movie recognized in print by critics and by the Sunset itself. One of the posters hanging in the lobby was a close-up of its lead character, staring blankly through crisscrossed wire that kept him separate from the outer world, the words the 400 blows stacked one on top of the other on the right-hand side. It was the poster itself that had made Nathan want to see the movie (*each time I enter the lobby*) – the intense mix of hopelessly lost but somehow still resolute lining the boy's face.

Nathan arrived at Bobbie's house at the end of a long stretch of Indian summer, and as they started off, he could see the fog above the ocean in the distance. Nathan mentally prepared himself for the gray overcast that would greet them after the matinee. (*Black and white movie into a dimly lit world.*)

"How's it going with your father?" Bobbie asked, taking Nathan's hand.

Nathan heard the concern in Bobbie's voice, and in response, leaned closer. "Oh, okay. Well, the blow-up at the diner's over. It took me awhile, but I realized that was really all me. I mean," Nathan shrugged his shoulders, "I did 'steal' his camera. He obviously hadn't planned to show me pictures of himself and Nira. Just," Nathan shook his head, "I still can't believe how that happened. What incredibly bad timing, or bad luck. Not sure the right word."

"It *is* pretty amazing. Almost fated. Like a Greek tragedy."

"Hmm, a Greek tragedy? You mean, maybe somehow, I willed it?"

They walked in silence, both lost in the same difficulty to understand, to find the right words to describe such an odd twist of fate. Nathan finally continued, "Well, anyway, I wrote my dad a letter to explain all of that, or at least to try. And to apologize. He hasn't called yet, so I'm half-guessing he's maybe written something back. Hope it's not a goddamn poem." Nathan shook his head in reaction to his cynical thought. "One way or another, I need to see him. *And* he wants to meet you." He gave her hand a squeeze.

They bought a big bag of popcorn and made their way to the front. They both smiled when they saw the third-row empty. They sat in the same two seats as before and set the treat in between. It was still ten minutes before movie-time, and they eagerly started in on the popcorn.

"Perfect music, don't you think," Nathan said, tilting his head back and forth to the plunking keys of a French honky-tonk piano. "It's from another Truffaut film. The only one I've seen so far. For a depressing film, I really liked it."

"Hey, Nathan, been meaning to ask. How do you afford all the movies you see? You see more than anyone I know! All the popcorn, bus rides, must add up."

"Independently wealthy."

"Oh, quite the allowance is it? Better be careful. Shouldn't get on the wrong side of your old man. Be careful what you steal from him."

"You are *so* mean, and whose old man you calling old?" Nathan stuffed a handful of popcorn into his mouth. "Boy, this is good. Speaking of money, I didn't tell you, I'm starting a job here. Beginning in October. First official job, so no longer just a moocher."

"How many hours a week, big shot?"

"Well, not many. Not even 20. Just two, maybe three, days a week. But I can sneak watching parts of movies all the time, and Herb said if things work out, free passes to any movie that doesn't sell out. I'll be able to put a serious dent in my must-see list."

"Hey, no more popcorn. We'll be finished before the end of the first reel." Bobbie grabbed the bag and rolled the top up tight.

"The first *reel*? You're sounding more and more like the real deal, a true aficionado. But talk about me seeing too many movies. What's this? Our third?"

"No, fourth, I mean fifth. Two the first date. Then, you wanted to see the new Bond."

"What can I say – always a sucker for an action flick."

"And *Bonnie and Clyde* a couple of weeks ago."

"Damn. Five in two months." The dimming of the lights and music interrupted Nathan. "And *this* movie will be the best."

• • •

Like the afterglow of a bright light, it seemed to Nathan that FIN was indelibly burned onto the screen, even after the image left. Even the slowly plucked violin strings and the sound of soft lapping waves on the beach lingered. He couldn't move. He had been slowly pushed back and down into his seat by the unrelenting portrayal of the character captured in the poster – a young teenager relentlessly searching through all that went wrong. Nathan swallowed hard as tears filled his eyes – not as sadness but as emotional release, an immediate and lasting connection with this boy. (*Down to a damn messed-up parent*.) As the house lights slowly came up and the piano music quietly began again, Nathan sat motionless, elbows on armrests, hands holding chin and cheeks, both knees high on the seat in front, the final blank look of Antoine's stare fixed in his mind.

Bobbie waited, patiently. She too had been moved by the story, deeply, but not nearly as Nathan had. Letting go her hand, he had 'left her' early in the movie. She had snuck glances. His intensely focused gaze bordered on frightening. No, not frightening. Otherworldly.

"Hey," she finally broke into his spell softly. "Let's take a walk. On the beach. Our beach."

As if woken from a dream, Nathan turned toward her. Bobbie saw his eyes brighten. "Yes. Let's." He smiled, reaching out to take her hand. "Hey. I love you."

The words caught Bobbie off guard, and she didn't know quite how to respond. She raised Nathan's hand to her lips. "Wasn't sure if you were ever going to move."

They walked slowly up the aisle, hand in hand, the last to leave. An attendant was already picking up cups and bags and throwing them into a can on wheels.

"That's me in a couple of weeks," Nathan joked, followed by his short laugh, which hung in the air as a punctuation.

The Sunset was no more than a five-minute walk to the beach. As Nathan had anticipated, the fog had indeed begun to cover the western edge of the city, more a high overcast than a thick dense blanket. Luckily, the wind was light. They crossed the street and then the high dunes before reaching the flatness of the beach. Still held by the movie's final scene, Nathan and Bobbie ran hand-in-hand across the hard-packed sand to the water's edge, to the endless ocean.

"God, I'm lucky," Nathan said while locked on Bobbie's eyes. "I have parents who may not be perfect but I'm damn sure they both love me. And I have you." He took hold of Bobbie tight, placing one arm around her back, the other arm raised to hold the full back of her head in his hand, as he bent down to her lips, to her mouth, for an infinitely long kiss. A kiss that slowly gave way to the

95

sound of the surf at their feet. Bobbie pulled away from Nathan enough to bury her head in his chest.

"Hold me, Nathan. Hold me, or I'm sure to fall."

They stood, arms wrapped tightly around each other, slightly rocking side to side to the gentle sound of the ocean's reach, breathing in the air heavy with salt. Eventually, they took each other by the hand and started to amble just outside the surf's edge.

"What do you think will become of Antoine?" Bobbie asked.

"Hmm, funny you should ask. I just read an article in Sunday's pink section that Truffaut has asked that very question. And is answering it. Not really sequels as much as continuations of his life. Not sure why that wouldn't be a sequel, but that's how the article put it. Anyway, Antoine appeared in a short film after *400 Blows*, and a full-length movie's in production. So, we'll find out soon!"

"That's interesting. But what do you think?"

"Me?" Nathan asked. (*God, your questions never disappoint.*) "I think . . . I think that Antoine will be just fine. He's such a tough nut, you know, in this movie. With a little luck, he'll find a way, a path forward. In his life that is. But I wonder about love. That's his riddle. Maybe, a life-long one."

They walked, holding hands, then swinging their arms to the rhythm of their walk. Each gentle swing grew in larger and larger loops. Then, all of a sudden, Nathan twirled Bobbie around and around, and around once more. They both laughed out loud at the silliness, but also at the ease and grace of the spin. Dancing on the beach.

"Hey, did you hear? You must have. Terry Dwyer has chosen his fall play."

"I did hear, but I don't know the play. *David and Lisa?*"

"I know the movie, from a few years ago. I saw it one afternoon on TV. So-so, second tier, maybe not even. It's a story about two teenagers who are, well, troubled, I guess you'd say. They live in, not really an institute, kind of a halfway house for kids, teenagers who don't function that well in the 'outside' world. They fall in love, or at least are attracted to each other, and by the end of the movie, they're not cured, but there's a way forward. So, a basic love story, but one in the context of mental illness."

Nathan's words faded into the sound of the waves lightly falling upon the sand, ending their long journey halfway round the world. This stretch of city beach hardly ever featured waves large enough for surfing, and the weather was far too cold for most to swim. The quiet surf was more suited for children, or a walk along the shore, accompanied by the music of the sea. Nathan was lulled by this sound and assumed that Bobbie was likewise. But after a moment he sensed a change. (*Is she looking down more than me?*)

"You okay?" he said after another moment had passed.

"Yeah."

"Hmmm. Not completely convincing."

"Just thinking."

"About?"

"What you just said."

"Which was?"

"Mental illness."

(*Oh.*)

They walked in silence, Nathan now focusing on the way each step left an impression in the damp sand. A slight give to each step. (*Where is this heading?*)

"Nathan, I haven't told you this, but I had another episode of, you know, how our first date ended. Not exactly the same, but similar, or at least not a good place to be. I was having an argument, a fight really, with my mother, and I got to a point where I just couldn't say anything. I just shut down. Inward. Like I did with you."

"You're being too hard on yourself, kiddo. It's okay to be emotional, to be upset with yourself, even really upset."

"That's just it, Nathan. It's not being emotional or upset. Just the opposite. It's a sudden, overwhelming lack of feeling." Bobbie continued to walk with her head down. "And . . . I should add, there was another time. Before the time with you."

"But how are you otherwise? Now, I mean. You've been your normal wonderful self today."

"No, I wasn't even thinking of it until you mentioned the play. Mentioned what it was about. 'Mental illness.' Being not well, emotionally. Should be called, emotional illness."

They walked again in silence. Nathan tried hard to think of what to say, but he lacked any real understanding, not only of what Bobbie described, but of any type of mental or emotional illness. Bobbie on the other hand was simply lost. Uncertain what these episodes meant and kicking herself for saying anything to Nathan. But at the same time, she thought, Nathan needs to know. Needs to know who I am.

"Oh, forget I said anything, Nathan." Bobbie blurted out. "You're right. I just have to learn how to handle this. Handle getting upset with myself. I don't want to ruin such a wonderful day."

"Nothing ruined," Nathan replied immediately, at the same time pushing back the questions that would not go away as quickly. He stopped. "And I certainly wasn't saying you just have to learn how to handle this. Bobbie – you know you can talk to me anytime. I want to know everything about you. You know that, don't you?"

Bobbie looked down shyly, then looked up. "Yes. Yes, I knew that. I know it more, now."

They had walked north toward the more crowded end of the beach. Even though the stretch of warm sunshine had ended, this section of beach was still filled with families, couples, large groups of friends, and the stray solo walker. The sounds had turned from simply those of the ocean to children at play and conversations ebbing and flowing as they passed others.

"Hey, Bobbie, I have an idea. Let's walk through Playland and then you can show me your favorite route through the park back to your house. You must have a secret path, or maybe even paths, living this close to the park."

Bobbie quickly smiled. "Only if you take me on the merry-go-round," she said pulling on his arm, wanting so to push away her uncertain thoughts.

"Absolutely."

"And I get to pick which animals we ride."

"With lots to choose from on that carousal. It's the best in the city!"

As they were waiting to cross the wide boulevard, Bobbie turned toward Nathan, "I forgot to ask. Do you know what part you have in *David and Lisa*?"

"You mean I have a part?" Nathan said.

"*Nathan*," Bobbie reacted, not quite knowing if he was teasing. "Mr. Dwyer said as much to Judy and me. Well, he said that you and Joseph Gavin were to be the two male leads."

"Joseph Gavin. Who's Joseph Gavin?"

"Sorry. I guess he's the other possible lead. I remember his name because I know his sister Rosemary."

"You're telling me more in a minute than Terry's told me the past two phone calls!" Nathan said grinning widely. "No, I'm teasing. Partly. He did tell me I had a part. And that another guy would have the other lead." They were about to enter Playland. "Just the merry-go-round, or a quick pop into the Fun House?" Nathan said, motioning to the nearest building.

"Absolutely not! I'm too short and get stuck in those revolving spin-dryer thingamajigs you have to walk through to get into the 'fun' stuff. And Laughing Sal? She gives me the absolute creeps."

As if on cue, a loud mechanical cackle erupted from around the corner.

"Oh, sweet Mary," Bobbie cried out, grabbing Nathan's arm.

That was followed by uncontrollable laughter. With Nathan putting his finger to lips, "Shsssh," and both looking over their shoulders, they carefully snuck around the Fun House to the merry-go-round and bought their tickets. Inside the enclosed carousel, Sal was gone, her cackle blocked out by the sound of the tinny pipe organ music.

"So, what'll it be?" Nathan said. Bobbie put her hand to her mouth in mock contemplation. "Not sure. I *love* the tigers, they're so beautiful. And low to the ground so even I can climb on. But they don't move, you know, go up and down. What fun is that?" Bobbie said. "Ostriches! – they go the highest."

They hurried over to the tall-standing birds adjacent to each other. Bobbie mounted the one with the stirrup lower to the ground. Once on, they felt the slight jolt of the platform as the carousel began to circle. Bobbie's ostrich slowly started to rise. As she looked over to Nathan, hers was much higher. He waved up at her from below, but then, in a second, from well above.

The carousel was nearly full, with all the other riders being young children. As they circled, Nathan noticed various adults watching the children intently. To him, the onlookers were as much a part of a merry-go-round as the riders. Both child and parent marked the circling repetition in split second recognitions, then eagerly waited for what seemed forever for that moment to repeat. He played a game of matching child to parent, most by their reactions, some by facial resemblance. After he had matched all he could see, he turned to look at Bobbie, whose head was tilted back, her long braid of dark hair falling straight down, as if the braid were enough of a weight to tilt her head backward. Her eyes were closed, and the slightest of smiles touched her face. He couldn't take his eyes off this picture of grace. (*She's my girlfriend?*) As the circle slowed, he saw her pull herself forward and turn toward him, opening her eyes. The last movement of the carousel left Nathan close to the floor, and as he looked up at Bobbie well above him, her smile had broadened ear to ear. Seeing Nathan looking up at her, with such a look in his eyes, she laughed and put her hand to her mouth, caught in the laugh of young love.

Chapter 12

Under the Bridge

Later that fall and at the end of the final performance of *David and Lisa*, as Nathan and Judy King returned to stage to join the rest of the cast, unbeknownst to even their director, they stayed in character for the briefest of encores. Lisa smiled at David and reached out her hand. David at first slightly withdrew, even tucking his arm closer to his body. Lisa responded by stretching her arm and fingers still further. Slowly, David relaxed into the beginnings of a smile, before reaching out his hand. After a final hesitation, the hint-of-a-smile grew, first partially, then broadly, and David took Lisa's hand with full commitment. The two turned to face the audience and bowed.

Back stage, Terry Dwyer addressed his cast and crew. "What can I say? Whatever I say will be brief. What a performance! As close to perfect as I've seen, by everyone. Honestly. Actors, lighting, stage crew – I couldn't be prouder. And Nathan and Judy – who came up with that encore bit just now? Thank you, each and every one. Now, go out and greet your audience. You deserve their praise!"

In a bit of a daze, Nathan followed his comrades-in-arms as they headed to meet family and friends in the large hallway outside the high school theatre. However, he held back to stay inside. (*Need a transition. Just for a moment.*) He stopped behind the last row of seats, looking back toward the stage. Nathan remembered standing in the same spot while giving himself a final pep talk for the audition. (*Ages ago. Or was that yesterday?*) What Mr. Dwyer said was true. Tonight *was* a great performance. They had hit it out of the park. But what did that feel like in the real theatre? This level of performance must be expected every night. (*How in God's name was that even possible?*) He finally pushed himself out the door to look for his parents (*together, at least for tonight*), but was already thinking ahead to the small gathering of cast and friends that would take place later that night across the city.

The Wine Cellar had become the go-to haunt for a number of the cast. It truly was a 'cellar' buried in the bowels of a recent renovation and having no windows. Once or twice a few of them, all underage, were somehow successful in ordering wine, adding to the mystique of a perfect hideout for teenagers ready to be years older. As Nathan and Bobbie arrived, the large circular table in the corner was already mostly filled. Judy motioned to the two seats she had saved.

"You sit next to your friend," Nathan said to Bobbie, then smiled. "I've been with her enough tonight."

Just as he was sitting down, someone approached the table whom Nathan failed to recognize at first. (*My God. Is that Jack?*) Jack Evanston, in turn, hadn't noticed Nathan, and was about to sit down next to his buddy Joe, who had played David's psychiatrist in the play.

"Jack!" Nathan called out, coming around the table. "What a surprise! Joe must have told you about the play."

"Yeah, Joe made me come. Just kidding. You guys were great," he said looking at Nathan and then toward Judy. "Even better than last summer." Jack turned to Joe, "But you, on the other hand, not sure you're the shrink type."

"How've you been?" Nathan asked. "How's school?"

"It's passing, as it should."

"You doing any theatre?" Nathan asked, the image of Jack's Rosencrantz still fresh.

"Naw. Transitioned."

"To what, pray tell?"

Jack raised an imaginary camera to his eye and clicked his tongue.

"Cool. I can just imagine – black and white, and edgy, right?"

Jack laughed. "Yeah, well, maybe too edgy. It'll take some time. You know who's teaching me? Lenny Fuckin' Lehane."

"Lenny does photography?"

"He does everything, man, but photo freelancing is his actual gig. The theatre stuff's just a hobby. You should see his studio. He'd love to see you."

"Is that an invite? Man, ever since I saw *Blow-Up*, I've been dying to see the magic of a dark room – watching images appear out of nowhere."

"Absolutely, man. I never tired of that. Though I have to admit, the more I learn the hardcore chemistry, the better I can wave the magic wand."

Nathan returned to his seat, and Bobbie greeted him with a whisper. "Nathan, we have a favor. Judy said it first just now, but I've been meaning to ask you forever."

"Hmmm, okay. You've got me curious."

"Well. You can say no, but . . you really can't. We've heard so much about your stories. I've heard so many tiny parts, but never a full-blown one. You know, the beginning-middle-and-end kind."

Nathan was caught off guard. "I love telling stories, but I've never been invited to tell one." (*Like being on stage?*)

"Well, this is what happens when you have a reputation. Please, it's such a perfect chance. All these friends at one table. One *large* table. And you're all warmed up, you know, from the play."

"You mean all tired and exhausted."

"*Please*. It doesn't have to be long."

Nathan looked past Bobbie at Judy, who was eagerly nodding. "Looks like no way out," Nathan paused. "It just so happens I'm beginning, and I mean beginning, to stitch a new one together. Based on something that happened during the summer. Actually, kind of connected to the workshop. Nowhere near complete. But wait, you said you wanted a beginning-middle-and-*end*."

"Who said that?" Bobbie and Judy were quick to change their minds.

Nathan, impressed by their insistence, shook his head, and gave in. "Okay. But I tell you, it's going to end mid-sentence. It really's not finished. No, let me be blunt – not even halfway done."

Judy elbowed Bobbie. "I'll announce. That way no one will think this is just a favor to the girlfriend." Judy stood and tapped a knife against her glass. "Everyone. All of you know how pushy I am? Well, I've just gotten Nathan to agree to one more entertainment tonight, one of his patented stories. Though one still being written, so not sure where it will end. It's called *The Tale . . .* "

Judy looked to Nathan, who sheepishly stood, curved his shoulders inward mimicking David, and shrugged, "No title yet, Lisa." Then stood upright. "I mean Judy. How about, *The Absent-Minded Angel.* Or, maybe better, the story of *The Good and Evil Identical Twins.*"

Jack and Joe immediately broke in, tapping their glasses loudly. "Hear, hear! *The Good and Naughty Twins!*"

Nathan shook his head. "Heckling? In the Wine Cellar?" As the table slowly fell into silence, Nathan took a deep breath. (*What the hell did I get myself into?*)

"There's a moment." Nathan paused and looked around the table. "There's a moment before each newborn descends from the heavens." Nathan looked up at the ceiling and paused again. "When its guardian angel pours *just* the right amount of grace into its waking soul. This story begins with such an angel, maybe not the brightest of angels, who was tasked with preparing a *pair* of infants, identical twin infants, for their journey to earth. The angel begins just fine, filling his oh-so-delicate spoon with God's elixir, and then oh-so-carefully pouring it into the soul of one of the newborns. To the last drop. Done. No, halfway done. As he re-fills the spoon . . . boom! He's startled by a sound in the heavens, or maybe, from down below? And he spills the precious liquid. Shaken, but not detoured, he fills the spoon again, but is startled again as he turns toward the two twins. This time though, he keeps the ladle steady. So proud of himself for *not* spilling a second time, he has lost track of which baby is which. And, as the twins are identical, he mistakenly delivers the second spoonful into the infant who had already received his share. And, so, the newborns are sent on their way to earth – but one without a single drop . . . of grace."

Nathan stopped. His eyes had been slightly unfocused, concentrating with all of his might on the story he had barely begun to write. He looked around the table and, surprised to see such attention, relaxed. (*I guess, so far so good.*)

"Well, there are identical twins, and then there are *identical* twins, pairs who bear not a single visible difference whatsoever. Michael and Sean were such twins. And growing up in the same family, in the same house, and attending the same schools, their shared world did little to shape the two differently. There *was* the one difference however (for which we can blame our bumbling angel). Michael's soul was doubly full of grace, while Sean's was, well, empty, barren, without a drop. What was the impact? Well, bit by bit throughout childhood, and certainly seen by adolescence, Michael was kinder, more dependable, greatly admired, while Sean, often in trouble, was mistrusted, and, indeed, came to think himself as cursed. And for those who are blessed to see auras, the colors of the spiritual world, an extra vibrant gold surrounded Michael, but a surprising lack of color, an outline of . . . emptiness defined Sean. Neither twin knew the cause of this difference, but both were very much aware that it existed. And not surprisingly, Sean grew to resent his brother. And at times, even despise."

Nathan peered at his audience again. "As I warned, this tale is truly a work in progress, so I'll jump ahead. Each twin grows to be successful – Michael because of his talent, love of career, and the reinforcement he receives from the countless lives he helps, and Sean because of his equal talent and a no-holds-barred fixation on success and his others-be-damned attitude. Michael is the manager of a large city park, in his office and hands-on in the field, a jack-of-all-trades biologist, guide, and teacher. Sean is the president of the firemen's labor union and has his hands in every lucrative pie and pocket, friend and foe alike.

"Now there's a bit of happenstance that connects these two jobs. The large lodge at the entrance to the park is co-owned by the Parks and Rec Department *and* the union. The upstairs offices are separate and kept locked to the other operation, and the rooms and kitchen downstairs are available to be rented for events. This proximity of offices brought to Michael's attention suspicions surrounding the union, and in particular, those involving his twin brother.

"On a night the union was hosting yet another large and extravagant dinner, Michael was upstairs quietly working late. As was his habit, he used only a small desk lamp, and his office appeared dark from the hallway. As the transom above his door was open, he was interrupted by the sound of loud and drunken voices, one of which he recognized as his brother's right-hand man, Robert Sullivan. Sullivan was spouting about how much these expensive dinners helped with recruiting, both for new applicants and for the already employed to join the union. But it was the next sentence that caught Michael's attention. 'If only the city knew how much its funding was helping the union grow,' followed by loud laughter. Michael wondered, the city's funding? What in blazes did that mean? Why would the union be receiving any money from the city? And how? And now that Michael thought about it, how did the union afford so many elaborate dinners? Then he heard a second voice boom, 'That young McMillan accountant Sean hired is just goddamn brilliant.' Sullivan quickly added, 'Yeah, but I tell you, it's Sean's idea that's the key – a little bit times a big number is still a big number, *and*, that little bits are never noticed.'

"Michael was well trained in the oft wanderings into the shadier side of life that his brother forever gravitated toward. He now sat quietly at his desk, drumming his fingers to the beat of the disconcerting words he had just heard – little bits and big numbers, little bits and big numbers, and then thought, just who is this McMillan? Something isn't right. I need to do a little nosing around. And I think I'll start with this 'brilliant' accountant."

Nathan raised his arms as if to stay the disappointment he knew his next sentence would trigger. "And this is where we need to leave Michael and Sean, for regrettably, the story is, well, still being written! And this storyteller has just hit the wall – I'm exhausted! But I'll leave you with the following tease. Stay tuned, because the rest of this tall tale is filled with revenge, embezzlement, graft, arson, and yes . . . a cursed murder."

To a mix of hoots and calls for more, Nathan slumped into his chair, muttering, "Boy oh boy, sure wish I were older. I could use a glass of wine." Instead, he raised a glass of Coke to salute his friends, "To all of you. You're the real thing," then whispered to Bobbie, "And you'll be the first to hear the rest!"

• • •

A month later and well into December, Bobbie was on the phone with Nathan. "So, how's the story? When's the next installment?"

"That's a joke, I hope. Haven't had time to even think about it. Way too much school," Nathan said. "Maybe I can get back to it during the break."

"Speaking of the holidays, Nathan. My parents are out tonight, and I thought we could celebrate winter break. Fire in the fireplace. Maybe a movie on TV." Bobbie's voice was so inviting, somehow even more lyrical on the phone than in person. She could be suggesting that he scrub her front steps and Nathan would say, "When?" But her invitation was perfect. He would be at the Sunset all afternoon. When he mentioned that, Bobbie exclaimed, "I'll make dinner for the two of us. It'll be like we're married!"

For the first time since he started working at the Sunset, Nathan didn't even think of sampling the just started movie and left as soon as his shift was done. When he knocked on Bobbie's front door, he somewhat nervously hesitated, aware of what might lie ahead. Bobbie and Nathan never had an 'inside' place to themselves, and for the entire evening. Only a few times had they ever been alone in either house, but it was always temporary, knowing that one or both parents would soon return. He hardly ever thought about what Bobbie might be wearing but did so now as he heard the door opening. His girlfriend couldn't have been dressed more casually, long-sleeved tee shirt with sleeves rolled up, sweatpants, slippers.

"Hmmm, looks like you've been watching movies all day long!" Nathan greeted Bobbie with a grin. "Actually, you look utterly delicious."

"Nathan Hughes – make up your mind. Are you insulting me, or buttering me up?"

"Buttering you up!" Nathan came in showing a big bag of popcorn from the theatre. "For the movie later." He came up to Bobbie, "Hey, you."

"Hey you back." They kissed tenderly before Bobbie broke off. "Not just yet. I spent too much time cooking dinner for us."

"Didn't know you liked to cook. What'd you make?"

"Better lower your expectations." Bobbie led Nathan into the kitchen. "Spaghetti, salad, but I did make the sauce. My brother taught me. He said everyone should know how to make a good marinara."

"Is he coming home for the break?"

"In a few days. Hopefully, you'll finally meet him." Bobbie paused and turned to Nathan. "No rush, but you ready to eat?"

"Starved – stayed away from the concessions all afternoon. What can I do?"

"You can start by taking off your jacket!"

"Oh. Sorry," Nathan said. "Guess I was distracted by your gorgeous outfit."

Bobbie returned his tease with a look of disgust. "And I'm the one feeding you?"

"Oh, come now, you love being teased," Nathan returned. "Now, what can I do?"

"Just sit down." Bobbie dished out the spaghetti, carefully covered it with sauce, and brought the two plates to the table. She set the salad bowl between the settings, along with a baguette, tearing it in two. Next, she reached up into a cabinet and retrieved a mostly full bottle of wine. "If we have a *very* small amount, my parents won't notice," she said as she lit the candles and sat down across from Nathan.

"Voilà," she said with her hands raised.

Nathan sighed and looked across the table. "You really are something."

Bobbie smiled and raised her glass, with Nathan immediately joining. She reached across the table, not to clink, but to gently rest her glass against his. "À nos vacances, mon amour."

"To whatever that means, *my* love," smiled Nathan. They let their glasses touch before Bobbie brought hers to her lips and took the briefest of sips. Nathan followed her lead.

"Something tells me this will be incredible," he said and twirled his first fork-full of spaghetti. Bobbie eagerly waited his reaction. "This is so good. The sauce is so light. And the flavors, they're amazing."

"It's okay. Not as good as using fresh tomatoes. But my mom buys really good, canned tomatoes and olive oil. She loves to splurge on good food."

"Hmmm, someday I'll have to thank her. Do they know I'm here?"

"Oh, I kept it vague. Said you might stop by, for a few minutes. God, how lucky I am you work so close." Bobbie took a big helping of salad. "Dennis also taught me his killer dressing."

As they were finishing, Bobbie said, "I didn't make anything else. Haven't gotten even close to trying desserts. But your popcorn is perfect. We'll have plenty of room for it later. Did you see what's on NBC tonight? *It's a Wonderful Life!*"

"I love Jimmy Stewart. And any story with a guardian angel..."

Bobbie started to clear the dishes, and Nathan quickly joined in. "Hey, let me help."

"Okay. You wash and I'll dry. Kind of romantic, isn't it?" Still holding the dishes, Bobbie reached up on tiptoes to kiss Nathan.

As they quietly stood next to each other at the sink, each enjoying the slow rhythm of the simple task, it occurred to Nathan that Bobbie hadn't mentioned any emotional difficulties the past month. (*Does that mean nothing's happened?*) He remembered Bobbie's answer on the beach, when he had insisted that she'd always be open with him. (*Would she? Better to ask.*)

"Bobbie."

"Hmmm."

"You haven't said anything in a while about, you know, what you were telling me on the beach a couple of months ago. Everything been all right?"

The slightest of sighs told him the answer wasn't simple. Bobbie stopped wiping the dish she held in her towel. "I was going to tell you tonight." She sighed again. "Another small episode, again with my mother. We talked later, and, well, we both came to the same conclusion. Best maybe to find someone I can talk with, someone who could help understand this . . . I don't know, tendency I have. Not a hardcore psychiatrist, but you know, more like a counselor."

"A great idea. Always helps to talk. I know it's hard sometimes."

Bobbie went back to drying. "That's what my mom kept saying. I know in my head that's true. But it's another thing to accept that I need, any help. Anyway, that's the plan." She paused, rolling her eyes. "Now all we have to do is find the right person."

As they finished the dishes, Bobbie laid her hand on Nathan's. "Thanks for asking, Nathan. I was going to tell you, but you asking makes it . . . easier." She paused, then smiled coyly. "Let's go to the front room – I have a surprise."

Bobbie led Nathan out of the kitchen and to the long sofa in the middle of the front room, directly across from the fireplace. He sat down and took his shoes off. Firewood had been piled over kindling over newspaper, and Nathan assumed that a cozy evening was the surprise. (*Man, talk about romantic.*) Bobbie did indeed go to the hearth and lit the fire. But then, as if reading his mind, turned back to him, smiling, then shrugging her shoulders, shook her head. She continued to the stereo cabinet and dropped the record she had set up before Nathan arrived. She picked up the album cover and, walking back to the sofa, handed it to him. "Just came out, two days ago. Back from the dead. *And* back to basics. Nothing electric. Guitar, harmonica, and, as always, lyrics to die for."

Not knowing what to expect, Nathan focused first on the cover's photograph, ignoring the words. It took him a second to recognize the scruffy guy in the middle, the one with his hands in his pocket and a bit of a what-the-hell grin. Just as he recognized the face, the nasal twang of *John Wesley Harding was a friend to the poor* against simple guitar confirmed who it was. (*Back from the dead? Oh yeah, his bike accident.*) Bobbie dropped down next to Nathan, pulling her legs onto the couch, snuggling close. She then sat up straight and reached behind to grab her long braid of hair. Fixing Nathan with her eyes, she slowly unbraided her hair, then ran her fingers through to disentangle it, finally giving her head a brisk shake. "All the songs are gems. But I like this the best," she said pointing to the last song on the second side. She smiled at Nathan. "Maybe we'll get to it." Then raising her eyebrows, "Or maybe we won't." She reached up to Nathan and gently pulled his head down toward her. Pulled his mouth close to hers. "Now, where were we? You know, when you first got here?"

Their kiss was continuous, riding the waves of giving then receiving, of taking then pausing, their lips pressed tight. Bobbie's small compact body pressed deep inside Nathan's thighs and trunk, seeking shelter from the storm of love. They had kissed longingly before, had held each other tightly before. (*But this is different. Night and day different. Nighttime different.*) Before long, Nathan knew, without question, that Bobbie had planned everything, the whole evening, the dinner, the fire, the music, for what was now fiercely underway. And what was underway was not just necking, not just kissing. Against Dylan's music, he remembered the words she said on the phone. 'It'll be like we're married.'

Nathan pulled away from Bobbie's lips just enough to whisper, "So, what's the surprise? The fire. Dylan. Or this?"

"All of the above."

"Maybe we should talk?"

Bobbie gave a short laugh. "Not the time for talking." She kissed him again, then slowly let her tongue move across his lips.

"You may have reached a decision, but not sure I'm quite there."

"Your mind or your body questioning?" Bobbie ran her hand between his legs. "Must be your mind."

(*Oh, sweet Jesus.*)

"At least, can we go to your bedroom? Your parents might be home early."

"You don't know my parents. But, if you wish, we most certainly can go to my bed, I mean bedroom." She went to the stereo, turned the record over and the volume up. "I want to make sure we hear that last song."

As Bobbie had led Nathan from the kitchen to the sofa in the front room, she now led him from the sofa to her bedroom upstairs. And directly to her bed, kicking off her slippers as she lay down, pulling him down toward her.

(*One more attempt.*) "Bobbie."

"Nathan, I know you love me. As much as I love you. So, love me." Bobbie encircled him with a commitment of arms and legs. "Make love to me." As they

111

once again dived into a never-ending kiss, Nathan could barely hear the music in the distance. Between Bobbie's forever circling tongue and the rhythmic waves of her hips, such persistent and perfect waves, as he grabbed hold of the elastic band of her pants and started to pull down, it was all too much, too wonderfully much, and he came. Mid-stream. Mid-motion. Mid-sentence in this ode to love.

Bobbie felt this immediately. "Oh, my. Oh, Nathan," she sighed, hugging him with arms and legs, body and soul. "It's . . . it's like . . . our wedding night."

As they fell into a shared and quiet breath, Nathan whispered, "I guess Jimmy Stewart was just a ruse."

"Yep," Bobbie whispered back. "No Jimmy tonight."

"Just Bobby?"

"Oh yes. Just *your* Bobbie."

As if on cue, Dylan's voice came faintly but clearly up the stairs. *Close your eyes. Close the door. You don't have to worry . . . an-y-more. I'll-ll, be-yourrr, baby toni-i-ight.*

• • •

Bobbie pulled into the driveway at Nathan's house, never an easy maneuver off the busy street, especially late afternoon. Nathan had been waiting and was in her car before Bobbie had completely put on the hand brake.

"So, where you taking us?"

"You're a senior in high school and you don't know what the word 'surprise' means? I told you – this is your Christmas present."

Bobbie crossed town, avoiding the traffic on the major streets. As she entered the northwest corner of the city, Nathan wondered if they were heading toward the bridge, but the route Bobbie was taking was new to him. When he finally saw the first grand tower, he realized they were heading toward the *base* of the bridge, where it entered the water and well below the roadway high above.

"I've never been here," he said in awe.

"It's a fort, built long before any bridge. To protect the entrance to the bay. You must have at least seen pictures of it." Bobbie pointed toward the promenade that lined the water's edge. "That's where Kim Novak jumped into the water."

"Kim Novak? What do you mean?"

"Oh my God, Nathan. I've seen a movie you haven't? You've never seen *Vertigo*?"

Nathan grinned sheepishly. "I tell you, I have a long list of must-sees."

"Well, my oh my. My day's made." Bobbie got out of the car and went around to the trunk. As Nathan got out, he saw Bobbie closing the trunk, holding her guitar. (*What the...?*)

She raised it up. "Present time. Over there."

She led Nathan to the promenade and sat down on a bench, on the end nearest the bridge so that Nathan would see her with the majestic structure as the backdrop. She made sure that her tuning an hour before was set and played a few chords while 'unwrapping' her present for Nathan.

"Several weeks ago, this song came on the radio, and right in the middle of our conversation, you just stopped. I lost you. Completely. You were so focused on the song. Remember?"

Nathan smiled and nodded. (*Oh, yes, I remember.*)

"I've never seen you so moved by a song, so I knew I had to learn it. To sing it to you. And play it. It seemed so simple at first, only four chords, all in E. But then, the picking patterns. Oh my." Her random strumming stopped, and positioning her fingers on an E, she looked at Nathan, "Not the whole song. And I've changed a few of the words. For *us*." She started a delicate pick to a beat of six, with her eyes on the strings. After completing the first measure and knowing these notes would have confirmed the song, she looked up with all the love she felt inside, for Nathan to see in full display.

"Suzanne takes you down to her place by the *water*"

Only the first line. (*Her voice, it's perfect.*) Nathan clenched his lips.

"You can hear the boats go by, you can spend the night forever"

His eyes quickly filled with love. (*Won't make it through.*)

"And you know that's she's *half-crazy* but that's why you want to be there" (*Really won't make it.*) A first tear falls.

"And she feeds you tea and oranges that come all the way," Bobbie tilts her head, motioning beyond the bridge and toward the ocean, "from China"

This silliness calmed him, just so. (*Maybe, maybe I can.*)

"And just when you try to tell her that you have *no* love to give her" (*The other night?*)

"Then she gets you on her wavelength

And she lets the water answer that you've *always* been her lover" (*The other night!*)

"And you want to travel with her, and you want to travel blind" (*I do! I must!*)

"And you know that she will *trust* you

For you've touched her perfect body with your mind"

Then Bobbie played an interlude, "Just for you" – part Cohen's, mostly hers – before returning to the chords leading back to the chorus.

"And you want to travel with her, and you want to travel blind

And you know that *you can trust me*"

Bobbie stopped. She looked deep into Nathan's eyes fixed in love and tears. For several seconds. (*Forever?*) Then, without guitar, she sang the last line, almost, but not quite, pausing at each word.

"For I've touched your perfect body . . . with my mind"

Then, looking back down to her guitar, she played the intro again, twice through, and finished with a pinch harmonic, its vibration floating high into the late afternoon air. Where the music hung long and pure. For both Nathan and Bobbie. Then slowly faded, into the sound of water lapping against the promenade's stone wall, all under a bridge that reached into the heavens.

1970

Chapter 13

From There to Here

Nathan and Bobbie lay naked on his bed on a mid-week afternoon in early January. The sunlight through the window fell squarely on them and was too warm for Nathan after the heat of making love. He got up to close the curtains.

"It's such pretty light, Nathan," Bobbie said softly. "Leave them open a bit."

While up, Nathan went over to the stereo, flipped over the record, then pointed to Bobbie, singing, "You'll come running to me," then lay back down to the sounds of acoustic guitar and drums, followed quickly by the trebled pitch of an Irish cowboy, *By-the-side-of-the-tracks where-the-train-goes-by. . .*

"So, tell me again. When do you go back?"

Bobbie rolled her eyes. "Nathan. You just don't listen. This Saturday. My classes start next week."

"Right." Nathan half-grimaced. "I do listen. Just don't want you to leave."

Nathan ran his hand gently along Bobbie's arm, over her hip, along her leg as far as he could reach . . . *I say, hey, come running to me* . . . then let the back of his hand reverse the long path back to her shoulder. Then, to begin again.

"Nathan, how do you see our relationship when we're apart?"

(*Such a Bobbie question.*)

"Are we heading for a serious discussion?"

"I don't know. Just curious if it's changed for you."

"Hmmm. Has it for you?"

Bobbie remained silent, then opened her eyes. "It has. Some changes subtle and probably not important, others, not so subtle and . . ." She stopped mid-sentence. "Yes, it has."

Nathan's hand completed the downward stroke along Bobbie's side (*as if my hand had a mind of its own*) and reluctantly dropped it to the bed. "If this is a serious talk, we need to get dressed. Your body is way too distracting."

Bobbie smiled, but didn't say anything. She rolled over to the edge of the bed and sat up. "Probably best," she murmured and went over to pick up their clothes, tossing Nathan's toward him and starting to put hers on. (*Hmmm, more than most Bobbie questions.*)

"Let's go downstairs and talk in the back room," Bobbie said, looking down at Nathan, still lying on the bed as she stepped into and pulled up her jeans. Nathan wistfully watched the pale skin of her calves, knees, then thighs disappear into a denim replica. (*Goodbye, sweet legs.*) Bobbie added, "It's such a nice room when the sun's out."

"Nicest room in the house, no matter the weather."

As they walked down the stairs, Nathan asked, "Should I make some tea?"

"Tempt me."

"Oh lord, that would take hours. No way I could list all the crazy teas my mom's collected."

Bobbie laughed, "I can just see your mother trying every new blend of women's tea that comes out. Keep it simple."

"Open some windows back there. It can be such a hot house."

In the back room, Bobbie experimented with opening various combinations of windows, top or bottom, differing amounts, keeping curtains opened or closed, before finding just the right combination. She sat down out of the direct sunlight and closed her eyes before reluctantly giving in to the waiting inevitable – this was not going to be easy. Much of what she needed to say was more feeling than thought, all of which had slowly materialized over the now endless months of living apart. She was determined to talk in person, so now had to be the time. But the time for what? To express unclear feelings? As they shared tea in this lovely, bright, private room in the back of Nathan's house? And leading to what?

Bobbie watched Nathan approach from the dim kitchen into the sun-bright back room. She thought, he has no idea.

"Kept it simple. Peppermint. And nothing else," Nathan said and waited a moment, feeling the perfect mix of cool air and warmth from the sun. "Great job with the windows. I can never get them right."

"If only life were as simple as opening windows," Bobbie muttered to herself. Then she thought, not just yet, this is all so lovely. Soon. *Soon.*

"I know you don't like your tea strong, maybe another minute?" Nathan sat and looked at Bobbie. She was somewhere else – he could almost see thoughts swirling inside her head, as if her skin and bone were transparent. But he sat back in his chair, knowing full well she would begin when ready. (*By the looks, soon.*) He momentarily looked at the print of the woman in the blue dress. No chaotic thoughts circling inside that quiet head. Today, the lady on the wall was meditating, a perfectly balanced serenity. He looked back at Bobbie to see her eyes searching out the window. Then, they shifted to his.

Just dive in, Bobbie thought. "I'm confused, Nathan. I'm so, broken in two. At college and here, with you. And unfortunately, most of me is at school. Staying down south last summer, that's when I felt . . . the balance tip. And this semester, my life has only continued to grow, more and more away from here, from you. And all this distance." Bobbie stopped to find the right word, if there was one. "I've started to see differences. Or more, to feel them." She could see Nathan was simply taking words in. "And the differences frighten me."

(*Differences? Between us? In her? Me?*) To distract himself, Nathan filled one cup, then set the pot down to continue to steep. He turned the filled cup's handle toward Bobbie and said, "Not sure I understand, Bobbie. Differences? Between us?"

"Yes, between us," Bobbie said quickly. "There's so much more in my life now, Nathan. Not only classes and friends I've made, but also outside of school." Bobbie paused. "The times we live in are so incredibly powerful. Every month seems more and more intense. The March in November was immense. The fight for civil rights never ends. The UFW strikes. We have to do everything we can.

Not simply protest, but whatever it takes to change all this stupidity." Bobbie could feel her passion getting in the way. "Sorry, I always get so caught up. I didn't tell you. Right before I came home for the break, I was in a rally organized by the Chicano Moratorium. Actually, *in it*. A friend from school invited me to sing. The only white girl on stage." Bobbie smiled sheepishly. "I did my alto version of *Saigon Bride*. You know," Bobbie briefly singing, "*I'm going out to stem the tide*." She fixed her eyes on Nathan's. "We're both blessed with talent, Nathan. I know you are. We need to use those talents. Not just for ourselves and our friends, or even to entertain 'the public,' but for change. Real change."

(*So, this is it. This is where it's heading. She is, I'm not?*) Bobbie's passionate connection with righteous causes was nothing new to Nathan. Her intense commitment was maybe at the core of his love for her. "But Bobbie, you've always been more dedicated to the 'good fight' than me. I love your passion. You know that. You inspire me. I don't see what's different."

"Have I inspired you, Nathan? I haven't seen that for a long time." Bobbie sunk back in her chair, struggling between what had been true in the past, and her feelings and ill-formed thoughts now saying otherwise, that their relationship had changed. Was it a matter of degrees? Relatively small and acceptable differences when younger, but bigger differences now – and no longer acceptable? All in the context of being apart? So many ways we can change, or *not* change, Bobbie thought. But all led to the same nagging contrast inside her head – Nathan is a storyteller, while I'm steeped in . . . reality.

Bobbie turned to Nathan. "I know this will sound petty. And worse, judgmental. But much of what you tell me simply doesn't resonate, or when it does, only partly. I guess, Nathan, I need more from you than just stories. As wonderful as they are. Take the one you told me the other day, about the Dickens Fair. The three of you 'beaming down' into 19th century London. Fairy dust entrances, lasers across Trafalgar Square, Joe doing the Spock Shuffle. No idea what that is but it sounds hysterical. Jack's 'Good God, man, I'm a doctor, not a fish peddler!' And you, you as the perfect over-acting Kirk. "Cratchit, damn it, you either believe in yourself, or you don't. Take a stand!" What a funny, funny story. We all need that magic. Believe me, Nathan, I know that. But the balance, where is it? I need the 'other' part of life, the honest-to-goodness more important here and now. I just haven't heard any of that from you in a long, long time." Bobbie looked into Nathan's eyes, and then past them, deeper.

As much as Nathan knew that Bobbie was not judging him, he still felt backed into a corner. "Maybe I need to dedicate myself completely to magic, to be the magician, to be the storyteller," he said softly, looking straight ahead.

"I don't believe that, Nathan Hughes. There are always opportunities to do both. Remember Joseph? You had the same choice as he did when registering for the draft. We talked so much about that, and you still chose to simply register, rather than commit to being a conscientious objector. I was relieved to hear your number was crazy high, believe me, but that was an opportunity to take a stand. If you wanted to. I mean, what if your number had been 10? What would you have done? Would you really have gone north? Or to jail?" Bobbie looked hard at Nathan.

Now he was cornered and returned to the previous summer, to the few weeks that Bobbie was home and to their marathon walk the length of the park, from his house to hers. How they went through all the various bits and pieces – the moral arguments, which did he truly believe, and how exactly would he defend them? What were his options if he were drafted? As an objector or not? And what were the practicalities of registering as a CO. Forms, essays, letters of references, anything else? Nothing insurmountable, but who exactly would he list as references? He wasn't like Joe who had long staked a solemn oath as a pacifist. How many times had he gone back and forth, both during the walk and then afterward, continuing to waffle for weeks, until he had simply run out of time. He hadn't really decided at all, had simply left himself without a choice by not choosing. That phone call to Bobbie was a tough one. She was not sympathetic then, and certainly not now.

"Not my finest hour," Nathan said, staring down on the wood slats of the floor. He looked up. "Bobbie, I see the view from too many sides. And what's worse, I then connect with those too many views." He paused. "Great for storytelling. Bad for making decisions."

Neither spoke. Nathan heard faint voices from a neighbor's garden through the open windows, which interrupted his thoughts. He returned to Bobbie's first words. (*I'm so confused.*)

"You don't sound confused, Bobbie," he said quietly.

She looked at him, not sure of what he meant.

"That's how you started, 'I'm so confused.' But what you've said seems all too clear. Not that I agree with it, but what you've said is anything but confusing. It sounds . . . definitive. That you know the next step." Nathan waited for Bobbie to look at him. "Do you?"

Confronted by Nathan's question, Bobbie thought – a couple of years ago, I might have disappeared inward, shutting myself off. As confused as I am, at least I'm stronger. I've grown. But have we? And what exactly is the next step?

"Do I look like I know the next step, Nathan. Do you think that making love upstairs was part of a next step?" she pleaded, her eyes filling with tears. "All I've said, all that I feel, is real. But does any of that matter?" she said, looking away, and then in the softest of voices, barely audible but all too clear to Nathan, "I still love you." The profile of Bobbie's face was softly illuminated as the once-bright sunlight now dimmed over the tops of the neighboring houses. "I just don't understand – if we're changing, if our lives are becoming different, how can our love remain the same? If we, our lives grow, doesn't love also have to grow?"

Nathan had no answer. No answer for the only girl he had loved in his still young life. *His* girl, whom he had lain beside an hour before. (*Can still feel her arm, her hip, her leg. As far as I can reach.*) Now, their gaze held true for the longest moment, confirming that love, but then broke apart, under the weight of Bobbie's unanswerable question.

• • •

Nathan and Joe walked up the residential street angled at such a pitch as to beg for handrails. They had been challenging each other for several months to find the best 'hidden' walk in this, their native city. They had thought they knew each nook and cranny, but every excursion proved them wrong. And now they added a new component, not in the original rules – the walk had to lead to a view of the city that was both unexpected and agreed upon spectacular. By this definition, all walks were now up then down severe changes in elevation. No shortages of such in this city – someone had once claimed 41 individual hills defined this peninsular land.

Led by Joe's map to guide them along a curving path of streets connected by short and long stairways, they continued their climb up. Their goal was a small park at the very top and its tall obelisk base, which once held a crowning statue marking the geographical center of the city, at least at the time of its construction. The statue, eroded from decades of neglect, had recently been taken down, leaving only its tall base. Rumor had it that daredevils had scaled its walls to gain the most spectacular views of the city, even if still partly obscured by the uppermost limbs of cypresses now encircling the park.

They almost missed the next-to-last staircase that narrowly weaved its way among tightly spaced houses and apartments. (*Well, at least the definition of 'hidden' has been met.*) Joe led the way single file to the top which exited onto a one-way street. Directly across the street, up a final set of steps was the stone base exposed to the elements, a daunting 20 feet or more into the cold afternoon wind. Nathan and Joe looked at each other and, in unison, shouted the name of the only person they knew who would even think of attempting the climb, "Jack!" Laughing, they hurried up.

Much of the view of the city from the final landing was indeed blocked by trees and houses surrounding the park. However, a partial view due north caught their attention, Nathan pointing first. Framed by two nearby cedars and rising above the expanse of parkland in the distant northwest corner of the city, the two towers of the bridge reached skyward through a wispy overcast. Perfectly aligned between this hill and the far bridge towers, cathedral spires marked Nathan's high school. He was mesmerized by the overlay of these structures that meant so much to him. Their superimposition defined an imaginary line straight from where he stood, through the front doors of the cathedral to the central span of the bridge in the distance. He imagined being able to see even more from the top of the foundation behind him. From such a height, in his mind's eye, he should be able to spot his house, which also lay looking northward. And he knew in his bones that the house, the one he had lived in his entire life, would fall neatly on this same line, keeping intact a straight path in space. (*In space, yes, but also in time. From childhood to now. From been-there-and-done-that to here-in-this-moment.*) He let this image of intense urban beauty dissolve into a meditation.

"Man, if only we were crazy enough to climb the base," Joe said, breaking the momentary spell. "Each view, in every direction, I swear, would take the prize."

Nathan smiled, nodding his head, "Yes, buddy-boy, but close only counts in horseshoes. Though, I got to say, the walk itself has been our best so far. Talk about hidden."

They remained standing still, gazing at the partial views, before Joe stammered, "Man, it's cold. Let's get out of this wind for a few minutes before we head back down."

The two friends walked halfway down the steps to find a stone bench set into the hill and out of the wind. "Cozy," Joe said, then remembered, "Hey, Nathan, I think I have half a joint somewhere in my pockets. The perfect time and place?"

"Absolutely."

Joe found what remained of the joint. He held it in his teeth, struck a match and quickly cupped it, then barely touched the flame to the front edge to minimize any waste. They both took long hits, Nathan holding the warmth in the bottom of his chest, enjoying the earthy bitterness on the back of his tongue. He eventually pushed the last of the smoke past rounded lips, watching it slowly disappear into the cold air.

"Man, sometimes even a hint of a high is all you need."

Nathan sat cross legged with his back straight against the wall and his eyes closed, surrendering to the lightness penetrating his body. He opened his eyes slightly, "You have a smoke?"

"I do.'

"Do you mind? I just need a taste."

Joe reached inside his jacket, pulled one from his pack, and handed it to Nathan, who held it aside for a moment.

"Joe, do you think we do drugs too often?"

Joe snorted, "You crazy?"

Nathan tapped the end of the cigarette on the cement seat. "Bobbie thinks so. Or at least she was questioning why so many of my stories begin with us getting high."

"Yeah, well," Joe said matter-of-factly.

Nathan nodded, lighting the cigarette. He inhaled deeply, as if it were more weed, then exhaling, handed the cigarette to Joe. "She and I had quite a long afternoon last week before she went back to school. It was, well, a *long* afternoon."

"Man, Bobbie saying that about drugs surprises me. She's no goodie two-shoes."

"Anything but," Nathan said. "You know, it wasn't about drugs. The long afternoon, I mean. God, I wish it were that simple." As he dived headlong into Bobbie's concerns, and how at one point he even thought she was about to end their relationship right then and there, Nathan was thinking at the same time as telling his tale, how lucky he was to have Joe as such a close friend. Ever since that play together way back when, they had been inseparable. Their connection so tight that lengthy descriptions could be reduced to a single word, or that one would laugh before the other's punchline was delivered. These feelings of closeness drifted into an image of Joe at the Dickens Fair, in white face, marked uplifted eyebrows and pointed ears, hands behind his back, a tiny grin, slowly giving way to the music, falling into barely a movement, then not quite a dance, and finally – into the Spock Shuffle. Now, as Nathan continued to elaborate the difficulty with Bobbie, he smiled to himself as he saw Joe reach into his pocket to pull out a cigarette, just as he was feeling the urge for another himself.

"So, it all came down to, if two *lives* change, can *love* stay the same?" Nathan said, finishing his afternoon-with-Bobbie tale. "I'm not much of a scientist, but I think I remember something about the law of mass action."

"Nathan, man, you mean the law of mass balance," Joe said, striking a match.

"Yeah, well, there you go. I'm no scientist."

After Joe took a first, then second pull, he passed the cigarette to Nathan. (*See, he didn't even have to ask.*) "Was the important question, how can love stay the same? Or was it the other one, about your too-many stories? Even I know Bobbie well enough to know how dedicated she is to 'the cause.'"

Nathan accepted the cigarette, nodding his head. "Absolutely. Both questions are part of the same reality – we don't spend enough time together. Writing letters and talking on the phone just aren't enough. I don't know. When I was banging my head against this yesterday, I nearly reached the point that the only solution is to goddamn accept reality – we *are* living separate lives."

"*You go your way and I go mine?*"

"*Then time will tell who has fell.*" An aching sadness rose in Nathan's heart as he softly cursed, "Not ready for that, Joe. All this intellectual crap about balances and differences. I love her!"

After a long pause, Joe looked at his friend. "How'd you guys leave?"

"Didn't really. I mean we just said we'd call. I think I said something about going down to see her, but nothing was set."

"No, I mean, how did you actually say goodbye. Like lovers?"

"Oh," Nathan paused. "Yeah. Like lovers do." There was not enough of the cigarette left for even the hint of a last drag, so Nathan roughly rubbed it across the cement, barely catching himself before also rubbing his thumb against the unforgiving surface. "Maybe lovers saying goodbye."

"Hey, Nathan, on a brighter note," Joe said, slapping the back of his hand across his friend's arm, "let me tell you how love ends before it can even get started." Joe reached into his jacket pocket and held up a folded paper. "I've finally said, enough is enough. You know, caught up on goddamn Cypress Avenue one time too many."

More than grateful to take his mind off Bobbie, Nathan smiled, knowing of Joe's all-too-long Theresa obsession. He turned his full attention to Joe unfolding what surely was a new poem.

"It's called, *I Am the Milkman*," Joe said, clearing his throat. "*Thoughts that have floated over are fading, escaping like water from a glass, leaving an empty glass, an invisible eddy in the air, and enough distance in between to end all this nervous love.*" Joe took a short breath and changed his voice to matter-of-fact. "*Please disregard any previous unsatisfactory attempt at communication. Return the letters, collect any present, erase all dry throats and stutters. Leave any poem or any of the love you don't want on the doorstep.*" A second pause. "*I'll come by and pick them up in the morning.*"

"Damn."

Joe barely snorted a response.

"No really, great poem. So how did you deliver the milk, I mean, the poem?"

"Haven't yet. I was hoping that the story-man would know the right way."

"Oh, man, that's easy. Roll it up, nice and tight, stick it in an empty milk bottle, and hand it to her. And, oh yeah, find one of those white hats, and you know, kind of tip it as you leave."

Joe smiled broadly, "Perfect." He reached over, grabbing Nathan's head by its thick hair, and looked into his eyes. "I'm so sorry to hear you and Bobbie are struggling. You guys have been such an amazing couple, for so long. I mean you still are. All true love goes through hard times. Part of the territory of living life to the fullest."

The two gave each other a long hug. "Great walk," Nathan said, fixing his gaze on his friend. "And almost a great view. But sitting here with you has been the best part."

"Amen to that, brother," Joe returned. "Speaking of friendship, you thought about my idea? You know, Europe. This summer. The three of us?"

"Oh, right. Jesus, sorry, Joe. I had been thinking about it. Until last Wednesday. Fantastic idea, for sure. In principle, yes, absolutely. You said 800 for airfare? I think I can manage most of that. Might have to ask my folks for help. Has Jack said anything yet?"

"Jack's in, man. We're targeting June and July, so not too soon to grab plane tickets."

"Right, right. I'll let you know. Tonight, tomorrow at the latest."

Without a word, Nathan and Joe stood in sync to walk back down the hill. The wind had died, and a mid-afternoon sun was trying to fight through the overcast. They walked down the few steps to the one-way street and looking across the street, searched for the narrow entrance to the longer staircase. Surprisingly, neither could see the opening. Then, in unison, they pointed, laughing, "There it is."

"Oh," Joe said as they crossed the street, "I forgot to tell you the name of this hill."

"Yeah . . .?" Nathan said smiling, immediately trusting the punchline Joe was about to deliver.

"Mount Olympus. No really, I'm not making it up. We've just spent the afternoon," Joe said, "on the home of the gods." With arms tight around shoulders, the two friends squeezed through the narrow opening together, to the stairway now downhill, smiles fixed by all they had just shared – the challenge, the poetry, the ready support of the last few hours – in the years of friendship now turned forever.

Chapter 14

Low to High

Nathan sat in the student union café, waiting for his father while daydreaming out the floor-to-ceiling windows. The large expanse of grass in the middle of campus was empty in the late afternoon, and he found himself focused mostly on the background of cedars and pines bent but resilient in the steady wind. (*God, I love those trees.*) Nathan thought back to his last year in high school when State served as a fallback option. Now he felt lucky he was here. The idea of a dual major made more and more sense, with the bonus that Vincent Pioli was on both faculties, dedicated to playwriting from both the creative writing and theatrical arts sides. Vince had been a quick choice for advisor and then had become a godsend in encouraging Nathan's idea of a stand-up storyteller as a career path. As he sat waiting for his father, Nathan forced his thoughts to the matter at hand. He tapped his fingers in front of an empty coffee cup, ticking off all he wanted to cover. The difficulties with Bobbie. (*Maybe just maybe, he has some insight.*) Suggestions about Europe. (*Countries on his list?*) Joe taking his dad's class. (*What did he think of 'Plum Wine'? Such a great poem.*) But most of all, about his mom dating. (*Christ, Frank of all people? And oh yeah, how could I forget. Nira. No way we can get through all this in an hour. And now he's late.*)

"Looks like you're trying to plan out the rest of your life," his father's steady voice startled Nathan as he approached from the side. "Sorry being late," he added, seeing the empty cup on the table.

Nathan stood up for a quick hug, saying with a bit of a smile, "Just realizing how much has happened since I last saw you."

"Tell me about it. And I now have less than an hour. Have to get back to the office. You want another cup?" his father asked, heading over to the counter.

"Sure. Might help get through half I want to talk about."

As his father made his way back to their table, Nathan had the chance to observe him straight on. (*Something's different.*) He was not only *not* wearing his old leather jacket, but wearing what looked like a brand-new sports jacket. (*My God, it's almost stylish.*) "I don't think I've ever seen you in such a jazzy coat, Dad. Where did . . .? Oh my God, you shaved your goatee!"

"I did," Tommy replied. "You know the damnedest thing, Nathan, it's been a full week now, and I still find myself stroking my chin. A damn phantom goatee."

Nathan's observations then crystallized – his father looked like a different person, and Nathan sat back shaking his head. "Next thing you know, you'll be losing those ancient glasses of yours. Maybe contacts next?"

Tommy Hughes laughed. "Now that would be a change too many. I'd be in front of my class pushing glasses up my nose *and* stroking a beard, both of which aren't there. Wouldn't do that to my poor students."

"So, what got into you?"

His father pursed his lips, "You have to swear on a stack of bibles, not to tell your mother. She was forever letting me know, one way or other, I needed to retire my leather jacket. And that my glasses blocked my beautiful brown eyes. Though I'm not there yet." He paused, defiantly pushing his glasses up his nose with a slight smile. "Nira convinced me. And helped pick out the jacket."

"My god, Dad, that's quite a commitment," Nathan said, eyebrows raised, "like getting married?"

Tommy raised his eyebrows, "You've always been older than your years, Nathan. That comment has more than a bit of truth in it. Though losing the beard was my doing."

"How are things with Nira? Other than the haberdashery adventures."

"Plural? Singular. Haberdashery adventure." His father sighed slightly, looking out the window for a moment, then back to his son, "I think 'well' might capture our current state of affairs. Nira has officially and regrettably relegated her poetry to second-class status and sent in her law school applications." He looked back out the window. "It feels like we're in a place of suspended animation. Or I should say that's how I feel. Nira's plunging full-steam ahead. Long term . . . I wonder." He glanced at Nathan. "Nira understands me differently

129

than your mother does, but . . . ." His father stopped himself, then looked back out the window. "Or maybe it's me acting differently. Sometimes it feels as though I'm on a different planet." He sipped his coffee, then fixed his look on his son. "I'm guessing you want to talk about Frank."

"Am I that easy to read?" Nathan replied, shaking his head. "I swear, one day I'm going to catch you off guard."

"No question about that, boy-o. You already have, too many times. Not that mysterious. And certainly nothing to do with just you. It's about *us*. The bond between father and son."

"So, did you see this coming? When Mom mentioned Frank, it blew me away."

Tommy smiled to himself. Why should Nathan have any awareness of Frank's long-time infatuation with his mother? Tommy knew far too well it would be sooner rather than later before Frank was knocking at her door.

"Your mother's a very attractive woman, son. I was well aware of what I was risking. As for Frank, no, not surprised. From Frank's point of view, that is. Did I think your mother would reciprocate? Not sure I would use the word 'surprise.' I know Frank can be a bit of an odd duck (*that's putting it mildly*), but he can be charming and his fiction's outstanding. One of the strengths of our department actually."

"I won't be taking his class anytime soon."

His father laughed, "That certainly would be awkward. Though your reluctance's a bit ironic, considering Frank's gift for the narrative – his fiction is all about story."

"All I care about is keeping his interest in Mom fictional."

"Well, it's really about your mother's interest in him, isn't it?"

Nathan looked down, his gaze somewhere between the two cups, but his focus inward – just what was the right word to capture his feeling about Frank Strum. "Can't quite put my finger on it, but I know Mom can do better. A whole lot better."

"Not to change the subject, Nathan, but how are things with Bobbie? I didn't get a chance to see her over the holidays."

(*Hmmm, next time, no need to make a goddamn list of what to talk about.*) Nathan looked at his father, the clean-shaven face now younger in appearance, much closer to the image from childhood. ('*The bond between father and son.*') "You and Mom started dating young, right? I know she was still in high school. And you had just started college?"

"Yes, that's right."

"And after you started dating and became a 'couple,' you both always lived *near* each other, close enough to always be with each other. I mean you were never really ever separated?"

"Like you and Bobbie are now? No, we were lucky. Your mother and I never had that to deal with." Tommy Hughes hesitated, almost adding the words, 'until now,' but that wasn't the point. "It must be hard."

"Damn straight. Simply being apart has been hard. But now . . ." Nathan looked outside at the distant trees, trying to decide how much he wanted to say, needed to say to trigger whatever wise insight his father might have. "Bobbie told me how hard it's been for her, the last afternoon during the break. Caught me completely by surprise. But the more I've thought about it, the more her words make sense." Nathan paused and looked at his father, "And being who she is, makes all the sense in the world she'd see this first. While I was blissfully content in the status quo."

"Not sure how much you want to delve into details, son. I appreciate that being apart is no fun, but I assume it's not the simple distance you're referring to. That, being apart has led to some . . . issues?"

"Oh yeah. Leading us to, grow apart." Nathan realized that the phrase 'grow apart' could be misinterpreted. "How can I say it. That we're growing, changing, while apart, separate from each other. Put a better way . . . we haven't been sharing much of anything. For a long time now. I mean if we were apart for a week or two, or even a month, no big deal. But it's been a year and a half! And what's scary is Europe, this summer, which I want to talk more to you about."

Nathan hesitated. "Maybe I could go on like this for however long it takes to be back together, living in the same place. But even if I could, *and* if Bobbie could, where would our relationship, our love, be? Teenage love, back in high school?" Nathan paused, realizing his thoughts were jumping, not flowing, one to the next. "Does any of this make sense?"

"Not sure. Much of it sounds like mental gymnastics. That you're thinking too much. That you're worried about what's going to happen before it happens." His father waited for Nathan to look at him. "I assume you still love Bobbie?"

"Absolutely."

"And Bobbie still loves you?"

"That's the riddle, Dad. Our love is very much in place, but it's defined by where we were two years ago, and our lives, well, to paraphrase the poet, our lives *they are a changin.* Bobbie and I, both of us, are anything but standing still."

"I see," Tommy Hughes said quietly. "You two were only together for what, barely a year. I still think your concern might be premature. What about more visits?"

"In principle, maybe, but in practice? There are the costs, where do I stay, and then the biggie, finding the time. Like I said, we both have plans. Ever since Bobbie laid it all out, I haven't been able to put together a path that gets us back to living, sharing our lives together."

"Lives together?" Tommy paused. "So, here's an idea." (*I knew it. I knew he'd have something.*) His father looked at Nathan with a small but satisfied smile. "If you can't do that one weekend at a time, then, Bobbie should go with you to Europe, this summer."

"What a fantastic idea." (*Why didn't I think of that!?*) "Two whole months. In Europe no less! You know, I hadn't even told Bobbie about my plans. I was worried about her reaction – that we wouldn't have any time together for a second summer in a row. This changes everything," Nathan said, laughing. "At least I can tell her now! God, I hope she hasn't made any plans." Nathan closed his eyes, taking a deep breath, and said, mostly to himself, "Need to lower expectations." Then looking at his father, "What a perfect idea."

"Here's to a bit of luck and the smarts to make it happen." Tommy raised his nearly empty cup to toast his son. "Nathan, not to change the subject, but there's one thing that I need to talk to you about."

"Absolutely," Nathan said, though he was already thinking of the phone call he would make that night to Bobbie.

"Vince was telling me about the story you're working on for his playwriting class. *The Tale of the Good and Evil Twins*. Catchy title," his father said. "From the little bit he told me, it sounds like you're borrowing heavily from our epic walk a few years ago. And from what I managed to track down through phone calls and a trip downtown to City Hall."

"And the rest, as they say, is *just my imagination, running away with me.*"

"Yes, well, that's what I need to talk to you about. Nathan, you wouldn't be the first in our family who could tell a powerful story. And imagination is a great skill, essential for a storyteller. But you have to know how to use it." Tommy Hughes paused to lock eyes with his son. "If one is mixing fact and fiction." Another pause. "Especially if the facts involve public figures and the intent is to tell the story in public. Understand where I'm heading, son?"

"Ahh, well, does the word happen to start with 'lie' and end with 'bull?'"

"Cute, son. Libel. This is serious, Nathan. You can't just fabricate stories, especially malicious ones about a real person. About a public figure who could hear your story. Or even, hear about your story. A lot of ifs, but here's the rub: if you want to make a living as a storyteller, that means people, in public, will hear it. You can't tell a story like the one you're writing if it ends up being, well, public knowledge. Yes, it would be libelous. And maybe worse, dangerous."

"Even if only parts are true?"

"Especially if only parts are true! Nathan, my God, son, do you really think that Pat Scanlan killed his brother?"

"Dad, I don't think that way. It's all about the story. How it evolves. The story, if it's any good, always takes on a life of its own. That's when I know it's

133

going to be good." Nathan looked intently ahead, quickly thinking, trying to react to his father's concern. (*Wasn't expecting this.*) "What if I change details, you know, names, occupations, locations?"

"Nathan, you'd have to change more than that, like the fire, and certainly the murder, and then, well, there goes the heart of your story."

"So, I'll change all the names, tone down the plot, and the story will only be for my project and not the public. I've already written too much not to use this. It's a great tale. And I love telling it!"

Tommy Hughes looked hard at his son. "Nathan, maybe I should read the story before you perform it, even if it's only for your class."

"No need, Dad. I got the message," Nathan said. "Loud and clear." Though once again, his mind was working on more than one level, with much of his attention already turned to constructing the 'plot' of his phone call to Bobbie – the need for the perfect intro, how the logic would unfold just so, and then the all-important punchline. By the time he and his father were well up the path through campus, Tommy's musings about Frank Strum were barely a background sound. Instead, Nathan was walking in the same dim evening light, not here in his home town, but through the long, manicured park that fronted the Eiffel Tower, arm-in-arm with the love of his life, dreamingly deep within their summer-long European holiday. (*Sharing the adventure of a lifetime. No, more important, sharing our love . . . together.*)

• • •

"Damn straight this is a reason to celebrate," Nathan shot back at Jack.

The three friends sat together outside the two-room cottage that Jack rented deep in the avenues. The rental was situated well back of the owner's house and hidden down a long driveway, protected from the wind and neighbors by a high wooden fence badly in need of repair. The property was actually a bit of a dump, but that was its charm, as Jack would off-handedly brag to anyone who would raise an eyebrow. The late winter day was only moderately cold, and the three sat comfortable in light jackets, smoking cigarettes, and discussing plans for the summer. The front door was wide open as the guttural pleadings of Joe Cocker reached into the high foggy afternoon. *Ohhh, dear landlord, please don't put a price on my soul . . .*

"Before we go off celebrating," Jack broke into Nathan's plans, "let's get on the same page. Believe me, Nathan, we both think the world of Bobbie, but the original idea was strictly a guy thing, you know, a serious road trip. So, expectations. Are you seeing this more as a honeymoon now? If so, Joe and I need to plan accordingly."

"Hey, man, speak for yourself," Joe jumped in. "Bobbie joining's a plus. She adds class to us bums."

"It's a fair question, Joe," Nathan said leaning back in his chair. "I hadn't thought about her effect on the two of you. Or really on the three of us. I've been completely focused on Bobbie and me, on solving our problems. And by the way, this ain't no honeymoon. More like, life or death."

Joe shrugged. "So, we break the trip into times we're together, and times me and Jack keep the Kerouac thing going, and you and Bobbie are, well, on your honeymoon."

"Give me a frigging break," Nathan said with a grin. "Anyway, hard to imagine we all want to go to all the same countries. So, we'll be together in the E coupon cities like Amsterdam and Paris, but we can separate in, you know, the A or B coupons." Nathan paused to light another cigarette, then said while inhaling. "And maybe there's a country, or city, that Bobbie wants to explore, but I don't. Might be good for us to take breaks. Then the three of us can have time together, alone. Or is that alone, together?"

"Yeah, yeah, that's all obvious. Just have to get used to the idea the whole trip's different." Jack flicked the end of his cigarette across the cement some twenty feet directly into a metal bucket half full of butts.

"Man, you're looking at it all wrong," Joe said. "Not different. Better." Then, to change the focus, asked, "So, what are your top three destinations, Jack?"

"Amsterdam. To Athens. To Crete. Then staying put."

Nathan and Joe looked at each other, shaking their heads at their friend's ease of reducing everything to such simplicity.

"With a layover in Corfu I assume?" Joe added.

"Or past tense *laid*-over, absolutely, man. As many laid-overs as possible. But the focus is to get to Crete. End of the line. Beginning of the trip."

"So. As I think I was saying, one way or another, I'm celebrating Bobbie saying yes, and here's my idea." Nathan said, leaning forward toward his two friends. "You know my friend Leonard?"

"The tall skinny dude?"

"Yup. The one you said looks like a long strand of DNA. Well, he told me that he has a source, totally trusts, for psilocybin."

"Well, why the fuck didn't you say that in the first place?" Jack broke in.

"Not sure about you guys, never done mushrooms, but I've heard it's *all* about context. Even more so than acid. The better the ambiance, the better the high. So, I was thinking, what could we do that was all about positive vibes? One hundred percent guaranteed simpatico." Nathan looked at Joe and Jack.

"There's a certain type of movie classic that, when shown at the Sunset, not only sells out, but becomes more than just a random group of people watching a movie. I'm talking sold-out charged electricity from a packed theatre of like-minded enthusiasts, addicts really, who interact with the movie. They know the story, every detail. So much so, they'll cheer and cry and echo all the famous lines. It's almost religious. Like a call and response, with the movie the preacher."

"And?" asked Jack derisively.

"And, for the next three nights, we're showing such a movie. Maybe, the greatest call and response movie ever. Certainly, the most universal. It has everything. War, romance, intrigue, betrayal, and, in the end, the melting of a jaded, good-guy bastard's heart, leading to his salvation. And for all those leaving. Or staying. In . . ." Nathan waited a perfect beat. "*Casablanca.*"

"So," Jack said in his indelibly sarcastic snarl, "we eat mushrooms and go watch a fucking movie?"

"Trust me, Jack. Not a movie. A portal. To a total and complete transformation. Plus," Nathan added with a shrug, "the high lasts longer than the movie, so what we do before and after is up to us. And I think the three of us have imagination in spades."

"I *love* that movie." Joe said. "And watching it in a packed house while tripping, well, not sure I'd ever have put *Casablanca* and psilocybin together in the same sentence, but I love it! Tomorrow night, for sure. Jack?"

"Saturday night at the movies," Jack dead-panned. "Okay, but I'm holding Nathan to his promise of a doorway. To an early Sunday morning awakening. Now that I'm think of it, been way too long since I've been to church."

Chapter 15

Screen and Stage

"The Surf Theatre." Herb Malakoff mulled out loud Nathan's idea of changing the name of his movie house. As with all such planning sessions, the two sat in the exceedingly small office tucked underneath the stairs that led to the projection room. Nathan never tired of looking at the densely covered walls above his boss's desk. Hanging on the wall opposite was Nathan's favorite photograph – Herb, more than ten years ago, the new impresario wearing a look of utmost satisfaction, standing underneath his first marquee, *The Virgin Spring* and *Wild Strawberries*. Herb leaned back in his chair and smiled across the desk in answer to his young 'right-hand' man's quizzical look. "Needless to say, I'm more than used to the name 'Sunset.' As wedded to it as to my wife. But I must say," he paused, appreciating Nathan's anxious curiosity of his verdict, "the 'Surf' does have a certain ring to it."

Nathan could finally exhale. "I can only imagine what the name 'Sunset' must mean to you," he said, "but it's always seemed, at odds, you know, with the weather. I mean I know the sun has to set, fog or no fog, but sunset implies being able to actually see the sun go down. Which isn't often. Hardly ever really out here."

"Hmmm."

"Plus, I love sensually rich words – words that evoke more than one sense. Surf is one of the few words I can think of that's tied to all five. Legitimately tied. Not forced. *Seeing* the ebb and flow of the tide. *Hearing* the waves break. *Smelling* that distinct mix of salt and seaweed. *Tasting* the saltwater on your lips. Or walking barefoot and *feeling* the back and forth wash of the tide."

"Yes, I see."

"And I really like one syllable words – short and sweet. 'What's playing at the Surf tonight?'"

"All right already, Nathan. You've convinced me. To think it over that is. Now, anything else before I get to work?"

Nathan paused, wondering, if not now, when? His boss did not always have the patience to tolerate 'off-the-wall' questions, and Nathan knew his question was anything but usual. It had been lingering in his head for weeks, and Herb Malakoff was certainly the best person to provide any feedback. (*Plunge ahead. It's now or never.*)

Nathan leaned forward and set his gaze across the desk. He lowered his voice, not because he was worried someone might be listening, but simply because what he was about to say was, he thought, utterly fascinating.

"Have you ever heard of . . . the lost Hitchcock film?"

Herb Malakoff was caught off-guard. "Not sure what you mean, Nathan. Some of his movies from the fifties are out of distribution, and I guess could be called 'lost.'"

Nathan emphatically shook his head.

Herb tried again, "He had several ideas, I think even draft screenplays, that were never filmed."

"No, no. This is different. I've been told there was a movie, more or less completely shot in secret, only to be closed down during editing."

"And exactly where did you hear this?"

"Yeah, I know, more than far-fetched. I heard it from a good friend of my drama/film teacher at State. I completely trust my teacher, so I pressed him, hard, about his friend, and he swore by him." Nathan looked at his mentor. "This guy said his girlfriend had a bit part in the movie, which was shot in '49 or '50. Supposedly, everyone had this dead-serious no-kidding nondisclosure clause in their contract. So, everyone involved, from actor to costume designer, only knew as much as was needed. Therefore, the girlfriend didn't know much about the plot. But what she did know sounds amazing."

"Ok, Mr. Storyteller, cut to the chase."

"It seems that the construction was a movie within a movie, with the 'outer' movie centered on a famous director of murder mysteries – in other words

Hitchcock – who's filming a new murder mystery. The film goes back and forth between actual scenes in the new movie and the director filming the new movie, you know, directing the actor who is playing the murderer. But the 'inner' movie is the kicker. The actor, not the character he's playing mind you, the actor himself is planning a murder. Of whom, you might ask? Of the director! So, the Hitchcock character becomes the would-be murder victim. Wild, huh?

"But here's the real kicker. Who played Hitchcock? Orson Welles! My God, can't you just see him? His obsession with make-up and costumes. He was playing aging round men all the way back to Kane, right? And his own experience as a director? He'd be perfect. Who do you think played the actor/murderer?"

"I need a hint."

"Think Welles *and* Hitchcock."

Herb immediately smiled. "Joseph Cotten. I must say, if this is true or made-up, it sounds brilliant. Did the friend say anything about why it was never finished?"

"Only that the girlfriend heard the project started as a collaboration between Hitchcock and Welles. And that there was more than one day when shooting ended early, and abruptly. So, maybe the quintessential clash of egos? Two enormous egos." Nathan paused. "And I do mean enormous. Both of them!"

Herb gazed up at the ceiling. He knew in his head this unlikely anecdote had to be fictional. Something like this could not be kept under wraps all these years. But he smiled nonetheless at the one in a thousandth chance it was true. A lost Hitchcock film. And one with a plot and actors that could maybe push it near the top of his movies.

"I wonder..." he sat back with hands folded across his jacket. "This would have been right at the demise of Hitchcock's company. In the late forties. What was it called, Trans-something Pictures? If this was truly a collaboration of 'equals,' and it ended with a no-win battle royale in the editing room..." Herb mused. "What would have happened to the film stock?"

"Of course, that's to say any of this has even the smallest grain of truth, which, well, I think we'd both say, no chance. But still, it's worth exploring, don't you think? With all your connections? I'd say if you can't find any hint that would back up the story, then…" Nathan paused, letting the consequence of this chain of events settle in his thoughts. "Say, worst case scenario, you find no evidence for any of this, that the guy's girlfriend was just yanking his chain, I could turn this into a story. Maybe even write a screenplay." Nathan let out a short laugh. "It'd be like a 'found script.' Like remembering a great dream, and then turning it into a poem or story."

Herb marveled to see the machinations of Nathan's mind at work. This young man really does see all of life as a story, he thought. Or at least, fodder for the beginning of one.

"It seems, Nathan, that you'd rather me *not* find any proof of this lost film," Herb Malakoff said quietly, with a bit of a smile.

With just the slightest look of embarrassment, Nathan quickly replied, "Oh, good God, not in the least. I'd much rather be sitting front and center at the grand opening. Could you imagine standing underneath the marquee outside, 'The Lost Hitchcock Film'? Might be even more satisfying than that picture over your head, of the opening night of the Sunset!"

Herb sat for a moment, a bemused look on his face. "Or at least just as. Which would be quite the feat considering how proud I was that night. Someday, I should tell you how the Sunset came to be. It wasn't easy. By the way, Nathan. You didn't mention a title. Did the friend mention what this was to be called?"

"Another mystery – the girlfriend said it was always referred to as, *The Project*."

"Well, make no mistake, my young friend, truth or fiction, I'm most definitely hooked. Trust me, I'll be making phone calls and writing a few letters. We'll see how this story ends. On our marquee or in your typewriter," Herb said while looking into Nathan's sparkling eyes. "So, what should we call this film until then?"

"Well, they both liked their titles short and sweet, right? How about *Lost and Found*?"

"*Lost and Found* it is," Herb repeated, nodding. "Oh, I almost forgot, one more thing. Last Saturday night, at the late showing of *Casablanca* . . . I've never seen such an audience reaction in all my life. At the Sunset or anywhere. I was here in my office, and all of a sudden . . . such an explosion of singing! I hurried inside and couldn't believe my eyes, or ears. The French national anthem? Here in the Sunset? It was as if the audience had merged with the film! I thought I was hallucinating." Herb could see Nathan was clearly enjoying this review. "That was the showing you saw with your friends, wasn't it?"

"Yes, sir. It was. The damnedest movie experience ever, in all my life. Hallucinating – great description," Nathan said, biting his lip. "Only one problem."

"Yes?"

"I'll be forever trying to match it."

"Yes, well, maybe we'll just have to unearth *Lost and Found*."

"Yes, maybe we will," Nathan softly replied. He could already feel the gears of imagination engage. He had never considered writing a screenplay, but what a script this could be. Yes, maybe Mr. Malakoff *was* correct – some part of him did want this to be just a crazy rumor. Then it would be all his.

• • •

"Sean Murphy stormed into the front office, 'What's all this about my brother snooping into the payroll code?'"

Nathan Hughes stood on stage looking out into the dim light where the small audience of Vincent Aioli and his fellow classmates sat. He was halfway through his performance. The fool of the angel had sent the twins on their way to earth, filled with grace or not. They had grown through childhood and adolescence and had found their way into successful careers. Nathan knew the juiciest twists and turns were now his to tell. Time to put the engine into full throttle, liability be damned. He looked hard and mean at the audience.

"The tall, gangly but rugged man quickly covered the twenty feet of office floor, and putting both hands down on the desk with a thump, hovered over his right-hand man. 'Damnit, Robert, three different people are telling me he's been asking questions down at City Hall. In the goddamn payroll department. What the hell is going on?"'

The memory from the night in the grove three years earlier of Pat Scanlan's voice still rung in Nathan's ears. Now the harsh gnarly voice of Sean Murphy hammered his words into the air.

"Robert Sullivan looked up at his boss knowing he had no room to wiggle. 'I just heard about this myself, Sean. I spoke with McMillan not thirty minutes ago. He's going to, ah, discretely talk to our contact in payroll and see what questions Michael's been asking. And what answers he's been given in return. If any.' Sean Murphy quickly shot back, 'Do we know who Michael's been talking to? To our contact? Or someone else, which will just lead to more goddamn questions?' Sullivan squirmed a bit in his chair and looked away. 'We don't know for sure, Sean. But it sounds like it wasn't our contact.' Murphy banged again on the desk, 'You come get me when McMillan's back. I want to hear it straight from him, myself.'

"Well, it didn't take long for Sean Murphy to be convinced that his brother Michael was prying into his business and asking questions. Too many and all the wrong ones. When was McMillan hired and what was his background? How many union bank accounts existed, and just when were each opened? When was the last audit performed on their books? And most concerning – why did the union have any access to the payroll code used by the city? But all that was foreplay to the knock on his door a day later. A knock that didn't wait for an answer as the door opened and Michael Murphy stepped inside, closing it behind him, making sure he heard the click of the latch.

"Michael stood tall, his six-foot-three frame blocking the door. He looked at his twin sitting behind the desk for a drawn-out moment before continuing, 'Apologies for barging into your office, brother, but there's something we need to talk about. Something that can't wait.' Sean returned his brother's stare before replying, 'Well, I'd ask you in, but you clearly aren't waiting for an invitation, are you now?' His smile was molded into a snarl by years of tension between the two.

Michael moved a chair close to the desk. 'Sean, I know we've had serious discussions before, but never as serious as this. In the past, it's been more about best practice, or you doing more harm than good.' 'Whatever you say, brother.' 'Never about outright breaking of the law.' Michael paused. 'About felony.' Another pause. 'About grand larceny.' Sean held his ground and remained silent, putting the burden on his brother to state his concerns, to lay out all his cards."

Nathan portrayed the two brothers on stage by a slight turn of direction. He used the same gravelly voice for both twins, except that Michael's pitch was raised a bit, with just the slightest lilt. For the narrator's voice, he used his own natural tonality, a baritone, made confident through his lifelong practice of telling tales.

"Well, it was crystal clear to Michael that his brother would battle him, tooth and nail. Or at the start, battle him with his silence. To be expected, he thought. No need to beat around the bush. 'I'm pretty damn sure, Sean, that your union is stealing from the city. Siphoning off payroll into some bogus union dues account. In working with a couple of lads in City Hall, the latest backtracking I've done myself says maybe to the tune of a hundred grand per, but probably more.' Sean Murphy showed no emotion, not even a raised eyebrow. Though impressed by how accurate the amount of money was, he simply stared back at his brother. Expressionless. Waiting.

"Michael knew his brother as well as he knew himself, from their 56 years sharing an identical make-up, with ethics as different as night and day. Good and evil, pure and simple, Michael thought. He knew Sean well enough to again cut to the chase. To present the endgame. 'There's enough evidence to warrant an independent audit of your books, which I'm certain would lead to enough evidence to charge you and whoever else is in on this with grand larceny of the city's coffers.' So, now to the end, Michael thought, to what my silent brother is waiting for. 'Sean, I should not do this, but you are my flesh and blood. My identical flesh and blood. One alternative and one alternative only. You rewrite the payroll code, now, with hard proof of the changes, and I'll keep all I know to myself. To my grave. Word of honor. On our poor parents' souls.' Sean Murphy's response to the last words was a defiant snort. He stared at his brother, then asked, 'And what about your 'lads,' down at City Hall?' 'Not a concern. No one suspects anything. To them, the payroll balance is as it should be.'"

Nathan quickly scanned his audience, pausing a second longer on his teacher's face. (*Damn, everyone's engaged.*) He also took stock of the clock on the wall and noted his pace was a bit slower than planned. (*Time for the climax.*)

"Sean glared across his desk, thinking to himself, you're damn right you'll be keeping this to your grave. and replied, 'I need a night to sleep on it.' Michael gave one short nod as he rose to leave, 'Tomorrow then. A final decision.'

"After his brother's footsteps faded down the hallway, Sean Murphy quietly cursed out loud, 'Just how in the hell did he even know to start snooping? Damnit. Goddamn son of a bitch.' With that, he grew silent, keeping the rest inside. 'There's just no way he's taking this money from me. And worse, he can swear all he wants on our damn parents, I know he'll always keep this hanging over my head. No, this has to end. Permanently. And I can't trust any hired thug. It's got to be me. I have to kill that self-righteous bastard myself.' And with that most cold-blooded of thoughts seared in his brain, Sean's attention was drawn to the violent sounds of another winter storm rattling his windows. 'Was that a tree falling? Christ, when are these storms ever going to end?'

Nathan lowered his head for a count of three, then pantomimed knocking loudly on a door, while stamping his heal on the floor with each knock. "Robert Sullivan knocked loudly on his boss's door early the next morning, but didn't wait for an answer before rushing in. 'Sean, have you heard yet?' 'What the hell, man. Heard what?' 'A body's been found up the far slope of the grove, underneath a fallen tree.' Sullivan swallowed hard. 'Your brother's body, Sean. He's dead. Michael's dead.' Sullivan had known Sean Murphy a long time, knew how he could hide all emotion inside, with nothing showing on the outside: lips, eyes, the deep lines of his face still. As he looked at his boss in the brief silence, he couldn't tell for sure. Though maybe? Did he already know? Sean finally spoke, 'Is the body still there?' 'I have no idea, Sean. Billy said that the police got there 15-20 minutes ago, along with the EMS. So maybe. Probably, yeah.' 'Then we should go see, shouldn't we?'

"As the two walked quickly through the cold, wet winter park, the heavy-set junior partner barely keeping pace, Robert Sullivan dared to break the silence. 'Christ, Sean, I mean what happened is terrible, but what a fuckin' godsend. This certainly puts an end to his nosing around.' 'That wasn't a problem, Robert. Michael came by yesterday, and he found nothing. It was all a dead-end.' 'You mean he didn't find out anything in Payroll?' Sullivan was astonished. 'Nothing to find out. End of story,' Murphy said with a cold finality. 'Jesus,' Sullivan mumbled, shaking his head, 'and I thought our feet were surely in the fire.' After another minute of barely keeping up with his boss, 'Christ, what in God's name was he doing out in that storm anyway? It was truly vicious.' They were now close enough to see a small group of police and medical staff forming a loose circle. As they approached and were greeted by a policeman, Sean Murphy spoke first. 'I'm his brother.' Without as much as a pause, he walked over to the body. The head badly cracked and body very much motionless, lying not a yard from the once towering eucalyptus equally motionless on the hillside. He turned to another cop and asked, 'Was he found like this, or was his body moved, pulled from underneath the tree?' The cop turned to a man in coat and tie, who stepped in and said, 'You must be his brother. The head of the firefighter's union?' 'That's right. And you are Detective...?' 'Mullins. The body hasn't been moved. Found just like that. Strange, don't you think? Head caved in, but no part of his body under the tree.' 'I don't know, Detective. Massive tree. He could have been knocked to the side, away from where the tree landed,' Murphy said, then muttered something to himself. He then moved just a whisper to the side and bowed his head. From the detective's perspective, a brother saying goodbye. Even though Michael's head was crushed, the impact was in the back of the skull, allowing the detective to be impressed by the identical facial appearance of the two brothers. He could only imagine how this man must feel, what he must be thinking standing very much alive a few feet away from his spitting image, very much dead. After another minute, Sean Murphy turned and said quietly, 'I'll be in my office, if there's anything you need. Detective.'

Nathan maintained the look of a heartless, expressionless man as he gazed into the audience. He then relaxed his stance while locking his fingers together, his palms up as his arms hung in front. "A few weeks after the burial and the return to a sense of normalcy, Sean Murphy carefully weighed all the pieces of what had happened, to ensure no loose ends remained. First and foremost, he had to discover who his brother had talked with in the city's Payroll Department. His contact in Payroll was a sharp fellow, and painstakingly vigilant, so after intense questioning of this man, Murphy was convinced that his brother's words were true – not even a hint of suspicion had been left behind. However, separate from his brother's meddling, Murphy realized that, in reviewing the scheme itself, the paper trail of member dues might become an unfortunate clue, or worse, hard evidence if ending up in court. Although he knew his brother was not just some dumb fool, someone had uncovered the scheme, and therefore someone else might in the future. This paper trail was a problem. Why not simply make it disappear?

"'But how?' Sean wondered. He went to the room where all union records were kept. 'Jesus Christ, this is goddamn immense. No way could I carry all these records out of here and not be noticed,' he muttered, then realized, 'What the hell am I thinking! Why would all these records up and walk out. No, they can't just disappear.' Then, only when forced into this corner, did the answer present itself, and Sean Murphy let curl a most satisfyingly devious smile. 'Of course, the records don't disappear, they'll simply be destroyed,' followed by a short laugh. 'This old building has needed remodeling for much too long. All the records conveniently in wooden cabinets. Not a shred of evidence would be left after a fire.' The smile grew more crooked. 'No real urgency, more a safeguard. Plenty of time to upgrade the insurance coverage for maximum payoff. And make sure I come up with the most foolproof of plans.'"

With the end of his story in sight, Nathan jumped feet first into the finish. "And so, several months later and deep into another gala dinner to celebrate another successful recruiting class, Sean Murphy and Robert Sullivan 'accidentally' engineered a spill of cooking oil in the kitchen, carefully spiked with an even more flammable chemical 'that would be long gone and never detected.' The central core of the old lodge, which just happened to be the kitchen directly below the room full of records, exploded ferociously into flames. Murphy loved the irony, a fire at a Firemen's Ball. These firemen were all proven professionals with years of experience, and Murphy knew that any chaos would only occur in the initial explosion. It would even give the new recruits real-life experience! At the height of the fire, Sean and his sidekick stood outside, well removed from the burning lodge, watching the flames and smoke twist through and into the night fog. 'Like something out of Dante,' Sullivan said in awe. 'You know, considering everything that's happened these past months, you'd have to think a guardian angel is somewhere watching over us, Sean. Except for the grace of God, we should be sitting in jail right now, awaiting trial, don't you think.'"

Nathan paused to maintain the rigid look of the emotionless Sean Murphy one last time for the audience to behold its cold-hearted splendor. 'If there are two things, I can tell you for certain, my friend, are these. One, guardian angels do *not* exist,' Murphy snarled at Sullivan. 'And two, there sure as hell is no such thing as . . . the grace of God.'

"And *that*," Nathan said emphatically, "is the tale of the *Good and Evil Identical Twins*." With his arms opened at his sides, he took a deep bow toward the audience, feeling both the utmost satisfaction in his telling of the tale and an equal amount of uncertainty about how it was received. This contradiction was addressed before he even rose. Classmates and teacher were on their feet in loud applause. (*How could so few make so much noise!*) He somehow managed his way off stage to be surrounded by classmates and questions.

When the theatre appeared to be empty, and just as Vincent was about to add his praise, a student Nathan had barely spoken with the entire semester approached. "Great story, Nathan, but I have to ask. Didn't some of that actually happen?"

(*Christ.*) Nathan imagined his teacher's eyes were drilling a hole through his skull. "Yeah, maybe a few bits and pieces."

His classmate continued. "I grew up right across the street from the Grove, and I remember when the park director was killed in the storm. What was his name? It was Irish, started with an 'S.' Sullivan?"

"Scanlan. John Scanlan."

"Yeah, that's it. And then a few years later, the lodge did burn down. I remember how odd that was. Nothing at all in the news. And what was left was immediately fenced off, I mean, within a day or two. Then rebuilt surprisingly quick, and with no expense spared. I can see why you used that – what a great foundation for a mystery. Not to give away trade secrets, but how'd you come up with the idea of identical twins."

"Well," Nathan said, still caught off guard, "like you say, trade secrets."

"Yeah, yeah, understood. Hey, I interrupted. Great job." The student turned and disappeared as quickly as he had appeared.

Nathan stood in disbelief. The last thing he expected was to be quizzed about John Scanlan, or anything about the fire. Luckily, the student seemed to have no idea of who *Pat* Scanlan was. His thoughts quickly turned to what his father had warned him about and had discussed with his teacher, who now stood by his side, apparently waiting for an explanation. (*No idea what to say.*)

Vincent Aioli was not, however, waiting for Nathan to say anything. On the contrary, he was equally perplexed at what *he* should say. As Nathan's teacher of how to write and perform plays, his inclination had been just that, to praise the story and the storyteller. However, he now felt more of a responsibility. But of what, of a father? Wasn't that Tommy Hughes' job. What an odd situation to be in. Oh, the hell with it, he thought. Nathan needs to hear this from someone *not* his father.

"Nathan, let's sit," Vince said, pointing toward the front row. "And before I say anything about what Mr. Tomasini just said, first things first. I mean, what a story and what a performance." His teacher leaned forward in his seat. "You know, I found myself asking, more than once, why does this work so well? Why a one-man story, and not simply traditional theater. And then it hit me. In telling a story, even on stage, it's still a story. Still a combination of dialogue and narrative. Whereas theatre is only dialogue and some action. Certainly, no omniscient narration. How well you wove your dialogue and narrative together. It's all in your voice, you know. Your resonating baritone establishes the narrative, and then your facility with dialect brought the dialogue to life. Really quite perfect.

"Well, anyway," he paused for a split second, then dove in, "I do have to respond to Phil's comments. I know you know your father and I have talked about this. But what I have to say is strictly from me, a teacher's point of view." Nathan nodded. (*Here we go.*)

"So, the critical question. Where do our stories come from? Well, of course, from everywhere. From our lives, dreams, other stories we hear, bits of fluff we piece together because somehow we sense they're connected." The teacher looked at his student. "I want to make this clear, Nathan. It's not wrong to use actual people or events in your writing. You simply need to understand the risks. Or put another way, you need to understand why you're writing what you're writing. At one extreme, if you believe, or maybe even can prove a crime's been committed, well, that's not fiction. That's investigational journalism. If you want to make a point about a real-life shady character in a fictional novel or play, you need to walk a fine line. If the end-result is purely to entertain, well, I wouldn't take much risk, maybe none. My sense is that your *Twins* is pure entertainment. I assume no connecting the dots? In pursuit of solving a crime?"

Nathan let out a short laugh and shook his head. (*Well, I am connecting dots, but only the dots of a story.*)

"Nathan, there's no question you have talent. My recommendation would be to call *Identical Twins* a success and move on. I'm guessing you already have at least one or two ideas brewing." Vince quickly saw the affirmative in Nathan's slight smile. "I have to agree with your father about retiring this one. I noticed that you did try and tone down the plot in this telling, by having the cause of Michael's death ambiguous." (*That's because that's what the story's telling me now – I just don't know.*) "But I can't see the story ever being changed enough *not* to present a problem for the real and very much alive Sean Murphy, whatever his name is, and still retain enough to make it work. To hold the audience spellbound. Do you agree?"

Nathan had heard every word. (*It does make sense, absolutely, but...*) He agreed that *The Identical Twins* had come to an ending of some kind (*for now at least*), and another story would take its place. But even *Lost and Found* would take a back seat to what loomed directly ahead.

"Thanks, Mr. Aioli. For all your support. Actually, I won't be writing any stories for a while. Not sure if I told you, but I'm off to Europe in a few weeks. Trip of a lifetime. At least, up until now."

"Well, there you go, Nathan. Knowing you, and having been to Europe myself, I predict you'll come home with more beginnings that you'll know what to do with."

That may well be, Nathan thought. But there's only one story that concerns me now. The one that ends, *and they lived happily ever after.*

Chapter 16
Kismet

"Maybe I should give up this crazy idea of being a storyteller, Bobbie. Follow in my dad's footsteps. Be a poet. Sefaris writes, *the poem is everywhere.*" Nathan gestured toward the endless night sky. "Let's see. How many poems are staring me in the face?

"*The stars are calling out to me,* that's one for sure.

"The mast of this ship – *it's the center of the earth,* is another.

"And the old man up there on the upper deck? *He's like a slowly moving block of stone from the Acropolis.* Look, *he's dragging his chair like a stubborn mule.*

"And then there's you, in the moonlight, *your face aglow like the moon herself.* That's the best."

"You're silly. And sweet," Bobbie said. "But for all my criticism of your stories, you *are* a storyteller. Not a poet."

"Not even when inspired by such a romantic setting as this?"

"Well . . ." Bobbie began. "What you should write is a romantic story. After that last one about such a horrible man. Not to change the subject, but I'm glad we're taking the night ferry, even if we don't get much sleep. I've never ever seen so many stars. My head is swimming."

Nathan and Bobbie sat legs outstretched on the lower deck of the walk-on ferry from Athens to Crete. Their journey was barely a week old and already much had changed, some before they had even left home and another just hours earlier. The impact was still a best guess – news of Joe and Jack arriving on Crete might be waiting for them at the American Express in Chania. Or Heraklion. Or not. As much as Nathan was eager to see his friends, he didn't mind the uncertainties that now charted their course. How could he, sitting next to his one and only.

"What did that Israeli couple say about scooters on Crete – amazingly cheap. We can make Chania our base camp and explore the island by moped. No telling where Joe and Jack will be."

"But remember what else they said about the bikes – 'every third person is a walking mummy, scraped and bandaged from head to foot.' Sounds romantic."

"Hey, look at it as the price of admission. Becoming truly one with the land of Crete."

"Hmmm, I'd rather pay in hard currency. Mycenaean gold if I have to."

The weather that night was calm, as was the steady rocking of the ship. Soon, both travelers were asleep. They were awakened in the early dawn by the bellowing horn of an outbound ferry, a friendly wake-up call that their ship was fast approaching Chania. Nathan struggled to open his eyes. Although they had been traveling through Italy then Greece for a week, he felt he was waking on the first morning of their travels. Maybe it was coming off such a vast sea into the protected harbor. Nathan had little interest in the explanation and sat in awe of the simple beauty brilliant in the early morning light.

"I wonder if Jack knew how amazingly beautiful Crete would be," he said.

"Probably not," Bobbie laughed, "but we still have to give him credit. Whether he knew or not, Jack is why we're here."

• • •

No letter at the American Express. Either in Chania, or in Heraklion the next day. A friendly woman perched behind the counter suggested they search along the southern coast of the island. "Many beaches where, hmmm, young travelers like you end up. Go to Matala, and maybe small village Plakios. Beaches are beautiful. Where are you staying now, please?"

"In a hostel in Chania," Bobbie said.

"Oh, hostels in Rethymno are nice, too. And from there, much more easy trips to south."

"Can you get to the south of the island on a moped?" Nathan asked.

"Hmmm, might take few hours. Only 80 kilometers, but some of road very, hmmm, how you say," the woman weaved her hand back and forth.

"Windy?" (*Or does she mean windy?*)

"Yes, windy. If you don't mind sometimes very slow, then okay. Cars will want to pass. So," the woman shrugged her shoulders, "slow sometimes is, hmmm, better, no?"

Nathan and Bobbie both smiled, "Yes!"

"Oh, mopeds, very important. Some rentals are no good. Some *very* bad. Make sure you test scooter first," the young woman smiled, nodding her head.

As much as the no-message from Joe or Jack was disappointing, as soon as they were outside, the couple turned to each other with the same thought – the plans just laid at their feet were an unexpected blessing. "Shall we?" Nathan smiled at Bobbie.

"Slow? Absolutely," Bobbie quickly returned. "I know we'll eventually find Joseph and Jack, but in the meantime, it's our trip! Only one request. You have to promise . . . only really good bikes!"

After re-settling from Chania to Rethymno and finding the right scooter rental for the morning, Nathan and Bobbie went to bed early, still tired from the short sleep on the ferry. They rose with the dawn and prepared for a leisurely trip south. Filling day packs with water, fruit, bread, and a full cup of olives, they were over the island's central hills and heading downhill by late morning, the expansive sea once more in full view, without a single spill-out or fall from their scooters. The closer they came to the sea, the more their focus was on its hypnotic blueness, and closer still, on the contrasting blue-green surf line close to shore. When nearing Matala, they could see the sandstone bluffs that rose from the beach. The bluffs that were pock-marked with countless holes of varying sizes. The caves of Matala.

Nathan motioned Bobbie to pull off to the side of the road. "This calls for a glass of wine. Let's celebrate at the first café we come to."

While barely straddling her bike, Bobbie leaned over, balancing herself by grabbing onto Nathan's arm, and with helmets knocking, answered him with a deep kiss. "I like your logic."

"No logic. Just feeling," Nathan replied, his eyes locked onto Bobbie's. "Say, you lead the way."

Bobbie returned a big smile, nodding her head, then gently pushed off Nathan's arm, giving it a squeeze. Bobbie rejected the first café they passed – 'no logic, just feeling.' But the second was perfect, relatively quiet in the late morning, with simple tables and chairs, brightly colored, spilling out of a small hole-in-the-wall onto the street. She raised her arm, pointing emphatically.

Sitting down, they looked at each other with knowing smiles, as if the past week, even months, comprised one long journey. To here, and here alone.

"We made it," Bobbie said.

"All the way from that afternoon in the back room of my house," Nathan replied. "Where all we talked about was that damn distance. Not anymore."

"Lots to toast."

"I hear that Crete has been making wine for a very long time."

"We deserve nothing less."

Nathan turned around, peering into the interior of the café. A man stood behind the bar, hair and scraggly beard a warm strawberry blonde, and skin clearly white even underneath a suntan. (*Hmmm, looks American.*) Nathan called, "Do we order here or inside?" The man nodded and came outside.

"Either way. You two love birds just drive over the hills?"

Nathan grabbed Bobbie's hand, raising it to his lips to kiss. "Yes, and not a single spill. Two glasses of wine to celebrate!"

"Ah, to be young, unfettered, and alive. And without a dent," Redbeard teased. "So, two glasses of wine. Red or white?"

Nathan said, "Red" and Bobbie, "White" at the same time, then laughed. "Sorry, we're being silly. But, hey, that's who we are," Nathan said pretending to be slightly embarrassed.

"To paraphrase extremely questionable so-called literature, young means never having to say you're sorry," Redbeard said with a deadpan face. "Best-selling authors, what do they know? You need anything to eat with your celebration?"

Nathan and Bobbie looked at each other. Bobbie replied, "Not yet. Too many toasts."

"You know, sometimes..." Redbeard said, then paused, "sometimes we toast to nothing, as my old lady likes to say, and that's okay. But drinking with a purpose, man, that's the best," he said and headed back inside.

"You know how sometimes you know, I mean know for certain, that all the stars in the galaxy are aligned," Nathan said, almost whispering. "That you are exactly where you're meant to be?"

Bobbie's eyes sparkled. "Which is here."

"What will be our first toast?"

"To us!"

"And the next?"

"To the lady at the American Express."

"And then?"

"Maybe this guy here? Oh, it's your turn, Nathan."

"Well, my wonderful impossible dad. I hate to admit it, but us being together in Europe, anywhere in Europe, was his idea."

"Then maybe he should be the first!"

"And we shouldn't forget Joe and Jack. If they hadn't fucked everything up by not leaving messages, we wouldn't be here, just the two of us. By ourselves."

"By ourselves," Bobbie repeated, then added, while getting up, "I need to make room for all these toasts!"

As she entered the café, Bobbie stopped at the bar where Redbeard was opening a bottle of wine. "Say, I have a really crazy question."

"Crazy questions – my fave."

"I noticed the guitar over there, and, well..." Bobbie hesitated. "I've been wanting to sing a song to my boyfriend ever since we started our trip, and everything today has cried out, *today's the day*. I was hoping maybe that, I could borrow it, for just one song?" Bobbie looked past all the red hair and into a pair of striking blue eyes. For a long second, she had no idea how he would respond.

Then Redbeard smiled. "Well, it's not my guitar. But it is my old lady's. She and a girlfriend are off exploring the nearby isles, so what she doesn't know won't hurt her. Just kidding. She's like me. She'd be honored to be in the service of love. Especially, young love. And she's hardly playing it anyway. Totally into her dulcimer. So, you'd be doing her a favor keeping it in tune."

Bobbie shook her head, thinking, nobody better wake me up. "Thank you *so* much. And your girlfriend!"

A few minutes later, Redbeard returned to the table with two much-larger-than-expected glasses of wine, and set them down, saying, "It's clear to any fool that a regular glass of wine wouldn't do, not for all those toasts. Extra's on the house."

"That's so generous!" Bobbie said, with Nathan following on top, "Now we can toast both you and your café."

They turned to each other with glasses raised. Nathan cleared his throat, then raised his glass higher still, "To Thomas J. Hughes. Sometimes a royal pain in the arse. But I hate to say it, smarter than I. He saw the obvious when I was blind. That I needed to share this trip with you to save our relationship."

After several toasts, Bobbie reached across the table to take Nathan's hand, "Do you know what today is?"

"Ah, Monday?"

"No, what date."

"Well, I know it's still June. And we left on the 14th."

"June 22nd. Ring any bells?"

Nathan knew he was fast failing this quiz. "I need a hint."

"Three years."

(*Three years. Three years. Three* . . .) "Oh! So many ways to mark a beginning," Nathan realized. "First meeting, first date, first kiss, first, ah, et cetera." Bobbie smiled. "First day we met. At the Y. I like it. It's so . . . definitive."

"We need to celebrate. But not with wine." Bobbie showed the briefest of smiles, then stood and walked inside. Nodding to Redbeard, she reached over to the back counter for the guitar. As soon as she held it, it felt familiar, and Bobbie immediately saw it was a Martin, the same D-28 as hers back home, the one she had saved two years to buy.

"So," Bobbie said, back at the table. Quickly testing the guitar, she thought, boy, this is in incredible shape for not being played. "I told you I took a jazz guitar class this semester? One of the projects was to take a song written as one type of jazz and re-do it in another style." Then she thought, I don't have to do a darn thing to this guitar, it's absolutely perfect. "So. An old Cole Porter, turned into . . . a bossa nova. For you." Bobbie closed her eyes and took a final slow deep breath, and then, corrected herself, "No. For *us*." She started to play. The ch-ch, ch-ch-***ch***-ch-ch rhythm from her thumb, three fingers, thumb, three fingers striking the strings and filling the air with the sweet upbeat sound of Brazil.

"Night and day, you are the one

Only you 'neath the moon, or under the sun

 Whether near me or far,

no matter, *darling* where you are

 I think of you, night and day"

Ch-ch, ch-ch-***ch***-ch-ch

"Dia e noite, por que é tão

Que este desejo por ti segue para onde quer que eu vá

No barulho do trânsito

No silêncio do meu quarto solitário

Penso em ti, noite e dia."

Ch-ch, ch-ch-***ch***-ch-ch

"Night and day, under the hide of me

There's an *oh such* a hungry yearnin' burnin' inside of me"

Then slower.

"Its torment, won't be through"

Slower still.

"Til you let me spend my life"

The guitar stopped, and Bobbie whispered, now to the beat of her heart.

"Making love to you"

Ch-ch, ch-ch-**ch**-ch-ch

"Day and night, night, and, day," Bobbie's last word fading into half-closed eyes and the softest of smiles.

"What was it you said on our very first date? *Oh, my,*" Nathan said, gazing at Bobbie. "And when did you learn Portuguese! We need to find a room. Now."

"Yes," Bobbie's return smile a perfect mix of coy and shy. "A room with a bed. But first I need to return this to our wonderful 'host.' And, I'll have you know, I have not learned Portuguese. Barely that verse."

Bobbie didn't have to walk far. Redbeard was standing, arms folded, leaning against a post just inside the overhang, waiting with a look Bobbie didn't quite understand.

"Never heard that guitar play Brazilian. I'm telling my old lady for sure."

"Oh, please do. That'll be a big thanks for letting me play it at all."

"All I can say, your boyfriend is..." Redbeard then said the next three words extremely slowly, "one . . . lucky . . . dude. One other thing. Hope this isn't being too forward. Dinner for you guys, on the house, with a *bottle* of wine included, if," he paused, "if you play a set tonight. We have a little spot right over there for music."

Bobbie had to put her hand on the back of the chair next to her. "I thought my head was spinning looking at all the stars the other night," she said, half to herself.

"Oh, come now. You've played to an audience before."

"Well, kind of. A song or two. But 'play a set'? It sounds so, so professional," Bobbie said softly laughing. "I'm just a student, a beginner."

"Hell, we're all students. And you ain't no beginner, lady. Your voice? That has nothing to do with beginning, middle, or end. It just is. It's amazing. It's so amazingly..." Redbeard stopped himself from saying 'sexy,' as he saw the color of Bobbie's face had already warmed. "Christ, I'm trying to talk you into playing for my café, and all I'm doing is embarrassing you. We should introduce ourselves," he said, walking her back to where Nathan sat.

"Nathan, it seems our miracles are never-ending," Bobbie said in a mix of wonder and disbelief. "I've been invited to play music tonight. Here. I mean over there," she said pointing to the small stage off to the side.

Redbeard broke in. "Considering this might be the beginning of a beautiful friendship," he said in a tough-guy drawl. (*Casablanca?*) "I should introduce myself. Dominic Kuske. One-man show here. Manage, bar-tend, cook, even wait," he said with a smirk, which changed to a thin smile as he reverted back to the drawl. "So, who are you two? What were you before this trip? What did you do and what did you think?"

"You sure your name's not Rick?" Nathan quickly returned.

Dominic laughed at Nathan's quick connection. "Not that far off. Close friends call me Nick. Which you two should. So, really, who are you guys?"

Sensing Nick's interest in Bobbie's music, Nathan said, "You first."

Shaking her head, a bit exasperated at the attention, Bobbie plunged in, "Well. My name is Bobbie McGregor and been singing since before I can remember. Tried countless instruments. Finally latched onto the guitar, halfway through high school. You know, all the obvious 'J' influences. Joan, Judy. And of course, Joni."

Nick smiled as if he held an inside joke. Then said, "Interesting. All more soprano than anything, which your voice is most definitely not."

"Well, they're all inspirational for many reasons, are they not?"

"C'est vrai, mademoiselle." Nick then looked at Nathan, "Et toi?"

"Jeez, tough competition," he said, tilting his head toward Bobbie, half-disgusted, all in-love. "Nathan Hughes, storyteller deluxe. Been spinning yarns 'before I can remember,' at countless 'venues' when I was little. Fireside chats, family gatherings, who-can-shoot-the-biggest-bull with the winos across the street. Graduated to theatre in late high school. Now I'm following in the footsteps of the old-time greats. Mark Twain. Will Rogers. Like me ohld man always says, set your sights 'igh."

"That doesn't sound like your father at all, Nathan," Bobbie broke in.

"Hey, did I interrupt you?"

"Say goodnight, Gracie. And you too, George." Nick said, shaking his head. "I have an idea. For tonight. Bobbie could do three or four songs, then Nathan, sounds like you might always have a story ready, and then Bobbie another handful of songs?"

(Oh, Christ, Bobbie and me sharing the same stage. How goddamn perfect!)

Bobbie looked at Nathan, eyebrows raised in a mix of a little questioning and a lot of answering. Nathan returned her look.

"I take your goofy looks as a yes," Nick said. "Have you guys had calamari yet? And Kriti's amazing tomatoes?"

"No, yes, Christ, I don't know, but more importantly, Nick, are there any hostels or cheap hotels near here?" Nathan replied. "We should find something this afternoon. Sounds like we're staying the night."

"Hmmm." Nick hesitated. "Don't usually do this, but I have a small room in back I use only occasionally, when I get tired of 'back to nature' in the caves. Which you have to explore by the way. I'll throw the room in with the dinner? For a second set?"

The young lovers held hands. "Yes, yes, and *yes!*"

• • •

After all toasts were complete, and after Nick had 'spiffed up' the back room, Nathan and Bobbie lay in each other's arms on a small twin bed, still not believing their good fortune.

"Maybe guardian angels do exist. And somehow, maybe both of ours met, fell in love with each other, and decided to go crazy overboard."

"Oh, Nathan, no stories now." Bobbie pressed her mouth hungrily against his. "Let's pretend we're on our honeymoon."

"Pretend?"

After love, after passion and the lull of soft touches had led to a short, dreamless sleep, Bobbie rose and peered into a small mirror hanging on the wall. "Mirror, mirror, on the wall, who's the luckiest girl of all? Nathan, do we work now, or go to the beach? Or see those caves. I should really practice. At least, pick out the songs to sing. Do you know what story you'll tell?"

"That's easy. *A Night in Casablanca.* And I don't mean Groucho's!" Nathan said, pretending to flick a cigar.

Bobbie grinned, but then noticed a small polaroid pinned next to the mirror. She recognized Nick, with a woman close to his side. Must be his girlfriend, she thought. Then, "Oh, my!"

Nathan immediately reacted to Bobbie's surprise and jumped up to see the photo himself. "Jesus F. Christ! You've got to be kidding."

They looked at each other, yet again in disbelief. Pointing to the photo, Bobbie said, "That must mean," then pointed to the guitar on the chair behind them, "that's *hers.* No wonder it's so amazing."

Nathan and Bobbie remained sealed in a look of utter incredulity. Finally, Bobbie teased, "This explains why you've been singing *For Free* our entire trip."

Nathan laughed. "I've only felt this way once in my life, Bobbie – that I'm experiencing something too unreal to turn into a story."

"Nathan Hughes! You'd better not turn this into a story. Or even mention it to anyone. Ever!"

"Oh, *not* what I meant, Bobbie. Just my poor attempt at describing how surreal this entire day's been," Nathan said. "And it's only half over!"

"Let's put that photo out of our heads. (*Easy for you to say!*) This is just a Martin guitar," Bobbie said matter-of-factly, carefully lifting the instrument, trying to convince herself. "That's all it is. Just a guitar. Back to the task at hand. Picking out songs."

"And I have to make sure I can remember all of *The Reason I Threw Plum Wine on Your Window Shield*," Nathan mumbled. "Damn title's longer than most poems," And to these words, Bobbie thought, why would Nathan need to remember Joseph's poem?

• • •

Nathan stood near the bar where Dominic was busy preparing drinks and coffee. Bobbie was on her last song. His turn was soon next, but he was lost in her simple version of *La Vie en Rose*. "Never heard her sing this before. Isn't she something?"

Nick nodded. "Like I told her this afternoon – you're one lucky dude."

(*I'm one lucky dude?*) "Hey Nick, I should tell you. I'm dedicating my story to you, for your quotes from *Casablanca*. My all-time favorite. You think enough folks here are familiar with the movie? Really know the ins and outs?"

"Man, no idea, but fuck the patrons," he grinned. "*I'll* love it. You know that Criti was also occupied. Twenty-five years is a lifetime for us, but it might feel like yesterday for someone who lived through it." He paused. "But no singing *La Marseillaise*. There might be German tourists here tonight. Hate for Renault to close us down," he drawled.

Nathan laughed. (*Funny. But . . . no need for me to sing it? But I need to. That might be the punchline.*) Then he realized that Bobbie was motioning him to the mic. (*Crikey, not even a minute.*) Nick's words about the War and twenty-five years swirled in his head along with Edith Piaf, scenes from *Casablanca*, being high on psilocybin, Joe's poem. (*What ties all this craziness together? What's the goddamn story? Maybe not a story – just commentary? Yeah, but what about? Should have planned this more.*) Nathan's head was still down, thoughts churning, as he took the mic from the stand. He looked up. (*It's showtime!*)

"Hard act to follow," Nathan began. "Not sure whose idea it was to match up a singer with a storyteller, but anything's possible, right? It really just depends on how the two are . . . connected. So, a story that begins with just that, connections, then a short tale of . . . perspective, but then finally, back to one final connection. And, oh yeah, maybe also a poem. (*I'm rambling. Better find a focus. Now!*)

"This afternoon a new friend, Dominic," Nathan raised the mic in the direction of the bar, "couldn't stop dropping lines from *Casablanca*, which happens to be my all-time favorite movie. (*Thank God – at least a few cheers.*) And just now, unannounced, my girlfriend ends her set with a long-ago romantic French ballad that connects here and now to long-ago France, to Paris, and so again, back to *Casablanca*. Here's looking at you, kid," Nathan said looking toward Bobbie. "You see, this all makes sense because Occupied France and Occupied Casablanca were not unlike . . . Occupied Crete. All in the same black-and-white battle of good-versus-evil.

"True story. A few months ago, I wanted to celebrate Bobbie's and my plans to travel to Europe together, and . . . (*hell, it's 1970, okay to talk about drugs*) well, a friend just happened to have scored some psilocybin. One and one equals two, right. I heard that psilocybin is completely dependent on the *context* of the trip, so I had to frame the celebration in the most positive experience possible. Then I remembered that the film house where I work was playing *Casablanca*, and . . . not sure how many would put the words *Casablanca* and psilocybin together in the same sentence, but there you go. Boy oh boy, were they ever in the same sentence. (*Christ, is this working? That guy's smiling, but too many blank stares. So much for connections.*)

"So much for connections. Now shift to . . . perspective. We think of psychedelics as mind-*altering* drugs, and, yes, they certainly do alter the mind. They also intensify how we view the world. And so, that night, the psilocybin intensified how my two friends and I saw the film. My friend Jack, a no-nonsense, hard-nosed guy, I mean his art is black and white photography, saw the movie as just that. The glory of black and white. In all its amazing clarity. My friend Joe, a righteous renaissance-man poet, saw the movie for what *he* thought it is, the ultimate fight of good versus evil. Me? I was simply celebrating my girlfriend agreeing to come with me to Europe. And *Casablanca* at the end of the day may be the greatest love story of all time. Perspective. We see what we want to see.

"But what was amazing was how these three different perspectives led to the same exact incredible climax. Hopefully, most of you have seen the film. Picture the scene leading up to *La Marseillaise*. Rick and Laszlo are in Rick's office, negotiating those infamous letters of transit. Appreciate the affect of psilocybin on the three perspectives. First, the heart of the love story, 'I suggest that you ask your wife. I beg your pardon? I said, *ask* your wife.' It's also the heart of the good versus evil story. In the middle of the Germans singing their war song, 'Play *La Marseillaise*! Play it!' And it's the very epitome of black-and-white brilliance, full-frame glorious black-and-white close-ups. One on top of the other. Of Rick, of Renault, then Laszlo, next Ilsa, then the trumpeter, and finally that damn beautiful woman playing her damn beautiful guitar. So, what was the climax that night? The night of *Casablanca* under the influence of psilocybin? Monsieur Rick nods, ever so slightly, the trumpeter raises his horn to his lips. And, cosmically connected with the citizens of Rick's in 1942, us three musketeers jump to our feet, in 1970 and (*Oh, damn any German tourist*) ..."

"Allons enfants de la Patrie," Nathan's rich baritone filled the café in a cappella. But he had not appreciated the power of his story, its effect on Bobbie. He had not realized how moved she had been by the story over the phone many months before. She was ready this time. She was the woman in the film, guitar raised. And when Bobbie and guitar joined Nathan, 'de la Patrie!,' this was a song to be sung by all, here in this Criti café. Joined one by two, two by table, table by waitresses, and yes, even by Monsieur Nick. All arms and glasses raised! "Vive la France! Vive la Criti!"

When the singing and cheers fell away, Nathan saluted with his mic, saying quietly, "To connections," and with a quick bow, looked for Bobbie to join him onstage. Bobbie, however, could sense the audience needed a breather, held her hand open with fingers and thumb spread.

"A five-minute break before Bobbie sings a few more songs. *La Marseillaise* must have worn her out more than Edith Piaf." Nathan smiled to the audience and headed to the bar.

Nathan spoke first as the two reached out to take hands. "I had no idea you were going to join in! That was so perfect."

"I wasn't sure you would sing the anthem. But I was ready!"

They held each other close. Then Nathan said, "Boy, was that uneven. A lesson that I'm not ready yet to ad lib. At least, not an entire performance. Thank God for the French national anthem."

Bobbie smiled, paused, then asked, "At the beginning, you said something about a poem. You didn't get to it, but what poem? *Plum Wine*? What's *that* connection?"

"Oh," Nathan realized, "you don't know the story behind that poem, do you? Joe wrote it that night, *after* we left *Casablanca* and went to Jack's place. I'll tell you the whole story some time." Nathan paused, still holding Bobbie's look. "Might still recite it tonight. You know, in the second set."

Bobbie pulled back, still in the hug, her hands now on Nathan's chest. "I don't understand – it was going to be part of your story? As your poem?"

Nathan immediately understood that Bobbie was questioning his authorship, and smiled, shaking his head slightly. "You still don't get it. After all these years. It's not about who wrote or said or did what. It's always about the story."

"But Nathan, this isn't a line or joke you're using. It's Joseph's . . . beautiful, amazing poem."

(*God, I love her. She's so goddamn consistent. And persistent. And those eyes...*)

"Hey, not the time, or place. Objection heard. Acknowledgements will be made, if and when, during the second set."

"Harrumph," was all Bobbie could manage, and not at all in jest.

• • •

Nathan stood at the mic just before midnight. He had finished *Plum Wine* and, somehow, had remembered not only the entire title, but all the lines. As he smiled to the audience, about to acknowledge once again his friend Joe as author, he noticed people standing in the street looking in. Then a neck-twisting double take. Joe and Jack stood the closest, both intensely riveted on him. (*They found us! Christ, how long have they been standing there!?*)

"Thanks," Nathan said looking around the café. "*And* Joe thanks you." He quickly smiled toward his friend. "The second poem is shorter. I wrote it to my friend Jack. *Midnight Miles*. A sonnet.

"*The sun sets. We jump the fence to cross the hours that always haunt our lives; the hours we hope will bud and blossom in a midnight rain. There is nothing we want that doesn't make perfect sense.*" Nathan nodded toward Jack. "*More desirous than morning's call, these midnight miles have no end. As day collects within our blood, we're left with night to lose or gain. Every act expands as hours bend. We want nothing less than all.*" He closed his eyes to whisper the closing couplet into the mic. "*We cast our eyes beyond the light and drive the miles toward midnight.*"

Nathan was greeted by his friend's intense gaze. Jack was first to release this joining of souls with his patented oh-so-slight smile and nod of head that meant, yes, damn it, *goddamn yes*. Nathan again thanked the audience then said, "It's now after midnight. But still miles to go. Bobbie has a last song. And then?" He looked past the tables at Joe and Jack, eyes afire. "Or, I should say, the night . . . it's just beginning."

Chapter 17

Lost in a Forest

Half a week later, on their first full day in Athens, the four sat mid-morning in an outside café sipping coffee under a soon-to-be sweltering sun, planning the day's activities. The main event was to take place that night, dictated by a Parisian Jack had met – a short trip just north of the city to the Daphni Wine Festival. "Jahck, eet's museec, dancing, and vin infinit. Formidable!"

"So, what's on the agenda today?" Nathan began.

Joe quickly answered, "I'm staying right here. Actually, inside, out of the sun. I have at least half-dozen postcards to write, and a poem I've wanted to start for the past week."

Nathan looked at Bobbie. "We're doing the Parthenon, right? You okay with the heat? It's funny – same temperature as Crete, but it feels ten degrees hotter."

"It's the city – all the buildings and streets trap the heat," Joe jumped in.

"Funny," Jack said, "why doesn't our city do that? The only thing it traps is the goddamn fog."

They all laughed, immediately returned to their hometown, somewhere on another planet. "Pretty amazing," Joe said. "Outdoors in a café, in the morning, sweating."

Nathan looked at Jack. "And what pray tell are your plans?"

"Man, I've got a whole carton of film that's weighing down my pack. I've barely shot a single roll. So, I guess, like Joe, I need a break," Jack said, lighting a cigarette. "To walk the streets. Turn all this illusional color into black and white reality."

"So, tell me again," Nathan asked his two friends, "just what happened in that van headed to Turkey, the one with a couple pounds of hash?"

Jack and Joe broke into laughter, and Jack pulled hard on his cigarette, eager to go into details, when a young exotic-looking woman walked up to their table.

"Jack. Joseph. I've been looking for you all morning. I thought you had said the café on the square. It's a good thing I remembered this one," she said slowly, her voice a mysteriously melodic blend of accents. Seeing the look of surprise on both their faces, she continued, "Oh, don't tell me you two have forgotten. Today is the 26th, isn't it?"

Jack and Joe looked at each other, momentarily puzzled. Jack spoke first. "Oh, shit, Anni," he said by way of apology, then, standing up, took her hand and warmly kissed her cheek. "We were to meet. No excuse. You won't believe the last few days."

Joe stood up, too, and greeted Anni. "Nathan, Bobbie, this is Anni Lee. Anni, our closest friends, the ones we told you about." Turning to Nathan and Bobbie, "We met Anni in Paris, the first night, wasn't it, Jack? Then again, here in Athens, right before we headed down to Crete."

Anni reached across the table to gently take and hold each hand for a short moment as she said, "Nathan" and "Bobbie. I love your name." Then, "So glad to meet you both. I've heard much about you two. So much . . . talent at one table," she said, gently waving her hand across the table.

(*Justa like-a, justa like-a, justa like a ballerina.*) Nathan was hypnotized. Bobbie, too, was captivated. Just who was this creature, they both wondered, though their inflection points were distinctly different.

Joe finally grabbed another chair, putting it between his and Jack's. "Can I get you a coffee, Anni?"

"Oh, yes, please. But not that nasty Greek coffee. Maybe a cappuccino." Then turning with a twinkle in her eye, "So, Jack, I'm surprised you forgot about me so soon."

"Forgot you?" Jack squirmed in his seat. "I tell you, Anni, I just forgot the date. Certainly not you. That would be impossible." Nathan had never seen Jack react so vulnerably, and for a second, enjoyed the revelation. Then, he jumped in.

"Anni, I can attest to the last few days on Crete. I've never experienced anything like it in my life. It's all been one big blur of (*what's the best word?*) . .

. life. With a capital L. And don't be hurt by their 'forgetting' a date. Bobbie and I were stood up by these two in three different cities, over five or six days!"

"Oh, all right, I forgive you, Jack," Anni said teasingly. "It doesn't matter now. I found you, and we're still going to that wine festival tonight, aren't we?"

"We most certainly are," Nathan chimed in.

"Lovely," Anni said quickly, smiling enticingly at both Nathan and Bobbie. "We'll go as two couples, Nathan and Bobbie, and Jack, Joseph, and Anni."

"Sounds, ah, perfect," Nathan said, as Joe came up with a coffee topped in beautiful airy brown and placed it before Anni. "We were just confirming . . . our dates, for the festival, Joe," he said, all the while unable to take his eyes from the goddess sitting across the table.

"Thank you, Joseph," Anni said. "So, what is everyone doing this afternoon? It's much too hot to be outside. I think I would prefer to stay . . . indoors." She placed her rounded lips on the edge of the cup, and slowly and longingly sipped the coffee from under the foam, while her gaze circled the table, pausing at each pair of eyes, each fixed solely on her.

● ● ●

Nathan and Bobbie were back in their hostel room to quickly change before meeting the others for the bus to Daphni.

"Did Jack and Joseph say anything about Anni Lee when you three were alone on Crete? I mean, you know, talking guy stuff?" Bobbie asked Nathan.

Nathan shook his head. "Do you think she's sleeping with either of them?"

"You're kidding, aren't you. She's fucking both for certain. The only question I have, is it at the same time?"

Nathan was taken aback. "You sure?"

"Nathan, for being such a great storyteller, you can be pretty naïve. You really couldn't tell? It was written all over their faces. And more, their bodies."

"Jeez," Nathan replied. (*Guess no one can call me sexually sophisticated.*)

"Just be careful tonight. Not sure her plans don't also include you."

When the five boarded the bus, Nathan, Joe, and Jack went straight to the back to sit together, with Bobbie next to Anni Lee directly in front of them. The two women turned to the back row while waiting for the bus to leave, and the five chatted about what little they knew of the night ahead – the price of admission covered entrance to the festival and an empty wine glass. Once inside, all wine would be free, and free-flowing.

As the bus started to depart, Bobbie and Anni turned around to face forward, with Anni admitting, "I can never sit facing backwards on any kind of transportation. Car, bus, train. I would get sick to my stomach," she smiled demurely.

"Oh, me too," Bobbie agreed. "Say, mind if I ask? Your accent, it's beautiful. I know it's a mixture, but I can't quite hear the pieces."

Anni smiled. "Long story. Well, my life that is. I was born in Hong Kong and lived there until I was about ten. Then we moved to New York City, where I stayed through high school. After that, I went to Paris, for college and to study dance. Ballet."

"Are you still in school?"

"Oh no. Dance is hard, but hard I can take. Ballet is much too competitive. You know, dancers put glass in other students' slippers," she said, politely smiling while looking down. Anni then looked up at Bobbie and said, "I like your hair, your braid is so long. And even braided, I can see that your hair is beautifully . . . full. Not like my hair. I don't like my hair. Too straight. No body at all."

"Oh. But it's beautiful. It's *so* black. It's mesmerizing."

"You think so? You're kind."

Bobbie looked out the window and watched the cityscape disappear in the evening light. She could see countless trees far up ahead, and thought, forests in Greece? Oh, of course. *Midsummer's Night Dream.* She turned back to Anni.

"How did you meet Joseph and Jack?"

"Meeting was easy. How we became . . . friends is more interesting. On the night we met, Joseph recited one of his poems. The one about plum wine. I *love* plum wine. Then, one thing led to another." Anni smiled. "I like them both. They're very different."

"It's funny. I thought I was the only person who called Joseph by his full name," Bobbie said, then turned toward Anni. "Why do you call him Joseph? I'm sure he didn't refer to himself that way. And I know Jack wouldn't have."

"Oh, that's easy. I always call people by their full names. The question you should ask is, why do I call Jack, only Jack."

Bobbie thought, Jackson? "So?"

"Because that's what he told me! 'Just Jack'," she said imitating Jack's dry delivery, and both laughed. Anni paused for a moment. "I don't know your full name. I know it's not Bobbie." Anni looked straight into Bobbie's eyes and gently touched her thigh, much higher than anyone had ever done except Nathan.

"Oh, I see I'm embarrassing you," Anni said quietly, leaving her hand on her thigh for a long second before removing it. "I'm a funny person. When I like someone, I show it." She took her hand off Bobbie's leg with a lingering brush.

Bobbie's heart was pounding, and only partly from surprise. Largely, in response to such a lovely hand so high on her thigh, with the lightness of a faint evening breeze. Just, where am I? she thought. Then Anni's last words fully registered and without thinking, she whispered, "Oh, please, you won't seduce Nathan tonight, will you?"

Anni looked down. Her face, no, more a mask, thought Bobbie, showed the slightest of smiles. She looked back at Bobbie, "You don't have to worry about Nathan, Bobbie. It's clear that he loves you." To which Bobbie thought, yes, I know, but that's not what I asked.

• • •

The five stood just inside the entrance, wine glasses in hand and each deeply curious of what lay ahead – a simple celebration of wine or a forest of make believe?

"I feel we're actors just offstage," Joe said.

"Took the words right out of my mouth," Nathan said.

"Well, it is night and in the middle of summer, isn't it?" Jack added.

"Oh, let's spend this night dancing through the trees, in twos and threes," Anni said, her long arms extended perfectly parallel to the ground. "To switch partners every time we meet."

"And never to wake from this dream?" Bobbie whispered to Nathan.

Anni, in the middle, linked arms with Joe and Jack, as the three headed slightly downhill on the path to the right, leaving Nathan and Bobbie to choose theirs.

First thing first, Bobbie thought. "Listen, Nathan. After we've all drunk too much wine and Anni waltzes you off alone into the night, and I know she will, you have to promise. Do *not* let her go too far. Or I should say, lead you too far. Off the path. Figuratively and literally."

"Bobbie, you're being silly."

Bobbie brushed Nathan's words aside. "Promise me. If she starts to whisper into your ear. To kiss you. Or puts her . . . amazingly lovely hands where they don't belong, you have to stop her." (*Amazingly lovely hands?*) "Promise me."

"Bobbie, do you think you know something I don't know? Or is it, you actually know something?"

Bobbie gave a short laugh. "Nathan, I don't know what I know, but *you* know me too well. Which doesn't change a single thing, actually makes it all the more important. You have to promise. Do not let her seduce you."

Nathan's was tempted to say, Well, only after the first kiss, but Bobbie seemed concerned. (*Is Bobbie serious . . . she could lose me to Anni?*) "Of course, I won't, Bobbie. I promise." Then he grabbed her hand. "But let's not get too far behind. In drinking or dancing." And he spun her around, and then around again, and around once more because the third time's always the charm. Bobbie's worries vanished into spontaneous laughter deep within Nathan's arms. At least, for the moment.

• • •

"Oh, do tell me about Kriti," Anni pleaded, as she and Nathan walked slowly and more than a little drunkenly side by side a few hours later. "No. First tell me the best story."

"Best story?" Nathan began, only to pause. "You know, once or twice in my life I've experienced something I just can't put into words. My first inclination is to . . . leave it be, leave it alone." Nathan smiled to himself, always enthralled to talk about what enthralled him. He had also lost count of the glasses of wine. "But I must admit, my struggle is this experience was so extraordinary, I'm incapable of making it more so. And as I always say, 'Can't add to it, then the story ain't mine.'" Nathan smiled. "Am I making any sense?"

Anni smiled back, putting her arm inside Nathan's. "So, don't tell me a story. Just tell me . . . facts. Tell me how you and Bobbie finally found Joseph and Jack."

"Oh, it was Jack and Joe who found us!" Nathan stopped. (*Anni's arm's inside mine. Is this what Bobbie was worried about?*) He noticed they were passing the wine station that offered the deep rich red, his favorite so far. "Well, it's quite a long list of facts, so maybe a refill. Have you tried this wine yet?"

"Yes, it was, so-so. I like sweeter wines. But you should re-fill your glass."

After their stop and as they meandered again, Nathan noticed that Anni had not retaken his arm, but instead walked close enough that her arm brushed against his with every step, in an impeccably timed beat. (*Of course, ballerinas even walk in perfect rhythm.*) Feeling the measured soft stroke of Anni's arm, Nathan lost any residual focus as they headed down another path neither had yet taken.

"How did Jack and Joe find us?" Nathan returned to Anni's question. "You'll have to ask them. But I think it was our angels. That's how Bobbie and I ended up on stage that night. A day- and night-long script our angels must have slaved over. For months."

"Angels are not facts, Nathan. They are the beginnings of a story."

"You're right," Nathan said emphatically. "So. Facts. Let me count the ways, I mean, facts. But only extraordinary facts!" Nathan took a long drink of wine and recited all the miraculous steps-by-steps on Crete, from the American Express to standing on a stage at midnight. "And there they were, just as I was reading my poem to Jack, *Midnight Miles*. Facts!"

"Hmmm, midnight . . . my most favorite hour. You must tell me this poem," Anni smiled, then pointed down a smaller path. "Let's see where this one leads." As they moved even deeper into the woods, Nathan realized that the sounds of the festival were considerably fainter. (*No, barely heard.*) Then Anni spoke. "I know this feeling of kismet. Of what you mean by . . . angels. And fate. But we can control our fate, too. Who knows who or what would have greeted you at the *next* café, if you didn't pick, who did you say, Dominic's café. By the way, who is this Joan Mitchell you said? The one whose guitar Bobbie found to play."

"*Joni* Mitchell? You've never heard of her?"

"No. Oh, I told Bobbie. I live in Paris. Haven't lived in your country for many years."

"She's actually from Canada. Though not the French part," Nathan laughed at his confusion, "not sure why I said that. She's a great folk artiste. Guitar and piano. And her lyrics are . . . true, *like ice, like fire.*"

"Ah, folk music. I only listen to classical. A weakness of mine. I need to broaden my interests." Anni again placed her arm inside Nathan's. "I'm wondering if you can tell me about Joseph's poem. *Plum Wine.* I can't remember the entire title, but it's a very lovely poem. I think you know him very well and, maybe, you know how the poem was . . . written?"

(*Oh yes, I know that story.*) But before Nathan could respond, he realized that he no longer heard any music or sounds from the festival. Only the sound of being deep within a forest, and very much by themselves. (*'Off the path?' Good God, Bobbie was right after all.*) Anni stopped their slow walk and turned to face him, with room for only the slightest breath between them.

"I can tell you are close to Joseph, and you are both very handsome." She touched his hands with her fingers. (*Amazingly lovely fingers.*) "I think you somehow like Joseph, in a romantic way?" (*I do?*) Then she took both his hands in hers. (*Amazingly lovely hands.*) "You know, Nathan, the French *menage à trois*?" Leaving her lips open from *trois*, Anni turned her head slightly as she brought her face even closer. (*Amazingly lovely face.*) Her lips barely touched his, then slowly joined, first dry but soft, then rounder, then opening. A captivating hint of moistness. Then, more than a hint. Anni pulled away slightly enough to whisper, "It's easy to fantasize, Nathan, making love, with both of you, with both of you, making love with each other. Comprends?" Her breath *(amazingly lovely)* – a dizzying mix of mystery and such a lingering of sweet wine.

● ● ●

Bobbie and Anni sat close at a small table near a crowded wine station that featured a mavrodaphne. "Now this is a wine that could get me into trouble." Anni laughed in sync with the music of the night. "What is the first line of Joseph's poem, '*Time itself is drunk*'?" She finished her glass in a long slow swallow. "Do you like it, or is it too sweet?"

"I'm not sure what I like tonight," Bobbie replied. "My head is in such a whirl."

"You sound like Nathan, when he was trying to tell me about Kriti."

As tipsy as she was, 'tell me about Kriti' rang in Bobbie's head. "Oh, what was Nathan saying about Crete?" she asked as nonchalantly as possible.

"He didn't know how to tell the story!" Anni quickly replied, happy to veer away from her intimacy with Nathan. "I told him to ignore the story and simply tell me what happened. Les simples faits clés. So, he compromised. Des faits extraordinaires."

But just how extraordinary? Bobbie thought. Maybe if I play the flirt. She leaned closer to Anni. "I'm curious, Anni, what caught your attention most?"

"Oh, his telling me about kismet. How your angels were spinning," Anni gracefully spun one of her long arms in the air, "extraordinary tales of fate."

"Yes, that *was* magic. Much like tonight," Bobbie said, still pressed forward, chin in hand and eyes on Anni. "But tell me. Which part was the most extraordinary?"

"Hmmm. Finding the café that you found, Bobbie. And all that was . . . waiting 'inside.' Dominic, and you and Nathan performing that night, and you playing the girlfriend's guitar." (*Not* the guitar, Bobbie thought.) "Whose guitar? Sorry, too much wine. Joan somebody? You tell me. You're the one who borrowed the guitar!"

Joan somebody exploded in Bobbie's head. She did her best to hold her smile, taking all her strength to keep her voice from cracking while at the same time thinking furiously, Nathan promised me. "Did he say anything else about her, or her guitar?"

"No, not really. Just that you sang a wonderfully sensual song to him," Anni responded, staring back into Bobbie's eyes, once again happy to divert attention away. "I hope that you can sing me such a song."

Why do I feel I'm playing a game of chess? Bobbie thought. "Maybe, but not tonight," Bobbie returned. "No guitar." She smiled at Anni, while thinking, no story, at least he didn't tell her a story, allowing herself a small sigh of relief. Then a slight laugh to herself, how ironic, she doesn't even know who Joni Mitchell is.

It was only then that Bobbie wondered, what else did Anni say to Nathan? And Nathan to this . . . creature of the woods. This seductress. This sexual . . . Puck. Had they touched, kissed, or even . . . the rhyme too painful to even whisper.

• • •

Bobbie and Joseph followed, a stone's throw behind the larger group of Nathan, Jack, Anni, and Jack's latest newfound fling Patty, along with the troupe of Patty's friends. Although the festival was still crowded, the revelry was subsiding, allowing Bobbie to hear the laughter and loud voices ahead, and occasionally, Nathan's resonating words. Not surprising, she thought, once again the center of attention. Bobbie had just finished confiding to Joseph her match-play conversation with Anni. Earlier in the night, she had told him for the first time the details of Matala and who Nick's girlfriend was. That she had made it clear to Nathan how important, no essential, that the girlfriend remain her story, not Nathan's. That it wasn't even a story, simply a gift from the heavens that should remain as such.

"I can understand how he might have slipped and told Anni. What's the phrase? Loose lips sink ships? So many ways to loosen lips tonight. Endless wine. This enchanted forest. The spell of a temptress. My God, Joseph, I've never met anyone like Anni. Did I tell you she even made a pass at me on the bus?"

"You wouldn't believe what she said to . . ." Joe barely stopped before saying, Nathan.

"What did she say to who?" Bobbie immediately demanded.

"Oh," Joseph said thinking quickly, "to Jack and me on that first night in Paris. A first for both of us, is all I'll confess."

"I knew it. I said as much to Nathan."

They walked without talking, both trying unsuccessfully to fit Anni into their limited sexual experiences.

"I have no idea what went on between Nathan and Anni, but my intuition says something happened," Bobbie continued, noticing Anni inching closer to Nathan in the group ahead. "But it's funny, that doesn't bother me nearly as much as Nathan telling her what happened in Matala. His damn stories!"

"But Bobbie, you just said that the little he told Anni was just a slip of the tongue."

"I know, I know," Bobbie said self-consciously, "I'm all mixed up. Having a hard time telling fact from fiction. That's why I get so infuriated with Nathan. I've never felt so much a character in a play. And you know me, I never wanted to be an actor on any stage!" Bobbie then noticed that, rather than continuing to the front gate of the festival grounds to leave, the group ahead had turned off the main path and was now walking downhill. "Where in God's name are we heading now?" She then saw a signpost at the top of the path, words on top of each other, αμφιθεατρο, amphitheater, 0.4 km. Imaging the stage at the bottom, she thought, Do I really want to follow them? Was this timeless fantasia to be officially blessed not just on any stage, but with the certainty of theatrical antiquity? Then, as if pulled by a rope tied tight around her waist, Bobbie muttered, "No choice" and began the descent, led by a foreboding that this dizzying Shakespearean comedy was heading downhill. Into what? A Greek tragedy?

• • •

Without hesitation, Nathan hopped onto the floor of the stone stage. (*Greece – the birthplace of theatre!*) His mind was racing; it made such perfect sense that this night-long fantasy had guided him here. Jack had seen the signpost first. "Nathan, a story. And this one on stage!" As they hurried down the path, Nathan asked himself, so, what story to tell? His first thoughts were of the not-so-successful rambling improvisation on Crete. But then he realized, this is just a small group of friends. (*Anything goes. Just for the fun of it. Just . . . for free?*)

Now on stage facing his small but vocal audience, Nathan raised his hands, signaling for quiet as he consciously unlocked his last hesitation. (*No thought – all feeling.*) He began half-speaking, "So there I was," half-singing, "standing on a noisy corner. Waiting for the walking green. Across the street he stood. And he played real good. On his clarinet, *for free.*'

"A story. Of circles. Maybe spirals, but definitely, a 'round' story. Of what goes out, must always come back. Before I left for Europe, I listened to nothing else but *Ladies of the Canyon*. Over and over and over. Or, I should say, round and round and round. And yes, we *are* stardust. Golden. Caught in the devil's bargain. But sometimes, maybe in the arms of an angel? And caught, *For Free.* What a perfect song. That's the one that's been stuck in my head."

Just then, Bobbie and Joseph rounded the last bend of the path, pausing off to the side. Bobbie immediately recognized Nathan's all-too-familiar gestures, of arms, of hands, of shoulders, the intensity of his slight lean forward, pulling the audience in. And that damn deep music of his voice. *For Free.* She stopped, needing to remain unseen.

Nathan continued. "I've always been fascinated by what makes *place*. What is it that makes where we live special, familiar, *my* place. What reaches into our soul and grabs us, holds us. Calms us. Is it the land? Or what we make of the land? Or maybe, it's the weather? And if so, the weather year-round or a single season? Or perhaps, it's the absence of seasons. Or something less tangible in the air – a smell or even more vague, an essence, so that even if blind-folded, kidnapped, whisked to a foreign land and spun around, could still be identified by someone *who knows*. This is the first time that I've traveled for any extended stretch of time. So, a perfect way to understand where I live . . . by experiencing other places. To experience the sun-drenched glory of Greece. Of its sea. Of Crete. Of Kriti. Of here, on these ancient stones of theatre."

Nathan paused briefly, eyes closed, led by the rhythm of his free-flowing thoughts. (*Is this circle still going out? Maybe the apex?*) "I think the first time I fully appreciated connecting with a new place, that I wasn't just traveling through, but had arrived, was when Bobbie and I landed in Chania." (*Where is Bobbie? And Joe? They must have missed us turning down the path.*) "It might have been the slowness of the ferry. Or waking from a very strange dream. But arrived we had. It felt different, yet oh-so right. Physically. Mentally. Certainly spiritually. Kriti was where we were meant to be. But Kriti is a large island and where exactly, should we be? In Chania? In the central mountains? We had the excuse of looking for Jack and Joe. But was that enough? (*Time to start bringing it back.*)

"We can discuss, debate, argue how we found our place, found Matala. Our guardian angels or some amoebic waltz or just our own goddamn feet? Whatever it was, however it happened, one thing *is* certain, finding Matala was perfect. And where we were meant to be. Because finding Matala," Nathan paused in step with the natural beat of the story, "meant finding that café. And finding that café meant finding Dominic. And finding Nick meant that Bobbie and I..." Another pause. "Could play, just for the love of it. For an audience who didn't pay to hear us. To play *for free*. And..."

Don't say it, please don't say anymore, Bobbie whispered, begging to herself. This has all been fine, no, lovely. Please, please, Nathan, don't, don't!

". . . because all circles have to be made . . . whole. All circles have to come back to the beginning. To come back to Joni Mitchell and her very own, and so beautifully worn . . . Gibson D-28 guitar."

Bobbie turned at the word 'Joni' and ran. Around the corner and fast up the trail. Her sudden motion distracted Jack who was sitting directly in front of Nathan. And as Nathan was saying, "But that's a story...," he saw Jack's head abruptly turn, which immediately turned *his* head, to see the last wave of Bobbie's dress vanish in the trees.

"...for another time," Nathan barely finished his sentence, staring blindly toward the empty uphill path. In his mind's eye, he could still see Bobbie running. Her red dress billowing bright through the gray brown pine. Running through the never-ending trees of a now bewitched forest. His love forever. Running, fleeing, away from him. Smaller. Smaller still. Then . . . gone.

Chapter 18

Locked In

"Me name's Danny. Danny-O'Dolye-from-the-glorious-mud-and-green-o'-county-Kilkenny. But just call me Danny," the wild-eyed full-bearded leprechaun of a man laughed in a high lyrical pitch over the din of the pub. "And what be your names?"

"Nathan Hughes."

"Joseph Gavin."

"Ah, Iresh actors, pretendin' to be American."

Nathan and Joe laughed, and Joe raised his glass high in a salute, "To County Kilkenny. I was lucky enough to be at your beer festival. *That* was quite a night. Ages ago, at the beginning of my travels. And now," Joe sighed, "sadly at its end."

"To me place o' birth," Danny said, returning the toast, then draining his glass.

"Can I buy you another?" Nathan offered, finishing his glass. "I have a twenty-pound note weighing down my pocket that'll soon be of no use."

"You can," Danny returned. "Are you lads leavin' for home then?"

"Tomorrow," Nathan said, as Joe finished his pint, nodding. The three were seated at the bar, and as Nathan raised three fingers to the barman, Joe got off his stool in search of the restroom. Nathan continued, "Figure if we stay up all night, we might be able to sleep on the plane. Though, to be honest, I'm more trying to drown my sorrows."

"Your romance go off?"

Nathan looked down. (*You might say that.*) All of a sudden, he had an uncontrollable urge to embellish the last few weeks. To turn the cold reality of the letter Bobbie left on their bed into something, anything more unreal. To lie his way into making all of this nightmare untrue. He was drunk enough, and this slight Irish man intrigued him so. (*I should tell him, 'So much worse, Danny. Just got a telegram my girlfriend was killed, back home, in a car wreck.'*)

Nathan shook his head. (*What the hell am I thinking?*) He shook his head even harder. (*This ain't no damn story.*) He stared straight ahead, eyes unfocused. (*No need to embellish it. This story's bad enough.*) "About as bad as it could be. We were traveling together. Our European odyssey. Didn't even get through the first two weeks before I fucked up. Broke the worst of our ten commandments. She up and flew back home. A month early, and, my God, it wasn't cheap." Nathan turned toward Danny, though without looking at him. "I shouldn't be surprised. She's never been one to take any shit."

Joe returned just then, and by Nathan's posture and the look on his face, immediately knew what Nathan had been saying. Joe thought, maybe it would do Nathan good to have someone new to talk to. I certainly haven't been much help. And this Danny fellow, not only does he have charm, but he seems the real deal.

Joe put an arm around Nathan. "Time for me to call it a night, bro. I have way too much to prepare for. This way, one of us will be up bright and early. I'll knock on your door in the morning to make sure you're awake."

Nathan, still disgusted with himself, replied, "Unless I stay out all night and knock on yours first."

Joe noticed the third pint sitting on the bar. "I'm sure this won't go to waste." He slid the beer between Nathan and Danny, giving Nathan's head a rough shake, and reaching his hand out to the Irishman, "Until we meet again, Danny O'Dolye, on the streets of Kilkenny."

"Now that'll be a long time from now, Jahseph," Danny said with a sparkle in his eyes. "You'll likely be there before I."

After Joe left, Nathan shoved the full glass nearer to Danny. "Man, I need to apologize. What a bunch of crap I just laid on you."

Danny waved his hand, "No need to apologize. If we stay 'ere long enough, I'll be matchin' your crap with plenty o' me own."

Nathan grinned, "So, tell me, Danny, what time do pubs close in London?"

Danny nodded his head, "Now that's a great question. And the answer is, it depends. If you're just someone off the street, then most pubs, like this one, close their doors to ya at 11. But, if you're a regular, like yours truly, well, there's somethin' called 'locked in.' And locked in means just that. Sometimes for a very long time. If the bartender ain't tired and knows ya well." Danny finished with a sly grin and another nod of his head.

Nathan smiled. (*I could listen to this sweet music all night.*) "Now that's just what the doctor ordered," he said, tipping his glass slightly toward Danny.

Danny met the top of Nathan's glass with his and said, after a pause, "And so, what's your sweetheart's name?"

"Bobbie. Bobbie McGregor."

"Bahbbie. Lovely name," Danny said. "So, do you want to go on some more about her, or should we move onto another topic?"

A light switched on in the gloomy darkness of Nathan's mind. (*The perfect confessor for a wayward storyteller?*) Here was someone who had the advantage of *not* knowing him, coupled with the Irish wonder of story and gift of gab, made fast by the quick connections of the previous hour.

"You know, Danny, I think maybe a little bit of both." Nathan pulled out a cigarette, then offered one to his new friend, "Do you smoke?"

"I do, but tryin' to not."

Nathan struck a match, then paused, holding it. "I'm one of those lucky bastards who can smoke whenever I want, but never needs to." He lit his cigarette. "Though when I drink this much . .. ."

"So, a little bit o' both, ya say?"

"I mean I don't need to talk about Bobbie herself, but I sure can use help in understanding if there's any hope of keeping our love alive."

"And what exactly was that mahrtal sin you committed?"

"Ah, well, as you say, interesting question. I assume you were raised in the church?"

"Do we Iresh like to tell stories?"

(*Reads minds, too.*) "Not sure if I committed a mortal sin, but I did break our most serious commandment. Though, now that you mention it, Bobbie likely thinks of it as a mortal sin." (*Not sure how to tell this – from whose perspective?*)

"Damn it, boyo, gerronwiddit, what'd ya do that was so damn wrong!"

(*Boyo. That's my dad's word.*) "Sorry. Just trying to figure out how to tell this. (*Gotta be from Bobbie's view.*) What was the commandment? Thou shall not tell a really private secret to the whole world. From a goddamn stage no less. And after specifically promising never to tell anyone. And worst of all, never *ever* trivialize that secret simply to dress up a story." Nathan paused, inhaling his cigarette smoke deeply. "*And* doing so after going through months of similar issues doesn't help in the confessional."

"Me oh me Nathan, that's one foehckin' long commandment. Not sure if I could remember it all, let alone break it. Don't tell me you actually did all that?"

"I did, Danny, I did, and more. I also let an amazingly beautiful woman seduce me. After Bobbie explicitly warned me that she would try and made me promise not to give in."

"I'm thinkin' I'm understandin' why Bobbie went thick on ya. When you say seduce, did this beour screw ya?"

"Well, let's just say we didn't quite break the sixth commandment, but went *way* beyond the ninth." Nathan finished his cigarette before emphatically grinding it out.

Danny shook his head and drained his pint, then reached for the one Joe had abandoned. He looked at Nathan. "And just where was ya when this all happened. From the sound o' it, ya must have been mighty high or drunk, or more likely, both. No one sober could have done such a splendid job o' foehckin' it up."

Nathan didn't know if he should laugh or cry. Danny's words rang truer than true, but he knew he had only scratched the surface. He had yet to even hint at his addiction to story, the main issue with Bobbie. (*Maybe the curse of my entire life.*)

"No drugs, just drink. Unlimited 'tasting' at the Daphni Wine Festival. Danny, have you ever felt like you've been dropped into the middle of a play. But without a script."

"Ah, Nathan, not sure I have, but I've spent half me life feelin' as if I'm as mad as an hatter. Drunk or sober, mind ya." Then with a light nod, Danny added, "And that's the gospel truth."

Danny's words were the final bit of string that tied Nathan's heart and soul to this man. Even the hint of vulnerability somehow made immediate and perfect sense. This slight confession also begged questions.

"Danny, why did you move away from the 'mud and green'? And why London?"

"Questions that would take more time than we have. Mighty kind of you to ask, Nathan, but I think we should stay focused, given you're leavin' for home in a few hours. Have you talked with 'er yet, on the phone, since she left?"

"I tried. Not even sure where she is now. Anyway, I did speak to her mother. God knows what she was thinking – all she said was Bobbie wasn't home. It was a very short phone call."

Just then, the bartender leaned over the broad wooden counter. "Say, Danny, will yer and yor mate be stayin' the night, then?"

"We will, Stephen. We will indeed."

Nathan looked around. The few patrons who remained were sitting in booths, hands wrapped around their pints, each fixed in conversation. He looked at his watch. Eleven fifteen. One bartender was at the front windows, letting the blinds down as if to hide a secret gathering. When finished, he went to the front door and turned the deadbolt.

"As simple as that, Nathan. The pub's closed." Danny smiled. "We're lahcked in for the night."

Everything inside Nathan's head fell away, save Danny's final words, the perfect answer to his needs, resonating with the music of the Irish tongue. (*Locked in for the night. Here. In this dark and ageless London pub. Dedicated to the baring of souls. Focused only on Bahbbie and me. With this new friend, this*

186

listener, this ancient teacher. Eyes ablaze and framed by such wild and fiery hair. Oh, lucky man!)

"Oh, Danny, I'm such a lucky man! If ever I could even begin to understand how I got into this mess. Let me make sure I got this right. The pub's closed from the outside, but it's still 'open' inside?"

"'Tis," Danny nodded hard.

"Sweet perfection. I still have all this soon-to-be-worthless English coin in my pocket. And such an aching in my heart."

The two held each other's gaze, caught in an awareness that they were balanced on a transition – from a lovely introduction to something deeper. (*On the cusp of a . . . one-of-a-kind friendship?*)

Nathan broke the momentary spell, then dove headfirst into the depths. "I need your help, Danny. I need your help in understanding my goddamn addiction to story."

"Addiction to story!? Now why do you say that? You make it sound like that's somethin' wrong." Nathan could hear Danny's accent grow thicker, the music flow even smoother. It might be from Danny's umpteenth pint, but Nathan took this as a gift, of Danny letting go, baring himself completely. He looked up to catch Stephen's eye and raised two fingers.

"And maybe we should add a whiskey?" he asked Danny.

"I wahn't say no."

"No idea what to order."

"At *this* stage o' the night? It dahn't matter much. Powers would do just fine."

"So, Danny. I'm not saying there's anything wrong with telling a story. My God, just the opposite. But I have no control. For me, everything's fair game. Fact, fiction, your truth, my truth. Innuendo. Exaggeration. Whatever the story calls for." Nathan paused to look Danny in the eye. "Even if I swear never to tell a soul."

"Well, first off, what ya just described, that could be almost any Ireshman at the bar while on 'is fifth pent." He was about to elaborate, when Stephen placed the new pints down and picked up the empties.

Nathan looked up and let the rhythm of Danny's voice filter into his own words, "And if we can have two Powers, Stephen, I think we'd be set just fine." Then he turned back to Danny, "Even the part about swearing never to tell a soul?"

"Absolutely! Come 'ere to me. Stories and the drink? They go hand in glove. Under the influence, even the most sacred pledge can always fall away."

"But Danny, I can be stone cold sober and still be 'intoxicated,' have no control. Now, the Daphni Wine Festival, *that* was one of a kind. My God. I was most definitely under . . . multiple influences. But there've been many times, countless times, going back into childhood, that the only 'influence' has been the story itself." Nathan paused, taking out another cigarette. "Never sure if the spell is from the story, or the *telling* of the story. You know, I think both. When I'm 'writing' a story for sure, but there's been many-a-time when I add something in the saying that gets me into trouble. Some spontaneous ad lib, a where-in-the-fuck-did-*that*-come-from. Catches me off guard even while I'm saying it!" He paused, thinking, then lit the cigarette and took a long pull. He turned his head and looked at his new friend. "Danny, why are stories so goddamn powerful? Where do they come from and why do we love them so?"

"Why are stories so mighty powerful, you ask? Ah, Nathan, don't you know, they are the very framework o' our lives." Danny's fire pierced Nathan, past his eyes, connecting to his innermost being. "Without stories, much o' what we do is simply random walks. We almost always build our tales to make a point. To give our lives structure. The structure of a beginning, a middle, and, when we can't avoid it, an end."

Danny barely took a breath followed by a long swig of beer. Nathan leaned on the bar, marveling at the force coming from such a slight man. "Without stories, we're simply going from some meaningless point A to some different meaningless point B. And where in the foehck did letters even come from? Well, each letter is a story in and of itself. The letter A?" Danny pointed both his hands up, chest width apart, "Ya see, these lovers," slightly shaking his two hands, "are a nightly two," then slowly raised his hands from his belt to above his head, while bringing them together as if drawing the letter. "They sneak *over* the line, the line of what's taboo." He nodded to Nathan to make sure he followed this short story. "While the letter B." With his right hand in the air traced the curvature of that letter, emphasizing each quick falling of the arch back to the staff. "We find ourselves deep in summer and winter, after glidin' on the edge of spring and fall. Or *whatever* story you want to tell. Or make up. We tell our stories *to make a point*." Danny pounded his fist soundly on the bar. "Or at least, it's our foehckin' attempt to understand why we do what we do. So, I ask you again, why do'ya say you're addicted? It makes as much sense as sayin' you're addicted to breathin'."

As if choreographed, Stephen placed the two shots of whiskey down near the pints. Danny's shot glass hardly rested on the bar before being raised back in the air for a toast. "To the letters, A and B. To their stories – how they got 'ere, what they mean, *and* why we love them so."

They both downed their whiskeys, while Danny tilted his head and squinted his eyes in question. "But Nathan, why all this talk of story? You make it sound it's your lifelong passion."

"Oh, but it is, Danny, it is. Not only my passion, but . . ." Nathan hesitated. (*This will sound ridiculous to someone like Danny.*) "I'm hoping it will be how I make a living. On stage. As a storyteller. If I have the talent." Nathan looked sheepishly at Danny. "Are there Irish professionals? Storytellers, that is."

"Ahh me, yes. Plenty of Iresh make a livin' spinnin' tales. Dave Allen, Jem 'Awkins. Eamahn Kelly, not only a great actor, but a marvellous storyteller. No, you don't just have to be standin' at the bar to have an audience. You can fill a theatre, each one of them payin'."

Danny's words hung like fairy dust in the air of the smoky pub. In the lull that followed, Nathan realized a trip to the john was long overdue. As he stood

189

up, the full effect of the pints hit him. He laughed as he steadied himself by grabbing the edge of the bar, saying, "If I don't return in a few, call out the dogs."

He squinted his eyes as he made his way in the dim light down the back hallway. (*So, you say, 'from point A to point B.' From the bar to the john?*) He pushed the door open and staggered to the urinal wall. (*Or has this walk been the entire summer? From the ferry with Bobbie to these wild eyes of Danny. Random? Not a story that makes any sense. God, I'm still missing her! Missing every single damn thing. Her hair. Those kisses. Waking by her side each morning. That laugh. That infectious laugh. Her music. Her goddamn every-note-is-perfect music.*) Nathan stood finished with an endless pee, his forearm leaning heavy on the wall above while Bobbie's music disappeared into a vision of a red dress running through a forest of pines. (*I can't be alone for a single foehckin' minute before . . .*) He pushed himself away and stumbled out the door. In a blur of the moment, he turned the corner and returned to the present – Danny and Stephen across the pub, against the backdrop of mirrors and bottles. (*So, what is Danny's A to B? Must be quite the tale.*) As he neared, the Irishman's voice rang out followed quickly by Stephen's laugh. (*Will there ever be another chance to hear that glorious sound? Another night like tonight? But wait, tonight . . . it still is!*)

"Danny, how about a change of scenery? To one of those booths. They look so, I don't know, cozy."

"A grand idea."

"I have enough money for one more round." Nathan turned toward Stephen. "Two more pints, sir." They waited at the bar for the full-to-the-brim glasses and carried them to the corner booth tucked into a quiet darkness.

"You've been very generous, Nathan, with all the pints. You must know that I plan to catch up with ya on every last one."

"Damnit, Danny. Your constitution is mind bogglin'. And your bladder! Don't you have to pee?"

"Me bladder's been well trained, it 'as. Ya see, Nathan, we Iresh never want to miss a story with unnecessary trips to de jax. I'm talkin' years o' habit. In the context o' a pub bein' a *communal* gatherin'. A verbal free-for-all, where you never know when a seanachie will be so moved."

Nathan leaned back in the booth, enjoying its support after hours on a stool. His thoughts turned back to when he almost uttered the ridiculous lie about Bobbie dying in a car accident. Nathan leaned forward. "Danny, you know I was saying my stories sometimes . . . take over. With a life of their own? Well, here's an example.

"Way back when you asked if my romance had 'gone off?' I was so pissed at myself. Wanting the last month to be just a terrible dream, that I made up an even worse story. I was this close, a split second from . . . it's hard to even say it. That I'd just learned my girlfriend had died in a car accident. Back home. Just got the telegram."

Danny didn't bat an eye. He held Nathan's gaze as the calm eye of the storm. When he was sure Nathan had finished, he said in a quiet steady voice, "But ya didn't tell me Bobbie had died, did ya. You didn't tell me a story t'all, you simply told me what happened. What really happened on your travels together."

(*Self-control? But I was this close to spinning that lie.*) Nathan nearly dismissed Danny's words, but something held him back. "I don't know, Danny."

"What do you mean, ya don't know. Tis a fact. You didn't." Danny raised his pint for a drink, keeping his eyes fixed on Nathan. "So, you tell me, why didn't ya when you were so close? And mind, ya had more than a bit of drink taken, so ya were mighty primed."

(*Something did stop me. Right about that. Tis a fact. A goddamn fact.*) "Disgust." Nathan said out loud, looking near but not quite at Danny. "I was disgusted with myself. I had to draw the line." (*Now that's a first.*)

Nathan gazed at the mostly full pint in front of him. The head had settled to a thin layer barely covering the top. He remembered reading once about addiction. No one can kick until reaching the absolute bottom of the darkest journey. Are all addictions the same? (*Storytelling's an addiction.*) Was the tale of Bobbie's death rock bottom, his refusal to verbalize, a turn of the corner?

Nathan looked up into the unblinking eyes of an unmoving face. (*Unmoving, but I can tell, caring. Friend or brother? Or father? Just how old is Danny? I had thought just a bit older, but, maybe, years? Those eyes, God, they're ageless.*) "Enough about me, Danny. I need a story. Tell me a whooper."

"A whooper is it?" Danny replied quickly, but then paused, looking past Nathan. In just a few seconds, he refocused. "I've another idea. Let's you and me, we build a tale *together*. We'll start with just the idea, the foundation, tonight, and then, over time, over however long it takes to bring us back together, the one beginnin', ya see, will turn into two stories. And the next time we meet, we'll compare how each story is the same, but each be different. How each plot, will fit snug and fine against our different lives." Danny stopped and smiled, and raised his glass, "So how 'bout that, then?"

Speechless, Nathan raised his glass, then forced out, "I don't know what to say, but it's fucking perfect. No, 'tis foehckin' perfect." He banged the entire length of his glass against Danny's.

"'Tis," beamed Danny, "if I don't say so meself."

"This is your house," Nathan said emphatically, "so you have the first say."

"If I have the first say, then I say it's foehckin' time I buy me first round. *And* take a trip to the jax." Danny pushed himself out of the booth and, stopping at the bar, called out, "Stephen, two pents and two wheskeys, if ya please." After the back and forths and after settling himself again into his seat, Danny looked Nathan in the eye and said, "The pents are for the task at hand, but the wheskeys, they'll have to wait, for when we're fully done. So, Nathan, one more thin'. I really shouldn't but I'm goin' to anyway. I'm goin' to ask you for a fag if you don't mind. I've fought the temptation all night, but we're way too into this, don't ya know."

Nathan grinned broadly and dug out his cigarettes. After two were lit, and Danny had taken a very long pull and even longer exhalation, he said, holding up his cigarette, "As we were talkin' addiction. Nathan, if I ask for one more, you may oblige. But if I'm *after* asking for another, you may not. Ya listenin'?"

"I am."

"Good. So, we're on then," Danny took another drag and began. "There's been these beginnin's of a story brewin' in the back of me head, steepin' in the far corners of me mind. The perfect occasion to bring them out and we take a sip." Danny nodded his head toward Nathan, who returned the nod in sync. "Now ya have to understand, Nathan, 'tis a rake of bits and pieces, it is. But in the middle of it all lies . . . a romance. Or I should say, romances. A mess of a love tale, but still, a story of passion." Danny took a long swallow of beer, hungrily finished his cigarette, then continued. "Though not quite sure if this be light comedy or, well, dark tragedy."

Nathan immediately latched onto the extremes. "That could be our two versions!" Then he looked across the table. "Sorry, jumping ahead. Continue, the bits and pieces."

"Firstly, a young colleen. The only child of a widowed mam. About twenty I'd say, give or take. All in all, a most beautiful lass. And as young as the first rain of spring. She may be in university or she may not, but, no matter, headstrong and mighty independent, but still, knitted to her mam. Knitted with a tight stitch. A mixed bag of emotions *that* relationship be." (*I know that mixed bag feeling all too well. Bond between father and son be damned.*) Danny nodded and smiled as he ticked off the next. "And then, the other side of the coin. The mam, just about double in years. When her daughter's age, a one-o'-a-kind, like your beour, the one who seduced but didn't screw ya. With hair as red as the settin' sun. Now, not quite so bright in color, the years have worn her down more than a bit, but the same spirit deep within." Danny nods the last time. "And then, there's the one in the middle. The single man, let's say about thirty. A stunner he be with a wit to match, though a bit of a boy-o if truth be told. We'll have to see if he's more the innocent or more the conniver. That is, once the story unfolds." Danny pauses. "So, a 20 and a 40 and a 30 – can ya see where we're headed, Nathan?"

"I think I do. A twist on the tale where the son's betrothed falls in love with the handsome father." (*Or maybe, the son seduced by his father's young mistress? Thank God Nira never made a pass at me. That Portuguese dialect . . .*)

"'Tis. But you agree don't ya, that having *two* female hearts and souls lend much more complexity to the yarn. A much richer cloth for the weaver to weave."

"Oh, Danny. I do, I do. And what do you call these bits and pieces?"

"At this early stage? Only that."

"But we'll need something to refer to. You know, in our letters we write. Let's call it . . . *Like Daughter, Like Mother.*"

Danny laughs. "And so we shall. But, in your version, the daughter meets the man first, does she."

"As you said, to be written by our separate lives."

"I see. You'd be givin' us a broad canvas?"

"A broad canvas works best for me, Danny O'Doyle!"

Nathan finished his beer and thumped the glass down on the table. "Danny, this has been a night of nights. You have any travel plans? Like, to the States?"

"Not in the cards I'm afraid."

"Well, I guess there're always letters. I hope you like to write."

"I do," Danny said, then smiled and nodded, "as much as I love to read."

"Even endless pages?"

"All stories have endings. At least, in the tellin'."

"And tonight? Do we have an end tonight?"

"Let's say no to that. At least, not yet. In fact, let's have another toast." Danny placed one of the whiskeys near Nathan and raised the other. (*Isn't this how the trip began? Endless toasts?*)

"But not a toast, 'tis a poem from me. A poem that's called *The Blink. Much that doesn't, does happen. Much is said to ourselves. We are what's left o' the same mind. What we see, we see perfectly. Our friendship lies on this blink. We are in . . . repeated agreement.*" Danny raised his glass higher, ready to wait or ready to drink.

Nathan quickly responded. "A poem back." (*Joe won't mind.*) "*Nine Ways to Dance – Homage to the gods. Ice wine from a bed. Snapping fingers. Bird drunk on berries. Arm chanting. Dizzy kiss. Wild hands of friends. Respect to death. Mad boots of proof.*"

"To mad *as an hatter* boots o' proof," Danny said reaching his glass to Nathan.

"To endless pages," Nathan returned. "Wait, to all stories, with and without endings." The two glasses met as one in the thick air of a locked-in London pub, and for a moment, the entire summer condensed and crystallized, gloriously and painfully, in front of Nathan, with Bobbie at the center of this enchantment. (*Damnit, Danny, don't take your hand down. Don't. Stay locked like this. Stay!*) But Nathan watched as Danny took down his hand to effortlessly tip his glass, and reluctantly, he did the same. And with this toast, the vision of the past two months that had unexpectedly materialized and hovered before his eyes vanished, instantaneously and completely.

(*And so, too, does Bobbie.*)

1973

Chapter 19

On the Edge of the World

"The older I get, the more I think *I'm* a pair of identical twins, fused together in my mother's womb. A freak genetic event. A one in a billion roll of the die." Nathan tossed down the rest of his bourbon, then looked at Joe and Jack. "Either of you ready?" Both were sipping their drinks slowly and hardly replied. He walked over to where Eddie was holding court behind the bar. After briefly listening to him (*once again for chrissake*) tell the story of being pulled out of the bay under the bridge, Nathan returned with his glass refilled.

"I feel like two goddamn forces are constantly fighting inside me."

"Good and evil?" asked Joe. "Never seen your evil side."

"No, more like 'in control' and 'free-willing.' Like, who's telling the stories tonight?"

Jack took the bait. "So, who was it tonight?"

"Me, myself, and yours truly. In full and total control. Each word, each pause. Every fucking inflection point. The more subtle, the more perfect the nuance. Which felt great, but there's no crazy magic when everything comes out so crisp. Timed to bloody perfection. Unlike that impromptu show a few months ago. I had no idea where half of that stuff was coming from."

"That's easy – from the weed," Joe said. "That shit was incredible."

"Not that simple," Nathan replied. "Maybe a little, but I was already in that other zone before you even came in. And if I remember, I only had one hit."

"Sure, sure," Jack said, before noticing a bob-haired woman draped in a silk robe enter from the backdoor stairway. "Monika. With a *k*. Stunning as usual. Break time?"

The woman barely managed the briefest of smiles, signaling immediately that the clientele in the topless nightclub directly above were not on their best behavior.

"Hard night?" Joe asked.

Before he got out the 't' in night, Monika responded, "Don't even ask."

Joe jumped up to give her a hug. "Well, at least you only have another couple of hours."

"Tell that to my tits. We're absolutely depressed. The three of us. The crassness that passes as civilized man. In 1973 no less. And even the slightest sense of real humor? Christ. Sometimes I wonder if a bartender is any better off than a dancer on stage. Maybe worse; I'm supposed to talk to those morons. Mind if I bum a cig?" Monika said, reaching for the pack on the table, then remembered. "Hey, Nathan, wasn't tonight your big night, your first 'real' gig? I mean a paying audience and everything?"

"Well, sold out it was not, but considering a few tables had folks I'd never seen before, enough to officially celebrate." Nathan raised his glass to himself.

Joe quickly added, "Nathan's downplaying the numbers. The hall was at least three quarters full. I did a quick count; closer to a hundred than fifty."

Monika looked at Nathan, clearly impressed. "And you were just telling stories? Clearly you weren't showing off your boobs. I mean, no music or jokes or nothing?"

"Plenty of nothing," Jack added.

"Some may argue, all of nothing. Or I guess that would just be a black hole. Didn't feel like a black hole," Nathan smirked.

"What did one black hole say to the other?" Jack quickly asked.

"See you in the light at the end of the tunnel?" Nathan tried.

"I didn't know you were . . . a relative?" Joe countered.

"Didn't say anything – just a wave."

"Speaking of black and light," Joe quickly steered the flow away from the absurd, "when's your show opening, Jack?"

"Less than two weeks."

"And what's it called again."

"Self-portraits, comma, et cetera."

"Cool. You showing your signpost 'self-portrait,' I assume."

"Absolutely."

"You a signpost, Jack? Tell me, which way is up? I keep forgetting," Monika asked, adding a long trail of smoke to the densely filled room.

"Oh, you've got to see this photo, Monika," Joe jumped in. "I've seen it a dozen times, and it always blows me away, you might say. No idea how Jack did it. And he won't say."

Nathan laughed and explained. "It's a photo of Jack holding onto a signpost, arms, trunk, legs, all completely outstretched, his entire body parallel to the sidewalk," he said, then paused for a second. "Jack, being blown away. As if he's holding on for dear life in a hurricane or something. It's unreal, like a goddamn cartoon."

"I mean you have what, 10 seconds at most after hitting the shutter release?" Joe said. "How in the hell do you have time to get into that position?"

"Fuck the time factor, how does he get into that pose at all? And stay in it! I mean I know he's stronger than I am, but it's just crazy."

"Owe it to all my years being a dumb jock. Before finding 'the light.' Three years of high school football can last forever. And Joe, you can adjust the self-timer on any decent camera."

"The enigma speaks! I never knew you were a jock," Nathan exclaimed. "Jack the Jock. I can see it, looking at your build, but football? The last thing I would have guessed. You may be an arrogant bastard, but you sure ain't dumb."

"More mean than dumb. It was my way of getting back at my old man. For all the shit he laid on my mom. Though seems even slamming quarterbacks wasn't enough," he muttered and abruptly got up while grabbing his empty glass and headed for the bar.

Nathan looked over to Joe, asking quietly, "What brought *that* on?"

"Tell you later," Joe whispered back, then turned to Monika. "You really should see Jack's show. It's not just that one photo either. You want a drink?" he said, getting up with his empty glass.

Monika snorted, "Tempting, but not a good idea. Though maybe I'll take a sip of yours. As a homeopathic boost for the final shift."

"Homeowhatic?"

"You never heard of homeopathy? A smart boy like you?"

"Teach me, sis," Joe smiled as he headed to join Jack, who was talking and laughing with Eddie, which led Joe to think – man, always quick to bury his troubles.

"So, Nathan, I was serious. You just tell stories on stage? I've never seen a show like that. What sort of stories? What was tonight's menu?"

"Two longs, and a bunch of shorts. Started with my bread and butter, *The Identical Twins* – a tale of good and evil. Then pretty much free-wheeling commentary. Short stuff. Mostly social, some political. And yeah, a few jokes. Then I brought out the 'world-premiere' of my latest, *Like Daughter, Like Mother*. More than two years in the making."

"*Like Daughter, Like Mother*? Sounds right up my alley."

Nathan laughed out loud, shaking his head. "How long have we known you, Monika. A couple of years? Seems forever," he said as Jack and Joe sat down with their refills. Jack took his hand from behind his back and placed a second filled glass in front of Nathan, "Just to make it clear I'm not just an arrogant bastard."

"Great timing! Monika needs to take her lisbeopathic sip from my glass."

"Jesus Christ, *homeo*pathic," Monika smirked.

"Using our Lord's name in vain."

"Your lord maybe. Sure as hell ain't mine," Monika said, raising Nathan's glass to him, and taking a healthy sip. "Here's to your mom and daughter."

"Monika, with a *k*, when are you dumping your girlfriend?" Jack asked longingly. "On second thought, I'm a liberal guy – keep your girlfriend, but, I'm beggin' you, sleep with me."

"Jesus *Fucking* Christ," Monika said looking at Nathan, who just shrugged his shoulders. "No more – the apes upstairs beckon! Jack, no fucking affair. Or any other kind for that matter. But do let me know about your show. Maybe I'll see something in your self-portraits that'll change my mind." She left with a teasing brush of fingers across her lips sent across the room to Jack as she retreated out the door and up the stairs.

"One of the many reasons we spend so many nights here," Nathan said with a deep sigh. "Good old Eddie's. What's the full name of this dive? I can never remember."

"Not that hard," Joe said. "Eddie's Museum of Inferiority Café."

"It makes no sense!"

"I've explained it to you, man. That little, tiny hole-in-the-wall alleyway outside is Adler Place. Alfred Adler is the shrink who came up with the concept of an inferiority complex."

"Inferiority I get, I mean why else would you come here to get plastered," Jack said, "but 'café'? Where the hell's the espresso machine?"

"I actually asked Eddie once," Joe said. "He said his plan was to open a European-style café, you know *all* types of drinks, but the espresso machine cost a fortune. He had every intention of saving up, but it never happened."

"Life, what a bitch."

"Yeah, but it's still a great name. So bohemian."

"Bohemian, shehemian. It's the location. Tits upstairs. Gold Rush across the street. The Theatre down the street. *My* gallery a few doors down from that."

"You ever think you'll end up across the street, Joe. You know, in Gold Rush. Maybe even in the front window?"

"Still haven't had a single poem published."

"It'll come. We're just graduating college! And you did win the poetry contest at State."

"Big deal. And that was over a year ago."

"Hey, the writing program at State has one of the best reputations in the country, and my dad said there're close to a hundred applications."

"Nathan." Joe looked at him in disbelief. "I'm talking formal publication in a recognized journal. A hundred? Thousands send their poems to get published. To top-rank places, tens of thousands." Joe shook his head, "Talk about inferiority complexes."

"As I said, that's why some of us are here." Jack raised his drink.

"Screw you, man. At least you have your show coming up."

"And you have a functional life from what I can see. Rather that, than a goddamn show of a few photos." While Jack reached for the communal pack of cigarettes, Nathan once again looked at Joe, questioning Jack's bitterness. Joe discreetly shook his head. Jack lit his cigarette and continued while nonchalantly flicking the match across the table into the middle of the ashtray. "And you're the only one with a real girlfriend."

"Shit, three's not a very large sample size."

"No, but two years is impressive. And Nathan, when the fuck you going to start dating again? Tell me, how many copies of *Blue* have you worn out now? Is it three or four?" (*What the hell?*) And which side is it you wear out, one or two? Oh yeah, must be one. *Carey* then *Blue*. The high then groveling in the low. Just like an addict."

"What the fuck!?" Nathan looked hard across the table, right into those empty eyes. Cold. Unblinking. (*Just who the hell is this?*) He shook his head, grabbed the cigarettes, and pounded the entire pack on the table. "What's gotten into you?"

Joe looked at Jack. "Man, you gotta tell him."

"Shit, you tell him," he said, downing his bourbon then slamming back his chair and heading toward the door.

('*Lots of laughs. Lots of laughs.*') Nathan's hand shook as he lit his cigarette. He took a short then a very long pull. ('*Hell's the hippest way to go.*') Then looked at Joe. "Well?"

"He had a fight with his dad."

"You're kidding. That's it!? Who the fuck hasn't?"

"No, not 'a fight.' A *fight*. And his dad lost. Lost like, he's in the hospital. It just happened. Two nights ago."

('*Gonna take a look around it though.*') "Christ. Joe. What happened?"

It was Joe's turn to grab the cigarettes to steady his nerves. "No details. Well, I guess enough to get the picture. He went to his parents' house. Not planned. Caught his dad, ah, 'smacking his mom around' were his words, I think. He said he lost it. Doesn't remember anything until the cops and the ambulance arrived. Not sure which first. From the sound of it, he kept on slugging, *after* he had knocked his old man out."

('*Been to sea before.*') Nathan took in what Joe said through the image of *his* father's arms around Nira, his goddamn girlfriend. (*When will that ever end. He said...*) Shaking his head. Barely able to comprehend Jack's world. "Wouldn't want to be on the other end of that fist." ('*Crown and anchor me.*') He finished his drink. "So much for celebrating." ('*Or let me . . . sail . . . a . . . way.*')

"Yeah," Joe said.

The two sat in silence, slowly smoking their cigarettes. Both trying to make it a simple but mindless task. The singing in Nathan's head somehow shifted from *Blue* to *Carey*, but the needle was stuck on the last line. Or more accurately, on the first half of the last line. ('*Oh, you're a mean old daddy.*') It couldn't jump to the second half. No complete sentence. No complete thought. Broken record, broken life. (*Wouldn't want to be on the other end of that fist.*) He was startled by Joe's voice. "So, Nathan." He looked up, as if from a long-ago dream. "When *are* you going to get over Bobbie? I mean, really get over her."

(*Bobbie?*) The needle skipped backwards then stuck again. ('*Beneath the Matalan moon. Beneath the Matalan moon. Beneath . . .*')

"You know it'll be three years. *Three* years. That's a long time to go without a soulmate. For a romantic like you."

Nathan refocused on Joe, taking in his new short, now wavy combed-back hair, seeing it clearly for the first time since he had cut the locks that had draped his shoulders just a few weeks before. (*Take me back. Take me way back.*) He was taken back to when they had met in high school, taken back to being in a play together and then the countless late afternoons spent together, locked away in his room. (*'This closely fit, we hadn't thought to miss each other's youth.' Whose line was that? Which poem? Which story? Did he hold the innocence and I the spark. Or, was he the incense, and I the match? Joe, Joe, you still there?*)

"Nathan, you here?"

Nathan blinked, then said as if in a trance, "*Lies on this blink.*"

"*In repeated agreement.* From your Irish guru, from Danny's poem, right?"

"You know me. I'll steal from anyone."

"So, *shall I open your blindness?*"

"*Shall I walk you home to the dark?*"

A short laugh escaped from somewhere hidden inside Joe's heart. "At the risk of competing with Danny, isn't it you and me who are *what's left of the same mind?*"

Nathan looked at his friend, blinked, smiled, blinked quicker, then madly. Slowly, his eyelids came to a stop. "Seriously, to answer your question. I am over her. I will *never* be over her."

"That's all well and good, Nathan. Be as obtuse as you want. But when are you going to date again?"

"Date? You mean like Jack? Not looking for his kind of date. No romance in that. Anyway," Nathan laughed sarcastically, "I did try that kind. Don't you remember? All the girls with names starting with 'B'? And they all somehow played an instrument. After Bobbie with her guitar, I tried Bonnie with a cello, then Betty with her piano. Who was the next?"

"Bridget. But what did she play?

"Yeah, Bridget. The Nazi. She played *me* like a fiddle. God, that didn't last long. She was the last straw. Get me to a nunnery. I mean, monastery."

Joe looked at his friend, half exasperated, mostly understanding, completely in love. More than a brother, not quite the lover. At least not in a physical way. Maybe for a moment? Lost deep in a forest somewhere long ago? Oh, fuck that shit, way too young to reminisce. "I really don't see you as a monk," Joe grinned slightly, shaking his head. "But Nathan, there's a fine line between needing a break from the search and still keeping your heart and mind open, you know, to whatever the new day might lay at your feet."

"Heart *and* mind? High bar."

"High bar? It's been almost three years! You know, man, Jack can be such a prick, but I gotta say, there's more than a little truth in what he said. Just not in the way he said it."

"You sayin' it's time for a girlfriend, or time to put *Blue* away?"

Joe laughed. "You know Joni Mitchell does have another album. And over a year ago."

"Yeah, but no dulcimer on it."

"Don't you hate it when your fave keeps trying something new."

"Especially when new doesn't work. Like *Hard-On the Highway?*"

"Yeah, that was such a boner."

Nathan drummed the table, "Ba-dum-bum-*ching.*" Nathan looked deep into Joe's eyes. "God, I'm lucky to have you."

Joe returned the look. "Let's make sure we *always* speak the dance. And dance the things we never say." Joe paused and smiled. "I can steal, too."

"That reminds me. I've been writing a poem to you about a plum tree. Writing it around the last line, 'I can plum, too.'"

"Can't wait," Joe said, then stood up. "Say, I've haven't gotten you a drink yet. You know, to celebrate. Can't have Jack the Jock outdo me."

Nathan watched Joe make his way over to Eddie, watched the two of them yuck it up as Eddie did his business making the drinks, as his own thoughts drifted to Bobbie. Or more to the point, to the realization that he couldn't remember the last time her face had magically or mysteriously or even tap-on-the-door appeared inside his head. (*Maybe I am over her?*) Her living down south sure made it cut and dry. He hadn't even seen Bobbie since last summer, after she had graduated and was up visiting her parents. But he wasn't just being cute (*obtuse?*) when he said he'd never get over her. Deep down, Bobbie was the one he compared *all* women to. At least when the occasion arose. But Joe was right (*and Jack too, damnit*) – that hadn't happened for a long time. (*Maybe just need to find someone whose name doesn't begin with a goddamn B.*)

Joe was back, a drink in both hands and a grin on his face. "Thought you deserved a step-up from a Beamer. Mr. Daniels." (*Jim to Jack. Maybe a J name for a change?*)

"Sweet! Cheers!"

"Cheers back. Speaking of your guru, you still in touch with Danny?"

"Absolutely. Got a long letter about a month ago. Still in London. Still hasn't been back to the sweet green 'n mud. Not sure if you noticed, but I recorded the second half of the show tonight. The entire *Like Daughter* now on cassette," Nathan said, sitting back, extremely content thinking of earlier that night. "I had this idea a few weeks ago to 'write' my next letter to Danny as a recording. Jack pointed out that most cassette players now can also record. Then it was only a hop skip and jump to the idea of recording *Like Daughter*." Nathan took a long sip from his glass, then shook out one of the last two cigarettes from the pack. "Must mean our night's about over," he said, flipping the pack toward Joe. "I do have this nagging question. Would Danny rather wait and hear it 'live,' you know, in person? I mean, we kinda swore on our grandmothers' graves that we'd tell each other our stories the next time we meet. And man, I *love* my grandmother. But I have no goddamn idea when, or if, I'll ever see Danny again."

"Oh, man, you gotta send it. He'll absolutely love it. And then you'll get his version back in the mail. And being a selfish SOB, I can hear it!"

In the brief lull that followed, Eddie's deep voice cut through the thick air. "Last call. Bar's closing in five. Front door in fifteen."

"Say, Nathan," Joe said. "I saw your dad pull you aside after your show tonight. I remember you telling me how he feels about your 'Twins' story. What did he say?"

"Christ, I can't believe he's still harping on the same old same old." He took one final hit off his cigarette then put it out. "You know, Joe, it's funny to have a father who's pretty cool and famous and all that, but still's just a nagging 'old man.' That's who he was tonight. To be sure." Nathan finished his drink, sucking on the ice cube in his mouth for a second. "I think he's actually worried about my safety. He went on and on about how weird the city has gotten."

"You mean all the murders?"

"And that kidnapping. The newspaperman's daughter. Man, that's fuckin' surreal."

"Just our tradition," Joe said. "The gateway to the edge of the world. And a gateway into and out of. Social, political change, even chaos for the hell of it. But this latest shit? Hard to argue with your dad. The last couple was killed just down from where Samantha lives."

"On that note, we have a long walk to . . ." Nathan began, but was interrupted by the sound of Eddie's exasperated voice. "Hey, you two, whaddaya think this is, England? No one gets *locked in* after closing."

Joe looked at Nathan, "Sounds like the furniture yelling at the kids."

The two picked up their glasses, ashtray, and debris and brought them over to the bar. "See, we even bussed our own table, Eddie," Nathan said, "so don't give us such a hard time. Say, next time we're here, instead of hearing for the tenth time you rag on about ending up in the bay, I'd love to hear how you ended up underneath a topless joint. I mean, which came first?"

"Here's the short version. It was all one business way back when, maybe the most famous Italian restaurant in the neighborhood, but, hey, you're not the only storyteller here. Always happy to tell the long version. Say goodnight to Jack for me. He sure left in a hurry."

Outside in the alleyway, they bundled their jackets against the cold, grateful for the brief transition before being hit by the heavy late-night wind coming off the boulevard. Joe nudged Nathan, pointing with a tilt of the head to the street sign on the side of the brick wall, Adler Place.

Nathan grinned. "All in all, buddy boy, not too much of an inferiority complex tonight."

"Yeah, even Eddie seems to know about your stories. Beginnings of a reputation?"

"Maybe. Maybe," Nathan shrugged. "It's been a long night. First things first. Let's see if we can remember where we parked. And without being killed!" The two buried their hands deep in their jackets and braced themselves as they turned onto the wide avenue. As they made their way into the wind, they became slowly aware that the background noise of the city had changed, punctuated much more now by the sound of distant and not so distant sirens. (*Police, ambulance, fire? Christ, I think I hear all three.*) Slowly but surely, Nathan had to acknowledge that Joe was right. That they were walking on a boulevard deep within a city that now teetered on the edge of the world.

Chapter 20
Straight on Till Morning

Tom Powers came through the front door at Sixth Avenue, unwrapping the cellophane on a new album. "Hot off the press. You gotta hear this song, man. It's so die, no, *mite*." He held up the cover as he made a beeline to the stereo, eyes twinkling behind the large wire-rimmed glasses under the electrified Caucasian afro crowning his head. "The dudes from the other side of the bay demand an answer to that age-old musical question, Wha'is hip?"

Nathan still marveled at the boundless joy of all things music that overflowed from his not-so-new roommate. All types of sounds, but especially rhythm and blues, soul, or funk. (*A mix of all three? Too much for the poor boy.*) And even more if the sound was all about bass, drums, and never-ending brassy horns.

As he placed the record on the turntable, while bopping to the music in his head, Tom sang in a high falsetto, "Tell me, tell me, if you think you know," effortlessly dropping the needle gently onto the intro grooves. He stepped back to pause, raising his finger, as if to say "'cuse me," and looked down at Nathan sitting on the couch under the opened front window. In the glow of a bright morning sun, Tom dropped his hand in perfect timing to a churning rhythm that started on the first note. He fist punched each emphatic beat, with every part of his body locked into the rhythm of the horns. Then, perfectly mouthing, "So ya wanna jump out of yo trick bag. Ease on into a hip bag. But you ain't just exactly sure wha'is hip." Dadadada-da-dadada.

Nathan slid further into the couch, surrendering himself completely to the Tom Powers' experience, and to the infectious sound that now overwhelmed the room. (*Man, Tom is always right about music.*) Almost giggling, Tom put one hand to his mouth, dada-dada, while pointing the other directly at Nathan, dada-dada "you into a hip trip" dada-dada "maybe hipper than hip" dada-dada "but, wha'is hip?" Music swelling into so much trumpet, all the while Tom's head nodding incessantly to the beat. "Hip-ness is" dadahdada "what it is," dadadada, "Hip-ness is" dadahdada, "what it is," then raising his hand, pointing to the ceiling, shaking his head, "And sometimes hipness is wha' it *ain't!*"

The wall of horns reached higher still into a cresting wave that washed over and into and through the warm morning air entering the open window. Tom doubled over, grinning ear to ear. He lifted the needle back onto the arm rest, still shaking his head, 'Tell me, tell me,' the echo of the horns ringing in both their heads. "A tour-*dee*-force, I'm sure you agree."

"Goddamn," Nathan said. "Who's the new cat?"

"The singer? Lenny Williams."

"Tom, somehow you *gotta* get into the music biz. We all love music, but you? You're just nuts. Where'd you go for this 'hot off the press'?"

"Where else, all the way cross town. Tower Records, of course."

"Powers to Tower for the new Tower of Power."

"Shee-it. Hadn't thought of that one."

"That's my job. Your job is to know which music to buy. You just have to find a way to translate that into making a living."

"That's the plan, my man."

"Hey, haven't seen you for a few days. We're having a dinner party Friday. You around?"

"Not sure. May be driving south yet again. What's the poison this time round? Prose or poetry?"

"Man, that's why you have to be here. I already got a cassette back from Danny. He must have had his version of *Like Daughter* finished and ready to send."

"Tell me, tell me."

"Maybe hipper than hip. No, it's amazing. No way to summarize, you got to hear it yourself. All I can say, this idea, this 'project' to write the same story, but from our two different life views? Might just be the coolest thing I've ever done! In Danny's words, 'How each plot will fit snug and fine against our different lives.' So true!"

209

"Man, I can't say it enough times. What a find Sixth Avenue has been for me. A non-stop trip through Wonderland."

Nathan looked at Tom with his mouth scrunched up. "Joe's always on my case calling it a non-stop trip through Never-Never Land. He says that's why he moved out. I know he's just kidding, but . . . always a grain of truth. Whatever that is."

"The grain?"

"No, truth. But enough of this Flakey Foont routine – I gotta get moving. We have a matinee today and I haven't even had breakfast. Let me know if you're here Friday and I'll set you a place."

"Later," Tom said, his eyes still sparkling behind his glasses. As if the past few minutes were just a pleasant distraction, he was immediately back to business, back to the stereo to hear the entire album from start to finish, lifting the needle, his head already back in sync with those horns from across the bay. His falsetto still a gleeful plea, "Tell me, tell me, if you think you know . . ."

● ● ●

"Hyperbole be damned. There's nothing I like more than our dinner parties." Nathan turned to Joe after all ingredients for the main course had been laid out on the kitchen counter. "When was our first one?"

"Three years ago," Joe answered. "September 1970. And the theme was our trip to Europe. Jack had his photographs. Me, my poems. You, you had your stories, but never told them, locked away in that trunk somewhere upstairs in your cortexual attic, never to escape. Still haven't, have they?"

"Damn straight."

Not that they had any real talent for cooking. Nathan had his curry chicken, and Joe his three-layer vegetarian lasagna, both respectable. All other aspects in the art of the dinner party, though, were notable, including the famous dinner table. Joe's father had always dabbled in woodworking, enough to hand down an interest and a few tools to his son. Joe used the souped-up jigsaw to cut a kidney shape from a one-inch thick piece of oak plywood, which could be slid upright behind a cabinet when not in use. As a table, it was heavy enough to remain stable on cinder blocks, guests seated crossed legged on the rug. They once were able to squeeze ten around this table. When asked why a kidney shape, Joe simply shrugged his shoulders. But he wasn't happy when one friend noted that it looked more like a limp penis.

"Fuck you," was his ready reply.

"Not with that you won't," the retort.

Over time, various paraphernalia were found, tried, and kept if they added to the desired ambience. One was a cigarette dispenser Nathan picked up at his favorite second-hand shop – a gold-plated canister that opened upward like a flower to unveil a fan-shaped collection of slots, each intended to hold a cigarette. Usually, such as for tonight's dinner, many of the slots would hold joints, freshly rolled during the afternoon preparations. In addition, for this dinner, Joe had finally found a store that sold Sobranie cigarettes, which he had discovered in Europe. They were expensive, but nothing was spared to create just the right mood for their dinners.

A notable talent that had been revealed was Nathan's knack for just the right music always at the right time. This was directly tied to a record collection stemming from too many hours lost in used record shops and occasionally 'borrowing' older recordings from his parents. Tonight, of course, after dinner, there would be a different kind of recording, the centerpiece music of Danny O'Doyle's story. But for now, as Joe and Nathan faced the adventure of preparing a souffle, the decidedly upbeat *Sinatra-Basie* filled the entire lower floor of the flat. This was the first dinner they had hosted since Joe had moved out a few months before, and they were having a blast. "So, tell me again, why's Samantha in Arizona?" Nathan asked Joe. "Is it really for college?"

"The short answer is her father. The long answer is her father. He clearly wanted her gone from my life. His 'dictum' about her needing to explore school, and in Arizona, was a feeble excuse. You know, the type A start-you-own business type doesn't jive too well with some twerp doing his master's in creative writing."

"Hey, you're talking about my best friend!"

Joe laughed. "Tell that to the judge."

"But your old man *is* the judge."

"And *he* didn't give me any grief about Samantha! Pop's charmed by her beauty. Say, you sure we can make the souffle base this much ahead of time?"

"That's what the cookbook says. I shouldn't tell you this, but you know where I first met Samantha?"

"Not sure I wanna hear."

"Iris Inn. It's a nudist camp down the peninsula."

"What!?"

"We were both single-kid 15-year-olds, parents wanting 'only the best' for their one and only. I think my parents actually believed that. You know, wanted me to have a 'healthy' view of the human body. Not sure about Samantha's dad. I think he was simply on the prowl for a new mate. Her parents got divorced not that long after."

"Jesus, Nathan. A nudist camp? That's weird. Hey, you said no yoke in the whites." Nathan was cracking the eggs, doing his best to separate them.

"The book says it's okay if a teeny tiny bit escapes."

"I think 'the book' is saying whatever you want it to say. Anyway, was it strange to be walking around naked? In front of girls your own age?"

'It was and wasn't. We had gone there throughout my childhood, so I was used to it."

"Were you attracted to Samantha? You must have been."

"Yeah, but most girls that age are pretty damn gorgeous. You know, in a nubile kind of way. We never did anything if that's what you're asking. So, we're all set. We have the base and the egg whites ready to whip. We can put it all together when everyone's here, then bake for 25 minutes, and voilà!"

"Yeah, right, voilà. I can't believe we're attempting to make a souffle for the first time for a dinner party. What's the Irish slang again for idiot?"

"Hey, there's always the pizza joint on the corner," Nathan said, then paused, holding up his hand and counting his fingers. "How many are coming?

I keep forgetting someone. You, me. The guests of honor, Herb and his wife. Jack, your new poet friend, what's-his-name, Dylan Thomas."

"Jake. Jacob Williams and his girlfriend. Doreen somebody. Haven't met her yet. Except in Jake's poems. Which, given Jake's poems, she must be something. You're only half right about Dylan Thomas. More like the marriage of Thomas and another Williams. William Carlos. Here's a short one. Called *Wedding Day*. On paper, long and skinny. *How to measure the distance between grace and chance occurrence. The circumstance of her lace and his raw silk pants. Is there a truth in the passing of clouds or the fortuitous meeting of strangers? How should one measure the collection of milky white raindrops? Just open your mouth.*"

"And you call *me* obtuse! Nice, but I like your poetry better."

"You're just pissed at your dad for setting up that reading with him and Jake."

"That should have been you! Anyway, that's seven, but I know there's eight. Who's missing?"

"I can't believe you're saying that, Nathan."

"No really, who am I missing?"

"Jack's bringing her. Someone visiting from France."

"Oh. You're right. I am an eejit."

"I guess you have the excuse of *not* having actually slept with her."

"You mean the two of us, together, never having slept with her. God, I mean, it's like it was yesterday. Not sure what I remember more, her lips or that heavenly breath. I'm swooning all over again." Nathan reached out to grab Joe's arm.

"Wait, you can't have it both ways. Forgetting she's coming, in an hour for chrisssake, and now fainting over her."

"Yes, I *can* have it both ways. I can have my cake and eat it, too. And please, explain exactly what that means."

"Man, it's, 'you can't eat your cake and have it, too.' Anyway, we've done it again. The art of the dinner party has many components, but there's no question we always ace the most important – who's sitting around the table. Which is why I left my table here. Your guest of honor? A stroke of genius, man, having Herb and Ruth."

"Well, that was obvious. Herb's been so amazingly supportive. In all ways. But especially in my off-the-wall story-telling career choices. I haven't told you half of what he's doing for *Lost and Found*. And he and Ruth coming last month to my show? The next day at work, he almost demanded that he hear Danny's version of *Like Sister*. Sorry, I mean *Like Mother*, whenever it arrived."

Joe nodded and stuck a cigarette in his mouth, holding it in his teeth as he dug out matches from his pocket. "I really like the combo of Herb, Ruth, and Anni. They're each so, cosmopolitan. What's Herb favorite line? 'Ahh, variety, the spice of life'? That's Anni, in spades!" He lit his cigarette, then said as he inhaled, "The only wild-card is how Jake and Jack will hit it off. Something tells me . . . but maybe Jack will be too distracted by Anni."

"Hell, that's a goddamn given. Time to roll the joints and set the table? Or make the salad? I'll flip you for it. Should it be heads for the joints, or heads for the lettuce?"

"Good God. I'm heading out the door."

● ● ●

After finishing his last bite of the main course, Nathan sat back against the set of drawers and let the success that lay before him soak in. To his right, to his surprise and utter delight, Jack was knee-deep in conversation with Herb Malakoff, who had taken on the impossible task of convincing Jack that the beauty of Ingmar Bergman's black and white images was more than enough to overcome Jack's visceral intolerance of the Swede's addiction to unresolved angst. Anni Lee hadn't changed much in the past three years. (*Slightly fuller in the face? Even more beautiful.*) Though tonight, she wasn't playing the temptress. Seated beside Ruth at the opposite end of the table, the two were locked in conversation about which cities in Europe had the best cafes. From the espresso-to-décor-to-the most-charming-of-waiters point of view. Joe sat in between Jake and Doreen. Jake's poetry might be a fusion of Thomas and Williams, but his voice, at least in the one short poem he shared, was all ethereal Thomas. At the moment, Joe and Jake were spellbound listening to Doreen describe how to make the simplest spaghetti sauce with three ingredients and three ingredients only – fresh sage, garlic, and olive oil.

Nathan lightly tapped his wineglass with a knife, adding, "Attention!" with the French pronunciation. "Time for the main attraction. But first, a decision is needed. Joe and I recognize that this Roman-style sitting is *not* what our 20th century bodies are used to, so we have a choice. We can bring in pillows to lean against, or adjourn to the couches and chairs in the front room. It's *essential* that everyone be comfortable when listening to our guest reader. His *Like Mother* is a full 30 minutes. Timed it yesterday."

Herb Malakoff assumed Nathan was in fact addressing him and his wife and responded immediately. "As much as sitting cross-legged brought Ruth and me back to our younger days, I will use my age-before-beauty privilege to adjourn to the front room. If no one objects," he said, smiling.

"Decision's made," Nathan replied. "Everyone, bring what you need with you. Help yourself to either choice out of the canister. And there's more wine in the kitchen."

"Nathan, before we adjourn," Anni said while ascending in one graceful motion, hands stretched out toward her host, "I want to say, the souffle – c'est magnifique!"

"Hear, hear," Herb and Ruth added immediately.

"Boy, oh boy, did we ever get lucky," Joe quickly replied. "I couldn't believe it when we opened the oven. It was like a goddamn picture in a magazine."

"Not lucky. All in my little black cookbook," Nathan added.

"Jesus," Joe muttered, shaking his head.

After everyone had settled comfortably into their seats in the front room, Nathan finished lighting the candles he had placed around the room, then turned the lights out. "All for the tale of romance. Or, I should say, romances." He circled his gaze one-to-the-next, connecting with guest. "Not much to say. For those of you who know the story, well, you know the story well. For those who don't . . . I met Danny O'Dolye only once mind you, and for only one night. But it was a night that held a foehckin' lifetime, pardon me brogue." Nathan paused. "Danny's story is a poem, all in the meter of Ireland. A short introduction with a wee bit of rhyme, then the story itself in such a lovely meter, but no rhyme. And little reason. Only the reason of a . . . Iresh love story. Nathan paused. "And you'll notice the order is switched in the title. From my title, that is. In Danny's tale, the mum falls in love first."

Nathan bowed, turned, and pushed the 'play' button on the cassette player. Nothing. Or was this the sound of distance? As if the sound waves were traveling half-way round the world. Then, a voice from far away, but oh so close. The voice, the sound of Ireland.

"Like Mother." A singular pause. "Like Daughter." Then, music rang. (*Snug and fine against such a fiery life from the mud and green.*)

• • •

Nathan and Joe sat on the small balcony outside of Nathan's bedroom upstairs. Their backs against the outside wall of the neighboring flat, legs outstretched across the width of a twin mattress, and a large ashtray piled with cigarette butts in between, along with a loose pile of Joe's poems. Joe was enjoying the last of the Sobranies he had saved for just this moment. The two friends were knee-deep comparing notes from the night just ended.

"So, what were *your* top three, man?" Joe asked.

"Danny of course was on top. No, over. I mean how different can a story be and still be the same. Then having Herb and Ruth in my home, getting to know Ruth better. She was *so* complimentary on the name change from Sunset to Surf. I know that was Herb's decision, but Ruth must have had some influence. Third? Same old same old. Another successful dinner party. And to think Bobbie's never been to a single one!"

"So, tell me, whadda you think of Jake?" Joe pressed his friend, ignoring the Bobbie reference.

"Hmmm, strong cup of tay, ah must say."

"Yeah, but tell me, what did you *really* think?"

Nathan laughed. "You know, it's hard when there's been so much build-up. You have to wade through all that just to see what's in front of your face. I can see why you like him so much. Hard to imagine, but he might be even more of a Renaissance man than you. God, with his knowledge of science, the metaphors must be endless."

Joe quickly responded, "He wrote an entire poem just of metaphors," and in a high lyrical voice, "*The Argiope geometer divides airy circles invisible to thistle seeds and insects.* And on and on. He told me he wakes up nearly every day, switching back and forth between sticking with writing or changing to biology."

"Well, biology sure won't hurt his poetry."

"And likely make it easier to find a job! At least that's what I wonder, for myself that is."

"So, what about Doreen? You must have been as curious about her as I was about Jake."

"Absolutely. Talk about preconceived notions. Jake's written so many poems about her. *Love Shot*? My God, how could you not have any notions! Anyway, I guess my biggest reaction is that they seemed somehow to be, I don't know, at odds with each other? Jake hadn't said anything to me about problems. Did you pick up on any hints?"

"No, but you were talking with them more than I was."

"Hey, I forgot something. I think downstairs," Joe said.

The last notes of *Closing Time*'s trumpet and piano had just faded into the early morning night, and Nathan followed Joe to pick out the next record. Not wanting to ruin his streak of perfect transitions from one album to the next, he carefully thumbed through the thick stacks resting on the floor of his bedroom. He was still focused when Joe came back into the room, holding up a new pack of cigarettes, "It wasn't in the kitchen. Had put it on top of the . . . Holy shit, Nathan, look – the mattress's on fire!"

Nathan turned and looked out the door to see the middle section of mattress in flames. Bright yellow against the night sky. Right where they had placed the ashtray and pile of poems. Nathan saw Joe grab the heavy blanket on his bed and run back onto the balcony. He flew into the bathroom, looking wildly for any large container, grabbing a bin and filling it in the tub. He could see through the doorways that Joe had mostly smothered the flames, but still rushed out, sloshing water, and dumped the entire bin on what was left. Thick smoke filled the porch.

The two friends looked at each other in shock. "Way beyond eejits," Nathan said, shaking his head.

"Yeah, and some of those poems had no copies! Fuck. *Fuck*!"

The two looked at the mess of wet charred sheets and mattress, smoke still hovering. "Sure hope none of my neighbors saw that," Nathan groaned.

But as they poked around to make sure no embers smoldered in the debris, sirens blared from a distance. Nathan and Joe turned to each other, dreading to hear if the high pitch grew in intensity. It did. Soon, they knew for certain that more than one fire truck was on the street in front, as the sirens began to fade.

"Goddamn lucky Tom and his brother are away," Nathan muttered as he hurried inside to run downstairs. He opened the front door just as the first of the firemen stepped into the enclave. Several more were right behind, all fully garbed in heavy jackets and pants, their helmets firmly latched under chins, each face grim.

"Fire's completely out," Nathan managed, before anyone else spoke.

"You better show us," the first instructed. Nathan headed back up the stairs, in front of the line of firemen fast on his heels.

After all sense of danger was put to rest and Nathan was standing more than a bit numb in his bedroom, one of the firemen walked in, filling the room with his height and size expanded by the thick protective clothes and helmet. He seemed from another planet to Nathan. The fireman noticed the foot-and-a-half plastic statue standing on Nathan's desk, and pointed with a laugh, "Flash Gordon?"

Still in a half daze, all that Nathan could stutter was, "No. You, you are."

The firefighter laughed again. "Yeah, I guess this suit is a bit over the top. But, you never know when you'll need it." He continued to look around the room. The poster of Nathan's recent performance grabbed his eye. He went over to it and read out loud, "Nathan Hughes. A Night of Stories. From *Identical Twins* to *Liking a Daughter*." He turned toward Nathan, "Did you see this show?"

The question brought Nathan out of his daze, and he laughed. "Yeah, I went all right. I was the guy on stage."

"*You're* Nathan Hughes?"

"The one and only. Well, the only one I know. Probably more than a few back in the home country."

"You from Ireland?"

Nathan laughed again. "Sorry. Pure hyperbole. Well, some sense of truth. My dad was born there."

"Lots of us Irish in this city."

"No question about that."

The two stood looking at each other for a few seconds. Nathan was thinking that this man could be the big brother he never had, when the man's smile suddenly faded.

"Say, this *Identical Twin* story. I gotta tell you. Probably shouldn't, but I think you need to know."

"What?"

"The way I hear it at our station is that the main character in your story, well, he bears resemblance to the head of our union. A tall bastard of a man named Pat Scanlan. And, I really shouldn't tell you this, but Scanlan isn't someone you should be on the wrong side of. And seems that you are. On the wrong side. Someone heard him cussing you and your story left-right-up-down-and-inside out. Not sure why, but he's obviously taking the story personal." The fireman locked eyes with Nathan. "Not sure if you have anymore . . . engagements to tell this story, but if I were you, I'd cancel." He again looked hard at Nathan waiting for a response.

Back in a daze, though for a different reason, Nathan nodded slowly.

"And be more careful with your cigarettes or whatever you're smoking. I know the cops are kind of lenient with pot, but not when you burn the house down."

Nathan, chagrined, could only nod again. "Hey, sorry to put you guys through this. Guess the ashtray was too full."

"Yeah, well, you know what Smokey says. But, really, more importantly, stay clear of Scanlan. You hear?"

"I hear." (*More to the point, I see.*) Nathan's mind's eye was drawn back to another fire, years ago, and to the man who walked out from the inferno, stopping close enough for Nathan to be awed by an unfathomable darkness buried deep inside unwavering eyes.

Chapter 21

One Too Many

The fog was high and thin in the growing darkness as Nathan walked, exploring his new neighborhood. (*This edge of town. Used to think of it as a town. It's more a cold-hearted city.*) He had just finished a late afternoon shift at the Surf Theatre and, instead of heading straight home, he was in the middle of an aimless loop. First through the fringe of the park, passing Bobbie's house with barely a pause, then along the promenade of the beach, and finally randomly past the monotonous block-by-block stucco houses that neighbored his new address. Most north-south blocks were defined by house butted against house. The block where Nathan now lived ran east-west where the houses were separated by pathways leading to modest backyards mostly featuring small courtyards. Nathan lived in a large make-shift single-room apartment that had been converted from a basement garage. As a bonus, he had access rights to the backyard patio. It reminded him somewhat of the place Jack had rented several years ago. Fences on sides and back created privacy. Bricked raised beds held well-established geraniums and fewer daisy plants, none of which thrived in the cold fog.

Nathan had moved from Sixth Avenue just over a month ago. The not-so-subtle repercussions from the short-lived fire had dovetailed with a close friend of Tom Powers moving up from the south and needing a place to rent. More to the point, Nathan embraced the idea of living alone. The framework of the once mythical now fully fictional Hitchcock/Welles collaboration was flushed out, but needed all chapters filled. (*Chapters? Not a book. Scenes in a movie.*) Herb and he had penciled in November as the 'premiere' month, and it was already late July. He had to have the script finished by early September, if not before, to fit into Vince's schedule at State to film the one-man performance.

As he now meandered back home, his thoughts focused on the gondola scene, one he had quite consciously lifted from the Ferris wheel scene in *The*

Third Man. The actors were the same, but the roles were reversed: Joseph Cotten as the wickedly conniving villain more than capable of murder, and Orson Welles the intelligent but gullible would-be victim. Cotten would play the murderer in the new Hitchcock thriller, while the role of the portly director was filled by Welles. The story was set in 1949 in this fair city. What should have been a short ride through the air from one headland precipice to another was interrupted when the gondola stopped unexpectedly. The Hitchcock character assumed the cause was a momentary glitch in the motor. Both the actor and director hovered 100 feet in the air directly over the Phelan Baths, which sprawled on a still lower bluff overlooking the ocean. The two could hear a distant foghorn, positioned north of them where sea entered bay. No music would be used in the scene, only the constant drone of this deepest of baritones. The wind was mild that day, and the car gently rocked back and forth in the high thin fog. (*Hmm, weather just like today.*)

As always, Nathan demanded that his story work on multiple levels. The primary purpose of this scene was the back and forth banter between actor and director discussing the motive behind the next scene to be filmed in the new Hitchcock movie. At the same time, it would be the first hint the audience was given that Cotten's character was not just an actor playing a murderer, but someone possibly dangerous, maybe even a murderer himself. Or at least someone contemplating the foulest of deeds. To add to the complexity, Nathan wanted to tongue-in-cheek remind the viewer of the analogous scene from *The Third Man.* (*Just to be cute – can't help myself.*) And that the movie, and this scene in particular, should be an homage to the city he loved. (*Christ, do I always have to give myself such impossible challenges?*)

Hitchcock stood firmly (*weightily?*) on the floor of the gondola, one hand calmly holding the banister between the windows. Camera takes in director from waist up. In his distinctive slow cadence, he says, 'Joe. It doesn't seem that you understand why your character is up here, in this gondola, riding back and forth . . . then back and forth again. We've gone over this before.'

The actor/murderer leans back against the wall of the gondola, even more at ease. Camera repeats the similar shot (same distance from subject). 'I think maybe it's you, Old Man, who doesn't understand why you and I are up here. Up here at all. And now, *dangling* in mid-air. Do you think we've stopped by . . . accident?' (*That's good. I like it.*)

Camera comes slightly closer to the director, taking him in from chest up. 'And what pray tell do you mean by that, Joe? Sounds like a line from some B-movie Warner was trying to palm off on me.' (*Warner? maybe RKO's better.*)

The murderer stands upright, slightly away from the wall. Camera shot is from chest up, and murderer walks slowly nearer to the director. 'Listen, Hitch, it's damn obvious you want me, my character, to be looking down.' He leans slightly out the open window looking down. First, a close-up of the actor, leaning out, then the camera itself looks down at what the actor sees. 'Looking down at all the people, the tiny people . . . going in and out of the baths below. And down the hill, to that restaurant there. Tiny people, in their tiny lives.' (*Too much like the Third Man, or even Shadow of a Doubt?*) He turns back to Hitchcock, as the camera takes a quick close-up of the face of the director, who, though remaining stoic, raises one eyebrow slightly, then cuts to close-up of the murderer's head and upper chest. 'You see Old Man, maybe I'd rather, for a change, have my character be . . . be more of an adventurer, looking out to sea.' He waves grandly toward the sea. 'That majestically immense and boundless sea.' He turns to the director. 'There's more to life than murder, you know.' He looks back to the ocean. 'One gets tired of having to play . . . only . . . murderers.'

Camera shot of director from waist up. 'But Joe, your character *is* a murderer. Maybe in our next film, you can, as you say, look out to sea.'

Camera follows the murderer as he slowly walks the entire perimeter of the gondola, occasionally looking out. 'But Hitch, I don't think you understand who your character really is in *this* film. I don't think you know how much your character has changed. Over the years. The many years. The *too* many films. *Your* too many films. Your character, always the same. Variations maybe, but variations on the same . . . slightly . . . looney role.' (*Looney? Come on, Nathan, that's not the right word.*)

Lost in focus on his story, Nathan started to cross an empty street. Then something caught his attention, quickly replacing the characters in his thoughts. He recognized something about the signpost on the corner, or was it, the house in the background? (*Is that the same post in Jack's self-portrait? Jesus, that's the house. That must be the signpost.*) Fascinated, he now mentally added Jack, across the street, being blown off the ground. Hung out to dry. Then he realized, given this view, that he might be standing exactly where Jack had set up his tripod. Without hesitation, Nathan looked down on the sidewalk. To his amazement, a small but quite clear *x* was etched into the cement. Was that Jack's mark? Could Jack have set up the shot in that much detail, wanting an exact distance and angle? (*Random? Does Jack do anything random? This x has to be his.*)

The image of Jack outstretched slowly faded in the cool evening, and Nathan shook his head one last time in amazement. He turned toward the park to hurry the few blocks back to his apartment, with his thoughts now solely on his friend. Before now, he had been vaguely aware of a gap in their friendship, that he had only seen Jack once since that night at the bar. And a dinner party was no place to talk privately. Nathan had heard Jack's dad was out of the hospital but living separate from Jack's mother. Nathan kicked himself for not having reached out. (*Selfish bastard. Lost way too much in my goddamn writing.*) Yes, Jack had been up north off and on. Yes, they had exchanged one or two cycles of short letters. He wasn't even sure where Jack was now. (*Got to check with Joe.*) When Nathan reached his apartment, he went straight to the phone to call Joe. The answering machine light was blinking bright in the evening dim. He thought for a second to ignore it, but out of habit (*spent too much money on this stupid machine*), pushed the play button.

"Nathan, you don't know me. I got your number from a mutual friend, Eddie Foelmer. (*Eddie? How does he . . .? Oh yeah, gave him my card.*) Name's

Harry Martins. I have a club down the peninsula, past Lincoln, almost to Grant. And no, the town's not Johnson. Sorry, I get that line all the time. Anyway, calling to invite you to give a performance. Looking for the same show you just did in the city a few months ago. Guaranteed packed club. Give me a call. 408-226-2424."

Overwhelmed, Nathan sunk into the chair next to the phone and looked blankly across the room. He had had no expectation of building a reputation this quickly. Then he heard the fireman's warning in his head. (*Does this guy want the exact same show?*) Nathan had been toying with a show where he presented both his and Danny's *Like Daughter, Like Mother*, but no way he could be ready with that anytime soon. Not with the deadlines for *Lost and Found*. (*Shit, I can't pass this up. Halfway down the coast, how would Scanlan even know?*) He listened to the message again, this time ready with a pencil.

• • •

Nathan and Joe had just taken the exit for the road that climbed up and over the coastal range and connected the north-south freeway with the much slower north-south coastal highway. When Joe had announced that his new used clunker had a tape deck, Nathan quickly recorded his newest favorites on Tom's system. Now far away from the fog of the city, car windows were down, and the immediate fragrances and warmth of summer filled the car. He pushed *Asbury Park* into the slot, noting the satisfying slight pull of the cassette clinking into the deck. (*'Cut loose like a deuce,' indeed.*)

"Hey, you want to take a quick detour up the road? I can show you where I met Samantha. You know, the Iris Inn."

"Wow, wasn't expecting that. I dunno, man. Not sure I brought the right attire."

Nathan laughed. "I didn't mean go into the place. Not likely anyone would remember me. And you have to be a member, anyhow."

"Be a member, or have one?"

"Jesus, and you complain about me? On second thought, probably not a good idea. I know it's somewhere off this road, but no idea even which exit to take."

"Man, every time I get out of the city during the summer, I think the same thing – why the hell do we live there? We all need two addresses, the one in the city from September to May, then *any*where outside of it for summer."

Joe stuck his head out the window, yelling as loud as he could, "It's so incredibly nice!"

"It's our puritanical British blood, Joe. Ninety-five percent of our life has to be spent in penance, for these few brief moments of pleasure."

"Ain't it the truth, *ain't* it the truth."

The plan was to arrive at the bar mid-afternoon so that Nathan could check out the room. (*Sans crowd, that is.*) How much room to maneuver, on and off the stage. How sophisticated the lighting. (*Was there any stage lighting at all?*) How far was the stage from the noise of the bar. Then they would drive farther down the coast to their friend Richard's house, where they would spend the night after the show. Neither had seen him for a good half year, though Joe had recently run into their mutual friend Renee, who had been wearing a tee shirt with large letters across her chest, Grand Opening arched above slightly smaller May 10, 1973. Just what did *that* mean, he wondered. Clearly, they had some catching up to do.

Nathan reached over to the tape deck to pull out the cassette. "Hmm, first time I'm hearing this during the day. Springsteen's way too into the night. Let's try this."

Percussion. Bongo and drum kit as one. A single bass note feeding into the hard, clear tickle of piano. Then, a string of guitar on top. *I've seen the bright lights of Memphis and the Commodore Hotel, and underneath the streetlamp . . .*

"And *that's* not a night song?"

"Just the *any-time-of-day* feelgood downhome honky-tonk. This came out the beginning of the year and still might be spinning on Tom's turntable. Whatever music's good enough for Tom Powers is good enough for me."

Joe laughed. "Man, can't argue with that."

Down in Dixieland. De-de-de-de-de-de-d-d-d-d-de.

They had reached the summit and were soon heading downhill, though most views were blocked by the thick mix of trees. Joe was focused on the road and its continual back and forth tight curves. Nathan was leaning back, eyes closed, enjoying the warmth and music. Soon the trees began to thin, and glimpses of the distant coast materialized around the bends in the road. After an especially sharp curve, and overwhelmed by the view of the entire coast, Joe immediately pulled into a turnout.

"Great idea," Nathan said, gazing at the panorama. They got out of the car and hopped up to sit on top of the hood.

"It's been a long time since I've been down here. We used to drive over to the boardwalk for the afternoon when we were at Iris for a few days. When I was really young, I remember all three of us would ride that huge roller coaster together. Me crammed between my parents. I wonder if it's still there."

"Oh yeah. And as popular as ever."

"Man, life sure is crazy. Two days ago, coming down here? It didn't exist, not even the slightest of inklings. Now, Christ. I'm in the goddamn way-back machine. Hadn't thought of my parents together in ages. Shit. Where's Mr. Peabody when you need him."

"What's the latest with them? I see your dad at school, but, well, not my place to ask him about Nira."

"He's saying it won't last much longer. But he's been saying that for years! She started law school, so who knows. Not sure if he's waiting for her to meet someone her own age, or if he's going to end it himself. But as you say, not my business."

"And your mom?"

227

Nathan looked at Joe with a huge grin. "Now there's good news. No more Frank. And I might have actually been part of the breakup – no Oedipus intended. Though, I suspect Freud would have a field day."

"What? Tell me."

"Man, it was like a bad comedy of manners. Frank has this small house up the coast and he said that I could always go up and use it. 'Never have to ask. If you need to get away for the night.' Told me where the key was hidden. So, about a month ago, right after all the hubbub about the fire, I drove up there for exactly that. To get away and think things through. I arrived late in the afternoon and the door was unlocked. Okay, I thought, door's unlocked, but no car, at least that I could see, must have forgot to lock up. I head upstairs to the bedroom. Cute little cottage. Great view of the ocean. And I walk into the bedroom, expecting that view, and, instead, great view of . . . my mom and Frank. Doing it. Hate to say it, but it was like watching two cars colliding. In slow motion. *I tell ya,*" Nathan pretended to straighten his tie a la Rodney Dangerfield, "*somebody could've gotten hurt.*"

Joe was in stitches. "Whaddya do?"

"Do? What could I do, I was paralyzed! Probably a split second, but, my God, it seemed forever. I finally somehow managed to turn myself around. Mostly because I was about to crack up laughing. Straight out of the house and into my car. I talked to my mom the next day and she said she ended it, right then and there." Nathan paused shaking his head. "This has to justify as a new psychological complex of some kind but haven't found the right name for it yet."

"I'm sure Frank has a name for what you did."

"Yeah, well, he has only himself to blame."

"Man, you could incorporate this into your show."

"Oh, believe me, I know. I just have to figure out how to hide *all* traces of identity. And I have to come up with a name for it. You know, for the punchline. I thought of, the motherfucker complex, but, well, much too crude. It's my mom, for chrissake."

"Hey," Joe said looking at his watch, "we'd better get going if you still want time scoping out the club this afternoon."

"Yeah, can't keep relying on my usual preparation for a show. You know, throwing up five minutes before curtain call."

"You still doing that? I remember that trick from *David and Lisa*."

"Ain't no trick, man. Nerves – they're the real thing. Gotta keep that tension nice and tight." Nathan's thoughts then turned to his performance, only several hours ahead. (*First time in a truly public place. A damn bar, no less. Hecklers? Absolutely.*) In response, long-ago memories quieted his nerves, returning him to early adolescence when, on more than one afternoon, he had waged good-natured verbal war with the winos in the Panhandle. He smiled. (*Lots of practice with bona fide experts on how to heckle. Tonight? Piece of cake.*)

• • •

Joe stood in the back of the club near the bar watching Nathan bring the 'Twins' to its close. Sean Murphy and his side-kick Robert Sullivan had just left the burning lodge and were watching the soaring flames and smoke mix with the swirling night fog, all surrounded by the towering trees of the Grove. Man, Joe thought, I can understand how seeing something like that would lead to a story like this. Having heard the tale more than once, Joe was able to keep a distance to watch how his friend told the story, rather than listen to it. It was impressive to see Nathan handle himself in this new environment. Luckily, no outright meanness, but people sure were talking. Damn loudly at times. Nathan not only effortlessly handled all surrounding noises and comments but seemed to feed off them. Even weave them into the story, as Sullivan responded to a loud uproar from a nearby table of drinkers, "I sure could use a small taste of the drink meself."

Nathan had just begun the banter of commentary and shorter stories. Joe heard a pause, then, "How a restaurant turns into . . . a topless club. True story."

Well, Joe thought, *Eddie's* true story.

Nathan continued. "Back before the beginning of time, there was a restaurant built in the city to the north. The owner had the good fortune of more than the usual amount of land, *and* the money to do it justice. A large structure with the added feature of a lower level for storage. This floor had its exit in the back, off a small alleyway, perfect for unloading food and the like, around the corner from the entrance to the restaurant itself, which, owing to the slope of the land, was really the second floor of the structure." Nathan was contorting himself, weaving his hands and arms this way and that, trying to explain where the two doors were relative to each other. "Have I confused you enough? The important features – two floors, connected by a stairway inside, and entrances on two separate streets. Well, if you go back into the archives circa 1910-1920, the *best* damn Italian restaurant in the great Northside neighborhood of the city. Then, Prohibition sets in, and well, this place was maybe even more perfect. Restaurant stayed on the main floor, and . . . you're ahead of me I can tell. The bottom floor now turned into a speakeasy that could be accessed via the stairs, or if you knew the right rhythm of the right knock, through the back door off the alley. But, as we all know, Prohibition was eventually, well, prohibited, and lo and behold, the owner still has a nice setup. A great restaurant *and* a great bar. 1930s through the 40s. Then, what-do-you-know, the owner ups and dies, and leaves the business to his two grown sons. Not exactly 'good and evil,' like that first tall tale, but let me tell you, they were different enough. Let's call the 'better' one Eddie and the 'not so' one Phil. When was this? A little over fifteen years ago, mid 50s, smack dab in the middle of the great beat of the renaissance, which was *all* about the Northside neighborhood. All about the tension between the world of poetry and art and that of well, the not so artful world of the low-life. The brothers decide that Phil would take the top floor and Eddie the bottom. It works for both, certainly for Eddie, who had always wanted to run a true European-style café, you know, serving *all* kinds of drinks. Though I'm told he's still waiting for that espresso machine to be delivered. Well, I bet you can guess what Phil's interests leaned toward. The restaurant-turned-nightclub he started in the late 50s slowly but surely stops headlining comics and jazz and starts featuring, ah, dancers. And as you can guess, the dancers were all women, and then, to this very day, they wore less and less. So, this still works great, and if you find yourself in Eddie's and you happen to notice a stunningly beautiful woman enter off the back stairway in a lovely silk robe, you now know how a restaurant can be transformed from a feast for the stomach into one . . . for the eyes."

Joe smiled broadly, thinking, man, he sure can steal with the best of them. I wonder how Eddie would take this? Probably flattered. Joe's attention was suddenly shifted to a short older man, maybe in his late fifties, getting up from a stool on the far corner of the bar. He watched as the man finished his pint, took one more look at the stage, shook his head once or twice, then turned toward the door. Oh well, Joe thought, can't expect everyone to be won over by Nathan.

Even if Nathan had shared the fireman's warnings about Pat Scanlan, Joe would be unlikely to have any suspicions of who this disgruntled customer was. Certainly would have no idea who had sent this man on a two-hour drive south of the city to watch only half a night's performance by a young and still obscure storyteller. The half-a-show in which Nathan tried his best to weave fact into fiction, to create story from reality. Scanlan's right-hand man would have to report, 'No. Hughes completely failed,' as the facts behind this tale of identical twins still shone through the tinsel of make-believe in all their glorious evil. At least, as seen through the eyes of one of the twins himself. The one who was still very much alive.

Chapter 22

Back to the Surf

"I ran into crazy Leonard and guess what?" Joe fixed his eyes on Nathan.

"Shit, don't tell me. Psilocybin? I got way too much on my plate."

"Man, Nathan, we may never get another chance."

"We? But Jack's not even here. We'd need the three of us for a redux."

"Don't I know. But I was thinking, Jake for Jack."

"Hmmm. So. What film?"

"I see you and Herb are showing a Bergman series next."

"Bergman? While tripping? You are kidding, aren't you?"

"Hey, man, where's your sense of adventure?"

"Sense of adventure!? Where's your sense of sanity? Do you want to end up in the psych ward like Bill? And which Bergman movie needs any of its . . . intensity heightened?"

Joe laughed. "None. But this isn't about any cinematic deficiency. This is a challenge, pure and simple. The ultimate challenge. His newest film. The one filled with *red*."

"*Cries and Whispers?*"

"Yup."

"You want to see *Cries and Whispers* on psilocybin?"

"Well, 'want' is not quite the word I'd choose."

Nathan sat across from his friend, trying to get his head around the idea. The more it made no sense, he had to admit, the more he liked it. Then, the flickering light bulb turned suddenly bright. "Hey, I've always wanted to do something no one else has."

"I knew you'd come around. Jake's in. And we already planned to head up to King's Point after. Jake's been wanting to show me Miwok's Lagoon. We can camp out."

"Camp out? Don't you read the news? Another two bodies were just found."

"But Nathan, you're not paying attention. They've all been couples. Heterosexual. The nutso must have a grudge against those who have what he doesn't."

"Well, that's quite a leap. So, a compromise. No camping. Anyway, which night?"

"You're the one who scheduled the retrospective! This Friday. October the thirteenth."

"Hmm, I better make sure my guardian angel's on call that night."

• • •

Most of the audience stayed through the entire closing credits. Likely because all were emotionally drained and couldn't move. Nathan turned to Joe, "I have no idea what I just saw. Just one long red blur." As the three exited slowly, as if in a dirge, few comments were heard. Joe was the first through the front doors, and when he felt the unusual warm night air of the Indian summer, he practically yelled, "I'm still alive!"

Nathan could only shake his head.

"Hell, I'm still in the beginning of the movie," Jake said. "I didn't know if those cries came from someone making love, or someone dying."

"Man, the whispers got to me more than the cries."

"Family feuds, what a bummer," Nathan said. "With lives like that, glad to be an only kid. Jake, you have any siblings?"

Ignoring the question, Jake changed the subject. "Hey, let's take a stroll on the beach. Before I do any driving, I need to lose this edgy edge. Not the high, just the edge."

"From the Surf to the surf," Nathan said, lighting a cigarette and taking a long draw. "You have talent, Jake. Me and highs? We don't mix one bit behind the wheel."

As they walked the few blocks to the beach, Joe steered the conversation to their favorite topics. Love and poetry. "So, man," he said to Jake, "is it *over* over? You and Doreen. Last we talked, you said there was a slim chance."

233

"I said that? Must have been delusional. No, that love's most definitely been shot. *But love, shot, as a bird, shot, hurts because it hurts the chance to come, and not be madly made, to love.* It's been over for months. Time for a new beginning."

"Ahem, you hear that, buddy boy." Joe reached out and dug his elbow into Nathan's side.

"Give me a freakin' break! I'm working overtime on my new film."

"You know, I tried to sneak in to watch you guys filming your thesis, but the door was locked. I couldn't believe it. Not even your best friend."

"Damn straight, not even best friend. Everyone had to sign a nondisclosure agreement."

"You mean, all three students?"

"Hey, four. You have to include the teach."

The three reached the beach and stood listening to the rhythmic wash of the surf across the sand. Jake broke in, "You know, the word 'surf' may be unique. I can't think of any other word that so easily evokes all five senses. We certainly can hear and see it." He bent down, brushing his hand across the surface. "Can feel it." Then licked his hand. "Taste it." Then took a deep breath. "And man, oh man, we sure can smell it."

The high of the psilocybin pulsed through Nathan's head. "Jake, man, you and me, this is the beginning of a beautiful friendship."

"What? You met him five months ago." Joe said.

"Yeah, but he didn't say *that* five months ago," replied Nathan.

"Say what?"

"Say exactly what I said to my boss to get him to change the name of his movie house. 'Sunset' to 'Surf' – it's my favorite word!"

"Oh," Joe said in mock disappointment. "I thought 'plum' was your favorite."

Nathan laughed loudly, "Oh, shit, I still owe you that poem, don't I."

"Let's do poetry," Jake sang out. "Now! The three of us. With the sea as witness. Nathan Five-Sense, you start. Then Joe."

Nathan immediately shot out, "*Five senses say you breathe about a need*"

"*That is secret,*" Joe shrugged his shoulders, "*or it couldn't be*"

"*Twitch stitched to every touch.*" sang Jake.

Nathan hesitated, then continued. "*When every hand without a hand will lose all strength*"

Joe paused, "We rhyming?"

Jake replied, "If the spirit moves you."

Joe nodded, then, "*Though you are only fingertips beyond arm's length.*'

Jake exclaimed, "New stanza!" Then immediately continued, "*All such odd love, such mystery,*"

Nathan wavered, then, "*Remains secret when each secret's freed*"

"*Or whispers into each rain, 'a little life must fall.'*"

Jake smiled, "Nice. Next stanza." Then, in an even higher pitch, "*Faintly, as when shadows of breaths meet,*"

"*About this airy silence, this silent moment,*"

Joe paused, thinking hard, then smiled, "*I sense no grief or woe, meant.*"

Nathan and Jake groaned in unison. Nathan said, "You *got* to be kidding. Woe meant?"

"You got a better rhyme for 'moment'?"

Shaking his head, Jake started again, "*For I have turned, and see first your feet,*"

"*Next your knees. Though my bashful glance,*"

"*Is but a secret.*" Joe finished the sentence. Then, "*Does this romance*"

"*Mean the secret's set? I should not chance*"

"*You seeing me.*" Nathan said, then with a grin, "*And so, I take my leave, quite quietly.*"

"Oh, man!" Joe shouted, falling back on the sand, "What'll we call it?"

"Gotta be, *Quite Quietly.*"

"Not that it matters. It'll be gone by the morning, like a fucking dream!"

"Hey, I'm not going to argue," returned Nathan, who then cupped his hands to his mouth and shouted to the crystalline night sky above, "I'm not going to argue!"

To which Joe exploded, "BLUEY TUNES! And I thought I had come on during the movie. I'm! tripping! NOW!"

Nathan threw his arms around Jake in a sudden wild dance, swinging them both, while singing a tune, a bluey tune spinning in his head, "I'm as mad as a hatter, mad as a hatter, I'm as mad as a hatter, I am, I am. I AM!" And both he and Jake fell to the sand spinning as they let go of each other, all three laughing and pointing at the moon that looked down on them. The unblinking almighty eye. But wait! did this cyclops just wink?

Nathan sang out, "Change of plans! Let's ditch the lagoon and make a tape for Danny! Me house is but a kiss away. *A kiss away. Kiss away. Ohhh, children! It's just a kiss away*!" They all scrambled to their feet, Nathan planting himself between Joe and Jake, throwing his arms around their shoulders.

"And maybe, just maybe," Joe chimed in, "we somehow, miraculously, remember the poem we just hallucinated, and send it to Danny. Each reading his own line!"

"Or if we can't remember it, then another! We'll simply write another!" shouted Jake.

And the three marched back across the sands, away from the sight, sound, feel, taste, and smell of the surf. Back into the edge of the city, now blanketed in an early morning darkness made soft by the occasional wink of an Indian summer moon.

• • •

"Joe, you have got to pin Leonard down on what-the-fuck drug we ingested. Not the same mushrooms as before. And it's not acid. No idea what it was, except fucking amazing."

After filling both sides of a cassette to Danny with stories, music, and poetry, complete and incomplete, with newest of rhyme and barely a reason, no one felt any hint of coming down. In response, Jake had returned to their original plan. "We can easily cross the bridge and get to Miwok's before dawn. And no edge anymore, I can drive." It was now pushing hard against four a.m. as they drove along the winding east-west road through the north county's countryside.

"Jake, tell me again – what's so special about this lagoon? Nathan should hear."

"What's so special? Ecologically, biologically, historically, metaphysically, or just plain poetically? I've only written a dozen poems about Miwok's, so unless you . . ."

"Whoa, Nelly. Jake, did you sneak in some speed somewhere tonight?"

Jake laughed, "Whatever we took must be doing different things to each of us."

"I'll help you focus. First, ecology. Something about a 'tidal exchange'?"

Within not even a blink of a moon's eye, they were parked at the trail head, each looking out into the foreground of dimly lit grasses and distant silhouettes of coastal hills. A small part of the large freshwater lagoon could be faintly seen off to the right.

"So, Jake, what was the last poem you wrote about Miwok's?"

"Thought you'd never ask. Called *Meditation of Grasses*." He took a deep breath, then oh so high. "*This scrubland, this scattering of purple hedge nettle. The path between the lagoon's flat surface and where cows lull and breed weaves our souls into distant dunes. Tall grasses – and your hair – wave in an ocean's breath, as we breathe to measure the airy weight of salt.*" Jake took another deep breath. "*We reach driftwood bare-footed on warm or even hot packed sand, still distant from a softer beach. Between there and here, the sands rise into a mediation of grasses. We find shade inside to be kept by a sacred sound – ocean wind through reedy green. Almost to the sea.*"

"Nice. Visually, long and skinny?"

"Exceedingly skinny."

"It's like one of your poems, Joe."

"Time to head out," Jake broke in. "We're here to live this poetry, not discuss it." Before Nathan could get out of the car, Jake and Joe were already well into the darkness. Jake called back, "There's only one path!" Then calling out again from farther down the path, his words fading into the distance, "If you don't catch up, we'll be waiting at the bridge . . ."

Nathan felt no need to rush. In fact, he lingered in the car with the door open smelling the ocean in the breeze coming across the lagoon. (*The airy weight of salt indeed.*) He was finally coming down from whatever psychedelic they had shared some eight hours earlier and so many miles away. On the edge of a city far removed from the unearthly quiet that now surrounded him. (*Or, really, this earthly quiet.*) Coming down. (*Always the best part of a trip.*) His mind now scrubbed clean of all built-up habits, the residue of day-to-day repetitions. (*Everything leaves a film. Always good to clean.*) Nathan closed the car door and squinted hard at the path ahead. He could see surprisingly well at least thirty paces ahead, although farther faded into a mix of shadow, darker grays, and then blackness. He started to walk.

The trail was a well-worn rut in the scrubland that was bordered by a fence and an uneven terrain of lupine, ferns, and low blackberry. The fence fixed the boundary of a dairy ranch to the south, and as Nathan looked to his left, he saw occasional rounded shapes low on the ground. Down the path, one cow was standing near the fence. As he approached, the large animal turned its head. Nathan stopped directly opposite it. He could clearly see two small eyes that failed to blink. These eyes returned Nathan to his distant youth. He smiled. (*Same eyes, different beast.*) He heard a calm soft snort and waited patiently for the animal to take in all she wanted. (*No need to free this beast. There's a fence, but it goes on forever.*) Just as a wind kicked up, something grabbed Nathan's shoulder. A sudden, strong grip. He quickly spun, shaking off the hold, but could see nothing, just a deadly quiet. The sudden commotion startled the cow. She snorted loudly and moved farther away.

Nathan's heart and mind raced. The imprint of the grip stayed strong. What had grabbed him? Or who? Was it from the drug? (*But hallucinations are visual, aren't they?*) No one had experienced any apparitions of any kind earlier that night, and he was no longer tripping in any sense of the word. Then Nathan remembered the recent nearby murders and couldn't move, almost couldn't breathe. To steady himself, he found himself focusing on the cow still close. Slowly, the hint of panic quieted, enough to push himself forward. (*They're going to wonder where I am.*) Luckily, as he walked, Nathan could see far across the flat terrain. (*Nothing tall enough to hide behind.*) Finally, in the distance, Joe and Jake came into view, standing near the bridge that Jake had mentioned. The bridge that connected the trails that ran along the two lagoons. Underneath the bridge, the nearby freshwater mixed with the brackish marsh that extended not quite to the sea.

"Where've you been, man?" Joe called out. "Communing with nature?"

Nathan approached, shaking his head. "You won't believe this." He stopped, realizing he was still panting and took a deep breath. "I *was* communing with nature. At peace, really. Then something grabbed me. I turned, right away, but nothing."

"Shhitt," Joe said. "Residual hallucinogen."

"No, it couldn't have been. I was so not high. In fact, as you two first headed out, I just sat in the car, blissed out. On coming down *off* the drug."

Joe turned to Jake with a look of 'oh, yeah, right' but saw his friend looking at Nathan, seriously. "Man, you believe him, Jake?"

"I do," Jake nodded. "I believe him because I've had similar experiences out here. Once kind of, but the other time, no question. And I wasn't high either time. Both times were at night. Very late at night."

"So?" Nathan said quickly. "What?"

"Not sure. My first thought was knee-jerk, a ghost. Then, something vaguer. Maybe a portal into the past. Or into a different world. You know, this entire place," Jake said, motioning to the surrounding panorama, "is *all* about transition. Sea into land. Saltwater into fresh. Soft sand into firm then hard ground into coastal hills. Migratory birds into local. Miwoks into . . . us, whoever we are. It's a powerful place." Jake lit a cigarette, his mouth and thin mustache suddenly brightly lit. After inhaling deeply and again in near darkness, he said, "Let's keep moving. We can get to the sea by first light."

"Hey," Joe responded, "remember Bergman's film *Hour of the Wolf*? This is it, man, the hour between night and first light. Might explain what Nathan felt."

Jake laughed. "No wolves here. Though plenty of coyotes and bobcats. And I saw a cougar once. But that was much farther out, almost to the Point."

"I think Bergman used the wolf as a metaphor, Jake."

"A meta-for-what? Who needs metaphors? Don't need no stinky metaphors."

The three made their way to the end of the formal path and the beginning of the open sand that bordered the northern side of the brackish lagoon. "Let's leave our shoes here," Jake said. "It's easier to walk and, man, the sand's still nice and warm."

As the three made their way across the flats, Nathan's attention was kept by the stark beauty of a landscape scarcely seen in the moonlight. He looked up to find the moon and was surprised to see it now low on the horizon, barely peeking over the dunes. (*Damn, it can still see us.*) This relentless eye reminded Nathan of suddenly being seized. Instead of returning to what had seized him, he thought of how he had steadied himself, by focusing on the cow who had moved away. (*Had she seen something?*). The cow seemed to be studying him. (*Making sure I was okay?*) Nathan then returned to the long-ago memory of the bison's small eyes, and the fantasy that grew from that magical encounter. (*What damn story will I invent tonight?*)

The three hiked up the final dune that separated the lagoon from the sea, the dune that at least temporarily blocked a tidal exchange. Was this long electric night finally coming to an end? Coming to an end by returning to the beginning. Returning to the sea, birthplace of all life. Maybe even the birthplace of an unexplained hand reaching out from a world beyond. At the top of the dune, the majestic waves and expansive beach were barely visible to the west. Nathan was first to turn and face back toward the east. He motioned Joe and Jake to join his gaze. Against the high night sky still filled with stars, the softest and thinnest of yellows lined the distant hills – the sun was beginning its ascent. More importantly, the moon had set – no longer to be seen. And, calming their lingering misgiving of the unknown, a moon who could no longer see them. (*Winking, blinking, or otherwise.*)

Chapter 23

Ajar

Nathan first heard about the latest killing on late-night TV. The next morning, he walked past the crime scene tape only two short blocks from his apartment. As Nathan headed to the Surf to meet Mr. Malakoff, he felt oddly comforted that this murder, so close to his apartment, had been tied to drugs, rather than the seemingly random homicides that had recently made headlines. Even the slaying of young couples hiking in the back country had a story of sorts – some lonely crazy taking revenge on what seemed impossible. (*The terror of random murder? With no explanation? Maybe I should add that to my next tale.*)

But even murder couldn't distract Nathan for long, as his life was now consumed with *Lost and Found*. Herb had set the schedule for a week and a half, with his film's 70 minutes sandwiched each night between two tried-and-true classics tied to Hitchcock or Welles or to his home town. First night, *Shadow of a Doubt* the early show and *The Third Man* last. Second night, *Lady from Shanghai*, then *The Lineup*. The final night, *Touch of Evil* first, with *Vertigo* showing last. (*Man, I must be nuts. Putting my movie between such gems.*). But Nathan's movie was not quite finished. What a crash course in filmmaking the past two months had been. Even for a film that mostly captured his performance on stage. It was all the damn sound effects Nathan had insisted on adding for just the right atmosphere. Like that foghorn. (*Was it really worth all the work?*) To add to the stress, the featured movies hadn't yet arrived. (*Have to call the distributor. And we still haven't agreed on the marquee. Jeez, why is that so difficult?*)

As Nathan entered the lobby, he could hear the radio playing in Herb's office. He immediately went to the small hideaway to find his boss bent over an enormous spreadsheet covering his desk. As always, the radio was tuned to the cool sounds of jazz.

"What would you do without 92.7?" Nathan asked. "*And* that ridiculously large spreadsheet?"

"The simple pleasures of life," Herb grunted. "You forgot to mention my box of number 2 pencils and the electric sharpener Ruth gave me years ago. You finished yet? With all your sound editing?"

"Really close."

Herb rolled his eyes, looking up at Nathan while tapping his pencil on the sheet.

"No, I swear. Almost there. We're still on for you to preview this Friday."

"And the six movies that should have been here by now."

"Calling Pete in a minute."

"Don't call Pete, call Harry, now, and tell him I'm not happy."

"Yes, sir." Nathan gave a half salute and headed to the phone behind the concession counter. Herb's close-to-lecturing response reminded Nathan that this crazy plan was enough of a risk to raise concern, even though he recalled his boss's dismissal from the previous week: 'Nathan, don't worry about me. I'd need more fingers and toes to count the number of disasters I've had. Remember *Zabriskie Point*?"

Nathan came back into the office a few minutes later. "Harry checked. All six just left. He'll double check with the shipper, then call back. But they should arrive Friday, Monday at the latest. So, really, plenty of time."

"All right," Herb said matter-of-factly. "And the preview Friday; that's here, right? We need to see how it plays here. How the sound is, here."

"Of course. Herb, you sound like Brando in *The Godfather*, worrying about Barzini. Am I supposed to lean toward you now and say, *What's the matter, Pops? What's bothering you.*"

Herb not quite smiled and said in a low gruff, "*Women and children can be careless, but not men.*" He leaned back in his chair. "We have to reach a decision on the marquee."

"Herb, whatever you want. It's your theatre, and you've been doing this nearly as long as I've been alive."

"Yes, but you're the one with the great ideas."

"Hmm. Remember, *Zabriskie Point* was my idea."

"So, we keep it simple. The marquee isn't that big a space. Just the name of the movies."

"Can we fit 'Hitchcock and Welles' on the top line?" Nathan said apologetically, realizing he was already backtracking on Herb making the decision. "That might help explain *Lost and Found*."

Herb put his hand to his mouth. He was reminded why they hadn't come to an agreement yet. "Shouldn't be this hard," he muttered. "My marquee is just too damn small. Barely one at all."

"How 'bout, 'Hitchcock, comma, Welles,' on the top line, then 'and *Lost and Found*' on the second?"

Herb Malakoff tilted his head back and forth. "Maybe," his boss said, then pulled at his lips. "We can try that and see how it looks. You know, Nathan, I think we're stuck because we're both thinking back to our original marquee fantasy, 'The Lost Hitchcock Film.' And that's just not the reality. Or, even a fantasy. At least, not the right fantasy."

"Fantasy," Nathan said, letting the word roll around in his head. "So, how about, 'Hitchcock and Welles' first line, and then, 'A Lost and Found Fantasy.'

Herb looked at Nathan, his eyes now twinkling. "I think you nailed it on the head. Yet again. Eight words. Should easily fit and says it all."

"Finally!"

"I must say, Nathan. We *do* make a great team. I'm lucky to have you. You and your damn enthusiasm."

For once, Nathan didn't know what to say. He squirmed, swallowed, then looking down, managed, "Not half as lucky as me." (*To have you. Boss, mentor, friend. The grandfather I never had?*)

"My oh my, Nathan, my friend. Don't think I've ever seen you tongue-tied before. I'll take that as a compliment." Herb could see that Nathan was struggling to keep his composure. "But enough sentimentality. One more clarification. You're still planning to introduce *Lost and Found*, correct? And I should briefly introduce you, right before your film starts. No need for us to say anything before the first movie, or the last."

"Agreed. Yes, no need."

"I'll set up a microphone in front of the screen. Do you think we should have a platform. Make it more of a stage?

"I like stages," Nathan said with a grin.

"I've noticed," Herb replied. "I have one somewhere in storage. We have had speakers here once or twice, you know. You won't be our first guest film auteur."

(*And please, guardian angel, wherever you are, make sure I'm not Herb's last. For his sake.*)

• • •

"No ands, ifs, or buts," Joe said emphatically. "Jack'll be back down *before* Friday. I talked with him last night. He sounds committed to working things out with his dad. Or at least, he is. He'll be staying with me until he can find his own place. And he's talked with the folks at Gasser's about getting his old job back."

"He knows about *Lost and Found*?"

"Absolutely. That's why he said before Friday."

"Let me know as soon as he gets to town. I want to see him before Friday night."

It was now Monday afternoon, and Nathan and Joe had decided to meet in a revisit of the small park on top of the still obscure Mount Olympus. Neither had returned since the hike up the steep streets several years before. Now they were sitting on the same enclosed bench built into the steps where they had sat before, protected against an equally cold wind. Though a different time of year, the weather was nearly identical.

"I can't believe that everything's ready," Nathan said, shaking his head and pulling on a cigarette. "The films arrived this morning. Herb gave his thumbs up after the preview. I even have my little intro actually written down. Man, I never do that in advance." He laughed nervously. "Probably not a good idea. Likely jinxed something."

Nathan noticed that Joe was looking down, distracted. "Hey, what's up, bro?"

"Well. I guess, good news, bad news." He fumbled out a cigarette and began fiddling with it, twirling it in his fingers. "Someone else is coming to town." He finally looked at his friend.

(*Not Bobbie.*) Nathan looked away. "Who might that be."

"I think you know. Rosemary's been in touch. But that's not all."

(*Christ.*)

"She's coming because she also has a gig." Joe finally stuck the cigarette between his teeth and lit it. "A music performance. Here in the city. On Friday night. And it starts the same exact time as *Lost and Found*."

"You're fuckin' kidding me!"

"I heard about it yesterday but didn't know how to tell you."

Nathan sat stunned, doing his best to absorb the news, but struggling. "Does she know about my film? Anything about it?"

"She does now. Rosemary filled her in."

"I can't believe this." They sat in silence. "Only one performance, Friday night?"

"Yeah, just Friday."

"So, she could come to the Surf Saturday. To see my film. Hypothetically." Nathan looked blankly into the fog that was thickening in the late afternoon. He felt numb, in body and mind. "That won't help my not being able to see her show. (*Her first show in this city.*) I can't believe this."

Another few minutes passed. Joe slowly smoked his cigarette, while Nathan's accumulated a growing tip of ash. Finally, he tapped it off, then turned toward Joe. "Anything else you couldn't tell me? Where's her gig?"

Joe grimaced. "You remember the Wine Cellar? They have a stage now, with weekend music shows. It's kind of a nightclub gig."

"Christ!" Nathan's thoughts instantaneously returned to long ago and the large round table in the restaurant. To Bobbie's face. So close to Judy, and the two high school friends begging him to tell a story. And not just any story. (*Let me get this straight. I'm going to miss Bobbie's first performance in her hometown, at the place where I first told the beginnings of 'Identical Twins.' And she's going to miss the first showing of 'Lost and Found'? Who the fuck wrote this script!?*)

Nathan turned toward his closest friend, his next of kin, almost screamed in a whisper through clenched teeth, "And who *the fuck* wrote this script? I swear, I'd kill the bastard."

• • •

Nathan walked back to his apartment late Friday afternoon. After thinking about nothing else all week, he knew he had to see Bobbie, the sooner the better. Joe had told him she'd be staying with her parents. Nathan had gone back and forth and back again on calling or simply showing up. 'Simply' had won out, but no one was home. He left a note slipped through the mail slot, one that he had written back at his place. (*A just-in-case note.*) As he crossed the street where the Surf Theatre waited quietly in the middle, he looked again at the marquee. Its simple message centered him, prepared him for the momentous night that lay ahead. (*My first film! Well, a film of sorts.*) He smiled at the luck of that morning, the luck of Jack photographing Herb and Nathan standing underneath the marquee. (*Man, can't wait to see that black and white.*) The smile remained as he then thought back to the subsequent hour spent with Jack in his apartment, recovering a friendship that had been partially lost the previous months.

Nathan turned down the walkway to his apartment, thinking ahead to a quick shower and simple dinner. (*Maybe just a sandwich?*) As he reached the patio in back, he noticed that the door was ajar, slightly but most certainly open. Did he not close it earlier? Unlikely. He pushed the door fully open and looked in. The dim outside light failed to reach beyond the center of the large room. (*This doesn't feel right.*) He reached inside and hit the switch to the ceiling light. Across the room, in the chair against the far wall sat the large frame of Sean Murphy. (*No, it's the real thing. It's him. Scanlan.*) The man's eyes were incandescently bright and instantly locked onto his. A baseball bat in his large right hand was striking the opened palm of his left. Nathan was suddenly pushed from behind. He stumbled fully into his apartment, as he heard the door bang shut.

"Enter, the storyteller." The immediately recognizable crusty voice filled the room. "The goddamn, snooping, why-don't-you-mind-your-own-business storyteller."

Nathan looked up. Scanlan looked the same but didn't quite match the memory. (*Christ, six years ago?*) Nathan was so caught off guard in the surreal moment of the character from his own invention sitting in front of him, very much alive, he at first failed to grasp the gravity of the moment: why Scanlan was here, in his apartment. It was all too bizarre, until he was struck hard across the back of his head from whoever was behind. He turned to see a much shorter man, similar in age as Scanlan. (*Sullivan? whatever the hell his name is.*)

"Mike Gallagher," Scanlan called out, "say hello to our storyteller."

Gallagher shoved Nathan further forward. "Glad to meet you."

"Make our guest comfortable, would you. Get him a chair, then you can excuse yourself and make sure no one's snooping down the alleyway."

Scanlan's right-hand man grabbed the straight-back chair from the table, pushing Nathan down into the seat and roughly pulling off his jacket. Gallagher then grabbed a length of rope from his back pocket and tied Nathan's arms around the chair back, his legs to the front chair legs, tugging at the knots to ensure they were taut. "I'll leave the door open a bit. Holler if you need me, Pat."

Scanlan waited until Gallagher was outside. Then waited another minute. All the while, he continued to gently thump the bat against his open hand, as if keeping time to his slow steady heartbeat.

"So. What do you think? Seem enough of a good story, storyteller?" A pause. "You must appreciate the irony. Up and coming young raconteur on the eve of his new release. Sounds like an even better tale than that of my damn brother and me. An homage to Hitchcock? I'd consider walking over to the movie house, after I'm done here, but I think they'll have to cancel tonight's showing, don't you? When the storyteller himself fails to show."

Scanlan could tell that Nathan didn't understand his plot. Or if he did, he was simply seeing this scene as flickering light on a screen. Or maybe, a dream?

"You look as if you need to be pinched, Hughes. You're not dreaming. And I'm no goddamn specter. Maybe we should start with this bat. Do you recognize it?" Scanlan held the bat closer to the overhead light and rotated it so that the dull red marks near the end were clearly visible. Somewhere, in the deepest drawer of Nathan's mind, he was standing on a ledge peering through a window. Seeing a bat. Seeing what had looked like blood. Hidden on the top shelf of a locked shed.

Scanlan was scanning Nathan's face for the smallest hint of awareness. Come on, damnit, he thought, show me. Show me! Then, he got what he wanted, a slight upward movement of an eyebrow, and smiled for the first time. But only for a second, and not at all friendly. "Ah, you remember," he growled. "Now we can begin."

• • •

It was early and the Surf was still empty of customers. Herb looked at the clock behind the counter. Five twenty. "Thought Nathan would be here by now. Probably, any minute," he assured himself.

Joe came out of the theatre. "I threw my coat and sweater across the entire back row, just in case. You think it'll sell out?"

"Joe, I gave up the job of soothsayer long ago. You just never know."

Ruth emerged from the hallway where the restrooms were located and looked at the two. "So, how many family and friends are coming tonight?"

"Mother and father. And of course, Vincent Aioli. And I assume the students who shot the film. Most likely other faculty and grad students. From both departments," Herb said.

"Jack should be here soon," Joe added. "He said by five thirty. Jake and his new girlfriend are coming tomorrow. I'd say about half of our friends are coming tonight, but I've been too busy to keep track."

"I guess Samantha's still at school?" Ruth asked.

"She is. And not at all happy about missing this. But what the heck. We can always have a private showing, right Herb?"

"Absolutely. Though I haven't given the future of this project much thought. Nathan and I have joked that we'll show it to the old man himself. Entice him to make his final masterpiece."

"Not sure he'd want his final film to be, well, so final," Joe said.

"Shhh, no more. Ruth hardly knows anything about the plot."

"Ooops, I'm not supposed to know either."

"Who needs a plot?" Ruth rhetorically asked. "I just love listening to all of Nathan's different voices."

"Do either of you want a coffee?"

They both shook their heads. "Too late in the day," Ruth replied.

A short pause followed, with the melodic sounds of jazz filling the void. "Who selected the lobby music?" Joe asked.

"Nathan. I would have used the soundtrack to *The Third Man*. You know, that zither is so contagious. But Nathan wanted old-school straight-ahead jazz." Herb glanced again at the clock, again muttering, "He should be here. I think I'll call him."

• • •

Nathan finally forced himself to take his eyes off the piercing blue eyes of Pat Scanlan and back onto the bat. "And?"

"Oh, so you're awake now, are you?" Scanlan stopped tapping his hand with the bat and held it quiet in both hands. The phone rang, but he ignored it. "Well, the short version is, Michael had managed to convince me that your story had no consequence, at least through your performance here in the city. But when you kept at it, down the peninsula, I had enough. I don't know how you figured out everything so damn well, but it's time to put a stop to it. *That's the 'and' of it.*"

(*Is he planning to kill me!?*) This was all too fantastic for Nathan to comprehend. Was he in a movie? (*Like Hitchcock in 'Lost and Found'?*) Nothing made any sense.

"If you're worried that my story is so obvious, won't the police think so too, and suspect the main character?"

Scanlan's laugh was more a bark, brief and vicious. "This story has nothing to do with the storyteller. It'll be the well-worn reality of yet another drug killing. Actually, the second half of the reality began down the street earlier this week. You see, I, too, can weave a story." Nathan looked on, bewildered, while Scanlan placed the bat on the floor and reached down into a bag at his feet. First to emerge were vinyl gloves, which snugly fit Scanlan's large hands. Next, a capped syringe, followed by a small vial. The tall man loaded the syringe with a colorless solution.

"You should appreciate this, mystery storyteller like yourself. A seven percent solution I think it is." He walked over to where Nathan sat, bound. Scanlan roughly pushed up Nathan's sleeve to expose his arm and emptied the syringe into a vein. "Cocaine is metabolized quite rapidly when introduced this way. So, we'll just wait, say 10 minutes, so all the bloodwork will be 'consistent.' Have to make sure you were high *before* you were killed. And then all the other evidence, such as this." Scanlan pulled out a large plastic bag of powder. "Will be 'found' around the room." Scanlan looked about the room for places to hide the various clues. "There you have it. You know you really do talk about drugs too often in your stories and commentary. No more storyteller; just another dealer/user trying to keep a little for himself."

Nathan felt the sudden hyped-up rush of stimulation swirl in his head. The drug on top of the more and more surreal acts left him speechless. He tried to yell for help, but nothing came out. Was it the drug or panic? What did it matter? He was feeling overwhelmingly helpless. He was held mesmerized by this evil twin muttering to himself as he wandered around the large room, pulling out

251

this, stuffing an envelope there, all the while setting the stage for the final scene of what Nathan now realized was deathly certain.

● ● ●

Herb looked up to see Nathan's parents, together for this evening, enter the lobby, immediately followed by Jack Evanston. That's it, Herb said to himself. Past five thirty and still no Nathan. Something was very wrong. He motioned to Joe across the room and then made his way to Nathan's parents, waving to his wife to join him.

"Tommy. Ava. So good to see you. Have you met my wife? Ruth Malakoff. Nathan's lovely" pointing to Ava "and famous" pointing to Tommy "parents."

"Ruth," Tommy Hughes said, smiling, "a pleasure. And where be the guest of honor? I expected to see him pacing the lobby."

"He called and will be here any minute. Last minute jitters. Ruth, take Ava in and save an empty row. I want to show Tommy something."

Herb led Tommy into his office, with Joe and now Jack close behind. The four huddled together in the small room. Herb wasted no time.

"Nathan hasn't called, Tommy. I didn't want to worry Ava. Joe and I think something has happened. I have no idea what, but I have a bad feeling. I saw him this morning. Jack took our picture outside. When Nathan left, he said he'd be here early. A little after five. I tried calling a minute ago, but no answer."

Tommy Hughes was following the logic as if he expected it. "Right," Tommy said quickly. "Joe, Jack, come with me. Herb, make some excuse to Ava."

As the three hurried outside, Tommy pointed across the street to his car, "We'll take my car. Not a second to lose."

● ● ●

"What's the line from that goddamn kid's story?" Scanlan snarled to himself, then looked across the room at the bound Nathan. "*The time has come, the walrus said.*" The tall man stood his full height and slowly crossed the room. "You need to know this. I've killed only one person, with my own hands that is. Or I should be specific, killed him with this." The blood-stained bat again tapping

252

his open hand. "You might ask, why keep the murder weapon all these years? Why keep it at all? Did Cain save the weapon he used against Abel? And what was that weapon? The Bible only says, *He rose up against his brother.* And I rose up against mine! My goddamn identical twin." Scanlan raised the bat high then crashed it down against the floor. "One blow was all it took! And you? You're not half the man my brother was. He went to his grave as silent as he needed to be." Again, the tapping of the bat. "NO MORE STORIES!" Scanlan bellowed. Then much slower, and almost in a whisper. "Your damn story ends now."

• • •

Tommy pulled sharply into the driveway. As the three jumped out of the car, Jack took the lead. "Better to split up. I'll take the alleyway next door."

Jack was immediately back to his high school football field of battle as he tore down the neighboring path, his mind and body prepared to jump the wood fence, the fence he had noticed just that morning during his only visit. Luckily, the cross studs were on the outside, so he managed to scale it in one quick jump step and swing of his legs, landing solidly on both feet in a crouch. The apartment door was slightly open, and he heard Tommy's and Joe's and another's voices yelling down the main alleyway. He barged through the door, his body leaning forward in a run. He was greeted by a devastating tableau frozen under the overhead light – a very tall man, old man strong, a bat raised high in both hands, and Nathan bound helpless to a chair. *All I have!* was Jack's only thought.

"Nathan!" cried Jack, barreling forward, focused solely on the exposed torso of the tall man.

(*Jack!?*) As Jack slammed into Scanlan's mid-section, the descending bat exploded in a blur, not at the apex, just off the crown of Nathan's head. Still bound to the chair, his head and shoulders badly slumped forward, as Jack savagely climbed on top of Scanlan. Not stopping. Repeatedly connecting. Driving his fist into whatever meat or bone he could find until Tommy was pulling him off, Jack now weeping, no sobbing, as Scanlan barely groaned on the floor, with Nathan collapsed in the chair, motionless.

Chapter 24

Circles and Squares

(*Jack!? Thank . . .*)

• • •

"Careful." (*car full?*)

(   )

(*smell strong stronger rotten!*) Nathan, still not responding in the back of the ambulance, involuntarily turns his head and vomits.

(*sounds. . . words?*)

(*sea surf, sea surf, sea . . .*)

(*sea sleep. no, not. nothing? breathe, breathe. bre . . .*)

(*. . . sleep?*)

(*light? open . . .open ...no*)

(*hand? warmth? gone.*)

(*pounding. just breathe. no! stop! stop. stop. . .*)

• • •

(*Sound. I know. Voices. I know. Sleep. Sleep now.*)

(*I am on a lonely road, and I am falling falling...*)

(*Awake no sound. No sound. No pain. Alive. Angels?*)

(*Hand. Warmth. I know that. Oh my, I know those!*) "Nathan?" (*Oh My!*)

(*Sound, sea, surf, sea, surf. Sleep. I can sleep. This is how...*)

(*Bright! Still . . . bright.*)

(*Unraveling it's the unraveling, the unraveling.*)

• • •

"Ja," Nathan mumbles.

(*'He said...'*) (*I said?*)

(*Pulse. Head. Pulse. Peace? Head. Hurts. Now not. Hurts. Not. Sleep again.*)

(*Dad?*) "Da?" Nathan barely forms half the syllable.

Tommy Hughes isn't prepared. He rises from his chair, dropping his book on the hospital room floor. "Nathan. Son. Good Lord!"

"Where'm," he slurs, his eyes open as if awake. Then, just as quickly, he leaves.

• • •

(*Alive. Wanna joo box jive. Applause your kisses your kisses...*)

(*Hand. Warmth. Different. Gotta. Got to. My . . .*) "Nathan! Can you hear us, son?" (*Fingers. Each. Me. My.*) "He's here, Ava. He's really here." (*I'm here.*)

(*Mom?*) "Mom?" Nathan completes the syllable.

Ava is prepared, her whole being focused on her son. She reaches for his hand. "Nathan."

"Im ir irs. Irsty."

Tears fill her eyes, here, drink these. She brings a cup – the doctor had said the tiniest of sips – to her son's lips. Nathan takes the smallest taste. He smiles weakly. Tommy focuses; will his son throw up again? As the first tear falls down Ava's face, she bites her lips, trying to breathe. Trying to catch her breath. She can't. Her tears flow, and she breathes, air and tears together.

• • •

"Unconscious for what, twenty-four hours? Could have been so much worse," Dr. Ahlbach says. The specialist is older than Tommy and Ava, head traumas his field of expertise. They listen as if he were a god. He shakes his head, nearly a shudder. "This may sound unbelievable, considering everything, the unconsciousness, the severity of the bruising, but I think this was more a glancing blow. A minor fracture of the skull. No drainage. Scary to imagine if the bat had come straight down onto the crown."

"Jack," Tommy says under his breath, then continues louder, "Nathan was hit on the right side of his head, away from the door. Jack must have tackled Scanlan just as the bat came down. Knocked him and the bat, just enough, a few inches." Tommy turned to his wife. "Good Lord, I didn't fully appreciate until now. Not only did Jack tackle Scanlan, but he saved Nathan's life."

Ava peers out the window. "And then you saved *his* life. That evil man's life. Even if he's locked up."

Ava looks at the doctor. "So now, two endless days later, Nathan keeps falling in and out of what? sleep, or in and out of consciousness?" They all turn toward Nathan, who lies still, eyes closed, little movement other than his rhythmic breathing.

Still looking at his patient, the doctor replies, "I simply don't know. We're not quite able to image the brain in real time. From my experience, I'd guess some middle ground. But there's no question that everything is heading in the right direction. Sorry. No pun intended."

"*All* puns more than welcomed," Tommy immediately adds.

"We could test your question if we wanted to," Dr. Ahlbach adds, looking at Ava. "We could try and wake him. But no need. Whether asleep or unconscious, he's clearly letting his body heal. We're monitoring everything we can. His speech is already improving. I see no need to rush." He pauses, looking intently at Nathan's still body. "Though there is the matter of the police wanting to question him. Especially about finding cocaine in his blood. I must admit I'm impressed with their patience. I'm sure that will have its limits."

"Don't worry about Mullins," Tommy says quickly, then stops. "Now Nathan has me confusing fact with his fiction. I mean Mitchell, the detective in charge. I've been talking with the police, seems from the moment they arrived at the apartment."

"What about other visitors?" Ava asks. "Joe says he's been getting countless calls. And then, there's Jack – he really wants to see Nathan."

"I'd certainly hold off on visitors in general. We're all obviously focused on the physical trauma. But emotional trauma is also a concern. Seems like he's blocked that out so far. Let's keep it that way for now." He paused. "His best friend – Joe is it? – can continue to visit. But his friend Jack? He's obviously directly tied to the trauma – so let's hold off. A few more days of sleep, or whatever we should call it."

"And when do we tell him what happened? Beyond being 'hit on the head.'"

"I want the staff psychiatrist to work with Nathan on that question."

• • •

(*Square. Circle. In middle, a door in middle. Still sleep. Keep closed. Soothing. Quiet red. Almost, not door. Just color. Just breathe. Breath color. In middle of square in middle of circle. Leave. Now, sleep. Now . . .*)

In early morning light, Nathan wakes. Or, he opens his eyes thinking he is dreaming of opening his eyes. No one in the room. Then, in his deepest soul, his truest heart, his sharpest thought, he wakes. Fully and utterly *conscious.* All is quiet, save for the electronic hum of the monitor. The window blinds are fully open. The softest light brightens the acacia tree across the street. (*In bloom?*) The hushed emptiness in his room comforts. He slowly looks at each shape, each part of the whole. The chairs off to the side where his parents must have left them last. He sees the residual trace of his father's hands pulling the chair back against the wall as he is about to leave. His mother turning one last time. He feels her gaze. Effortlessly feels them both, their spirits, in the room. All, his parents, himself, *part* of the room, part of this whole. As is the poster board on the wall across from his bed. The table underneath. The monitors to his right. Tubing. Wires. He calmly focuses on the call button resting on the small table to his right, pauses, then closes his eyes, returning inside, to a square inside the circle inside the square. His universe. His new . . . place. (*For now.*)

• • •

"And how old are you?" Dr. Ahlbach continues.

"Twenty-three. And," Nathan slightly stutters, "a, about a half. If that counts. If you want to count months. If you're asking. Since you ask."

"Sounds like a normal Nathan," Tommy whispers to Ava.

"Where did you go to high school?"

(*High school?*) "Oh goo, good God, must you remind?"

"No evasions, please."

"Jes, Jeshuit High. Not that far from here?"

"No, you're right. Just a few blocks. Up the hill. And speaking of geography, a bonus question. Which direction is west?"

"Hmmm, being ob, ob, observant, is, is that part of the test? Nah, not just memory? No mah, matter. Looking out that window, is to my mom's house, so loo, looking south. (*That way.*) Therefore, wah, west is that wall." Nathan points directly opposite his bed.

Dr. Ahlbach smiles and looks at Tommy and Ava. "He *is* observant, and his cognition is certainly functioning. Very encouraging, considering the blow was on the right side. I assume his memory is a hundred percent?" They nod, both smiling, no, beaming. Albach's smile slowly fades as he looks down in thought, as if to decide. Then back at Nathan. "What is the last thing you remember, Nathan? Before being here. Before being in the hospital."

"Ahh, the mill, million-dollar question," Nathan responds. "I remember watching my *Lost and Found*, with Herb Mal, Mala, Herb my boss, sometime re, re, recently. I also re, remember going to that small park, with Joe. Ah, Joe." Nathan pauses and smiles dreamingly. "Though not sure which was first. Oh, I remember *Lost and Found* was to be at the Surf Thea, Theatre. Along with several of my favorite moies, moies. Can't say it." Nathan frowns for a second, then looks out the window. "But, not sure when." He looks at his parents. "Did that happen? *Lost and Found*?"

Tommy purses his lips, shaking his head. "Not yet."

"So, slight post-traumatic amnesia. Maybe about a week lost. Not unreasonable," the doctor says to no one in particular. "Nathan, I'm getting close to not being of much use to you. Your speech has returned, amazingly quickly, improvement each day, almost to normal. Your employer's name and movies be damned. Headaches nearly gone, and no longer severe. Appetite fine, no more vomiting. Clearly, your long-term memory is fine, as is your cognitive function. No motor loss that I can see. Right now, the biggest concern is a bit of amnesia. A small fraction to lose, if irreversibly. Which I suspect is *not* the case. Considering the trauma, it's probably best to work with a psychiatrist to restore the memory. And, equally important, to process it. So . . . time for Dr. Brady to take over. She's our resident psychiatrist in Neuro." He pauses to assess any reactions from Nathan. "Any questions for me?"

"Besides, wha, what hit me?"

"Yes, besides what hit you. I'll let Dr. Brady help you with that."

"Well, you prah, prah, probably can guess my oth, other question," Nathan puckered his lips. "When the heck you letting me out?"

"Soon. Maybe by the weekend? Or early next week. Your blood chemistry is still showing slight markers. Your vision not quite back to normal. Very close though. Looking ahead, you should stay at your mother's house for an additional period. Maybe a further week or so. Though nothing strenuous for another few weeks. Can't have you jostling that head of yours. At all."

(*No, no jostling.*) "No worry 'bout that. Never been a ah, athlete. Dad tried to get me interested in his sport. Bay, baseball."

"I should add, for both you and your parents, we'll want to follow you for a longer period of time. Much longer than you'll feel necessary. Several months. Some symptoms may reoccur or may occur for the first time. Not to scare you, but you need to be aware of these . . . possibilities." (*Aware. Yes.*)

"Any specific symptoms long-term?" Tommy asks.

"Pretty much anything you would think of from such a blow-on-the-head. Slow response time, poor memory, different sleeping and dreaming patterns, learning issues. Some might be transitory. Some can be addressed, some adapted to. A myriad of variables, which leads to keeping close tabs on our patient." (*Myriad. Funny word.*)

"Oh, one last question, Nathan. Would you say you're back to what you'd call 'typical' dreams? Typical for you."

"Hmmm. Dreams? Sti, still having, well, you know, I wou, wouldn't call it dreams. But wha, whatever it is, it's still all I'm having. Sorry, nah, not making sense."

"No, I think I understand. You're having recurring images, but not really dreaming, correct?" Nathan nods. "Yes, good. It's definitely time to hand you over to Dr. Brady. Maybe she can meet you this afternoon. I'll talk with her."

• • •

Nathan sits upright in bed, fully awake. He looks out the window at the acacia tree, keenly focused on its intense yellow bloom. He closes his eyes, trying to remember if those flower clusters have a fragrance. Joe sits near the bed, shuffling the many poems he brought to read to Nathan. Ava sits quietly in the corner of the room, intent on her knitting. A wool hat to cover her son's head. For the coming winter.

Nathan opens his eyes with a start. "Joe, a memory just came back! Of you and me at the park last week, or when, whenever. You told me about Bobbie. About her show. At the Wine Cell, Cellar. Did that happen?"

Joe looks at Nathan's mother, who pauses. Dr. Brady said it was good to bring back memories, good memories. Ava nods to Joe.

Joe smiles at Nathan. "Absolutely. Last Friday night."

"Did you go? Who wha, went? How was it? Tell me."

Joe hesitates for the briefest of moments then replies simply, "No, I didn't go. But I heard it was fantastic."

"What did she sing? Is she still in town?"

"She had to go back south, for another show. I think it might even be tonight. But she said she'll be back as soon as she can." Joe sees the question in his friend's eyes. "To see you again."

"Again? What do you mean, again?"

Joe looks at Ava, who has stopped knitting to lock eyes for the briefest agreement to proceed.

Joe turns back to Nathan. "She was here. The first night. Last Friday."

"She was!? She was here? She came after her show?"

Joe's breathing turns suddenly labored. His eyes fill with tears. He swallows, looks down, then back at Nathan. "As soon as I called her. You ..." Joe can't speak. "The first sign of *any* life . . ." He stops, only again to force himself to continue. ". . . from you, was when she took your hand. When Bobbie held your hand." As Nathan's eyes also fill with tears, Joe thinks, yes, let them flow. "Your hand responded. *You* responded. You partially closed your hand, around hers. And your eyelids flickered, several times. We all saw it."

(*I know these!*) "And . . . she said my name," Nathan continues, nearly a whisper.

Ava Hughes is left with a single question – will I ever stop crying? Oh God, never, please, please never.

• • •

Dr. Brady has gathered Nathan's parents, Joe, and Jack in the hospital cafeteria. She has seen progress in the past few days and is confident the endgame is near. Not only had Nathan remembered more events from the previous week, but his recurring image has finally made sense to her.

"It's a map," she says, her eyes sparkling. "So utterly fascinating. Can't believe it took me this long. Has Nathan been exposed to, or have an interest in Buddhism? In particular, Tibetan Buddhism?" She glances around the table and is greeted only by puzzled looks or heads shaking. "Then it's as if he's somehow made the connection himself. My God, Jung would have loved this." She refocuses. "Do any of you know what a mandala is?"

"It's an art form, isn't it, usually religious. Geometric-based," Tommy Hughes says. "Extremely intricate. Sometimes three-dimensional when made with sand."

"By Buddhist monks," Ava adds.

"Oh, yeah, those posters," Jack says. "They're in all the head shops."

"Almost *too* trippy. Leading every which way," Joe continues. "Depending on your state of mind."

Dr. Brady smiles. "Ah, yes, the ever-present 'state of mind.' Actually, everything you've all said is correct. Especially what you said, Joe, 'leading.' In Tibetan Buddhism, a mandala is used in meditation, to guide one's journey to enlightenment. It's a map that uses circles and squares, inside and outside of each other, creating gateways to the middle. The Tibetan type is the five-deity mandala. Four deities on the outside corners; the fifth in the very center. The Lord of Death. But not death itself. The conqueror of death. When one conquers death, the life/death cycle is broken, and enlightenment can be reached."

"Are you saying Nathan is using Buddhism to deal with his trauma?" Ava asks.

"Not sure what I'm thinking, but no, not Buddhism itself. His mind is using geometric archetypes to focus. To organize his thoughts, his recovery from the injury. If we can understand his geometric 'logic,' then we can use that to help him remember what happened. And in a way that keeps everything 'upstairs' fully functional.

"I also work at the V.A., and we're seeing too many soldiers come back home, with or without severe head traumas, who are having a terrible time adjusting. What Nathan went through is similar. A horrendous attack coupled with a blow on the head. But he has the good fortune to have you here as support. And it would be such a blessing to use his own map to guide him."

"Circles and squares?" Joe says a bit confused. "How are those a map?"

The psychiatrist quickly finds a pen. She draws a large circle on a piece of paper, then draws a square inside of the circle, with each corner point touching the circle, and then another circle inside the square, touching the midpoints of the square's four lines.

"I'm not an expert on Buddhism or meditation, but what Nathan has told me is quite consistent with the little I know. At the four corners of the square sit four deities. These can be any four important forces, or factors you want them to be. The four seasons. The four elements. Four colors. Four emotions. Where the lines touch the inner circle, these are the four gateways to the space inside. Hence, the map. Remember the goal of meditation is to proceed from the outside in, from the macrocosm of the world to the microcosm within, eventually entering the middle, reaching into one's . . . center."

"And Nathan's mandala?"

"You mean, his specifics? Like, what are his five 'deities'? That's what I hope you can help me with. One idea comes from Nathan's talking so much about 'place,' where he lives. So, maybe his four deities are the four directions, and the center of his mandala is here, his home, this city. But he also talks about stories, and his struggles distinguishing fact and fiction. So, his mandala might be more metaphysical, with his center square being 'truth' and the four outer forces, I don't know, the four processes that help define truth? Observation, reflection, practice, dream?" Dr. Brady is silent. Then she remembers a critical feature of Nathan's map. "I forgot. The center of the mandala, his inner sanctum as it were, is now hidden, behind a closed door."

"Maybe a combination of both views." Joe says. "The 'truth' for Nathan is where he lives, which is surrounded not by the four directions as much as what forms his life."

"So why the closed door?" the doctor asks.

"Maybe the center of his map is literally where he now lives. His apartment near the beach. And the memory of last Friday is too horrific to remember."

"I wonder if Nathan's map is his entire life, or more, a 'smaller' one, something more specific," Ava puzzles. Then an idea comes suddenly. "Maybe it's just about this specific story? The identical twins story. About John and Pat Scanlan."

"And the closed door is what happened last Friday night," Joe adds.

Dr. Brady slaps the table. "I like it. But if the mandala is *The Identical Twins*, what are the corners?"

"I think we have to start with John Scanlan," Ava says, thinking back to her young son. "Nathan was always excited to tell me about this gardener. Repeating all the wonderful stories of the Grove. He was so troubled by his death, when Scanlan died in that storm."

"Died in the storm? Do you remember, Ava, how Nathan questioned if he was killed by a falling tree? Did he have a sixth sense? A premonition? Nathan was always precocious, but I never thought he was psychic."

"The next 'corner' in this mandala," Ava continues, "has to be that experience you two had. The fire in the Grove. When Pat Scanlan appeared out of nowhere."

Tommy looks at Dr. Brady. "I have never seen, before or since, my son, or anyone, look so, I don't even know the right word. It was powerfully frightening."

"Two of the four," Dr. Brady summarizes.

"I think I might be responsible for the third," Nathan's father says. "I filled his head with guesses and snippets, everything I learned from my snooping around City Hall. I must admit that I was pretty damn interested in understanding what was behind that fire."

"And the fourth 'deity'?" the psychiatrist asks.

"The fourth?" both Nathan's mother and father say in unison, while looking at each other. Ava Hughes turns toward Dr. Brady. "The fourth leg of this table has to be . . . his love of story."

Tommy nods his head and continues, "Though, maybe it was also a challenge – how could he concoct a tale from something so fantastic?"

"And I think we all agree," Dr. Brady says, tapping the center of her drawing, "that the fifth deity, behind the closed door, is the final chapter of that epic. Once Nathan retrieves that memory, he can begin the process of putting it to rest."

"To be added as a coda to *The Identical Twins*," Joe smirks.

"Coda? More another damn Nathan story all together," Jack adds.

● ● ●

The following afternoon, all members of Nathan's team sit around the bed that has been Nathan's home now for a full week. Nathan sits upright, dressed casually – sweatpants, tee shirt, and a thin sweater he had graduated to a few days before. All, including Dr. Ahlbach, had agreed that Nathan could likely be released soon if all went well today. Today being the trek through Nathan's mandala. Everything that Dr. Brady had heard from Nathan assured her that he viewed this hospital room itself as a safe haven. Combined with those he trusted, it was the time and place to open the door. Plus, Jack would supply one more piece of the puzzle.

"Nathan, I've drawn something that might be familiar to you."

Dr. Brady holds up a large poster board with a simple but handsome drawing of a 'bare-bones' Tibetan Buddhist mandala, including a central image within the inner circle of a closed door, rust red in color. The drawing she had meditated on the past few days. Nathan stares intently at the poster board.

"Recognize anything?" Dr. Brady asks.

"Yes, of course. My circles and squares."

"And your closed door?"

"My closed door and solid wall, you mean."

"We'll open the door. You and us. Together."

(*Group therapy, huh?*) Nathan's first inclination toward cynicism quicklydisappears as he focuses on the door at the center of the drawing. The drawing steadies him now as the image had the many days before, connecting the internal universe of the past week of recovery with the external world now present in this room.

"I've been preoccupied . . . with a mandala?"

"Yes, you have. Which leads to my first question. Have you had any experience using a mandala? None of your family or friends knew of any."

Nathan lets out a quiet laugh. "No, they wouldn't. I dated someone briefly who practiced meditation." Joe gives him a quizzical look. "After you moved out of Sixth Avenue."

"So, you know..."

"That it's a map," Nathan interrupts. "Yes, though not much else."

"And you know you enter the inner room through this gateway at the bottom?"

"Yes, the white gate."

"So, we'll start here, at the bottom left."

"And circle clockwise," Nathan adds. He closes his eyes. (*All is perfect. What I thought I saw, I now see.*) He takes an even breath, opens his eyes. "Lead on, Lama."

Dr. Brady's plan is to have Nathan's parents and friends guide him around the path that describes how the bits and pieces of fact grew into a fiction. And then, to lead him to where that fiction ran smack dab into the cold hard reality of last Friday night. She asks him to do his best to stay within each quadrant, to meditate on its message, to quiet his thoughts and not jump ahead. So, as Ava Hughes describes the first deity – Nathan's admiration for the head gardener of the Grove and the lessons he taught – Nathan simply returns to his childhood and adolescence, returns to his Mr. Scanlan. And when Tommy Hughes leads his son back to the endless foggy night almost as long ago, Nathan stays in his father's narrative, focusing as much on reconnecting with his father as with the apocalyptic meeting of the gardener's twin. He even stays in the moment of his father's search into the puzzle of a strangely ironic fire. And when Joe recounts how Nathan stitched these facts into what would become his magnum opus, well, there he is, knee-deep within this mandala of *The Identical Twins*. He stands before the white gate, its large wooden frame, the entrance into the inner sanctum. What were the words? How was he to enter?

Nathan looks at Dr. Brady. "Probably not, *Open Sesame.*"

The psychiatrist smiles briefly, then looks at Jack. "I think Jack might have the key. At least to the gateway."

Jack pulls out a photograph from the envelope he had placed under his chair, and hands it to Nathan, face down. Nathan holds it a moment, then considers each person surrounding him, all leaning forward in their chairs as if peeking around the edge of large white pillars to discover the smaller world inside. He has no idea what the photo will be. (*Only that it will be black and white.*) He turns it over.

Nathan stands arm in arm with Herb Malakoff under the exceedingly small marquee of the Surf Theatre which holds two short lines – 'Hitchcock and Welles' above 'A Lost and Found Fantasy.' Herb's smile is set in a well-worn look of satisfaction. Nathan's smile, simply ecstatic. Nathan now remembers. (*Jack, in the absolute middle of the street, camera raised, 'One more. And another.'*)

Nathan looks at Jack, here in this hospital room, and Jack nods in return. Nathan closes his eyes for barely a second, then looks at Dr. Brady. "I'm inside. Inside the white gate. *And* I'm heading home. To my apartment."

The psychiatrist holds his look. "We're right there with you. We're right *here*. With you."

Nathan leads the others from the Surf to his apartment. Down the path to the back of the house. And now the closed door of the mandala becomes the slightly open door to his apartment. He no longer needs the mandala. He stands before his door, knowing in his bones that what had happened, happened inside this door. Inside his apartment.

Everything that occurred, does so again. All the terror he felt, he feels again, in clear, sharp images, though each with the same unclear lack of understanding of . . . what? Fiction turning into fact? Or fact into fiction? Of not being able to accept one iota of this fact, this fiction? Even when being pushed from behind, being strapped to a chair. And like the ticking of a clock, that repetitive pounding of wood against the skin of a weathered palm. The resonating voice that alternated between words heard (*'storyteller'*) and guttural grunts. All this evil. But is *any* of it decipherable? And the unfathomable now layered with the frightening onrush of cocaine. Nothing made sense last Friday. Nothing makes sense in this replay. (*At least I'm remembering. Or is this just a dream. Within a dream. Within a dream.*)

Dr. Brady sees the confusion on Nathan's face. "Don't think, Nathan. Just say what you see." (*What I see. And what I hear.*)

"He's turning as he mutters, *the time has come.* And then, I see it. I've never seen one before. I see . . . his aura. Not bright. It's dark. The darkest black. Surrounding him. *Holding* him. Such a background for those eyes. Those piercing eyes. He's spitting out a story. From the Bible. Of Cain killing Abel? But

I don't hear it. Or it changes. Instead, somehow, he's taken my Dad's poem, the poem I hated, never understood. How does he know that poem!? *My son, come here*, he threatens, *the time has come*. He raises that bat. *My son come here, the time has come*. Those eyes, God, those . . . Jack? Jack!"

But it's Tommy Hughes who is now holding his son, hugging Nathan before anyone else can move. "Why didn't I stop this? *Any* of this. All of it! Should never have gotten this far."

Nathan looks into his father's eyes, their brownness calmingly familiar, washing away the memory of Scanlon's piercing blue. "But you tried. You tried so hard. I didn't listen. Didn't know how. Wasn't ready. It was *me*. *Not* you. It was me."

Ava quickly completes the circle of family, with Joe and Jack pressed close behind. After a bumbling gathering of emotions, Nathan tries to laugh, nearly cries, shakes his head. "Such a fool, such an eejit! Must have been an easier way . . . such a simple lesson. What a thick skull!" Nathan shakes his head again, then laughs before he says, "Though, maybe I deserve some credit for having the lesson truly . . . pounded into my head."

With that quip, the tension from the tale's horror breaks.

"Oh, man," Joe sighs, "back to normal."

"Maybe," Nathan responds, "but hopefully, not all the way back. Not back to the old normal. Never thought I'd say this, but a story's just a story. Life – that's the real thing." Realizing what he just said, Nathan can't refrain from one last pun. "*Coke-is-the-real-thing* be damned! I'll never do that drug again."

To that, his audience can only shake their heads in collective thanks. Held fast within this loving support, Nathan closes his eyes and returns to the waiting mandala, returns to its center, to his center. (*No more rust red. No door. Not even a damn wall. Simply, nothing. No, even better. A wonderfully . . . blank canvas.*)

Coda

The following day, the last full day in the hospital, Ava Hughes sits with her son and his best friend. She puts down her thermos with the latest in her endless search for the perfect tea, and once more counts her blessings. Just as Ava is about to run out of fingers, Joe interrupts her meditation.

"So, Nathan, two new movies coming this week. Considering the past two weeks, both have their merits."

"Tempt me."

"*The Exorcist.*"

"Don't even have to ask the plot. No. And no again! And the other?"

"Woody's latest. *Sleeper.*"

"Any plot? Or like *Bananas*, random stories strung together?"

"About a guy frozen, waking up 200 years later."

"Oh, I see. Been there. Though not quite 200 years." Nathan thinks for a second. "Sounds like a no-brainer, about a no-brainer, for this no-brainer."

"*Nathan.*" Ava responds in her exceedingly maternal way.

A soft silence sets in. Nathan re-crosses his legs and leans forward.

"I had such odd dreams last night. The first was me and Dad, walking somewhere in the Southside district. I was much younger, maybe 9 or 10, and he was taking me somewhere, no idea where, but, man, was I excited. Two things. First, the entire walk was filled with the overwhelming aroma of baking bread, like we were passing a huge industrial bakery. The other I guess was a classic dream thing. Each block we walked down was different, but each time we came to a cross street, the street sign was always the same, *24*. I mean, not street or avenue, just the number. Now what could *24* mean?"

Ava smiles quietly to herself.

"The second dream, right before I woke up, seemed a long time ago. I was alone, in a church, small, really just a chapel. Adobe walls. White, with dark wood framing. I was sitting in the last pew, and a family came in. Based on their dress, I wondered if I was in a mission church, maybe in the 1800s? Two small children with their parents. Mexican, though maybe Spanish. The kids were . . . beautiful. The mother led her children to the front to light candles. The father looked at me and nodded. I said, 'El nombre de esta iglesia?' 'San Francisco de Asís,' he said with another nod. Like I was supposed to know. I didn't, but thought, what more appropriate saint to honor this mission church. Then I woke up. And my first thought was a continuation of the dream. Why aren't *any* of the missions named after St. Francis? Such the perfect connection."

Both Joe and Ava's reactions are synchronous and puzzled – did I hear what I just thought I heard? They look at each other, Joe shaking his head, Ava with her eyebrows pressed heavy on her eyes. Joe speaks first.

"Nathan, did I hear you correctly? Why weren't any of the missions named after St. Francis?"

"What? Is that such an odd question?"

"Dr. Ahlbach warned us," Ava said, looking at Joe.

"Delayed symptoms, here we go."

"What? Why is that such a crazy question?"

"But, Love," his mother says, "one of the missions *is* named after St. Francis."

"It is!? Which one?"

"The mission two miles from here! Don't you remember? The entire city is named after him."

Nathan, in disbelief, looks out the window, as if the city view could somehow confirm what he just heard. His search leads to several faraway hills, and then inexplicably, to one particular smaller one. It takes him the briefest moment to recall its location and then its name (*Mount Olympus!*), and vividly remembers standing on top its height and the direction of his gaze, northward. The line from that hill to the distant bridge. The line that ran through the cathedral. The line, he now realizes, he still is on. Directly on. (*From there to here*.) Within the hospital two short blocks down the hill below the church. And the line of time that runs from his childhood to now. To now. (*To goddamn now*.)

"San Francisco." Nathan whispers the four syllables one to the next, as soft as a windless evening fog. As he does, the countless pieces of reality and rumor, the bits of truth and story, the tatters of fact and fiction gather in a whirl one final time, then gently, gently, fall into place.

About the Author

Edward Garvey began writing poetry, fiction, and plays in high school and started college as a creative writing major. After an half-century diversion within the wonders of science, he returned to writing full-time and has published several poems. This is his first novel. Born and raised in San Francisco, he has lived in Orange County, North Carolina, for a long time with his wife and family, blessed with all their many two- and four-legged friends.